THE LAND OF HONEY

CHINENYE OBIAJULU

TotalRecall Publications, Inc.
1103 Middlecreek
Friendswood, Texas 77546
281-992-3131   281-482-5390 Fax
www.totalrecallpress.com

Copyright © 2014 by: Chinenye Obiajulu
All rights reserved
ISBN: 978-1-59095-178-1
UPC: 6-43977-41786-2
Library of Congress Control Number: 2013956978

Printed in the United States of America with simultaneous printing in Australia, Canada, and United Kingdom.

FIRST EDITION
1   2   3   4   5   6   7   8   9   10

In memory of my late father,
Mr. T.T. Onyeaso

Acknowledgements

Writing this book was possible with the help of my sisters, who held me accountable. **Dr Udoka Onyeaso**, my fellow traveler who checked in to see "how far" and did the first read through, making many useful suggestions – I am grateful; **Dr. Ego Agbasi** played an indelible role, through her fervent prayers, and her contribution added flavour and colour. **Dr. Daisey Onuoha** and Emeka, her hubby, by example, showed that with God, all things are possible; God will reward your labour of love. **Barr. Nkay Mgbeoji** who sliced, and diced, and polished, and Prof. Ikechi Mgbeoji, thank-you for all the legal matters. My brothers and their lovely wives for whom I have semi modeled Zimako and Anuli; **Obi & Del**, (Obi many thanks for your work on all the associated elements) and **Nwach** & Ify, **OG** Onyeaso, thank you for believing in me.

I will not forget to thank my Aunty Mrs. O.E Odinamadu (KSC) for her support and boost of confidence; as well Dr. Uche Akwuba my Uncle, his suggestions during this process was invaluable.

I am very thankful to **Sigrid Macdonald**, who from the get-go picked this manuscript up and loved it. Her attention to detail and work on this book have been flawless. I would also like to extend my thanks to **Ben Henbest** for his work.

My thanks are incomplete without mentioning **"Mummy,"** my beautiful mother Mrs. K.O Onyeaso who bought our first library *Child Craft* and *Encyclopedia Britannica* and so many books.

Bruce Moran and the staff at TotalRecall Publishing have been fantastic, and have made it possible for my dream of having a book in print to come true.

For others too numerous to mention, on whose shoulders I stood to bring this book to fruition, I could not have done it without you, so please accept my thanks.

Finally my loving husband **Okey,** my soul mate, best friend and chief adviser. Your wisdom and encouragement as I toiled has been rewarded. "Baby, you were right!"

Preface

The purpose of this book is to draw attention to the plight of many immigrants to Canada. Many come from Africa and all over the world full of dreams, and are not adequately prepared for the changes that await them. Being a professional and an immigrant myself provided me with the essential ingredients for this book. It is my hope that while entertaining, this book also helps others who are in strange new lands that they now call home; and prepares others who will follow.

This novel revels in a particular play with the English language that is a hallmark of Nigerian/trans-atlantic fiction, and certain words in igbo language. To preserve the flavor of the culture, a glossary has been provided to help you translate the igbo words.

To God be all the glory!

CHAPTER ONE

Dear Diary,

I can't believe today is the day. The day I kind of become Mrs. Apparently of all the degrees in the world, this is the most sought after: master of romantic studies (Mrs) with honours. Zimako has honoured me by making me his princess. He says he'll be calling me "Obidiya." So this is how it feels to be intoxicated with happiness.

The excitement was palpable as dancers jumped down from a luxurious bus, which was showing signs of wear and tear from years of travel on the roads of eastern Nigeria, proudly bearing the inscription, "The young shall grow." The drum-mers upped the ante as soon as they espied the dancers. The Atilogwu troupe accompanied the groom's people all the way from Imeobodo. Costumed gaily in their colourful regalia of bright red, yellow, and green, they set up their stall under the fruit tree. They could not stand still; as they pranced on their tiptoes, their anklets jingled in rhythm to the percussion of ogene and udu by the musicians.

They were followed closely by two Hiace buses which offloaded Zimako's kinsmen from Imeobodo, led by *Ogbandiogu*, the go-between; he had mediated between the families. A convoy of prestige vehicles majestically made their way into the compound. Some village children trailed in pursuit; others gazed in awe as they observed the event. Passers-by and market women shouted, *"Ndi-ogo Nno, O,"* welcoming the guests and in-laws as they arrived for the *Igba Nkwu Nwanyi,* the traditional wedding rites and payment for the bride.

It was business as usual for the *okada* drivers. These daring motorbike riders served as public transport. They zoomed along the dirt road, raising the ubiquitous red dust that coated everything in view.

* * * * *

It was quite a spectacle.

Some *mmanwu, or* masqueraders, were out displaying their art. Their *otimpkus* surrounded them, plucking branches from trees, and in a display of supernatural endurance, flogged each other as they gyrated.

The scene was set. It was billed as the wedding of the year.

The cat that got the cream was the only way to describe how Zimako was feeling.

They had come all the way to the village, as is customary according to native law and custom. His parents, Ichie and Okpue-umu-agbala, his twin sisters, Makua and Chinazo, and of course his brother, Okwe, were key players.

He was the *diokpala*. The family were not to be outdone and had come in a *big way* for the ceremony.

* * * * *

Zimako pinched himself to be sure he was not dreaming. Anuli was a beautiful bride. She was his prized jewel and he was a very lucky man indeed to have won her heart. She was all he had dreamed of and more.

* * * * *

The elder kinsmen were in camera haggling about how much I was worth. They wanted the Ndi-ogo to know that I was a valued flower in my father's compound, in whom much had been invested. Now that I was yielding fruit, Ndi-ogo wanted to take me away; it is true that Ndi-ogo had shown excellent taste, but it would cost them. This banter was in good spirit and eventually they agreed on a worthy price.

Ndi-ogo brought out their chequebook and the elder kinsmen

became incensed. They demanded the payment in cash and extinct coins in *akpa-ego*. They argued back and forth on what would be a reasonable bride price, otherwise they threatened that it was over – they were prepared to leave. One allegedly almost came to fisticuffs with Papa Philomena. At this point, Prof (my father) spoke up and said I was not for sale and no price would make up for his loss; he was gaining a son, he said, and extracted a promise from Ndi-ogo that they would love his daughter like their own. That settled the matter. The parties sheath their proverbial swords, Prof had said it all.

The group made their way down to join the gathered guests, who were waiting with bated breath to know if deliberations had gone well. The MC handed the microphone to *Ogbandiogu*, who made a short speech and called for me to come out.

* * * * *

I came out dancing and smiling bashfully. As I approached the elders, I was handed the gourd of palmwine to present to the man who would be my husband. I knelt down before Zimako, took a sip, and then tenderly looked up and passed the gourd to him. Drinking from the cup with a confident swig, but leaving the dregs, he sealed our union as man and wife. The crowd clapped their hands in congratulations.

The eldest of the kinsmen was then handed the microphone, and he started to pray. Using Schnapps as libation, he prayed for good things that any newlywed couple desires. He called on the gods of the land present and witnessing the journey of the young couple to bless us with good luck, fruit of the womb, long life, joy together, and a peaceful home that welcomes strangers and prosperity. The crowd concurred, answering, "*Ise!*"

The formalities were over for now; it was time for Zimako and I to have our first dance as groom and bride. Zimako and I joyfully took centre stage in the central clearing, swaying to the rhythm. Guests sprayed us with naira and dollars, sprinkling the cash on us in a flamboyant display of generosity.

Soon we were joined by my friends in *aso-ebi*—gaily, uniformly dressed maidens instantly recognised as friends of the bride. These women, who had come all the way from the city to support me and celebrate with me, hoped to find a man of their own today if single. Meanwhile they showcased themselves, serving as hostesses for the day, and they danced and collected the money that was now lying in the dust.

The floor was open to everyone.

My mother strutted and danced as mother of the day. Her friends were identifiable by their own *aso-ebi*, which was fuchsia pink and gold head ties with matching *aso-oke* as sash. They sprayed her with cash as they danced along with her. Prof, my father was in full traditional ibo regalia – *Isi-agu*, joined her on the dance floor with his friends, spraying her lavishly.

Food and drinks were served.

Everyone was having a great time.

* * * * *

Zimako sat back in his mock throne under the marquee and grinned contentedly.

He cast his mind back as he smugly observed the dancers, elders, and invited guests who were here to celebrate with him and Anuli.

* * * * *

Yes! Yes! Yes!

Zimako made a fist and raised one leg, bending his knee. Then he jumped and punched the air.

"Yes!" he shouted again. He was filled with joy. Zimako and Anuli had been dating exclusively for over a year, and from the moment he laid eyes on her, he knew in his bones that he wanted to spend the rest of his life with her. She was everything he hoped for and more. He was a lucky man. After one year of courtship, he decided it was time to find out if she felt the same way about him. When she said yes, Zimako could hardly believe his luck!

* * * * *

Zimako felt his heart pounding. The prospect of approaching Anuli's father was one that filled him with trepidation. He knew Anuli was the apple of her father's eye. If he decided he was happy to accept Zimako as his son-in-law, that would set in motion the whole traditional wedding brouhaha. That was what he dreaded the most. He had heard urban tales of how that could make or break a full-fledged man. He knew that in-laws could be sly, demanding, obscure and weird, setting the bar high for an unsuspecting groom. It was a rite of passage that was not for the lily-livered. It was a journey that transformed boys to men.

Zimako had always hoped that when the time came for him to take a wife, he would know what to do and do it with dispatch. Now he was not so sure he was ready and able. It was a merciless process, and every action was subject to scrutiny from elders and in-laws alike.

First things first; he had to inform his parents of his plans to marry Anuli.

When Zimako phoned his father, Ichie Adiora, to inform him of his intention to take a wife, Ichie was pleased. The date was arranged for formal introductions, and he took Anuli back home to the village – Imeobodo, where his parents resided to introduce her to the family. This would also give them the opportunity to observe her and see how well she would fit into the family. Okpue-umu-agbala, as Zimako's mother was popularly known, had carried out the covert traditional tests to see if Anuli was wife material. She was required to cook *ofe onugbu,* a traditional Ibo delicacy of bitter leaf soup, and they observed to see if she knew *omenana* and understood the proper order for serving *kolanut* to the elders.

Ichie was satisfied with Anuli; he could see why his son had fallen for her charms. She was pretty and respectful and did not have any airs about her. Okpue-umu-agbala, however, had some reservations and was reluctant to give her seal of approval. No woman was good enough to take care of her boy; but in the face of Ichie's unstinting approval, she was cowed into silence.

* * * * *

I was dancing my heart out and having the time of my life. It was my day; I had dreamed of this day. Since being a flower girl as a child, I had subconsciously been planning this day. Zimako had done me proud. He promised and he delivered. If this was any sign of our life together, I was sure I was doing the right thing.

* * * * *

"I'm so excited! He proposed! On bended knees...!" I had broken the news to my sister Chiamaka. "Zimako asked me."

Chiamaka whooped. She sounded nearly as excited as I was feeling. She and I were very close. She more than anyone else knew I had fallen hard for Zimako, and in the early days she prayed he would not act like one of those Lagos boys who trampled on the affections and hearts of those who gullibly fell for them. They were now comfortably friendly, like brother and sister. She was happy for me.

"So, when are you getting married? Do you like the ring? Of course I'm going to be your maid of honour!" She said all this without stopping to catch her breath, then feigned a cough. It was no secret that I was Dad's favourite, and anyone who wanted to marry me had better be ready to answer to him.

"Zimako is in for it. Dad will chew him up and spit him out. Hmmm, I'd like to be a fly on the wall. Promise you will give me the low-down verbatim," Chiamaka said.

I had to agree with my sister. "I know, I have already warned Zimako. He knows it won't be easy." We laughed raucously.

"Mummy will be so proud of you; I want to be just like you when I grow up," Chiamaka said affectionately, giving me a tight hug. She was the best little sister.

That Saturday, we hit the Lagos–Ibadan expressway. Zimako was more nervous than I had ever seen him. He was dressed in a simple brocade Senegalese-style kaftan. He did not want to appear too ostentatious.

The first time we had gone to Ibadan, he was smartly dressed but did not wear a jacket. Prof asked him outright where his jacket was. That had been a tense visit; my two favourite men sparring with words, fighting over me, it seemed. Dad interrogated him about his career, his ambitions, his pedigree, and then his intentions. I remember being tickled by that phrase, "Are your intentions honourable?"

It was midday by the time we finally arrived. The one hundred and fifty-kilometre journey could be done in two hours, but the poorly maintained expressway was riddled with potholes. And then on arrival in town, the congestion and confusion that is characteristic of the Dugbe Junction added another hour to the trip. Mummy was worried and Prof was getting impatient.

My parents lived on the University of Ibadan campus. The house I'd grown up in was a bungalow on a quiet, tree-shaded avenue. Observing the campus and our home through my fiancée's eyes, I remembered him commenting on how clean and Old World everything seemed. The driveway was swept clean and neatly lined with Mummy's floral pieces, and the lawn was well-manicured; Mummy was proud of her garden.

As we got out from the car, in a show of solidarity, Zimako and I held hands, and I leaned in and kissed him lightly on the lips, him trying to deepen the embrace and me teasing, pushing him away with a promise to deliver more later, when he had passed the test. I reminded him, "Prof will try to unnerve you, baby. Don't let Dad make you nervous." Zimako squared his shoulders and indicated he was ready to make a good pitch to win my hand. I could not stop smiling. My fingers were crossed.

Prof was listening to the *BBC World Service News*, but as soon we came in, he approached us, gave me a warm hug, and offered Zimako a handshake. "You are looking just like your mother when I married her," he said, and we laughed and hugged again. He was more formal as he addressed Zimako. "Young man… "

I tried to read his body language, but found it difficult to interpret. I reached out to hold Zimako's hand and it felt damp with sweat.

"Mummy! We are here!" I called out as I made my way to the kitchen. I gave Zimako a reassuring glance, but that was the best I could offer him. The tension in the room was stifling.

Mama was cooking enough for a banquet. Her face lit up when she looked up and saw me. "*Omalicha nwam*, how are you? Hope the road was not too bad. How is work? You are looking very well." She rose to give me a half hug, holding the large wooden spoon in her right hand.

"I can't complain, Mum," I said. "Come, Zimako is in the parlour with Papa. You know he will grill him if you are not there." Mummy had a calming effect on Prof. She would stare him down when he tried to bully anyone she thought was the underdog. We chuckled.

"What? And take the fun out of this for your father? Let Zimako face the music. My daughter, men are funny creatures. If we don't make it tough for him, he will not value you. No, let's give the men some time. You know, you don't want him to think he is getting you cheap. *Nwam*, let him squirm and prove he is man enough to win your hand."

I looked around to see what I could do to help. "Mummy, you have already done all the cooking; there is nothing left for me to do."

"You are right, my daughter. Come to the room and chat with me while I get changed."

Mum and I made our way to her room that adjourned the master bedroom. My parents had never shared a bedroom. There was a connecting door between both rooms, and when the door was open they had a full view of each other's room. The smell of Mum's room was comforting. It had a faint smell of cotton and mothballs, and the fresh fragrance of clean washed clothes. She settled down on the bed and patted it for me to sit beside her. I sank onto the bed obligingly. I knew this meant that Mummy wanted to impart some pearls of wisdom.

"*Nwam*, congratulations! Chiamaka hinted at your news."

I smiled but was seething inside, mentally wishing I could strangle Chiamaka for stealing my thunder. Mummy read my mind. "Don't look so mad." Mama laughed. "You know your sister." So much for surprises.

That was just the beginning. Mummy had more to say. "Anuli,

I want to talk to you because many people go into marriage not being prepared, but I want you to enjoy a happy marriage like your father and me, even better."

She had my full attention. "You see, your husband loving you is all well and good. Indeed, that is the start. Your husband's love for you is very important, but... " She paused for emphasis, looking into my eyes, plumbing the depths of my soul. "If you want that love to last, you have to also win his respect."

I was listening closely.

"To achieve that, you have to exhibit maturity beyond your years. No matter how angry or upset you are, make sure that you always have his food ready and set out on the table for him. It is true that the way to a man's heart is through his stomach."

I wished I had a notepad in hand.

"Number two: whenever you are in public, let him enjoy the limelight—don't upstage him. Men's egos are very fragile and sensitive; keep your opinions till you get home."

I wanted to say something; this pandering to his ego was rather archaic. Once again, as if she read my mind, Mummy stared me down in that way she had. "Sshhh, I am still talking, Anuli. These things are true and I want you to take them to heart. You will not regret it. Three, do not give voice to your anger— calm down, and remember that he loves you and does not mean to hurt you. Speak honestly and tenderly to let him know if he hurts you. Do not be ashamed to reveal your vulnerabilities." Mummy finally took a deep breath. "Can you hear me? Are you listening? Do I still have your attention?" she asked. I nodded. She wrapped up, "Last, do not give him any reason to feel jealous or insecure."

Mummy was done. I had not realised I was listening with bated breath. I took a deep breath in and heaved a sigh of something akin to relief.

"*Nwam*, I think I have covered everything unless you have anything you want to ask me."

"Mummy, it is about infidelity... "

Mummy looked at me with concern bordering on panic. "No, no, Zimako has not been unfaithful. He is the most loyal and dependable guy, but you know Lagos women. What should I do if I suspect something is going on?"

Mummy had moved away to the dressing table when she concluded her talk; she came back to the bed and sat down beside me. "If you ever suspect there is a strange woman in your marriage, do not confront him; he will become emboldened. Use guile to introduce the discussion. Let him know that you will not tolerate it if you ever hear there is such a thing going on, and that he will lose your respect. He will not be sure if you know, but to retain your respect, he will work hard to end the affair."

Mummy looked really lovely when she was done. Her headtie *Ichafu* was very elaborately tied. We headed back to the parlour where Zimako and Dad were chatting over a bottle of palmwine. Zimako was relaxed. I was happy that he had somehow managed to hold his own. I caught his eye and gave him an enquiring look. He winked back and gave me a thumbs-up.

Mummy settled herself beside Prof on the sofa while Zimako and I sat in the two-seater loveseat. Looking at both of them swelled my heart with pride. Prof – my father had withstood all the pressure from his family when they insisted he send Mummy packing if she did not produce an heir. He stood by her, and did not let anyone bully her. He still teased her from time to time with their favourite phrase, "My beloved, in whom I am well pleased."

Prof turned to Mummy and asked, "*Nwanyi-oma*, a glass of *palmi* for you?"

Mummy replied, "No palmwine today. The occasion calls for something special, perhaps champagne?"

Prof chuckled indulgently. "*Nwanyi-oma*, you have very expensive tastes. Okay, Anuli, indeed this is a very special occasion. Go into my room and bring one of those bottles of champagne I've been saving."

I departed to fetch the drink; Mummy went in to the kitchen. With the assistance of Okwudili, the house help, they set out the food on the table.

By the time I got back, the conversation centred on the procedures for the traditional wedding. Prof was advising Zimako on the intricacies that had to be observed. "You and your people have to arrange to formally come and tell us that you want to marry our daughter. You know, when coming, you will bring *something*. For that formal visit, you can come with just your close friends and family, one of whom needs to be a respected elder."

Zimako acquiescingly nodded. His unspoken message was that no mountain was too high or river too wide to cross to make me his wife. We relaxed, chatted, and ate. The sun went down and too soon it was time to leave.

Mission accomplished; my parents bid us farewell with their blessing.

* * * * *

The afternoon skies were clear; the *Igbankwu nwanyi* was in full swing. The *Umu-Ada* seemed to be arguing over cloth and salt and dry fish in their corner of the compound. The band was keeping everyone entertained, and food and drinks were flowing. Zimako was exhausted and excited in equal measure. He could not believe that Anuli was now his wife and recalled all the obstacles he had overcome.

* * * * *

After that visit to Ibadan, Zimako promptly phoned his father, Ichie, to inform him of the success of his mission. He gave him all the details and they both agreed that their formal visit to the intended in-laws should not be delayed. Ichie offered his full support. "You must contact your Uncle Abel and let him know. He is our oldest kinsman in Lagos. He will accompany us to Ibadan for the *iku-aka*. I shall arrive in Lagos a day ahead. Of course, Okwe must come along, too his father instructed."

Okwe was Zimako's younger brother and a post-graduate student at the University of Lagos. Unlike Zimako, who tended to be measured and introverted, Okwe was some-what impulsive, living a fast life. He was one of the "UniLag happening" boys. The two brothers were as different as chalk and cheese but as close as twins. In different ways, both young men were captivating, exuding the confidence of inner strength, comfortable in their skin, tall and handsome,"easy on the eye," the flirtatious young women said of them.

"Yes, sir," Zimako responded, to his father's command, while wondering how Okwe would react to the news that he had been roped in without his consent.

Zimako was not surprised that Ichie had nominated Uncle Abel to accompany them on this most important call to his would-be in-laws.

Uncle Abel was a career civil servant and had been working with the Ministry of Works for over thirty years. He and Ichie were not blood relations, but had grown up as brothers in Ichie's parents' house-hold. He was well respected in the family as a fair and just man. His sojourn in Lagos was a success. He was a well-to-do man.

Ichie warned Zimako not to go empty-handed when he went to seek the support of Uncle Abel. "Take a good bottle of hot drink. Uncle Abel is a *big man*."

Within a week Zimako had called on Uncle Abel.

Uncle Abel was honoured to lead the entourage to the in-laws. "Thank you, my son. Marriage in our culture is a serious matter. It is not for small boys. I am happy to see that you have come of age. Are you aware that you have to engage a middleman who will be a liaison between the two families? I think I know someone who can do that job effectively, and he has experience with this kind of thing: Papa Philomena... He is from the neighbouring village. He holds a small position at the university and is versed in our culture and tradition. He will represent us during the mediation. You will need to approach him. Tell him I suggested his diplomatic skills. There is no shame in telling him I sent you, but you must find a way to compensate him for his services."

Zimako listened, his head was buzzing. The whole marriage thing felt like it was spiralling out of his control. It dawned on him that he had no choice or any real say in these matters. Uncle Abel outlined a list of things that would be needed for the visit and suggested they meet again within a fortnight. Zimako realised he was lucky to have people who would smooth the path and steer him in the right direction.

When Zimako called Papa Philomena on the phone to inform him of his intention and seek his expertise in acting as a "go-between," Papa Philomena listened attentively as he spoke. Then, once Zimako was done, Papa Philomena responded in a conspiratorial tone. "I have heard already that you intend to take a wife. However, there is a traditional procedure for me to act in this role. So go back to your uncle, tell him what I said, and do whatever he tells you to do."

Zimako was flummoxed. What was going on with all this traditional hocus-pocus? He was floundering. Now he understood why people called the Igbo marriage procedure a master's degree program. He called Uncle Abel again and relayed Papa Philomena's cryptic message. Uncle Abel laughed and then proceeded to tell Zimako what to do. "Go to Papa Philomena with a carton of beer, preferably Star beer, and put five thousand naira on top. He will not say no to your request."

Zimako thanked his uncle Abel, but he was livid. Why didn't Papa Philomena just say what he wanted—why the rigmarole? Was this the spirit of brotherhood? He put aside his irritation and phoned Papa Philomena to agree on a date when he would visit to discuss the matter like men.

On the agreed date Peters, his best friend in tow, Zimako headed to Ajegunle, a shanty town on the outskirts in Lagos. Zimako dreaded the trip. Ajegunle was known as a jungle within the city and was in a constant state of chaos. Special skills and radar-like alertness were required to navigate as wily pickpockets owned the streets, and the utter anarchy was symptomatic of the government's neglect of the area. Peters knew the area and offered to drive. Zimako was thankful as he felt on edge just observing the mayhem around him. Rickshaws, motorbikes, pedestrians, cars, heavy goods vehicles, and buses battled for the best parts of the road, which were by any reasonable standards not navigable due to inadequate drainage systems. The stench of urine pervaded the air; Zimako wondered how long he could hold his breath. Motorists hurled harsh words at each other, and demonstrated scant respect for other road users or the Highway Code.

"Are you sure we are not lost?" Zimako asked.

"No fear, man, we are on track!" Peters told him. "I laugh when I see cars advertised with satellite navigation systems; how will sat-nav guide anyone through this unmapped jungle? Some houses in the city don't even have an address. Imagine! I despair! Anyway, when I think it is no longer safe, we will park the car and board *okada*, but I hope it doesn't get to that."

Zimako was really uncomfortable. Peters was enjoying dodging the *okadas* who sped in all directions against the flow of traffic, rushing to God knows where. Just as Zimako was questioning the wisdom in continuing the trip, Peters brought the Passat to a halt in front of a kiosk.

"Let's park here. I don't want to damage the shock absorbers of your car, and it seems relatively safe. When we come out, we can *egunjerize* the kiosk manager who will have watched over the car for us to avoid malicious damage of theft."

Zimako swallowed hard. They took off on foot, bearing their gifts, to find an *okada* to take them the rest of the way to their destination.

They finally located the address after much back and forthing. The street numbering was not user-friendly in the least. Papa Philomena's home was in an old building with a darkened hallway. Dull electric bulbs brightened the hallway that ran though the building. There were rooms on both sides facing out onto a central corridor, with families of up to five persons living in one room. They were popularly known as *"face-me-I-face-you."* Ventilation and lighting were in poor supply. The odour of stale sweat, kerosene, and urine hung heavily in the dank building.

Papa Philomena was pleased to see Zimako. "*Nwam, nno, O!* Look how tall you have grown. Come, come in. Please sit down, and feel at home."

Zimako looked at his surroundings, and then indicated to Peters to take the armchair still covered in polyethylene wrap. Zimako sat gingerly on the threadbare sofa and tried to relax. He knew that Papa Philomena would not hesitate to interpret his discomfort as disdain and arrogance. Papa Philomena hollered to his wife to get drinks for their visitors, but Zimako declined politely. "Please sir, do not go to any trouble; let's get down to business."

Papa Philomena smiled at the sight of the gifts they presented. He was wearing a greying net singlet which must have started out coloured white, but had definitely seen better days. Scanty, kinky chest hair immodestly escaped through the netting. An old and worn print *wrapper*, a cloth wrapped around the waist to cover from waist to below the knee, was tied around his waist; he had seen life and life had seen him. Papa Philomena was weathered and worn. He explained the role he would play to help smooth communication between the groom's and bride's families. He knew Prof from the days when he was an administrative clerk in Ibadan. Prof was a good man. He promised Zimako that he would have nothing to worry about. Zimako thanked him and they agreed to meet the following weekend at Uncle Abel's, from where they would proceed to Ibadan for the *iku-aka*, the traditional Ibo engagement.

* * * * *

Zimako was happy when the *iku–aka* was successfully concluded. The bridal party was Prof, Uncle Chuka, who also drove up from Lagos, and Anuli's godfather. Zimako had come along with Ichie, Uncle Abel, and Papa Philomena, whom Zimako had trouble recognising in his traditional regalia, Okwe, and Peters. The formal proposal was tendered and they agreed to reconvene for the response.

The waiting time, it turned out, was really time for both sides to ask in-depth questions about genealogy and pedigree. Were there any known cases of mental illness in the family? Were they *Osu*? Did they treat their women with dignity and honour? Were the womenfolk fertile? Were there any land disputes? How did they handle family conflict? Each side sought answers to this unwritten questionnaire, and a yes to any of those questions could be a deal-breaker.

Once due diligence had been accomplished, and Prof satisfied himself that he had all the information he required, he contacted Papa Philomena, now known as Ogbandiogu; the appointed mediator, to convene a meeting to receive his response to the proposal.

On that day, they made their way to Ibadan for the response, bearing more gifts. It was a smaller group this time. Prof, Uncle Chuka, Uncle Abel, Papa Philomena, and Zimako were the only ones in attendance. Prof and Uncle Abel drilled down to specific issues requiring clarification. Banter turned to serious arguments and the atmosphere was charged. Zimako fidgeted as he saw his dream of making Anuli his wife slipping away. In his mind he bartered with God. *Please, God, if you do this for me, I will serve you forever!*

Just as suddenly as it started, the tension dissipated and Prof and Uncle Abel were laughing and hailing each other with their traditional titles. Once satisfied with the chronology and facts presented, Prof announced his consent. There was laughter and joy at the announcement. Refreshments were served and the discussion turned to suggested dates for the *Igbankwu nwanyi*.

It was the duty of Papa Philomena as the mediator to obtain the list of gifts to be given from the groom to various groups of people on the bride's side. When Zimako was presented with the A4 double-sided list, it was a miracle that he did not collapse. Discussing it with Peters later, he concluded that the whole marriage thing was a rip-off designed to bankrupt a hard-working, conscientious young man. "What! Do they think I am made of money?"

Peters was amused. "Now you understand what they mean when they say Igbo marriage is not for boys; it is for men—you are equal to the task!" Peters reaffirmed clapping him on the shoulders.

Zimako and Anuli sent out invitations, and preparations were in earnest. Both received calls from friends and well-wishers who were offering to help, confirming their intention to attend, or making their excuses.

A text came through to Zimako's phone that irritated him, and a frown creased his brow. *It should have been me. But know that I will never stop loving you. Ndudi.* Zimako furtively deleted the text. It was from his colleague at work. She had flirted with him at some point, and he had let it go on for longer than it should have. Now she just didn't know when to quit.

* * * * *

It was sundown, and Zimako and Anuli changed into matching white lace outfits and danced their last dance. They were escorted to the car, and Zimako took his bride away to his village.

Their white wedding followed three months later, where Prof handed Anuli over to Zimako to be his lawfully wedded wife.

They were now man and wife starting their new life together.

CHAPTER TWO

> *Dear Diary,*
> *I went to the doctor to discuss contraception. My husband (I love the way that sounds: my husband) and I have agreed to wait a few years, sort our careers out, and then start having children. It is so nice to be married to my soul mate. I feel secure and safe, knowing he has my best interests at heart. Life is so good.*

This is what happens when government takes an ostrich approach to the nation's problems. It was clear the government had no agenda to better the lot of the common man. Nonchalant disdain for the electorate, corruption, and cronyism were the order of the day.

Zimako was reading the day's copy of *Thisday* newspaper and did not know whether to cry or scream. Some Igbo traders had been burnt alive. He was ashamed of being Nigerian.

Nigerians had hitherto been a religiously tolerant people. Zimako was very concerned about the daily riots and killings that had started up north and were steadily working their way south. The government made ineffective noises, but failed to intervene. He now had a wife to protect and he was worried. Zimako knew it was time to act decisively.

"Anuli, I am really worried about our future in Nigeria. What do you think of these political-religious riots?"

It was not a new topic. I knew Zimako was exasperated with the way the country was going, but what could be done? He was not planning to challenge the status quo. "You mean the Boko Haram killings? What is there to do? We are helpless and the government seems to have no idea of how to safeguard us. Why? Are you thinking of running for political office?"

Zimako roared with laughter. "Not a chance, honey, but even better, I was talking to Obi, who was recently in the country. He is now in Canada. He told me we could apply for Canadian residency."

This was news to me. "Canadian residency?"

Zimako was very excited. "Yes, he explained it to me. We can file papers to become future citizens of Canada. He said it is a beautiful country and very organised!"

I was not convinced. "Babes, is it that bad here? We are not the only ones. Why do you think we should relocate? We are gradually building up capital. Let's be patient. Maybe the government will improve."

But Zimako was like a dog with a bone. "Sweetheart, things have not improved over the last decade, and there is no sign they will in the near future. Lack of infrastructure, corruption, even armed robbery I can cope with, but Boko Haram seems to be targeting Igbo Christians; we are no longer safe."

I wished I could allay his anxieties, but if I was honest with myself, I sometimes feared for our safety and understood his sentiments.

"But why Canada? It is so far away, and we do not have family there. What about our parents? What will they think?" I asked.

"Darling, the distance should be a plus. It will keep you from *Okpue*," he responded, giggling. "But seriously, processing the papers usually takes about three years. We are not packing our bags and leaving overnight, so there is ample time to bring them around while we watch the political climate and build our nest egg. I think we should start the process ASAP."

"Hold on, three years is a long time. When are we going to start a family?"

Zimako smiled. "Babes, we are still quite young. I think we should wait, so we can give our children the best!"

"...but, your parents. What will Okpue..."

"Let me worry about my mother." Zimako did not let me finish. Okpue harangued us about her grand-children during every visit, subtly hinting it was all my fault. Reluctantly, I gave my consent. "Babes, I trust you on this one."

* * * * *

The menacing actions of Boko Haram continued unabated. They seemed to be emboldened by the inactivity of the government. They had taken to throwing bombs into churches during Sunday service. Many churches now conducted security searches before anyone entered the premises. Zimako felt vindicated. Holding a copy of *Thisday* with the headline, "Boko Haram Rejects Amnesty," he shook his head.

"Honey, what is it?" I asked. Zimako threw the paper down on the centre table.

"I told you this thing was getting out of control. Can't you see? The government is trying to pacify these louts and they have rejected it. They'd rather kill people." I came over to see the article. A quick glance showed that talks had broken down, and Boko Haram was not willing to lay down their arms.

"I am so happy you had the foresight to begin processing documents for Canada." Zimako smiled broadly. "I told you," he responded with a smug smile.

* * * * *

After almost four years of a tedious application process, much money spent on English Language tests, Medical tests, fishing for documents long forgotten, and many anxious moments, the wait was over; the Canadian government issued the immigrant visas. It was such a relief and a momentous occasion. It was surreal. Zimako pinched himself.

He called Okwe to inform him that at last the letter from the Canadian Embassy had arrived. Okwe was ecstatic. He had not really believed it was possible.

"Ol' boy, c.o.n.g.r.a.t.u.l.a.t.i.o.n.s!" he bellowed into his cell phone.

Zimako sounded incredibly calm. "Honestly, I can't believe it. My heart is pounding so hard, so fast."

"My God! Na wa, O, so you are now a Canadian citizen? No more queuing at the embassy for a visa, like us common Nigerians, and being insulted by those clerks at the consulate office?"

"Hey, hey, I'm not a citizen yet, but I'll be on the road to becoming one once I land in Canada."

"*Kai!* Man… this is too much. I hear and read about this kind of thing, but never knew it was for real: to actually get *Oyinbo* citizenship. Man, this calls for champagne."

"No, this calls for reflection because I'm not even sure now what happens next. We have been waiting for and planning towards this for almost four years, but now that it's staring me in the face, I am not sure we are really ready for it."

"What? Of course you are ready, but we have to *wash it* first," he said in colloquial Nigerian speak. "At least let *awon* boys come and rejoice with you. The bill is on me. Just bring Madam; Friday, my place."

"No, no, no, Okwe, take it easy. I need to absorb this whole thing first."

"*You sef, haba na wetin.* Look, getting the papers is a big deal, no matter what you decide to do with them. It is an excuse to gather the gang. This party is going to totally rock, *O!* In fact, let me get off the phone so I can start calling around to tell the guys. This is ginormous! Man, I bow! You actually got it. Wow!"

"I know. I am still pinching myself. I held the letter in my hand, and did not want to open it for fear of rejection after getting my hopes up so high. After forty months, almost four years. God must have a plan for us."

"Yeah, man, that is why it calls for massive celebration," reiterated Okwe.

"I guess I cannot convince you that it is not necessary. Give the money to charity."

"I *don* try for charity," he guffawed. "This one is for you, big brother. Accept it graciously. I am so excited for you guys. To think that you accomplished this is just amazing. I am so proud of you, bro."

"Thanks, I am really humbled."

"So Friday night, my place?"

"Okay then, but please just don't call anyone today. I have to tell them myself. Maybe you can start doing the party invites by Thursday." Zimako was hoping that with such short notice, Okwe would be unable to gather the crowd required for a raucous jamboree. Okwe was not fooled.

"Ah ah, Thursday, the notice will be too short for guys to rally around, and they will have already made their weekend plans. Look, let me do it this way; I'll call and tell people to leave Friday evening open, but I promise not to divulge any details, okay?"

"All right, I give up. You win!"

Suddenly Okwe was impatient to round up the call. "Listen, I got to go. Give Anuli my best."

* * * * *

Okwe was of two minds. Zimako had been working on this visa thing for a while; Okwe thought it was all a pipe dream, and he had been wary of encouraging Zimako in case it did not come through. He had not wanted his big brother's hopes dashed by embassy clerks. Now the papers were in hand. It sounded too good to be true.

Zimako did not sound as excited as Okwe had expected.

The immigrant visa was gold, as far as Okwe knew. There were many people that would have given an arm and a leg to get it. For that matter, most Nigerians would be willing to make any kind of sacrifice to receive a second citizenship, preferably with one of the Western or "First World" countries. It was just the way it was. The conditions in Nigeria got worse every day, and consular staff had a field day rejecting even the most genuine visitor for a temporary visa with the now famous, "I am not convinced you will be coming back for reason of insufficient ties." It was the most ridiculous reason, given that 99.9 per cent of Nigerians had strong extended family ties. There were no orphans in Nigeria.

Okwe knew that if it felt too good to be true, more often than not it was a scam! There must be a catch somewhere; that much he knew. There was no such thing as a free lunch—nothing good in life came from nothing—but he had been proven wrong. Now, finally, the cat was out of the bag, and of course it called for celebration. Let all those naysayers come and see; he sniggered inwardly. His swagger fully on, he sidled quietly into the yea-sayer's queue.

He still did not get Zimako's reaction. He seemed to be developing cold feet. He did not sound wholeheartedly excited about the Canadian thing, considering how long he had been waiting for it to come through. He needed to get his mojo on, and let anyone with *bad-bellè* jump into the Lagos lagoon. At least that would have been Okwe's attitude if he were in Zimako's shoes. Knowing Zimako, he'd first take time to pray about the whole thing, and keep it quiet till he had "heard from God" before he decided what to do; but Okwe would not be dissuaded from throwing a party and painting the town red! His brother had accomplished something that was the envy of many.

He would throw the mother of all parties to celebrate his brother's good fortune.

* * * * *

Soon everyone would start arriving.

The gang, as he called them, the duo of Peters and a few others, would definitely be there. He had also invited a few friends from KC (the prestigious Kings College) and "Lag" (University of Lagos), whom he knew were also friendly with Zimako. It was open house tonight. No one was excluded, not even the twins, Makua and Chinazo.

The twins were not identical, either in looks or temperament.

Makua was the better looking of the two—slim, sexy, and flirtatious. When he phoned her, she assured him she would *"full ground"* with a few friends to *"make sure the party rocks."* Okwe and Makua were close. If she was inviting a few friends, then there would be enough hot babes to make it a great party. They saw eye to eye, Okwe and Makua. She also had his caramel complexion; they had the good looks in the family.

Chinazo was quiet and pretty in an understated way so that her attraction was less obvious. She promised to come with her hubby, Chuka, although she did not fail to add, "We are not party animals like you and Makua." She was old before her time. Party pooper, boring Chinazo. She was the younger of the twins.

Ireti was going to play hostess that night. Sweet, hot, and sexy

Ireti. He had landed the jackpot when she agreed to be his babe. It was going to be a great night. Nothing like a legitimate reason to get her over on Fridays; she had to spend the night.

Peters arrived early. Others followed closely. They generously came armed with some cartons of Star beer, the drink of choice for the happening crew, some bottles of sparkling wine for the women, and best of all, sizzling hot *suya*. It was going to be a beer, small chops, and suya party, unless of course "Mother Hen" Chinazo was kind enough to bring some *jollof* rice and chicken to feed the boys.

* * * * *

The mood was buoyant as Zimako and I walked in. I felt Zimako's arms go possessively around my waist. "You are beautiful" he said keeping his arms around me. I felt buoyed by his attention, as he closely regarded me. I knew he liked my features which he described as high cheekbones and almond-shaped eyes. I felt somewhat self conscious under his gaze. I had carefully applied my lipstick to full, pouty lips. Silky flowered top added color to my dress pants and golden brown skin had a tone that complimented Zimako. I recalled the first time Makua and I met, and she wondered aloud if I was "half-caste."

Our entrance was just what Okwe needed to jumpstart the party.

"My man!" he shouted, slapping a brotherly arm around Zimako's shoulder. "Glad to see you."

Zimako reciprocated the gesture. "If I didn't show, I know I'd not hear the end of it. By the way, Anuli has brought some stewed goat meat Zimako gestured. I knew Okwe would need help ensuring there was something besides *suya*, and made some delicacy for the occasion.

"Hey, I see you have not changed at all, ever the party animal." I said laughing with Okwe.

"*Haba*, this one has nothing to do with being a party animal, O. Sis, this is a big one. The news calls for some serious celebration. We have to wash it." Okwe guided both of us to the back of his bungalow in the medium-density Surulere area. The plastic chairs were arranged in sets of four around several white plastic tables under a mini-marquee; he was anticipating a good crowd. Buzo, another friend in attendance, and Peters had made themselves comfortable under the marquee and were already chilling with some of the lager. They waved to us as we joined the crew.

"Okwe, don't tell me this is going to be a big thing," Zimako said. "I thought you said it was just family and maybe a few friends."

Okwe laughed. "Listen, just relax and enjoy yourself tonight, okay?"

I knew Zimako's propensity to worry, and linked my arm in his. "Let's go and join the guys. I am sure Okwe has some loose ends to tie up before everyone gets here." The words were barely out of my mouth when we heard Makua at the front door.

"Hey guys, anybody home?" She arrived with her party entourage of three bubbly women, looking determined to have a good time, and her boyfriend of the moment. Their arrival signalled the beginning of the party, as they danced their way to the back where Buzo and Peters sat. As if on cue, the other guests started arriving.

Femi, another guest, found Okwe. "My man, longest time, *na wa* for Lagos life." They fist-bumped and did a manly handshake. Femi Kuti's "Wonder Wonder" was blaring in the background. The revellers got into the groove, greeting and hugging each other while congratulating Zimako on his good fortune. They were enjoying themselves, gyrating and swinging to the beat. The dimly lit back garden was alive with excitement. The party was in full swing, and everyone was moving to the beat, even Zimako. Food was abundant, and the booze was flowing; Okwe as host.

The venue was now chock-a-bloc with guests. Chinazo had arrived discretely at some point and, as predicted, laden with *jollof* rice, fried rice, *moin-moin*, and enough fried chicken to feed a village. After dropping her goodies in the kitchen, she found a seat beside her husband, Chuka, who was sitting with Zimako and I.

"I am so happy for you guys. Such a wait. Thank God it paid off. Four years, *abi*?" Chuka, Chinazo's hubby asked.

"More or less; I still can't believe it. Thank you, *O!* To God be all the glory."

"So how do you feel, and what are you going to do now? Will you quit your job?" Chinazo enquired.

"You know, I have been thinking about how we proceed now that this thing is in our hands. We have to be in Canada within three months. Otherwise it will lapse," Zimako replied.

"It seems like you have a limited time to put all your plans together if Canada is saying you must come within ninety days," chipped in Chuka.

"You are right," Zimako said. "It's not like we had not planned this. We thought we might both keep our jobs while we went over there. Then depending on what happens, we will decide if it is wise to resign or not. We are still talking through various options; the key thing is to land before the expiration of the three months or else."

"Actually, the main dilemma for us now is which city we should settle in," I added. "The system there is different from what we have here, and the reports are that it can be quite cold in Canada, even down to twenty degrees below zero Celsius. Can you imagine that?"

"Twenty degrees below zero Celsius? What? How are you guys going to survive that?"

"Those living there, do they have two heads? We will join them in survival of the fittest. Naija man can survive anywhere. Jokes apart, that seems to be what we have signed up for. Actually, Anuli is doing most of the research into which city we should land in. I am hoping to talk to Obi; we were mates back in UniLag. He did a master's program in Canada. I'm hoping he'll have some insider information that might be useful," Zimako said, and I nodded in agreement.

"Honestly, I envy you guys, but for God's sake, how does anyone survive in that brutal weather?"

As we continued to share and discuss our plans, Makua pulled up a chair and joined the group. She had ditched her partner somewhere.

"Hey guys, did you start the conversation without me?"

Her beauty and fun-loving nature belied her brains. She was an orthopaedic resident, but once outside the confines of the hospital, she was a creature of fun.

Chinazo hugged her twin sister; both were close, though they were very different. "Come sit beside me," she said, shoving her hubby away to make room for her twin.

"You have not missed much, my dear," I said. "We were just discussing the fine print of our journey."

"You guys are so blessed, Zimako, but I don't know what Okpue and Ichie will say. I'll miss you both."

Zimako smiled. "Yeah, yeah, if Lagos boys will let you." The conversation immediately turned to their parents, and how they might react to the news.

Okwe sensed a melancholy mood creeping in. "Break it off, guys. Hip hop hurray, yay yay." He did not miss a step as he coerced Makua to the floor to dance to Onyeka Onwenu's "Ekwe." It was one of Zimako's favourites; he stood on his feet and invited me to the dance floor, too. The music was a mid-tempo rhythm of African highlife beat.

The party pulsated on, and at intervals someone would clap Zimako on the shoulder in congratulatory salutation.

Dusk turned to night, inhibitions loosened, and the party took on a life of its own. Everyone seemed to be having a really good time.

Ireti, Okwe's girlfriend, arrived and dutifully came over to offer deferential greetings to the twins and me. She stepped easily into her role as the unofficial hostess of the party, and was bustling from one end of the house and backyard to the other, making sure that everyone was taken care of.

* * * * *

The time passed quickly. It was midnight when Zimako looked at his Breitling watch.

"Babe, we ought to be leaving," he indicated to me. "It's getting rather late."

Chinazo overheard him, and asked, "Are you guys already leaving? Now?"

"Yes, remember we got here early; moreover, I am tired. Okwe had to host this party today, and I am not complaining, but after a hectic week, I just need to go home and crash right now."

"Okay then, we'll probably talk to you guys before the weekend is over." I went to find Okwe.

* * * * *

Zimako watched Anuli's rounded bum swaying and glanced at his vibrating phone. He saw a new text from Ndudi who, despite his protestations, refused to stop bugging him. *"Heard ur news. Congratulations. I'll h8 2 C U go."* Zimako guiltily deleted the text. Some people had no sense of decency, he thought. He wiped the frown, then stood up to say goodbye to Okwe. He acknowledged that the diehard party animals would stay on till the wee hours of the morning. As he was en route to find him, he chanced upon Makua with Tony. Both of them exchanged a smile. It was no surprise at all. Makua was a great girl, and good looking to boot and her earthy nature made her likeable. Zimako smiled, Tony did not stand a chance. Tony, also a medical doctor, was a good friend from the UniLag days; he was at the stage where he had to be looking to settle down.

* * * * *

I observed Zimako as he made his way towards me, and I could almost read his mind. We were itching to match-make these two, but knew that with Makua's penchant for a good time, it was certain that Tony's heart would soon be broken if he ventured in.

Many hugs and kisses later, Zimako and I made our way to the car. At Chinazo's insistence I had taken a packed container of rice and a bottle of bubbly.

"You guys should have a quiet celebration when you get home." Chinazo and Chuka waved us away.

Zimako was the designated driver. He was driving his midnight blue Passat.

"How are you feeling?" I asked.

"Actually, very tired. Okwe is just too stubborn. He was hell-bent on throwing this party, no matter what." Okwe was well known in the family for his partying.

"Is it not Okwe again? Why are you sounding surprised? If you are tired, I can drive. Do you want me to take the steering wheel? Or can you manage to get us home safely?" Anuli enquired.

Zimako put his hand on her thigh and turned to me and smiled. "Anuli, I am able and capable. Get ready, darling, for tonight I shall ravish you!" He kissed me deeply and started the engine. The car purred to life as I responded by boldly caressing him. We shared a secret smile in that dreamy way couples do.

Zimako steadied himself and we zoomed off with a wave to Okwe and Ireti.

CHAPTER THREE

> *Dear Diary,*
> *It was so nice to be with friends and family tonight. Everyone was genuinely happy for us. I don't know if I feel ready to start a new life, learning to like new foods, making new friends, and partying with Oyinbo people who have no rhythm or soul. But as long as I'm with Zimako, he will take charge. He'll make it work. He is my hero.*

We were at the Alhaji Masha turn off Western Avenue. Although the roads were free of vehicular traffic, it was a seedy, run-down neighbourhood. Zimako was in a good mood but he was also tired. Somewhat distractedly he glanced up at the rear-view mirror and was blinded by the headlights.

It took a while before Zimako mentioned to me, "I think we are being followed."

"What?"

"I think we are being followed," Zimako repeated, with a tinge of irritation in his voice. Being out late was always a risk. He took another look in his rear-view mirror and a frisson of fear swept through him. "*Obidiya*, don't panic. Don't look back; just try to organise yourself. Remove your valuables and jewellery. Let's be prepared," he said, taking his eyes off the road and giving me a quick glance. "Do you have money on you?"

"Yes, just about fifteen thousand naira." Puzzled, I asked, "Why are you talking like this? Should I be concerned? Can't we outrun them?"

"I am just thinking of the worst-case scenario. There seems to be four guys in that car. If truly they are after us, we need to anticipate their moves. If we are lucky, they may find another meatier market and lose interest in us."

A very tense Zimako clenched the steering wheel as he stepped on the gas, not minding the treacherous potholes that dotted the roads as he tried to lose the car following closely behind. He was familiar with the neighbourhood, but did not want to underestimate the tail. They were still a good distance from home, and he did not want them on his tail when he got home. His best bet was to trust God and drive like a madman, and hopefully he would lose them or they would find him too challenging of a target and give up on him.

He cursed, never in his life had he wished so desperately to see a police checkpoint. It was all I could do not to look back.

It was now pitch dark, and there were no street lights to illuminate the streets. Zimako's primary concern was protecting me. I could tell from the way he kept glancing in my direction. He could handle anything on his own, but with me in the car, he felt vulnerable.

It was becoming obvious that the guys behind us had no plans of giving up. I watched anxiously as emotions played on his face probably playing out different scenarios in his mind, wondering what they could possibly want. I knew he would be prepared to hand over the car keys to these criminals if it came to that.

"Damn!"

"What?" I whispered now very frightened.

"I have my passport here. Oh God! How could I? They will go for that instantly."

My heart sank. We knew how precious our international passports were, and always left them locked up in the safe at home. We were both well travelled around Europe and America, and had a series of unexpired visas on their passports. This was not the time for admonition.

"Where is it?"

"In the breast pocket of my jacket. That is the first place they will check. Take it and put it somewhere private."

In that moment, a shot rang out, busting a rear tyre of the Passat.

Zimako briefly lost control of the car, causing it to swerve dangerously. That momentary loss of control, coupled with the now not-fit-for-purpose tyre, cost Zimako the distance he'd had over their pursuers. The beat-up Toyota 4Runner overtook us and now blocked our exit.

* * * * *

Four men jumped out, shouting simultaneously and cordoning off any escape routes by their captive prey. "Put your head down, and don't move. Jump down. Lie down. Put your hands where I can see… "

A much-shaken Zimako managed to whisper to me, "Please do whatever they say; don't try to be smart."

Before he could finish, the door was yanked open and he was forcibly dragged from his seat. A gun was placed to his head, right at the temple.

The gruff voice of one of their captors demanded the keys, which Zimako meekly handed over. He then set about running his filthy paws down Zimako, perhaps hoping to discover a wad of cash.

The other door opened and I was dragged out, too. "Get down!"

"Please, please don't harm her," Zimako pleaded.

"Shurruup!" the man holding the gun to Zimako's head yelled. "Get down on your knees and put your hands on your head." The fermented, stale odour of cheap alcohol, mingled with marijuana, hit Zimako as his captor shouted out orders.

The man dragged me out of the car and I tumbled out. I had difficulty regaining my balance.

"Please, don't harm me. What do you want? I have some money. You can have it."

This second man pulled me up roughly. "Shut up!" he commanded in a menacing voice. "How much do you have? Where is it?"

The third man in the gang was already ransacking the vehicle whilst the fourth stood aloof from the action as though keeping an eye out. He remained silent through the exchange.

They were all armed and masked. I sobbed louder, bile rising in my mouth from panic.

"Shut up," the man holding me growled again. "You talk, and I shoot your head off."

"*Moolah* no dey anywhere," the one ransacking the car called out, and then threatening gunshots rang out, causing Zimako and I to duck instinctively. "Where is the *dosh*?" the lookout guy, who was clearly the leader of the pack, enquired.

Zimako had beads of perspiration furrowing his forehead, despite the coolness of the night breeze. "I know where it is. Please let me check myself," he pleaded.

The Ransacker lashed out, giving Zimako a resounding slap and then proceeded to hit him on the head with the butt of the gun. "I say make you shurruup now or you are dead meat."

Zimako clamped his mouth shut with his hands. Ransacker seemed as wound up as a too-tight coil, which had to be the effect of the *Igbo* that gave his breath this dank, sour smell. This was a potentially deadly situation. I could tell Zimako was scared; I was trembling, dreading the outcome. "Please, God, help us," I prayed fervently. The gun still at his temple was held by a very unsteady, almost vibrating, hand and if he made any false moves they would probably be fatal.

"*Fyne gyirl, wey the wad?*" enquired the lookout guy.

I meekly looked up at the one I mentally labelled Godfather and offered to go and get the cash from the car. The men nodded to give me the go-ahead. I gingerly arose from the ground, and he escorted me eight few steps to the car, where I reached into the pocket inside the passenger side door and extracted a brown envelope. I obediently handed it over to my escort. As I handed him the envelope, our fingers brushed and a jolt of electricity stunned me; the softness of his hands and the simultaneous tremor in my nether regions shocked me. My eyes gazed at his, and I saw desire in his eyes behind the mask. He must have felt it too, because when he spoke his voice was a strange mix of gruff and tender. "Woman *wetin*? No seduce me before I show you 'somethin.' In fact, 'somethin' dey hungry me; I will deal with you when we finish!"

Suddenly Godfather, in between angry expletives, exclaimed that the brown envelope contained only fifteen thousand naira. *"Wetin dat one go reach do eh?"* Ransacker, in a chain reaction to this, kicked Zimako in the groin, elbowed him in the midriff, and then topped it off with another butt at the head with the gun. This must have torn Zimako's scalp and pierced his brain if the impact and bleeding were indicative of his injury. "Where the !@* is the money?"

Zimako swayed feeling faint. He attempted to mask his fear and pain, but his voice was tremulous. "That is all we have. Please, take my watch. It's a Breitling. You can get seventy-five thousand naira for it. We are not rich, so please let us go."

Ransacker snatched the watch off Zimako's wrist, bruising him in the process. Godfather suggested they were done. "Let's go! They have nothing to offer!"

The other two, who up till now had not said or done very much, perked up almost in unison: "Make we kill the man!"

"No, Jasper," shouted Godfather emphatically. "I don't want dead bodies here."

"Okay, but at least make we *chop* the bitch *naa!*" stated the last of the four, who looked frankly depraved as he roughly fondled my breasts leaving me feeling very scared yet angry and nauseated, I was helpless I never felt so defiled.

Godfather approached me and concurred with Depraved. "She resemble like she need '*somethin'*" strong. *Make I taste am first, then if she sweet una fit chop.*" In a single move, he grabbed me by the shoulders, and threw me against the car.

Beads of perspiration formed under my arms. I was trembling like a leaf, my silk blouse clinging to the sweat dripping under me arms.   I saw his voracious eyes ogle my cleavage hungrily and I instinctively reached up and covered my breasts, feeling very exposed. He flung my hands away and attempted to tear the blouse, reaching for the neckline. Zimako screamed a loud, "NoOoOo… " from where he was sandwiched between two of the men. "Leave her alone," he croaked. He would die before he played witness to my being defiled. He attempted to make a dash for me, but was overpowered by the determined arms of the captors. My well-made silk blouse by Monsoon proved to be its own defence. It did not give way, frustrating Godfather, who had just completed the task of undoing his buckle, opening his fly, and unleashing his caged erection.

"Leave her alone!" Zimako screamed as he lunged forwards again, this time throwing off the man who held the gun to his head. That was a mistake. Both men held a struggling and kicking Zimako to the ground, one holding his palm over his mouth.

"Man, leave this woman. We've stayed here too long. Let's go! This was not part of the plan," Ransacker said, suddenly the voice of reason.

The atmosphere had become tense as one of the robbers disagreed as to whether I should be raped. His comments stopped Godfather in his tracks as his turgid erection deflated. "*She look like say she go sweet.*"

"*You really really want chop am?*" he asked the dissenting Ransacker.

"*I no want am. Make we just go. We no plan for this. Make we look for genue market. This people no favour us, so we never get big money this night*; you are right. When we get the *dough wey* we find then, *we fit enjoy the bitches for there. Make we no waste time with this people.*"

"Let's go. *Gbagbuo* their tyres." Three shots deflated all three remaining tyres of Zimako's beloved Passat.

Ransacker, who had dissented regarding the rape, shot me an almost apologetic look. I knew I would never forget those eyes as long as I lived; he had saved me.

The men piled into their getaway car, slammed the doors, and sped off into the night.

I tried to stand up, but instead keeled over and buckled.

"Anuli! *Obidiya*! Anuli!!! Wake up." I heard his voice as though from a distance. I could barely move, and lay lifeless in his arms. Flustered, He did not want to leave, not even for a second, I tried to motion him to go, but found myself drained of strength; finally he made the hard decision and went to retrieve his phone. I heard him whisper, "Lord Jesus, please help me. Don't let my wife die; she's all I've got… "

I felt him lift me and carry me to the car still oscillating between consciousness and unconsciousness. Dialling quickly, he called the private hospital where we were registered. He asked for an ambulance, explaining his predicament. I tied to speak, but felt too weak. An attendant informed him there was none available. He must have advised Zimako to try and find a cab, or drive down. I heard him arguing, and kept repeating that his tyres were flat and his wife was unconscious. The phone went dead.

He turned to me; my breathing was comfortable and steady and I felt somewhat better if very weak and light headed. He found a bottle of water in the back seat; from a habit he developed to ameliorate the often unbearable Lagos heat. He sprinkled some all over me, not minding the damage to his car. It jolted me immediately.

"Oh, baby! Thank God. I am so happy you are alive! Are you okay?"

I still felt disorientated.

"Oh my God! Zimako, what happened to me? Did he? Did they… ?" The words died on my lips. I ached all over and refused to let my mind conjure up images. I could not be sure what was real, and what was not.

"No, *Obidiya*, nothing happened!" he looked earnestly at me, and cradled me close to his heart. "You are safe. They are gone. It's okay. We'll be fine. We survived."

I sat upright, for the first time and noticed the bleeding from his head. "Oh, look at you, Zimako. You are hurt. We need an ambulance."

He laughed, and explained what had happened. "I already called them. Now I'll call the police; we may have better luck with them."

He dialled the police. The constable took all his particulars over the phone, and asked him a few more questions. Zimako betrayed his exasperation with all the questioning, which only irked the officer and earned him more questions.

"Could you hurry? It is very unsafe here, and we are in danger."

The constable unsympathetically responded that he was not to blame and was only being thorough and doing his job. He suggested Zimako should accept that in the current climate, going out night crawling was an open invitation to unscrupulous marauders. Zimako swore under his breath. In a mock-polite voice the police officer suggested, "*Oga*, if you are not satisfy with my work, then police is not your friend. Try another place." Before Zimako could respond, the line went dead.

Without help from the ambulance or police, Zimako and I were truly stranded. I did not feel safe, and Zimako must have felt vulnerable with me by his side. He tried to reach Okwe, but that proved impossible, as the phone rang without a response. He decided to try and contact his mechanic, Blacky.

That was a lucky try. Blacky picked up his phone immediately. Zimako explained the situation apologetically and Blacky swung into action, in the way only a real Lagos area boy would.

"*Oga*, no *wahala*! Me and my guy, we come use tow carry your Passat to shop; meanwhile, *me I go carry una for my moto follow am; after we go drop you together with madam for house.*"

Help was on the way.

Where the so-called emergency services had let us down, Blacky was going to come through for us.

Zimako heaved a sigh of relief and assured me that within the next hour or so, we would be on our way home.

We only needed to stay safe till Blacky showed up.

CHAPTER FOUR

> *Dear Diary,*
>
> *Where do I begin? What a nightmare! Words can't begin to express the trauma of tonight.*
>
> *One minute, I was looking forward to getting home and getting down to some real good loving and the passionate embrace and gentle touch of my darling husband; the next thing I knew, I was being mauled by riff-raff—stinking, masked hoodlums.*
>
> *Oh my God! I will never, ever, forget being molested by that brute! His hands made me feel grimy. God, where were you? Why did you let it happen? Why, why, why?*
>
> *How can I ever cleanse my mind of this ghastly event?*
>
> *Are you there, God? I believed you were giving us a new beginning, so why did this happen?*

I couldn't stop wondering why what had happened that morning had occurred. My mind was in turmoil. I must have passed out at some point during the ordeal because Zimako was hovering over me when I woke up. I wished I had died. But Zimako said nothing happened that I should be ashamed of. He assured me he would rather have died fighting to protect my honour than let anything happen to me. He was being so brave, and did not mention the hits he took, but for the tell-tale bump on his bloodied forehead.

The hospital and police failed to respond to our SOS calls. Thank God for Blacky, the mechanic down the road! We were finally rescued by him.

Zimako insisted we try and get some sleep. He was eerily very calm and back in control. I was too tired and traumatized to even protest. We agreed to call our families and tell them what happened in the morning after visiting the hospital and lodging a police report.

To my surprise, I managed to fall asleep.

Morning dawned. Life continued.

* * * * *

We took a taxi to the hospital to see the doctor, who examined us. He said Zimako's head injury was superficial and minor and the risk of concussion was low. As for me, he was concerned I might develop post-traumatic stress disorder, but confirmed that physically there was no evidence to suggest sexual assault. Zimako had given him an honest but disinfected précis of the night's events in a matter-of-fact way, sparing my blushes.

On the outside I looked okay, but something inside me had died. My faith was shaken and my emotions were numb.

Zimako's first instinct call was to Makua.

He decided there was no point making a police report since we did not lose the car, the money was insignificant, and the wristwatch was uninsured and unlikely to be recovered.

I could see his point. Everybody in Lagos knows the police are in cahoots with armed robbers.

I felt bad about his watch. I had saved and made sacrifices to buy that watch for him. I had picked it out for him on holiday for our third anniversary and I had our entwined initials engraved on it. It was unique; I would recognise it anywhere. Oh well, thinking positively, it may have just saved our lives.

As though he could read my mind he suddenly said, "Anuli, let them take the watch; at least we are both alive. I know how you feel. Going to the police is a waste of time. After putting us through filling out all sorts of forms, they will sit back and do nothing. You and I know they will never locate those animals."

I nodded my head, not uttering a word.

"*Obidiya*, if you like, we will go to the police later. Your happiness is my priority. Just know that I love you."

I had a lump in my throat and tears welled up in my eyes as I heard him say that. His comment touched the very nerve of how I was feeling worthless and damaged.

He sensed my tears and turned towards me. He reached out, gave my limp hand a squeeze, and engulfed me in a warm, secure embrace which seemed to last forever; as I looked up into his eyes, unexpectedly he kissed me. Even more unexpectedly, I responded.

"Will you smile for me?" It was a tough thing to do, but I eked out a smile for him. I guess my smile reassured him, because he let out a sigh of relief.

"*Obidiya*, I will do anything to make you feel better. Do you really want me to get the police involved? Because if that's what you want, I will do it."

The thought of the perfunctory paperwork and rigmarole put me off. I recalled stories I had heard of people going to the station to report a crime and ending up being accused as suspects. "No, Zimako, I can see your point." I looked towards the traffic as I said that. Once again, the tears filled my eyes.

I knew Zimako was doing what was best for me, but I felt deep down that it was wrong for those hoodlums to get away scot-free. They should be made to suffer and pay.

Once Makua picked up her phone and heard the news, she panicked and imagined the worst.

"What?" she screamed into the phone. "You guys were attacked?"

Her reaction was hardly unexpected.

Zimako knew he just had to tell her, once he told her, she was certain to circulate it to everyone in the family.

It was trickier for me. I was still nauseated from thinking about everything, and wondering how to move on.

Suddenly, Zimako and I were the epicentre of news, both good and bad.

Once Zimako was done speaking with Makua, I broached this with him. "Will we tell the parents that we were attacked and that we are leaving for Canada in the same conversation? It will be too much for them to take in. It just seems too much is happening to us."

Zimako held my hand and lifted it to his lips, which always steadied me and in an inexplicable way brought me some comfort.

"God is in control, my dearest. I believe everything will work out perfectly." He smiled at me. That crooked smile of his was always guaranteed to set my heart aflutter as it did just now. Even after six years of marriage, I was as much in love with him as the day he proposed, perhaps more.

* * * * *

Zimako was concerned about my state of mind. I must have seemed overwhelmed and distraught by the events of the night. "Anuli, call your parents, and mention what happened, but please be gentle, okay? You do not have to burden them with the details, especially your dad."

Prof picked up the phone on the second ring.

"Anuli, how are you?" my father bellowed. He had the posh enunciation of the old grammarians, having attended grammar school of the old order.

"Daddy, I am fine." My voice broke as tears gathered in my eyes. "No, I'm not fine," I blurted out. The conversation had taken on a life of its own. Daddy seemed bewildered by my loss of composure. I am not sure he had seen me cry for years, maybe not since I was in my terrible teen years. I was widely regarded as the strong one in the family.

"You don't seem okay. What is wrong, Anuli? Do you need to speak to your mother? Is it Zimako?"

"No, Daddy, it's okay. I just called to tell you that last night Zimako and I were attacked by armed robbers."

"What!" The boom of his exclamation caused the phone to drop from my hand. I struggled to regain my composure, and retrieved my phone.

"Yes, Daddy. We were attacked last night."

"Have you reported the matter to the police? Are you hurt? Where is Zimako?" The questions kept coming.

"Daddy, we have gone to the hospital, and both of us are fine. Zimako is right here beside me. Do you want to speak with him?"

My father spoke with Zimako, who assured him that everything was under control, and that we would visit them sometime soon.

Once he determined that there was no further cause for concern, he gave the phone to my mother, who spoke with Zimako at length before handing the phone back to me.

"*Ewoo, ewoo,* hmmm. *Omalicha nwam,* how are you?" That question had suddenly become the most difficult question of my life. I knew I was lying when I said, "I'm fine, Mummy." I did not want to worry her. "We are already planning our next visit to Ibadan." I kept the conversation brief. Mummy is very perceptive; I did not want her dredging out answers from me.

"Mummy, when we see each other face-to-face we can talk about everything."

"Are you seeing your sister? Does she know?" My sister Chiamaka also lived in Lagos and Mum always took comfort in knowing we were there for each other.

"I will call her after talking to you, Mum."

* * * * *

We were now approaching the entrance into the gated community where we lived.

I put my BlackBerry away. Thank God they had not been interested in our phones. All my contacts were on it. I knew I had to call Chiamaka, but speaking to Mummy and Prof had worn me out. Perhaps later; yes, later.

Approaching the rented house we had called home for the past six years, a comfortable three-bedroom duplex in Yaba, I espied Chiamaka and Okwe under the fruit tree, anxiously awaiting our return. Clearly they had heard and had attended promptly, only to find us absent. Their facial expressions reflected sympathy.

"This is entirely my fault!" Okwe blurted as we made our way towards the house.

Chiamaka sidled up to me and whispered my name, and then she hugged me. I wanted to relax into her embrace, but as much as I needed the comfort she was offering, I knew I had to be strong. But being cuddled by my little sister really made me feel better; I think she sensed I needed the hug, so she further tightened her arms around me. She smelt clean and nice, the total opposite of those hooligans.

"Chichi, thank you. I am really fine, really; calm down."

"What happened?"

"Come, let's go inside. Zimako must be regaling Okwe with the details; you can hear it from the other horse's mouth." I laughed at my own joke and Chiamaka joined in. We collapsed in a fit of giggling. I almost wet myself.

This was the first time I had laughed since the incident and it attracted Zimako's attention. He looked up and smiled, as though trying to tell me it was all going to be fine.

"*Obidiya*, come here. Have you heard anything more ridiculous in your life? Okwe thinks it's all his fault."

Okwe and Chiamaka were regular guests at our home and there was not much required to make them comfortable. I sat down beside Zimako and felt his arm go around my shoulders.

"Okwe, you must not blame yourself."

"Mustn't I? Zimako never wanted that party. In this dangerous Lagos, I insisted. Now look what has happened. I'm so sorry."

"What party?" That was Chiamaka.

"Oh no!" Okwe, I could tell, was feeling guilty. He had not invited Chiamaka and Ogbo, her husband, to his "close friends and family" gathering yesterday. I could already sense an undercurrent and wondered how this would play out.

"I had a little get-together yesterday for Zimako and Anuli. You know, to celebrate the whole Canadian thing. I don't know how you guys skipped my mind. Honestly, just hold me account—"

He did not finish the sentence before Chiamaka interrupted him. "Sorry, am I missing a chunk of information? Just rewind a bit. What Canadian thing?" She turned to Zimako and me, repeating her question for emphasis. "What Canadian thing?"

* * * * *

"ChiChi... " I started, and then the doorbell rang.

Zimako jumped up. "Let me get that."

I knew Zimako was being cowardly, letting me handle the job of explaining to my sister why there was a major development which had led to a party and she had been left out of the loop. I tried to continue. "Where should I start? I guess I should take the blame. I was still coming to terms with the news myself and I planned to speak to you properly and get your point of view and now see… " My sentence trailed off as Chinazo and Makua, the twins, came in with Chuka in tow.

It did not get any more complete than that. I gave the twins a quick hug. I needed some time with Chiamaka. "Please make yourselves at home. Chuka, the girls will take care of you; I'm going upstairs for a minute. ChiChi, come with me, please."

I took her up to the bedroom Zimako and I shared. It was a light, airy room with an en suite bathroom; coming in here always lifted my spirits. I had picked out the soft furnishings individually and lovingly. Our bed was simple and understated. It had been handmade for us and was one of a kind.

I lay on my tummy on the bed and looked at ChiChi, who sat at the dressing table. We made eye contact indirectly through the mirror. I started by sharing the news about the Canadian residency, which I explained was the reason for the impromptu party which Okwe had single-handedly stage-managed despite Zimako's vehement objections. Conscious of the guests downstairs, I moved swiftly on to the post-party incident, sparing no detail. I was initially hesitant about discussing the groping of my breasts, but once I started, I wanted her to know everything. Telling her was cathartic and once I had vented my anger, I felt an inner peace, a sort of calm wash over me. ChiChi came and lay beside me, but did not say anything for a while.

Then she looked at me and asked, "How do you feel, sis? Honestly?"

I reflected on the way I was feeling and told her that, surprisingly, I felt fine just at that moment. I had not felt that way until I saw her this afternoon and suspected that I had drawn strength from her. She smiled and said she was proud of how brave I had been. We lapsed into our usual reminiscing of how we get our strength from our mother's side of the family, about being strong and resilient women, and making lemonade out of the lemons life offers sometimes.

I laughed. "So how is my life for a rollercoaster vacillating between extreme good and bad, eh?"

As we stood up, Chiamaka, with her thumb to the middle finger on both hands, simultaneously swirling her arm over her head, snapped her fingers and in a mock-serious voice exclaimed, "I reject, that is not your portion, O! I've heard all you said, the good and the bad. What I still don't get is how come I, your darlingest sister, did not know about this till now? Hmmm?"

"There's no excuse. Even if I said I was busy last week, that is not a reason. I called, but I didn't want to leave a message because I wanted to tell you myself. Then, of course, Okwe with his exuberance had a party planned from the second Zimako told him about it. The rest, as they say, is history."

"Oh well, that is what you get for going off and having a party without me. Now what is Ogbo going to say when I tell him this attack happened on your way back from a party held by Okwe, to which we were not invited? Hmmm?"

I knew exactly what she meant. I couldn't ask her to fudge the truth to get me out of Ogbo's *wahala*. Ogbo would feel slighted and Okwe would not be spared his displeasure.

"That serves Okwe right. He often leaps before he looks, so he'll have to deal with the fallout from this."

Chiamaka considered that and smiled. "Let's go back downstairs before your guests start to worry; I have monopolized you enough."

* * * * *

Zimako was doing his best to explain that we were fine when Chiamaka and I re-joined them. He caught my eye, and we shared a private look and smiled. I sat beside Okwe, while Chiamaka went to share the smaller sofa with Makua. Chinazo was sitting with Chuka. Makua started sharing the story of an unfortunate patient who had not been as lucky as we were, and everyone pitched in with the story of a friend of a friend; in Lagos everyone knew someone who had been a victim of robbers.

This was fertile fodder and soon the conversation veered to all that was wrong with our country. Nigeria was in a downward spiral. The government was making no effort to protect its citizens or provide infrastructure to cater to their needs.

Then Zimako spoke up. "Thank God for Blacky, who towed the battered Passat from his friend's workshop this morning to the VW auto shop. I guess they will let me know the extent of the damage and the damage to my pocket next week. My only consolation is that we are safe, Anuli and I." As though making a political rally speech, his voice notched up an octave and he continued. "Personally, this underscores my commitment to seek a better life in a decent part of the world. You guys know that I was ambivalent yesterday at the party when we spoke about leaving for Canada. Well, after all that has happened, I am now determined to do what it takes to protect my family. We will set in motion plans to leave soon."

It was quite a speech coming from my husband, and I could hear the emotion in his voice as he spoke. His siblings were quiet, and you could have heard a pin drop.

Okwe was the first to recover, and he spoke up. "Bros, I know you have said it is not my fault—of a truth, those gangsters were not my boys," he joked. "My hands are clean, *hair no dey my armpit*."

His lame attempt at a joke caught us unawares and everyone laughed. Okwe was not finished. "But jokes apart, I think this move to Canada will be good for you and Anuli, my best sister after my sisters, and this may have been a reminder of all that is wrong with Nigeria. I will miss you, bros, but there is no need for second thoughts. As for the rest of us, who you will be leaving behind, *aluta continua*, but we shall survive."

I liked Okwe a lot. He had a way of making light of potentially tense and volatile situations, and after he spoke, I could see the tension from Zimako's speech had been diffused.

To the question of how soon we were planning on leaving, and finer details of our arrangements, my husband vaguely suggested we might leave even earlier than we had planned, but "We are going to have to visit the parents and inform them of our plans first."

The conversation was overshadowed by thoughts of our

imminent departure and the effect it would have on family dynamics. Our families would have to adjust to our absence. Zimako was the oldest son and everyone's go-to person. His parents were advancing in years, and obviously the news of his departure would be a bitter pill. He was now the breadwinner for his parents. He was their pension plan, and they depended on him.

My parents were not young either, but Mummy was still working with the Ministry of Education. Prof was now only lecturing part-time at the university these days, and we all contributed a bit to support them. I knew they would find my departure difficult to adjust to. Zimako and I visited them more frequently than my sibling. My heart felt heavy and a wave of sadness overwhelmed me.

* * * * *

A new era was dawning.

I went to the kitchen, threw together a few ingredients, and rustled up some pepper soup and prepared some fried chicken. I arranged juice and soft drinks on the tray and took it out to my guests. We did not keep any alcohol at home as neither of us was a big drinker.

"No way, sis. Let's have something strong to drown our sorrows. How can I drink Coke at a time like this, eh?" It was Okwe again.

"Sorrows? Let us be happy. The future is full of promise," Zimako stated.

"Sorry, Okwe, not even for you." I laughed as I said it, knowing he was only pulling my leg.

As is the case when we gather together, time flew really fast. Chiamaka's phone rang; it was Ogbo, her husband. She brought him up to speed on all that had transpired, and he asked to speak with Zimako. Chiamaka tried passing the phone to Zimako, but Okwe intercepted it and immediately launched into an apology for leaving him and Chiamaka out of the party invite. Ogbo must have cracked a joke, as he accepted the heartfelt apology because Okwe laughed out loud when he handed the phone to Zimako.

When the call was over, Chiamaka stood to leave; we hugged and held each other tight knowing that we had very little time together.

"Listen, sis, call me on Monday, and let's arrange to do lunch, okay?"

Chinazo and Chuka followed in her wake. "Okay, guys, it's getting late. Let us know what the plans are. We might be able to travel to Ibadan with you guys on the weekend." There was another round of hugs as they departed.

Okwe and Makua relaxed and lingered. It seemed like a normal leisurely Saturday visit. We sat back, chilled out, ate, drank, and were merry.

The evening wore on, and Okwe, who used the facade of humour to manage his inner feelings, got serious and opened up as we all began to talk earnestly and share what the prospect of moving to Canada would truly mean for us all.

CHAPTER FIVE

> *Dear Diary,*
> *We are going to the village. This is a memorable journey and I need to have all my faculties focussed. I don't know when I'll travel this route again. I'm observing everything through new eyes. I'm even nostalgic about the rubbish roads and the street hawkers. The artistic inscriptions on the sides of the trucks amuse and entertain me to no end. I will not let Okpue get me down. I will humour her, I will be a model daughter-in-law, and I will triumph over this.*

We were on our way to the village. Crisscrossing the "expressway," dodging potholes and craters gaping so wide that they could comfortably house a shed-load of vagrants. Zimako shrugged his shoulders and sighed. "Will these roads ever be fixed?" It was a rhetorical question; I don't think he was genuinely expecting a response. He continued his monologue. "That is the problem with us. We lack maintenance culture."

It required certain dexterity to navigate and travel safely from Lagos to the eastern part of Nigeria. The roads were treacherous, having been ravaged by acid rain and erosion. The "east" was notorious for the disrepair of the roads, kidnappers, and highway robbers. It was not an adventure for the faint-hearted.

I didn't mind the bad roads as long as I was not doing the driving. Zimako seemed to handle the road masterfully. Before I knew it, we were approaching the famous Onitsha Bridge, the gateway to Igboland from the western part of the country. It was one of my favourite landmarks; it told me I was on Igbo soil and home was near.

The climate-controlled, air-conditioned Passat cocooned us

from the sweltering heat. Makua was singing along to Osadebe, one of our best known Igbo highlife musicians, who was singing "People's Club." She did some dance moves, really getting into the groove. I smiled at her. Makua somehow maintained a cheerful demeanour despite the emotional demands and mental and physical stress of her work as a medical doctor. Stress seemed to slither off her like water off a duck's back. Her work was compartmentalised away from other aspects of her life, and I really admired her ability to achieve what appeared to be the perfect work-life balance.

We had already been travelling for seven hours, and it was a pleasant journey so far. The sun was at its peak and if we maintained our pace, we would be home soon. I was of two minds about going to the village.

"*Obidiya*, we'll need to buy some fish and bread for Mama," Zimako reminded me. It was a given, practically engraved in stone, to buy provisions and fresh produce from Onitsha bridge-head before continuing into the hinterland. People at home expected travellers to come bearing these items as part of the gifts from *ndi-Lagos* whenever they came home. Arriving empty-handed was likely to be misinterpreted as an insult and would not go over well at all.

As Zimako slowed to park beside one of the ramshackle stalls displaying the wares of the roadside vendors, I peered out to catch a quick glimpse of the items on offer. Once Zimako came to a halt, the tenacious traders approached us aggressively, trying to get maximum exposure as they showcased their goods. The deafening cacophony of voices making a bid to outsell the competition was musical and irritating in equal measure.

"Buy yam, I go sell *am* cheap for you."

"You want bread? *E* fresh well well!"

"Banana, banana, and groundnut, sister, buy from me!"

"Na me first come!"

"Fresh fish dey, na today we catch am. I go clean am for you."

Some spoke Igbo to identify with the travellers.

I turned back to see Makua grimacing as she shrank away from the onslaught of the vendors crowding around our car. She did not care for the roadside market experience. "*Nne,* come with me, *biko,*" I urged persuasively. "You can offer me moral support and advice. You know better than I what *Okpue* and the aunties would like. Let Zimako stretch his legs."

Makua attempted a vociferous refusal before reluctantly giving in with a smile. "If you insist; only because it's you. These markets are just not my thing."

I attempted to open her door, fending off the vendors, hoping they understood that I had every intention of perusing the stalls and making my selections myself. As Makua pushed her way through the crowd, we were greeted with murmuring.

I was glad Makua was travelling down with us because my mother-in-law and I had a somewhat love-hate relationship, which was sometimes sweet, sometimes stormy. I definitely could use the diversion created by the cajoling and teasing presence of Makua. Having Makua as a captive audience also meant I could teasingly probe her about her love life, a discussion Zimako cringed to be eavesdropping on. Chinazo and Chuka had declined our invitation to come along, rather offering to come to Ibadan with us to visit my parents on our return to Lagos.

Makua and I blended into the fray, stall-hopping, bantering and bargaining with the vendors in response to cries of, "Customer buy from me. I will give you good price," "Take the remaining. Let me close market," "How much you *wan'* pay? Offer me better price *a beg.*" We haggled over the displayed produce, hoping to compromise on a favourable price. It was a sweet-talking process, requiring guile, in which only the patient and wily triumphed. The naive and prickly were invariably short-changed. I might have wanted to linger, but was conscious of my reluctant companion and the journey ahead. I could tell Makua was impatient with all the dawdling of haggling. I had insisted Zimako remain in the car, because it was a well-known fact that men did not triumph in market politics, often buying things at way above market prices because they were hasty and gullible.

My sophistication was merely a veneer. I had decided on my strategy. The vendors worked on the theory that those of us coming from Lagos usually had a little bit more cash, and they commensurately priced the items above the usual price for those they perceived as customers from Lagos. I whispered to Makua, "Brace yourself for this. Keep a straight face."

I smiled and addressed the woman wearing a scruffy, well-worn tee shirt over a threadbare, brownish, wax print *wrapper* in Igbo. "*Nwanyi ji ego ole?* How much for your yams?" I prided myself on being able to outsmart the vendor and get a great bargain. I had no intention of paying her asking price; my question was just the opening gambit.

"Special price for you, madam. These are mature yams, and see as them giant reach, you go pay me fifteen thousand *naira*, dozen price?"

Makua was rather amused and listened in with an air of nonchalance bordering on disinterest as I turned on the charm. The yams vendor and I bartered back and forth till we settled at nine thousand naira for the basket of twelve. Makua looked impressed that I pulled that off—a triumph for a woman from Lagos.

We also bought smoked fish, some loaves of Our Lady's, the distinctive malted bread, and some fruit, then made our way back to the car.

As we approached, Zimako helpfully grabbed the items from us as Makua brought him up to speed on the spectacle she had witnessed. She had not seen me in action before. "Zimako, you should have seen your wife; her spiel was worthy of an Oscar, honestly. She was like a pro. I bet you never heard her speak her street Igbo." Makua doubled over in laughter.

I tried to make light of it. "Oh, Zimako, you mustn't listen to Makua. You know how she exaggerates."

Zimako gave me an indulgent glance, and I winked at him and smiled slyly. Makua was excluded from our tender private bubble.

With our purchases stowed in the boot of the car, we set off again. Luckily there was little traffic to hinder us, and we crossed the Onitsha Bridge into eastern Nigeria.

* * * * *

Onitsha was the commercial hub of eastern Nigeria, rivalled only by Aba; it was a melting pot, a meeting of the old and the modern, at once a cosmopolitan city with new architecture, interspersed with the thatched huts and ancient buildings of yesteryear's pre-colonial period. The city welcomed us gaily; noise and the acrid smell of human excrement pervaded the air.

Ochoo passengers, as the bus conductors were known, indigenous touts popularly called area boys, and pedestrians commingled and jaywalked across the road as though it were an open-air rally. They had scant regard for approaching traffic. Zimako was unfazed by the chaos. He dodged the crowds, meandered through the narrow thoroughfare that was left of the dual carriageway, and skilfully navigated the potholed highway to continue our cruise to the village.

We embarked on the final leg of the journey with a mix of anticipation, trepidation, and excitement.

* * * * *

Okwe was also travelling up with Tony, but they were taking it easy. Tony had asked to accompany him as part of his game plan to demonstrate the sincerity of his interest in Makua. He frequently popped up, trying to include himself in intimate family gatherings. He was a gynaecologist in private practice and his work schedule was flexible. Tony and Zimako had been friends since their UniLag days, and Zimako was a motivated matchmaker. When the date was fixed for the trip to the village, Tony signed up, seeing it as a golden opportunity to formally register his amorous intentions and get closer to Makua.

Tony was good company, and Okwe was pleased to have him as co-pilot on the long drive. Glancing sideways, Okwe noticed his passenger had nodded off. He tapped him lightly. "Ol' boy, you dey snooze?" Tony was half conscious and mumbled an incoherent response. Okwe decided to let him be. Tony had worked the nightshift the day before, but insisted on making the trip; the lure of Makua was irresistible. His intentions were an open secret.

Okwe sympathised with Tony and respected his privacy. He did not try to pry information out of him. If he could give Tony one piece of advice it would be to quit while he was ahead. He knew it would be an uphill task for Tony to nail Makua; he smiled to himself, remembering all the guys who had befriended him to get close to Makua. Tony would not be the first one to travel this well-worn path to Makua's heart. Makua was a tough nut to crack.

Okwe figured that Zimako and his all-girl entourage had set off early and would very likely have hit Onitsha by now. They had a four-hour head start while he had waited to get Tony.

He planned a pit stop at Umunede, a small commuter town along the Benin-Asaba Expressway. It was his preferred spot for both drinking and passing water. A journey of this length needed planned breaks.

Lulled by the monotony of the scenery and the comfortable silence, Okwe let his mind drift. His thoughts veered to Zimako and his impending departure. He was happy for Zimako, knowing there lay great opportunities ahead for him, but amidst all the gaiety was a melancholy that swamped him in unguarded moments. Life in Nigeria was not going to be the same without his big brother.

It was going to be lonely.

He had always had Zimako around, apart from when he and Zimako had gone to different Federal Government Colleges. That was probably the only time they had schooled separately. Both of them had attended UniLag and had lived together in Aguda.

It was from their shared digs in Aguda that Zimako found his own place in Yaba just prior to settling down with Anuli. Shortly after that, Okwe also moved out of the flat in Aguda and got this one in Surulere.

He would soldier on. All things considered, life was good.

He had met Ireti at a party and was attracted to her bubbly and friendly nature. She was half Togolese, half Yoruba, and worked as a French translator with Alliance Française. Their relationship had started as a casual fling; he had not intended for it to last. He was not one for long-term relationships, but Ireti was special—so special she had broken a record, two years and counting. He engineered his relationships never to exceed nine months, where the attraction was strong enough, then maybe *pata-*

pata one year; that was the max.

He considered his relationship with Ireti. Was it really two years already? Time sure did fly when you were having fun. He really enjoyed her company. But, and there was a big emphatic but, Ireti had two serious shortcomings in his mind's eye. Firstly, she was not of his tribe, and although he prided himself on his metropolitan credentials, he did not see himself marrying a girl who was not Ibo. And then there was the other matter; of course one mustn't forget the other issue. He smiled to himself. She was just too good in bed to be wife material.

* * * * *

"We are nearly home," Zimako announced.

He was happy to be coming home. He always thought of Imeobodo as home. He had mixed emotions—joy at seeing his parents, but a heavy heart because he knew he bore news that would be tough on them. Okpue would be heartbroken and might even blame their Canadian expedition on me. Deep down, though, I sensed it was *Ichie* he was concerned about. He valued his father's opinion and more than anything, he needed his approval and affirmation. He knew this homecoming was different from all the previous ones. One way or another, it might turn out to be the last time they were together.

Ichie was a gentle giant, quiet and deliberate. He raised his boys to be God-fearing men, and to reach for the skies. He warned them against inordinate ambition. He lived what he preached. Peace of mind, he said, was a gift beyond all the money in the world.

Be still, my beating heart. I cautioned myself.

Zimako appeared both excited and anxious.

He loved the red muddy soil and dust that was a peculiar feature of eastern Nigeria. The red soil was both good and bad. It coated everything, everywhere, and could be a blight on the decor of modern painted homes; but the red soil was part of the unique character of home. He conjured up a mental image of the family home, with its ever-present fine dusting of red powder which caressed the walls and masked the paint. His thoughts seesawed between the sense of homecoming, the scenery, and the discussions he would have with his parents over the coming days would be difficult.

Makua intuited her brother's apprehension as we headed towards *Oye agu*, the central market in Imeobodo, which in the days of old served as a forum for farmers to barter their goods. She knew it would be difficult to break the news to her parents. Zimako was their devoted, successful son. Losing him to far climes would be an emotional challenge; tough times lay ahead.

She adopted a mischievous mood, making jokes to lift his mood and cheer him. "Hey, Zimako, do you remember the time you and Okwe tried to catch that goat?"

Zimako burst out laughing. That one was guaranteed to get him laughing out loud. "Makua. Oh no, please don't tell that story. Otherwise Anuli will never let me hear the last of it."

The ambience in the car had been overcast as each person was deep in thought. Makua lightened the mood with her comedic tales.

"No, I will not ask you to divulge family secrets," I said, shaking my head and smiling. Makua was glad her ploy had worked and she had sufficiently distracted Zimako. Job done, she turned her attention to the window and began people-gazing, looking to see if she could recognise any faces along the road. Passers-by also slowed to rubberneck, scrutinising the occupants of the unfamiliar passing car, almost as though with a sixth sense they could tell when one of their illustrious sons was coming home.

It was late afternoon, and it was *Oye* day. The market was bustling with activity. In Imeobodo everyone knew everyone, and nobody minded their own business.

Zimako informed us that he intended to stop at the all-purpose shop, which doubled as an off license, to buy some alcoholic beverages. The shop sold all forms of bric-a-brac. Zimako knew his father would not accept any excuse for not bring home some good bottles of Schnapps and White Horse. "Is there anything I can get for any of you?"

"Thanks, Zimako, I think I'm fine," I said.

Makua offered to go in with him. "You know I am the connoisseur of local hard juice," she said, making both Zimako and I roar with laughter.

"Go on, guys, I'll wait for you in the car," I suggested. I welcomed the solitary interlude to prepare to deal with the tsunami of emotions that was sure to be the hallmark of this weekend.

I idly reflected whilst absent-mindedly watching the human traffic go by. Life in the village bustled at a leisurely pace. Zimako's village was not much different from mine; okay, maybe it was more urbanised. For one, they had electricity and good mobile network reception. Pipe-borne water was a challenge, same as mine. They had a tarred road network of sorts. That was probably where the similarities ended.

I turned my mind again to the weekend ahead.

I was not looking forward to the barrage of emotions that would be unleashed once Zimako revealed we were immigrating to Canada. For goodness sakes, I was still struggling to come to terms with it myself; it was going to be challenging. Well, to be more specific, it was going to be difficult on my mother-in-law. She was obsessively possessive when it came to Zimako. Okpue was less clingy with Okwe. Zimako quitting bachelorhood to settle down had been a major trauma for her; you would think her son was dead, never to be seen again. Imagine how traumatic this would be for her. Since settling down with Zimako, I had tried and never quite felt that I succeeded in winning my mother-in-law over. This visit was not going to be different from all others in the past, with the veiled, somewhat snide, sarcastic comments interspersed with friendly familiarity; so while Zimako was excited to be seeing his parents, I was filled with trepidation. It was going to be a very long weekend.

Zimako and Makua came back to the car with the "hot" drinks. The journey resumed. We were no more than ten minutes from the family compound. Zimako's parents were expecting us.

"Okpue had better have my *ugba* ready, because I am starving," Zimako intoned. Makua said she had requested simple *jollof* rice and plantain with her secret-recipe of awesome vegetable stew.

Zimako reached out and held my hand. He was not unaware of my inner turmoil, but the excitement was getting the better of him.

As we approached the compound, more faces appeared vaguely familiar, and the passers-by waved at us with interest. It was obvious that sooner than later, the news would be all over town that there were guests at Ichie Adiora's compound.

Zimako stopped in front of the imposing gate of the family compound and tooted the horn. We waited for the gates to be opened.

Zimako and Makua were becoming irritated by the brief delay at the gate. He was impatient to see his parents and desperately needed to ease himself. After what seemed a lengthy wait, just as he was about to open the door and alight from the car, the gates were opened by Obegolu, the gateman.

Home, sweet home.

I made sure my smile was in place.

CHAPTER SIX

Dear Diary,

Please, God, give me strength. Give me patience.

It's going to be a long weekend. I had always said I would not marry a man whose mother was alive or was the bright shining light in his family. No offence meant, but the bonds between a mother and her son are difficult to fathom. I feel I'll need all my diplomatic skills to see me through. She may be his first love, but now he belongs to me and in his heart I'm number one. I need to keep chanting that as my mantra; I'm his numero uno. Let the battle commence.

Please, God, give me strength.

"N*no nno! Brother anata go!*" filled the air. "*Ndi-Lagos, e lu te go.*"

A whirlwind of copper-red dust trailed behind, the gate shutting quickly behind our Passat.

Letting their excitement get the better of them, Kene, Tochi, and Miracle ran alongside the car so closely I worried for their safety.

"*Broda, broda! Mama, broda na sista ha anatago.*"

We alighted, stretching our tired muscles, which were aching from the long trip.

I was headed for the boot to help unload our baggage and stuff when I looked up and sighted Okpue coming out to welcome us. She was beaming at her son and daughter. I flashed a warm smile at her. "Mama Nnukwu." I ran towards her, arms wide open for an embrace. It was going to be a mentally taxing weekend, but I would not be beaten. What didn't kill me would make me stronger.

The children came around to welcome me, huddling around my legs and touching me with their grubby fingers. Their bare feet were coated with red dust; they could barely contain their excitement. They had been street urchins but were now fostered by Okpue, whom they called Mama *Nnukwu*. They pranced about with excitement bordering on hysteria. They were deaf to the requests from Zimako to help with carrying the stuff from the car.

There were three of them: two boys, Kene and Tochi, and a girl, Miracle. No one knew their exact ages as their births had been concealed, but they were all probably about eight years old, give or take a year. They greeted me, "*Sister Lagos nno.*" They were openly warm and affectionate and tugged at my heartstrings. I remembered when I first met them as toddlers. They had been abandoned by their mothers: single women from the neighbouring village who had fallen pregnant and been made outcasts by their families. Their mothers were young teenagers who had not had access to contraception, a tragedy. Okpue's kindness and generosity had changed the lives of these children. That they were happy, clothed, and loved was a testament of hope. She had a big heart and I made a promise to myself there and then to persevere in my efforts to win her affection.

Makua ran to her mother and embraced her. "*Nne*, you are looking very well." She held her mother close. Makua and I flanked Okpue on either side; Okpue had her arms around us as she gazed lovingly at Zimako.

"*Nno,*" Okpue whispered, "*umum nno-nu.*"

"Mama, you are looking so good. You seem to be getting younger every day," I complimented her.

My mother-in-law was a titled lady, and outside the close family circles was hailed as Okpue-umu-agbala, which means "pinnacle of attainment for womanhood." This regal appellation acknowledged her outstanding achievements among the womenfolk in the local community. Her philanthropic work had earned her the title. At sixty-five, Okpue-umu-agbala was still a beautiful woman and something of a mover and shaker in the community, highly respected among her peers. I envied her a little. To her husband and children she was just Okpue or Mama or Mama *Nnukwu*. She was a matriarch who was fiercely loyal and very possessive and protective of her own.

Zimako's voice pierced my reverie. "So are you women going to stand there all day? Is anyone going to help get this stuff in?"

Okpue released us, and Makua and I went to help offload the vehicle; Zimako gave his mother a quick hug. "It's good to see you, Mama; you are looking well."

She chuckled; this was the compliment she had been waiting for. "Thank you, Zimako. How was the journey?"

"It was fine, Mama. Ichie *kwa'n?*" Zimako asked, wondering where his father was. The classic Mercedes 230CE he drove was not in the courtyard, indicating his absence.

"He should be back any time soon; he went for the meeting of the township development committee. I hoped he would return before your arrival. You made good time. Welcome. Come inside."

Everyone pitched in and soon the trunk of the Passat was empty.

We were grimy and exhausted. Once inside, we separated to our usual lodgings to freshen up.

Zimako and I were in the east wing, which was really the boy's half. Makua was in the west wing, which she usually shared with Chinazo.

The sun was going down, it was a cool evening, and the delicious smell of *ofe ora* cooked with *ogiri-ishi* filled the air and wafted towards the rooms. There was palpable excitement with the arrival of *ndi-Lagos*. The news had travelled and family members from the neighbouring compounds were stopping by.

It was the tradition; I guess out of respect, when people from out of town came home, the wider extended family in the village came to visit.

Okpue laid out the red carpet. She had mastered hospitality to a fine art. Well-wishers trickled in all evening, not giving any thought to the fatigue of us poor weary travellers; that was the joy of extended family. Zimako was in his element, meeting and greeting. After a cool shower, he had changed into a more casual kaftan and gone out to the obi, where the men were having heated discussions.

The obi was a modern outbuilding with a thatched roof out at the back of the compound. It faced the kitchen and, as there was no intercom, Ichie could put out his head and call for refreshments or attention.

Armed with a bottle of the White Horse to lubricate the tongues of the older men, Zimako walked through the kitchen out to the *obi* after exchanging pleasantries with the womenfolk.

"*Ndi okenye e ke ne'm unu.*" He greeted the elders and set down the "hot drink" on the centre table in the dimly lit *obi* beside the bowl of *kolanuts* and *ose oji*. The scene was set for gossip that passed for manly discussion. Zimako sat in the wicker rocking chair, chatting with his kinsmen, who quibbled and argued as they updated him on the inner family issues. He hoped his father would be back soon, because it was nearly suppertime.

The kitchen was really the hub of the house. It opened out to the backyard, where to one side was the well and vegetable garden, and directly across was Ichie's *obi*. It was the domain of the women. There was a comfortable sitting area with sofas upholstered in faux leather for ease of wiping. That is where Makua and I settled in comfy chairs, listening in on the hum of conversation around us, occasionally chipping in a comment or two. The ebb and flow of conversation, the companionship that was taken for granted, reminded me of all the things we would be leaving behind when we moved to Canada. A wave of sadness engulfed me.

* * * * *

Zimako feigned interest in the discussion, his mind drifting to his plans for a new life abroad. The voices of the women carried and he could overhear the harmony of raucous conversation as they chit-chatted, exchanging stories, sharing anecdotes. He would make new friends in Canada. The older kinsmen rambled on. They chewed *kolanuts* and rehashed the same old issues pertaining to the village. He wondered why his father was delayed. He was starving and eager to get the serious conversation out of the way.

The distinctive blaring of the horn of Ichie's Mercedes at the gate got his attention.

"*Ndi-okenye* – our elders, I think Ichie is back. Let me go and open the gate." As he made his way to the gate, he was overtaken by one of the little urchins—was it Tochi? Zimako could not confidently match names and faces with the boys; perhaps it was Kene. He gave up guessing and continued to the gate.

"*Papa a nata o yo yo!*" he shouted as he ran to open the gate.

Ichie sat patiently in his faithful old Mercedes Benz, tenderly revving the powerful engine. He had bought it brand new in 1989 and nurtured it like a baby. The gate was held open by the little boy, who turned out to be Tochi, on one side, and Zimako on the other side.

He brought the car to a halt as soon he crossed the threshold and smiled proudly at his *diokpala*.

Both men hugged and then held onto one another a little longer. Ichie finally broke the embrace. Holding Zimako at arm's length, he looked him over and nodded with pride and approval. "How's your brother?"

"Sir, Okwe should be here before the nightfall. He left late. But you need not worry. He is not travelling alone."

"In that case let us go inside. I am hungry, and your mother is always unhappy when I get back late from my meetings." They laughed conspiratorially and made their way towards the *obi*.

Ichie exchanged greetings with the men and settled down with them. The conversation continued in earnest, uninterrupted by the arrival of Ichie. The matter in contention was the decision by the Parish Council to site the expansion of the boys' secondary school on a plot of land that was in dispute. A lot of feathers were ruffled and court cases were threatened. It was deeply contentious and divisive.

All the visitors had finally dispersed. Dinner was ready. Ichie and Zimako had come indoors and were seated at the far end of the dining table, chatting as they waited for dinner to be served. The house was alive with sounds of happiness as we shared the stories from our journey. Tochi and the other children were really excited by the arrival of *ndi-Lagos*, as it was a distraction from the monotony of their daily lives. They were excited by the gifts and new clothes they had received.

"Ichie, you know there are some things I wanted to discuss with you. Our journey is laden with purpose; it is not something one can talk about on the phone," Zimako started.

"Can it wait till your brother arrives, hmmm?" Ichie asked, savouring a mouthful from his cup of palmwine. "This is good stuff."

"It can," Zimako said rather deliberately, "but the matter has very little to do with him directly."

"Still, it may be better to wait at least till after supper. Then we can all sit down as a family and hear you out. I am sure your mother will be very interested in what you have to say."

"You are right, Papa. I think it's best if Okpue-umu-agbala is here, too." He agreed.

It was already sundown, and the orange sun, a big ball in the sky, was lined by clouds in the horizon. The smell of rain was in the air and there was a light breeze, but it was clear the wind was gathering momentum.

Telephonic reception was affected by the winds, but through crackling and static had spoken with Tony and Okwe, who reassured us they would be arriving within a couple of hours.

Dinner was served. Okpue-umu-agbala planned a menu that had everyone's favourite dishes. She was serving *ugba* as a starter, followed by ora soup laced with ogiri-ishi and pounded yam as the main course, and finished off with freshly cut sweet pineapple served in its juice. Zimako settled down beside his father to enjoy the delicacies. Ichie was at the head of the table. Okpue-umu-agbala presided over the dinner table, occupying the seat at the other end of the table, close to the kitchen; I sat beside Makua across from Zimako at the table.

I could tell Zimako was nervous, and wanted to get the discussion over and done with. There were no two ways about it; the news Zimako had to share would be a bombshell, and I wished I could disappear.

"Okpue-umu-agbala, this is delicious," said Ichie. "You have again outdone yourself. This ora soup should send me to pay another bridal price on your behalf," he said.

"Mmmm, I agree. I have missed your cooking, Mama. See how I'm licking my fingers; it's a pity Okwe will have to make do with the leftovers," Zimako complimented.

"Just enjoy the meal, eh, and keep in mind I had the help of these two accomplished women." Okpue-umu-agbala smiled, generously sharing the compliments. "Anuli and Makua did most of the work, if you would know, and that fish they brought from Onitsha was *kposkia*: it made the dish special."

"Mama, it's your secret formula that makes it delicious," Makua chipped in. She knew how much her mother enjoyed being complimented on the cooking.

"Thank you, it is nice having people to cook for."

I had been quiet, deep in contemplation. "Are you enjoying the meal? You look worried." Okpue nodded to indicate she was speaking to me.

"Mama, please don't mind me. Forgive me for not complimenting the food. It is special, worth driving all the way from Lagos for; it just hit the spot."

"Thank you, Anuli. I know you must be very tired after that long trip from Lagos. Now let's enjoy the meal; maybe by the time we are rounding up, Okwe will arrive."

We continued our meal, with Zimako and Ichie dominating at the top end of the table, while Makua regaled her mother and me with stories that left us sometimes gobsmacked and often in stitches.

As soon as supper was over, we younger women helped the children clear up the dishes.

It was Ichie who opened up the conversation again. "*Ngwa,* let us go into the parlour and we can hear what has been bothering you, Zimako."

Ichie understood Zimako. He knew something was weighing heavily on his son's mind and he was anxious to hear it.

"Thank you, sir," Zimako responded.

"Mama, Makua, sweetheart," Zimako called out, "please come to the parlour. Papa is waiting." From the kitchen, Okpue-umu-agbala appealed to them. "You men should be patient. We have just finished eating. Let it settle before we rush into this serious thing you want to talk about, O!"

Makua took a tray of peeled oranges and set it down on the centre table. It was the after-dinner palate cleanser. The oranges were from one of the trees in the backyard, fresh and succulent. Makua was being very kind. She tried to catch my eye in an act of solidarity and encouragement. I was shaking on the inside; her surmise that I was a bundle of nerves was spot on. She had tried to get me to relax by teasing her mother and including me in the conversation over dinner, she succeeded a little, but the effect was short-lived. She, perhaps even more than my "Mummy's pet" of a husband, understood that coming to the village even at the best of times was still something of a challenge. I took a few deep breaths and counted to ten. I mustn't work myself into a state. Nothing had happened yet.

My husband had chosen the loveseat, I guess to make space for me to sit beside him as we shared our news. I wondered if they thought we were about to announce that we were pregnant with an heir apparent.

"Mama, we are all waiting for you, O!" Makua called out. It seemed Okpue-umu-agbala's female intuition it could tell the news was not good, and she seemed to be trying to put it off by delaying the discussions as much as she could. Did she know that we had life-altering news?

Maybe it was my imagination, but the mood in the house was morphing from joyful to tense; the children sensed the shift in the mood of the adults and withdrew to their sleeping chamber.

Okpue-umu-agbala came out from the adjourning room. "*Ngwa nu*, I am here. Ichie," she looked at her husband, "please lead us in prayers before we start this important talk."

They were good Anglicans, and prayer preceded major discussions and decisions at the home. Ichie led them in prayer, thanking God for all his kindness towards the family, and the privileges they daily enjoyed. Finally he asked God's guidance in the discussion the children wanted to have with them.

Prayer concluded, Okpue-umu-agbala took over.

"Ichie, thank you so much. You are God's blessing to this family. I have always said that if I reincarnate, and have the option to marry again, I will choose you all over again in my next lifetime". She paused for effect, and then continued "You children know how we started. We were not endowed with wealth, education, fortune, or fame. We had very little when we got married after the war. We struggled to make ends meet after your father returned from England, just before the Biafra war broke out. It is not news that father lost what little he had built up in Lagos and had to return home. God favoured us; we all saw the end of the war." She paused for composure as her voice broke.

Makua smiled to herself. It was almost poetic. Her mother always made sure she made this speech or a similar one each time there was an important family issue. Over the years she had found her mother's recounting of "The Speech," as it was known amongst the kids, sometimes inspiring, and at other times laughable. Okpue-umu-agbala continued, "But not everyone was so blessed. We lost family; we lost very close family, and friends. It was difficult for us. We went hungry, hiding and running, never knowing what the future would bring. Thank God we survived it. After the war, with the twenty pounds sterling that your father received, we went back to Lagos to try to rebuild our lives. We have always done our best to make sure you children received the best education we could afford. Not that we were rich, but that was what we could bequeath to you all. Now, you are all grown up. By the grace of God, Zimako, you are married. Thank God. You know what your father and I are expecting from you now, a new baby, and the next generation. Your sister Chinazo is expecting, thank God. Okwe and Makua, we are still praying for them to find God's choice for them. You are all very close and united. This is what we want for all of you, our children. To make us proud and to keep the family's good name. We always pray for you all. Ichie, I've finished. You can add, or let Zimako now say what he has to say."

The room was quiet after Okpue-umu-agbala spoke. The whispering buzz from the ceiling fan was all that could be heard. It was already dark outside and there was a light drizzle. Zimako held my hand beneath his and placed it innocuously over his crotch. I could feel an awakening and stiffening within. I was astonished! Don't get me wrong, we enjoy a passionate time in the bedroom and I know the smell of rain mixed with the dust always turns him on. But surely there is a time and place, and in my mind's eye this was not it. Men were strange creatures, I concluded, relaxing a bit. If my hus-band could be having lustful thoughts at a time like this, then it was a good omen, and everything was going to be okay. We had each other.

A flash of lightning preceded the roaring thunder; the gusty winds that followed carried cold air with it. Then without warning, lights went off!

"Ah ah, NEPA! Just what we need now." The room was plunged into darkness. NEPA was the National Electric Power Authority, which was the nation's electricity-generating parastatal, but the acronym was popularly construed as "Never Expect Power Always," as their services were at best epileptic.

"Shall I go and put on the generator?" asked Zimako.

"No need for that. We do not need electricity to talk," answered Ichie.

"You have heard everything your mother said, Zimako. I know there is something on your mind. You have been a good son, and your mother and I have never had cause to worry about you. What is the matter? We are listening. What do you have to tell us?"

It was time for Zimako to speak.

"Ichie, thank you, sir. Mama, thank you. I am proud to be your son. You have both set a standard and have taught us that the sky is the limit."

Both his parents nodded their heads in agreement.

"Well, I continue to believe that, and I have never been one to shy away from challenges. For the past four years, Anuli and I have been in the process of applying for Canadian residency. Recently, we received the final word. We have been accepted."

"That is wonderful, my son. We should be celebrating that."

"Yes, Papa, we should. I guess this is one of the rare occasions you and Okwe have agreed. Anyway, it also means that we will be relocating to Canada. We will be leaving Nigeria in less than three months. Maybe for good, mmmm, maybe forever if life favours us there."

There was a silence. The only audible noise was the blustery winds furiously raging outside. The parlour was pitch dark, and there was no way one could read anyone's body language. Zimako gave my hand a squeeze. I wondered how they were reacting to his bombshell.

"Papa, Mama... " he seemed to want to explain, to soften the blow.

Okpue-umu-agbala screamed, "Oh, oh, I am dead! Oh my son, how can you abandon me here? When did you start planning this? How can you be planning to leave Nigeria for good?" She was hysterical. "Why? You have a good job, great prospects. Why are you even thinking of leaving? Do you think that Canada is better than Nigeria? Why? How? Oh my God! What have I done to deserve this?" She was tremulous and jittery and had fallen to the ground, foaming at the mouth; I feared she might have a stroke or an epileptic fit.

"I will never carry my grandchildren. Oh! God, help me, this is not our agreement," she cried, waving her arms high above her head. "My son, why, why, my son? Anuli, is this your plan, who gave my son this idea? Ichie, please stop him. Oh... what will I do?"

I had guessed Okpue would assume it was my idea. But I could feel her pain. I stood up and walked across the parlour to where Okpue was now writhing on the floor and reached out and hugged her. "Mama Nnukwu, please don't cry." Makua and I pulled her up to the sofa and helped tie her *wrapper* securely. We three women huddled together, holding each other close.

Okpue-umu-agbala was inconsolable.

Ichie was stoically silent.

Zimako could not see his father's face. He knew Ichie was in deep thought. He wanted his father's approval. It meant so much to him.

"Papa, please, say what you are thinking. Speak your mind."

Okpue-umu-agbala interrupted. "Zimako, you have killed me. What am I going to do? Why do you want to abandon your father and me and go to Canada? Who has ever heard of such a place?

From where do you go to Canada? Where is it near? What type of people live there? What language do they speak? *Chei, e gbuo mu, O!* Please, my son, please. See the good life you have here and be satisfied with it. Do not go to Canada. Please, my son. Please..." Okpue-umu-agbala continued crying. "If Nigeria is bad for some people, you are not one of them." She could scarcely control her emotions.

Zimako appeared unruffled by his mother's melodramatic meltdown. He had anticipated this and refused to yield to emotional blackmail. Her histrionics would not sway him. He was more interested in what his father had to say.

Ichie was hurting inside, but kept a brave face. Going by the way he was feeling, he knew his wife was in agony. He agreed this was not the plan at all. They had never expected this to happen, for any of their children to join the brain-drain bandwagon of those looking for greener pastures in a foreign land and leaving the country. It broke up families, and caused untold hardships. They made sure the children had the best education in Nigeria, and they were all very successful. To hear his son say they were planning to leave the country for Canada broke his heart. Where had he failed?

"Zimako," Ichie began, "I am very happy for you. I know that you have a good reason for pursuing this Canadian paper, and I am happy you got it. Congratulations. It is true that Nigeria is not the country the British handed over to Azikiwe and Balewa. Things have deteriorated." He paused. "It was different in our day, but let me not digress. I do not know why you have chosen this route, so let me start by asking you why. My son, why have you decided that you want to leave home and go to another man's land?"

Makua jumped in. "Papa, that question is not necessary. Don't you see that he is going to be a Canadian citizen and he will have all the rights of any Canadian? Nigeria has not lived up to the promise she had in your days. Things are really declining. There is no functioning infrastructure; we have a failed government. We are the foot soldiers and we do not have a say. Many doctors have left, and truthfully, since Zimako got his Canadian papers, I have been thinking of also leaving for Saudi Arabia or the UK."

"Makua, no, let me answer. It's a good question. Papa is right. I owe them an explanation. So let me try. Ichie, Okpue, you see, there is something I did not tell you. Anuli and I were attacked by armed robbers about two weeks ago and they nearly killed us."

That news was another bombshell. I had not expected Zimako to reveal the incident to his parents because of the anxiety it was bound to cause.

"What?" yelled Okpue-umu-agbala. "You mean you children were attacked by robbers and you did not tell us? So until they tell us to come and identify your dead bodies in the mortuary, you won't tell us anything?"

Ichie was no less shocked, but he waited for Zimako to complete his explanation.

"Please, Mama, we did not wish to alarm you and Papa. It was frightening at the time, but the God you pray to was awake and he rescued us. As we were unharmed, we wanted to tell you face-to-face to reassure you that we were okay. However, that is a minor point. The truth is that we wanted to expand our horizons. To optimise our skills, and become the best we can be. Just like you have given us what your parents did not give you, we also want to give our children something more than what we have. We need you to be happy for us; we need your blessing."

Zimako's statement was simple. He was not expecting his father to try and change his mind, but he would be hard put to go without his father's tacit approval. I could feel his eyes boring into mine in the dark. I had remained beside his mother with my arms around her shoulder. There was a lone candle burning in the parlour, and the kerosene lamp was lit out in the corridor, providing sombre lighting to the room, suiting the forlorn mood that now settled over us.

Okpue-umu-agbala was weeping silently now, although her sobs were more subdued. I intermittently dried her tears with the edge of my loose-fitting Nigerian *boubou* dress.

"Papa, I know you understand what Zimako is doing," Makua said. "You schooled in England, and you know the difference it makes for one to have that experience. Mama, it may be painful for you now—it may seem it will be unbearable to think of Zimako and Anuli leaving—but they are not lost to us. They will come home from time to time. Let's rejoice and be happy for them."

Ichie considered the wise words of his daughter and smiled sadly. He knew that the decision Zimako had taken was what he considered best for his family. Zimako had been a worthy son, one to be proud of. If he did not lend his support to the young couple, Okpue-umu-agbala would give them a tough time, and the emotional blackmail would demoralise them. He had so much to tell his son. This decision had taken him unawares. All he had hoped for in his twilight years was to have his family around him, to share his old age with his wife and children, and to die and join his ancestors a happy man, having fulfilled his obligations to his family and town.

"Okay, Makua, I have noted your support for your brother in his decision. I take it Okwe and Chinazo are also in support?"

"Yes, Papa. We all knew when Zimako put in an application, but really, no one thought it would come to much, you know? It seemed impossible that a Western nation would be begging people to come and become their citizens. It has taken nearly four years or so, and finally they have approved them. Truly I am proud of Zimako and Anuli for what they have achieved."

It was heart-warming to hear Makua come to her brother's defence. Her cheery voice lifted the gloom that a minute ago had threatened to drown us.

I felt I had to speak up, to be heard. "Actually, Papa, I share your concerns. You see, this decision is not an easy one for us. Even now, I have yet to get my mind around it; how will we leave everybody and everything behind to go and start life afresh? We do not have any people we know there. The immediate loneliness and isolation is a clear and present challenge. We are used to having all of you to support and advise us. I know what my husband is doing takes courage, and we have been praying about it. We can only embark on this journey into the unknown with your support, blessings, and prayers."

"Thank you, my daughter Anuli. I know it is not easy. In fact, I remember when I was leaving for England for my studies those many years ago. My mother never stopped crying; it was tough on me, too. As soon as I graduated, I was back to Nigeria six months after. So I understand. It is just so unexpected. Let Okpue-umu-agbala and I think it through. We are not withholding our blessing; we just want to assure ourselves that this journey will be for the good. The night is far spent. Let us adjourn, and before you leave we will meet again. I can't be fairer than that."

Ichie was always very balanced. He was not going to let his emotions rule him, and the children trusted him to always guide them when things seemed overwhelming.

"Papa, thank you. Mama, it is well."

Ichie smiled, and was glad to see his son stand tall, as though a weight had been lifted off his shoulders.

"So, I hope we can now all relax and enjoy your visit?"

There was laughter all around.

"Where is Okwe? Did he give any indication of his ETA?" Makua asked.

"Trust Okwe to *gbuo* AWOL when serious discussions are taking place. He will arrive now and with *dogo turenchi*," Zimako responded.

We were still laughing at Zimako's comment, and it took a while to register that there was a horn tooting quietly, requesting entrance.

"That must be Okwe!"

"Tochi! Kene! *Gba nu oso, ngwa*. Go and see who is at the gate." Suddenly everyone became animated and strangely light-hearted. It was the Okwe effect.

CHAPTER SEVEN

> *Dear Diary,*
>
> *These past few weeks have been such a rollercoaster of emotions. It's been non-stop "gbaghalia"!*
>
> *I am excited about moving to Canada, but I'm of two minds. O, dear God I am so torn. I am leaving behind everything familiar and heading towards the unknown.*
>
> *Some think fortune has smiled on me, many wish they were in my shoes, but it niggles when a handful wonder why I'm risking a good life, reminding me that the life I lived had been charmed.*
>
> *I wish I had a crystal ball; is it sweetness and light ahead or will it turn out to be bleak and rocky?*
>
> *I am petrified but resolute. I hope it works out. What does my future hold?*
>
> *Are you there, God? Please, God, help me, please!*

I have spent the last weeks focussed on our move to Canada. I started researching where we should settle down and Toronto, Ontario, seemed to be the place. Every time I searched on the Internet for cities in Canada, the first place that popped up was Toronto. It seemed to be the place to go. Much like Lagos, it was the largest city in Canada, its financial capital. Another plus was that Toronto was very cosmopolitan; half its population was made up of immigrants. I read that it was the leading city for finance, telecommunications, and information technology fields, to which we could lend our expertise. When I first touted Toronto to Zimako, he nodded sagely and asked me to research all the major cities and provinces in Canada, listing their pros and cons. That didn't surprise me. Was not my darling Zimako, Mr Pernickety, meticulous to the point of obsession? Granted, it meant I had to do more work, but then he was right that we needed to do our due diligence and get it right. On his part, he had been talking to his friends who had visited Canada and had spoken to Olisa and Obi, old school friends both of who completed graduate programmes in Canada and lived their for a while before returning home.

It was strange to try to cobble together a new life from hearsay, picturing life in Canada through the eyes of others.

We listened to tales and pieced together various aspects of life in Canada. The jigsaw was slowly coming together, a bit like the six blind men of Hindustan trying to describe the elephant. I thought of my experiences in Lagos compared with those of someone living a different lifestyle from me, describing the same Lagos, knowing that even in the same city, people have different perceptions and see things differently. Deep down I knew we would never know Canada till we got there.

One day I told Zimako jokingly that we should just play blind man's darts, place a map on the wall and put on a blindfold, and just throw the darts at the map and go to whichever city the dart lands on. He did not see the humour in that. He been quite apprehensive, worrying about freezing cold temperatures, job opportunities, indifferent neighbours, and the entire adjustment process. One of my major worries was the weather. Was it really cold all year round in Canada? That would be unbearable. I wondered if I could soak up enough sunshine to last me a lifetime before we left.

"Anuli, the RH wants you to see him." Ronke cleared her throat as she stood patiently by the door. I had been so enraptured in my daydreams that I did not hear her approach the door. The RH is the regional head of our team.

Ronke, my secretary of three years in the financial services firm where I worked as Financial Advisor for high net-worth clients, stood silently. I loved my job, and the thrill of closing a deal still excited me. My bijou office was on the north corner of the tenth floor. I earned it. I put in the graft and deserve the perks. The decor was minimalist, with glass and marble, and the colour scheme was made up of shades of aqua-green: stimulating in an understated way. Our floor was the "power floor." It housed all the departmental heads of the company's conglomerate financial empire. Our office block was a twelve-floor, glass building with pizzazz. It was one of the few tall buildings that caressed the skyline in Victoria Island.

"Thanks, my mind was elsewhere. Have you been standing there long? I must have been daydreaming. Please tell him I will be with him shortly."

I had a few files I wanted to discuss with him, and there was the matter of deciding on my replacement so I could begin the handover process. I picked up the files and headed for Segun's office.

Segun, our RH, was genuinely a pleasure to work with. His encouragement helped in no small measure to ensure that our department had become the most profitable in the company. He was also a mentor of sorts to me. I could talk to him about almost anything. When we started making definite plans about moving to Canada, Segun was one of the first people I took into my confidence.

His personal assistant, Pius, was busy at his workstation just outside Segun's office. I liked Pius; he was a long-term loyal employee of the company. I smiled in acknowledgement to his greeting. "Madam, *Oga* RH is expecting you."

I walked briskly into Segun's office. "Hey, Segun, how is the day going?" I asked.

"Oh, the usual, back-to-back meetings. As soon as you and I are done I'm meeting the MD, and then a client."

"No rest for the wicked, eh?" I laughed. The chemistry between us worked well and he was one of the people I'd miss.

"I was hoping you had time so we could discuss some of these files. They are likely to present the most complications; of course, I intend to resolve as many of the issues as I can before handing them over."

Segun was very accommodating, and we spent time going over the detailed history of the clients I flagged. Two of them were particularly demanding, and we indulged them because their public profile gave the company the visibility that attracted other clients. Over the years there had been a decline in the performance of their portfolios, and we were trying to limit our exposure to them. I set my stall out, client by client.

"I think you are doing a good job, and I endorse your strategy. Have you got a contingency plan for the inevitable obstacles? These clients are high-maintenance, and could be difficult to handle when you are gone," Segun said.

We went into planning and strategising, discussing each file in fine-tooth detail. In my line of work, the devil is in the details, and though some may think Segun micromanaged us, I felt comfortable with his style and would not have had it any other way. Once we were done with the client's files, Segun wanted to know how the plans for relocation were progressing.

"Oh, that? Well, that takes up just about the other twenty-four hours of my day when you, my slave driver, are not whipping me." Segun roared with laughter at my response.

"Seriously? How are you coping?"

I brought him up to speed on how much I had accomplished.

"Well, you have made a lot of progress. I know you will take Canada by storm. It will be tough; you can take that from an old pro like me. Moving to a new country to start all over is never easy. But don't you ever forget the stuff you are made of. If you can make it in Lagos, you can find it in you to succeed anywhere in the world. *Capice?*"

"I hear you," I said, smiling. I knew he was very concerned.

"The next thing I will add is that you need a good support network. Life will throw so many curveballs at you, only the psychologically robust will emerge from the battle victorious."

He was looking at me strangely. "I know I have not spoken so openly to you before now, but you are like a daughter to me. Look, when you get there, consider your options, keep an open mind; try to understand the people and the system and don't be rash. Call me whenever you need to, okay?"

"Thanks, *Oga* Segun." I felt a little bit tearful as he spoke. I averted my face to hide my damp eyes; in the nick of time, his telephone rang, and I composed myself. It was a brief call; he dispatched the caller post-haste.

"Anuli, are you okay?" he asked.

I answered in the affirmative. "I'd better leave you to get on."

"One last thing, I wanted to talk about your replacement. At the management meeting yesterday we discussed it and finally shortlisted four potential candidates; we'd like you to be part of the interview process. Two of the applicants are internal candidates and two from elsewhere in the industry."

I anticipated this, but was still somewhat flattered and said as much. It was an affirmation of my performance for the firm. Segun and I talked a bit more about the qualities and skills we'd thought would be desirable in my potential replacement.

As we wrapped up, he casually mentioned that he knew a family in Ontario, and would speak to them about Zimako and me and perhaps put us in touch with each other. I thanked him and made my way back to my office.

I was pleased with the outcome of our meeting on several fronts, and looked forward to speaking with the family in Ontario. Every contact we could get in Canada would come in handy.

I decided to use the stairs rather than the lift. I needed to clear my head. There were too many thoughts swirling around in my mind.

I did not count on seeing Felicia.

Felicia had been with the company as long as I, or perhaps just a little longer, but her trajectory had flatlined. She had a reputation as tittle-tattle, so I tended to steer clear of her.

"Hey, Anuli."

"Felicia," I said politely, still walking on, intending to quickly go past her and continue on my way.

"Ah, how far now? I hear you are leaving us?"

Although it was no secret, I had not told a lot of people about my relocation. I weighed my response to her, sure that whatever I said would be repeated and possibly embellished.

"Mmmm, where did you hear it from?"

"So, is it true?" she asked.

"Oh well..." I said noncommittally, not wanting to lie outright, but also knowing that if I wanted to quash any rumours, this was the opportunity to do so.

Her curiosity was visibly etched on her features. I decided on my response.

"Listen, Felicia, ignore all the rumours on the grapevine. If there is any truth to such stories, I am sure that in due course it will become—"

Before I could complete my sentence she interjected.

"*A beg*, it's not a rumour *jo*. I heard this from the most reliable sources, so please don't patronise me with your evasiveness. Here I am, just trying to congratulate a friend, and you are playing politics with me."

I stood to my full height, squared my shoulders, and measured my response. "As you are so sure of your so-called reliable source, you do not need any confirmation from me. Believe what you wish. I have no more to say on that matter. I must rush." I sidestepped her and continued downstairs.

"Congratulations, O!" she bellowed after me.

I knew that my departure was being celebrated by certain members of the team—those who viewed my rise within the company as something of a meteoric aberration and would be glad to see the back of me. Felicia had rattled my cage. I struggled to regain my composure.

By the time I got to my office, I felt calmer.

Ronke came in with my messages. "Is there anything I can do for you? Drink? Snack? Divert your calls?"

"I'm okay for the moment, thank you. Did Monica call?" Monica was my best friend and we happened to work for the same company. She was head of Internal Auditing and was a good sounding board when I needed one.

"She did. She asked me to let her know when you return from your meeting with *Oga* Segun. Should I put a call through to her?"

"Yes, please; let her know I'm back."

I made some calls and caught up with my messages while expecting Monica. It wasn't long before she showed up.

* * * * *

"Anuli!"

"Monica, you are shining as usual; *a beg* have a seat."

"What can a girl do? Bring me up to speed; you have been so busy today."

Monica was my friend from school. We finished our youth corps together in Benin and decided to relocate to Lagos in search of job opportunities once we were done.

"See me see Felicia, O!"

Monica looked askance. "You and Felicia?"

I filled her in on my stairway encounter. We usually made contact at some point during the day to debrief.

"So, that is the rumour that they are circulating? Did she mention anything about the immigration?"

"No. I'm not sure who her sources are, but it didn't sound like she had full details. Look, my friend, forget all those *yeye yeye* people," I said, flicking my right hand, indicating I had little regard for petty gossips.

Monica was not willing to let it end at that. She found my confrontation with Felicia too juicy to dismiss. I knew she was going to milk it for all it was worth and I was not surprised. I had often done the same whenever she had a titbit I found interesting. I trusted her enough to let my guard down and did not mind gossiping a bit with her.

Ronke shortly appeared at the door, interrupting our chit-chat. "Madam, MD wants you to see him at 5.30 p.m. and Oga Zimako called; he said he is on the Island and will pass by the office after his meeting."

"Thanks, Ronke," I said to her retreating back as she shut the door behind her.

"Anuli, let me go back to my office. I guess your day is not yet letting up at all. The MD and now your hubby. You are really in demand, O! You are not an easy babe," she teased as she rose to leave.

"Everyone wants a piece of me. Let's chat later."

"Meanwhile," she said, "did I mention that you are glowing?" I was wearing a fuchsia skirt suit contrasted with a silk, multi-tonal, abstract-design grey blouse with a cowl neckline that somehow managed to flatter my cleavage whilst being demure. Monica was effortlessly chic in her elegant navy pant suit; her hair was an expensive-looking weave cut in a layered bob.

"Thanks, girlfriend, you are not looking bad yourself, as usual. Look, give me a call later, okay?"

I had a lot of stuff to catch up on and had to prepare for my meeting later in the day with the managing director. He was a brilliant man and a trailblazer. He had started up the company more than thirteen years ago and had built it into a top-notch financial conglomerate. I had a lot of respect for him and held him in high esteem. I'll be honest and admit that I was a little intimidated at the prospect of our meeting later in the day.

As usually happens when there is so much to accomplish, time flew by very fast. When I called Zimako to let him know I was meeting with the managing director later in the evening, he was surprised. "Do you know why he wants to see you?"

"My dear, not really, but I'm guessing it's to discuss some departmental profitability prospects. Anyway, just pray I'm composed and articulate."

"I will, I always do, but you'll be fine, darling. You are a star. I called earlier and spoke with Ronke, your right-hand man. I will be on the Island for a meeting with Siemens. When I'm done, I'd like to take my favourite girl out tonight. You up for it?"

"Count me in; that's just what the doctor ordered. I'll see you later. Love you, darling."

"Love you more," he responded.

That was the bolster I needed. Zimako worked really hard too, and loved his job as a project engineer; his contributions to the growth of his company had earned him encomium and a promotion.

I focussed my attention on preparing for my meeting with the MD.

* * * * *

By the time I arrived at the restaurant, Zimako was nursing a pint of ice-cold Chapman. I sat beside him at the table. It was a cosy, intimate set-up.

It had been a hectic day, and I could tell that he was also tired. I thanked God we had a driver; having them made conquering

Lagos traffic less of a palaver. The road network was diabolical; office buildings popped up everywhere, with the result that traffic was chaos. Indeed Lagos was an urban jungle. Zimako had said earlier that he was on the Island to attend a meeting. I thought I'd wait till we started our dinner before asking how it went.

He gazed into my eyes as his hand underneath the table discreetly stroked my thigh. "Babe, you are looking hot to trot... mmmm, so sexy. Pink suits you."

I smiled at his attempt to boost my morale by seduction and thought of a witty response. The waiter showed up with the menu, breaking the spell. Zimako had taken me to Chinaville, one of the upmarket restaurants in Victoria Island. He knew it was one of my favourite places, and that in particular I liked their shrimp cocktail. I was glad not to be slaving over dinner.

"Mmmm, you know how to push my buttons. Shall we just order our dinner first?" I started to unwind, already feeling very good about the evening. "So darling, what is the special occasion?"

"Well, you know me, babe, this was just one of those evenings I thought I'd relieve you of the menial task of pounding yam... but since you bring it up, why don't I just say it is our own private celebration of the goodness of God? I mean..."

He was about to continue when the waiter who had been hovering interrupted. "Are you ready to order or should I come back later? Perhaps you need some privacy?"

We thanked him, and Zimako once again focussed his attention on me. "*Obidiya*, admit it; we have been so richly blessed. Look at us. We are successful. Our marriage may not be perfect, but I think I'd say we are 99.999 per cent happy." He chuckled. I smiled in agreement and he continued, "And we need to remain thankful and not take anything for granted. Thank God for answered prayers, especially the Canadian immigration papers thingy."

"Amen!" I answered.

"And let's not forget he saved us from what could have been a terrible armed robbery incident."

"Double amen to that. Preach it, Pastor!"

Zimako was on a roll now. "And he granted us journey mercies to the east to see my parents, which was not too bad. Then he took us safely to Ibadan where we saw your parents, and that went very well."

"Preach on, our God is faithful," was my rejoinder.

Zimako paused. "Have I left out anything, or perhaps you have something you would like to add?"

"Yes," I said, pausing for effect. He looked at me curiously, wondering what he'd omitted.

"I'd like to thank God for blessing me with a man like you for a husband."

I could see that made him very happy. He grinned from ear to ear.

"Enough said now. Let's order before my head gets so big this restaurant won't accommodate it."

"I hear you. Have you decided?"

"Anuli, just choose for us. You know what I like." Zimako was meticulous about many things, but he was not particular about what he ate and it was always left to me to sort out the details. He might suggest the protein type like beef or chicken or seafood, but that was the extent of his culinary requests.

The waiter returned as if on cue. "Would you like to place your order now?"

I efficiently ordered our food.

"What will you have to drink; shall I get you our drinks menu?"

We did not drink a lot, but Zimako had decided it was our personal celebration, so I jettisoned my usual Coke as he perused the wine list. He settled on a bottle of Chateauneuf-du-Pape.

Orders placed, Zimako couldn't wait to tell me how his meeting went. I listened with rapt attention as his face lit up, telling me about the success of his meeting. I too had some news of my own and couldn't wait to share it with him.

"Guess what the MD wanted to see me about."

"Babes, you know I'm no good at guessing games. Spill the beans."

I was bursting to tell. The wine had loosened my tongue and I could feel the tension dissipating.

Our starters arrived. We shared the grace, thanked God for his provision, and dug into our meal. For me, this was the best part of the meal; I swear the shrimp cocktail got better every time. This was the life—good wine, great food, excellent company. What more could a girl ask for?

"Zimako, I know you are up to something, aphrodisiac plus alcohol; tell me what you want," I said in a husky voice.

He laughed. "You know now," was his cheeky answer. We enjoyed our first course in companionable silence. Miles Davis played in the background to soothe the patrons after a hard day. Our waiter popped back and cleared the dishes.

"Babe, how was your meeting with the MD? What was it about? Was Segun there?"

"Oh, that. Actually, it went very well. It was just he and I. He is not happy that I'm leaving. He said I have done a very good job for the firm and that he was sad to see me go. Then he went on to express his happiness at my good fortune, then offered me a safety net, saying the company's doors will always be open to me. He said that the firm would host a leaving-do for me in the next two weeks. I felt touched, especially when he concluded by saying the company would also do something for me to help with our settling down in Canada."

"High-five! That's excellent, Anuli!"

"Yes, I was on cloud nine when I left his office. Honestly, I knew the department was probably going to arrange a small reception to say goodbye, but I did not expect anything at MD level; that is just overwhelming."

"Do you now see why I said that God is so good? I am so happy for you, babes, *you dey, no be small*." We fist-bumped and high-fived.

I laughed, feeling really happy and enjoying myself. It had been a long day, and I was glad to be here now with Zimako.

* * * * *

"I have also done some more work on our plans. I made a checklist to help me with comparing the provinces like you asked. I'm starting to feel like a Canadian expert, hahaha. By the way,

Oga Segun knows a family there that he said he will introduce us to."

"So we are making progress, eh?"

"A lot, Zimako, a lot of progress."

"So what do you have on your checklist?"

I was about to respond when the waiter appeared with our main course. The delicious aroma had my mouth watering.

"Bon appétit."

"Thank you," we chorused.

After the first few mouthfuls, I continued. "Zimako, I would be honest and say that the whole planning thing can get overwhelming, but tonight, let's just enjoy ourselves. We can talk about this later."

"Babe, tell me, are you worried?"

I considered Zimako's question. It was hard to say how I felt about moving to Canada. I felt secure knowing that I would be making this change with Zimako beside me, but still, there was so much that we did not know, so many loose ends. "Zimako, I don't know how to answer that."

He paused, looked at me, and smiled. I could not read his expression, but I guess he found my answer perturbing, "*Obidiya*, you do not need to be worried. Look how God has been helping us. It will be challenging, no doubt, but I'm confident he'll see us through."

"I'll be honest. It's not so much worry or even anxiety; it's just the sense of not knowing what the future holds. I feel like the sand beneath my feet is shifting. We are going from a system that we have mastered and succeeded in to a new system which is unfamiliar. I am not even sure what the point of this move is, Zimako. I'm trying not to panic. I wish I had a way of seeing into the future. What will we find when we get to Canada?

"OoOoo, babe, I don't know why you are feeling this way. Is what you are reading about Canada causing you to have cold feet?"

"Zimako, okay, let me ask you. Did you know that our Nigerian degrees are not accepted in Canada?"

"What do you mean?"

"Well, if we are to get work in Canada, then we need to start now to apply to their regulatory bodies and send our transcripts to them to get them approved. Zimako, it seems so regressive. It is truly like starting over. And there's more. Do you want to know something else?"

"What?"

"I have been researching the provinces, and I found that each province has its own set of rules. The certification in one province does not apply to the next. Do you understand my trepidation yet?"

"Hold on, Anuli. Are you saying we have to go and start sending transcripts to all the different provinces of Canada? This is so tedious!"

"No, honey, I have not said so at all. My understanding is that any provinces we decide to settle in will require that our qualifications are ratified. So unless we just want to complicate our lives, we need to decide where we want to live even before we get there, because if we intend to gallivant all over the country, then we have to send out as many transcripts as there are provinces."

"Anuli, please tell me this is a joke."

"No, it's not."

"And oh, the weather… "

"Please, let's just enjoy our meal. Later we can settle down and discuss our Canadian strategy, because it is not going to be easy."

"No, it will not be, but for one, we have only about six weeks left, and I calculated my resignation to take effect in two weeks, so that does not give us a lot of time."

"Just eat, babe. I wanted this to be a light-hearted, relaxed evening, and then we'd segue into a night of sexual healing."

I laughed. "You definitely have a one-track mind. Don't you think of anything else?"

"Mmmm, maybe, occasionally."

"Really? What else does my swashbuckling stallion think of? Tell me, I'm listening."

Zimako laughed and gave me that crooked smile of his that melted my heart. I tingled with anticipation.

I did not know it, but Zimako's phone was buzzing in his pocket.

CHAPTER EIGHT

> *If you can keep your head when all about you*
> *Are losing theirs and blaming it on you,*
> *If you can trust yourself when all men doubt you,*
> *But make allowance for their doubting too...*
>
> *If you can dream—and not make dreams your master;*
> *If you can think—and not make thoughts your aim,*
> *If you can meet with Triumph and Disaster*
> *And treat those two impostors just the same...*
>
> *If you can fill the unforgiving minute*
> *With sixty seconds' worth of distance run—*
> *Yours is the Earth and everything that's in it,*
> *And—which is more—you'll be a Man, my son!*
> --Rudyard Kipling (1865–1936)

Zimako stirred, stretched, and yawned. Anuli remained fast asleep beside him. He slid out of bed and slipped on his pyjamas. Zimako usually slept in only his boxers, but this morning, even those were missing. He stood staring, mesmerised by the sleeping Anuli. Careful not to wake her, he leaned down and planted a kiss on her brow and tucked her in tenderly. "I love this woman, I really do." As he said it, he remembered the pesky Ndudi and her irritating booty call last night and scratched his head, thinking, *Why won't this woman leave me alone, for God's sake?*

He went into the kitchen and brewed himself a cup of tea in the old-fashioned way, using tea leaves; he liked his tea black, no milk and one sugar. Zimako was in a contemplative mood as he made his way into the living room. He drew the curtains and noticed it was not quite dawn yet, and in the distance he could make out discordant voices transmitted over various public address systems. He was familiar with the noises; one of them was the Evangelicals commanding the morning, focussed on defeating the devil. Another was the white-garmented *Baba Adura* chanting incantations from his megaphone, ringing his doomsday warning bell as he patrolled the street. Meanwhile the Imam sang the *azan*, calling the faithful to the first prayer of the day. Yaba was an interesting melting pot of religions. This morning, though, Zimako was not interested; all he wanted was a bit of peace and quiet to clear his head and think his thoughts. He sighed with disgust at all this noise so early in the morning.

"Why do they have to be so vociferous about their religious beliefs? Why must they wear their faith like an adornment akin to the Pharisees in the New Testament? Lord, have mercy!"

Closer to home, he heard the vendor outside hawking newspapers. He grabbed his wallet off the coffee table and walked outside to buy his copy of *Thisday* and remembered to get *The Punch* and *Ovation* for Anuli.

He planned to hunker down all weekend and review the issues that Anuli had raised about Canada. Zimako prided himself on paying attention to detail. He was not upping sticks and moving to Canada without doing his homework. He sat down at his desk and powered on his iMac. Internet reception was temperamental, and he knew the best time to get any serious uninterrupted work done was in the morning. Hopefully, he would cover sufficient ground before the speed slowed down.

Later in the day, he would go to the Internet café at Mega Plaza in Victoria Island and continue his research when it became impossible to continue at home.

Seeing as it was Anuli's preferred city, he knew exactly where he would start: Toronto, Ontario.

On his aide-memoire he wrote the keywords *jobs, cost of living, new immigrant*.

He began to surf the internet, greedy for all the information he could get. It was very interesting to read stories of different experiences as one web page led him to another. Some of the stories were deeply disturbing, some were success stories, and some were so-so. He even found some sad tales of shattered dreams of people who wished they never came to Canada.

It seemed to Zimako that the success stories were stage-managed, but he knew it could be his cynical suspicion that was leading him to that conclusion. The neutral stories had a ring of truth to them. His earlier enthusiasm was turning to ambivalence. It was not his intention to lead his family down a slippery slope, but it seemed there were no guarantees as far as moving to Canada was concerned.

Some of the excitement was wearing off. He cast his mind down memory lane. All the while he had been getting documents ready for Canada, he felt confident that it was the right thing to do, and that life would be much better over there. It was a structured society with checks and balances, effective law enforcement—with the net result that there was little or no corruption—a meritocracy, a fair society. Most of all, he felt it would offer their children a better life. It was clear that Nigeria was still going to get worse before, God willing, it began to turn around. The more Zimako thought about the Nigerian situation, the more melancholy he got. He shook his head in bewilderment. How could a country so blessed with such a wealth of human and material resources sink to this sorry state? Sad, really sad. Well, he was not going to dwell on it. He was blessed to have his Canadian residency within reach, and now he could wave goodbye to *jagba-jagba and nyama nyama*.

He blinked, returning his focus to the screen before him, and decided to try other provinces in Canada.

It was difficult. Unwittingly, he had become fixated on Ontario. Toronto was a city where he felt he could effortlessly fit in. To his mind, there was the potential of more jobs.

Plus it was true: Toronto had the largest percentage of immigrants compared to the rest of Canada.

He googled "foreign trained professional" and a bunch of pages popped up.

Each was a revelation. It confirmed what Anuli had said. His qualifications would require certification to make it comparable with similar Canadian degrees, and then there was the risk that they could be downgraded. What were the criteria? Nigeria operated largely from the British educational system, but Canada—was it the American system or British system or perhaps a hybrid?

He sighed. The one thing he had not prepared himself for was the downgrading of the years of education and wealth of experience that had facilitated his success in his career.

He jotted down the telephone numbers and email addresses of the institutions responsible for the review of foreign degrees in Toronto.

There were ten provinces in Canada, and three territories. It was mind-boggling. He knew it was practically impossible to send out an enquiry to all the provinces and immediately understood Anuli's frustration.

Which would be better? Ontario or Manitoba? Alberta or British Columbia?

How did one adjust from thirty-three degrees Celsius to minus three degrees Celsius? Should they opt for a province that had the easiest acceptance of foreign experience and qualifications? Or the one with the most welcoming and friendly people, where it was easy to feel at home? Or should job opportunities be the deciding factor? A real man needed to be a provider and be able to meet his financial commitments to build a secure future. Which economy was growing the fastest?

Zimako put all his questions down in black and white. He wanted to see the facts, although he felt overwhelmed by them. He pushed his pad away. "Oh God, I am so confused. I do not know how to navigate my path from here. You made Canada, and you know what will be best for Anuli and me. Please help me; where do you want us to go? Where is your promise for us? Please show me the way."

He settled back in his chair, just savouring the silence with his heart focussed on God. "I am so confused."

* * * * *

He did not hear me approach. His side of the bed was empty and cold when I reached out for a cuddle. I hopped out of bed, quickly donning one of his tee shirts and went in search of him. "Zimako?" I called. "Babes, are you okay?" I heard him talking to himself.

Zimako looked up and saw me. "Come over here," he said. "You look so adorable, I could eat you."

I knew he meant it, but that would just distract from the pain I had glimpsed in his eyes. "Zimako, what is bothering you?" I asked sitting on his lap. "Please share it with me, honey."

He looked closely at me. We strove to be independent, but also relied strongly on each other. I knew he never liked me to think he'd lost control, and tried not to betray the internal turmoil he was experiencing. He felt overwhelmed by all the information jumping out at him.

"Anuli, I am not sure I am having a good morning." His brows creased into a frown.

"What is it?" I also knew Zimako was resilient and would only cry for help when things became unbearable.

"You were right; deciding where to live is not so easy. Our qualifications will be subject to recertification in almost all the provinces to determine what they equate to by Canadian standards. It is frustrating. After jumping through all the hoops with the immigration people to get offered permanent residency, then, just as I was beginning to smile that we had breasted the tape, a new set of hurdles."

I was silent. It was not just what we knew, but what we did not know. The bogeyman might yet be lurking in the shadows. "Zimako, what do we do?"

Zimako did not know the answer to my question. When the process of this journey started, he was sure of the direction. Now he felt he'd lost GPS connectivity. He could feel his heart palpitating and fear, an emotion he was unaccustomed to, engulfing him. He gently set me on my feet and begun pacing.

"Now I understand that saying, 'fear of the unknown.' It's my ignorance that's fuelling my panic. Fear comes from ignorance.

We are confused because we do not know how to proceed. So, could this be the crucial crossroads that determines success or failure? What if this is the point where we are left to begin to chart our own destiny—how should we handle it?"

Zimako kept an eye on me as he paced back and forth. I felt forlorn and must have looked fragile and dishevelled in his shirt, with my hair tussled around my face. He forced himself to come to a halt before me, squatted down, and then reached up to frame my face. "We are going to Canada, Anuli, and nothing will stop us. Challenges will come, but we must soldier on. We will persevere till we conquer our fear. I do not know what awaits us, but I have prayed long and hard. If it was not the will of God, this paper would not be in our hands. Babes, yes we can!"

I was still silent, contemplating what Zimako had just said.

"What if this is the proverbial crossroads, the determining point of destiny, Zimako? Can we be sure we are on the right path?"

"Look, babe, we have entered the next phase of our journey to this strange land. Something tells me that choosing where we shall reside will be important. But one thing I, or shall I say *we*, must not do is to let fear dominate our emotions and dictate our actions."

"So what are you going to do?"

"Research!" Zimako announced. "See, I have spent the hours before you woke up just surfing the Internet to understand what life would look like, where we should go for a soft landing, you know, researching, but now the system is getting sluggish, so I think it's time I went downtown to VI. Come along for the ride and keep me com-pany; two heads are better than one. Shall I make you some coffee?"

I considered his request. It had been a whirlwind of activity since we got our papers, and time was not standing still. Much of what we had done was on an individual basis, briefing one another. Maybe if we spent time together doing our research and trying to figure out what to do, we might go farther.

"So two good heads?"

"You mean, my good head and your half-awake one?" he

replied, teasing me. I cheered up at his teasing, mock punching him in the chest.

"Okay, I think I will come with you. I was actually thinking of going to the market, then driving to Ibadan to see my parents, *but how for do now*? This one is more important."

"We can go to Ibadan tomorrow after church. Are your parents expecting you today?"

"I did not specify today, just that I'd try to see them this weekend."

"So call and let them know that we will '*full ground*' after Sunday service."

"Cool, babes, I'm on it!"

* * * * *

Okwe knew that Zimako and Anuli were in departure mode, and did not want to hassle them.

"Seriously, Okwe, you need to ask your bros. He might want to offload the vehicle."

Buzo had been pestering Okwe for a while to talk to Zimako about selling one of Zimako's cars to him. "The least you could do is put in a good word for me, man. I mean, your brother takes good care of his cars, and I'd rather buy from him than from those Berger guys."

Okwe could see Buzo's point of view, but Zimako had not indicated that he wanted to dispose of any of his vehicles and he did not want to seem pushy. "Why are you putting me in this difficult situation, man? Zimako *never tell me say im wan sell any of the cars. I go jus go begin disturb am to sell moto? E get as e be na. Like person wey sick for hospital, doctor neva talk anything, you begin ask am say whether e don write him will? Haba! A beg no expose my nyasch, O!*"

Okwe often spoke Pidgin English when was chilling with his guys. He was feeling pressured by Buzo. Approaching Zimako with such a request, in his mind's eye, was rather presumptuous. He did not like it one bit.

Ireti overheard their conversation, and couldn't help chipping in. "Buzo, *na wa for you sef. You* and Zimako *dey pally. Why you no* call am convince am to look your side if him want sell the moto? Call Zimako and ask him about it. Zimako knows you pretty well, and he might do you a good deal if he's looking for a buyer."

Buzo considered that. "You are a sharp babe. You know, that sounds like a good idea, but it's easier said than done, O! *Na how to introduce the matter be kpalava.*"

Okwe laughed. "You should have thought of that before bugging me, but what do you mean easier said than done? *U dey fear Zimako?*"

Ireti knew that Okwe did not want to get involved. He was such an easy-going guy. If he were willing to do it, he would not need badgering. She had gained some insight into his little bugbears as their relationship progressed. It was obvious he did not want to approach Zimako on this one.

"*How for do na?*" Buzo was flummoxed at the thought of approaching Zimako directly.

"Just call him, and ask him," Okwe countered.

"Just like that?"

"Well, yes. After all, that was exactly what you were expecting me to do just now, *abi?*"

Ireti chipped in again. "Which car are you wanting him to sell to you?"

"The Passat."

"*Ah ol' boy, your currency don land, O. That one na big boy's car,*" Okwe chimed in.

"Come on, my guy, *na softly softly catchi monkey.* I am only trying to move up, you know."

"But honestly, *that moto go cost sha.* How much are you pricing it?"

"*If im gree for two milla, I go carry am.*"

"You must be joking. He bought that car for 4.4 million, and has used it for only two years. You know how well maintained that car is. Better raise your budget, O."

"Well, I have to start from somewhere. Since you are hanging me out to dry, let me gather my courage and call him," Buzo concluded.

"Yes, call him, and please leave me out of the conversation."

"No *wahala*. You get him number handy?"

Okwe gave Buzo the number without any further fuss. "No doubt he'll know I gave you his number, but *nothin' spoil*, good luck."

Buzo left Okwe's place with the promise to keep him posted on the outcome of the negotiations. He couldn't resist a parting shot, though. "Look, if you like this babe, then you should have put a ring on her quickly, *you no see say she smart well well.*" He laughed, shutting the door behind him, leaving an embarrassed Okwe to sort that out.

He was barely out the door, and Ireti, knowing Okwe would be embarrassed by that parting shot, deftly steered the topic to a safer harbour. She couldn't contain her curiosity. "So why didn't you want to help him? You could have talked to Zimako and he would do it; you know that."

Okwe was still smarting from Buzo's departing wisecrack. "Exactly. That is the reason I do not want to get involved. It's Zimako's decision; he has not mentioned the intention to sell of any of his stuff to me. Why should I fast-forward and pressure him into selling his car at what sounds like a ridiculous price?"

"I guess. By the way, how much time do they have before leaving for Canada?"

"Two months, perhaps a little more, maybe a little less. I can't imagine how Zimako is feeling. Imagine leaving Naija at this mature age to go and start struggling afresh in no-man's land?"

Ireti came to sit by Okwe on the armrest; she put her arm around his shoulders, caressed his biceps, and ogled his rippling six-pack. She was throbbing in her nether regions and getting a bit wet and in the mood for loving. The room was dimly lit. There had been another of the commonplace power outages, or in the local parlance, "NEPA had taken the light." Though there was a slight breeze, it was a humid evening with temperatures around twenty-eight degrees Celsius, just the right ambience for getting up to no good. She tried to focus her mind on the conversation at hand. "So, it is not something you will consider at all?"

"You know me, darling… I am easy. I *no dey* stress. I am a Naija guy to the core. If I want to travel, I will apply for a visa. If they give me, fine, if not, *I go siddon jeje for here dey enjoy my life.*

"I know what you mean. Do you think he is making the right move? After all, they have always been able to get visas to travel whenever they want to. Both of them are professionals and they are doing well."

"Ireti, I get what you are saying, but Zimako is Zimako and he reasons in his own unique way; as for me, I *dey Naija* for life, no leave, no transfer."

The aroma of goat meat stew wafted through from the kitchen, reminding Ireti of her *"pot wey dey fire."* "My guy, let me make sure the 'touch and follow' I'm cooking doesn't get burnt."

Okwe gazed lustfully at her departing, well-rounded backside, giving it a playful smack. "When you are done, Martha, come and give me some Mary. Seems like my Lazarus is coming to life."

Ireti turned back, flashed her boobs at Okwe, batted her eyelids, and sashayed away, leaving him hungering for more than just goat meat. Okwe was the best thing that had happened to her as far as relationships went, not that she had a lot of experience, but men these days were such Lotharios. With Okwe she knew where she stood. If he ever popped the question, she was sure what her response would be. *Well, let's leave that thought for another day.*

* * * * *

Zimako and I were huddled in the cybercafé in the highbrow, low-density Victoria Island. The café hosted a fast food section, a beer parlour which came alive as a happening joint in the evening, and a mini-mart.

This all-in-one plaza was a meeting point for the resident young executives in the neighbourhood. An open space that served as a car park was jam-packed with luxury cars.

A lot of people were loitering outside, some with intent, others less obviously so. There were the gatemen popularly known as *abokis*, who had small-time table top stalls vending everything imaginable—from *suya* and cigarettes to chewing gum and pure water—and the nubile women peddling oranges, or whatever fruit happened to be in season, and sometimes more. Some of the people appeared dressed for office jobs, but wore a look of despondency and hunger. Zimako observed this disparate group from his vantage window position. I knew his mind was trying, but failed to fathom the business model that would synchronize these diverse businesses together. He mentioned it frequently and concluded that indeed strange bedfellows coexist in harmony.

It was almost 7.00 p.m. and the day was far spent.

"Well, I am glad we came out here to do this."

I looked at him and smiled. It had been a long day, and I felt a lot had been accomplished. The clouds of foreboding and the fears of drowning in a sea of mystery were dissipating. We had some answers, though others were pending. But all in all, it no longer seemed insurmountable.

At least we had whittled the list down to three cities we could reside in, and hopefully, once we decided on that, we could start sending out emails and making phone calls to give substance to our plans on settling down.

It came down to Regina, Vancouver, or Edmonton. We had finally decided against Toronto because of the high rate of unemployment and crime.

Zimako was jolted out of his reverie by his ringing phone. "Hmmm, who could be calling me?" he said, rising to his feet. "One sec, I'll be back," he mouthed.

Zimako exited the café and turned to his right, having espied a canopy of trees providing shade for some chairs arranged underneath them. "'elloOoO?"

"Hey, bros, na Buzo. *How far na*?" Buzo had decided to take the bull by the horn. He needed a car, and a classy one at that. The options open to him were limited, and Zimako was his first and last best hope to actualize his dreams. Although he had not said it to Okwe, he had figured that if he got Zimako's car at a bargain, he could proceed with his engagement plans.

"Buzo?" Zimako was caught unawares; he was not expecting a call from him, but was also relieved his caller wasn't that shameless hussy Ndudi. He wondered what might be the matter, although he had a sneaking suspicion he knew what the call was about. Buzo could only have pried his number out of Okwe, but at least Okwe should have given him a heads-up.

"*Yes, O, bros, na me, Buzo, where you dey now?*"

"Actually, I am on the Island. What's up?"

"We need to see. I want to discuss something with you. When will be convenient for you?"

"It depends. Is it an emergency or something that can wait?"

"Well, it's a bit of both. Can I see you today or tomorrow?"

Zimako suppressed his laughter. How could something be both an emergency and still be something that could wait? Ah, Buzo. "Well, tomorrow we are going to see Anuli's folks. Where are you right now?"

"*I dey* mainland, on my way home, but if you tell me where you are, *I fit block you now now.*"

"Okay, here's what we are going to do. Anuli and I will be heading home soon. What if you meet us at home in a couple of hours?"

"For sure, thanks, bros. See you soon."

Zimako hung up, wondering what the emergency could be. Buzo was strictly Okwe's pal, so he was surprised to hear from him. He couldn't wait to find out what it was all about. He looked up to see a mallam looking at him strangely.

A feeling of doom overcame him. He was tongue-tied for a minute, Then, making a quick recovery, he jumped to his feet and spoke up. "Are you okay?"

"Sit down, I want to talk to you," the stranger started.

Zimako was curious as to what this was about. He did not visit the cybercafé often, but an observant person may have noticed him previously. He wondered if this was an attempt to extort money from him.

"Listen, I do not have any money on me, so if your intention—"

The words were barely out of his mouth before the mallam cut him short. "I am not here to beg you for money, sir. I want to help you."

"Help me? Do I know you?"

The mallam pulled up a chair beside Zimako and began to speak. "I see things. You are a very godly man," he said, pausing to watch Zimako's reaction. Then he continued. "I see you are about to embark on a journey." He looked searchingly at Zimako. "There is a woman, I see a woman; she is going to play a big role in your journey, but be very careful—all is not what it seems. I see a tall mountain, and I see an open land." The mallam shook his head. "Who is that woman crying?"

It dawned on Zimako that the mallam was a sorcerer. "Get away from me, man; I reject all your words. My fortune and life is only determined by God!"

"Don't you want me to finish, and interpret for you?"

Zimako stood up, looking around to make sure he wasn't leaving anything behind. "Listen, this conversation did not happen. I did not meet you, and I completely erase your words from my life." He took a deep breath and walked back into the complex where Anuli was waiting for him.

His exterior did not betray the turmoil he was feeling within; he had had enough. It was time to leave.

* * * * *

I saw Zimako approaching, and from the purpose in his stride I could tell something was wrong. "What was the phone call about? Zimako, are you okay?"

"Let's get out of here now."

I was puzzled. Who could he have been speaking with on the phone that had upset him so much? I began to gather what I could while Zimako picked up the files. He seemed to be in such a rush to leave.

"Okay, I'm ready," I said, grabbing my Louis Vuitton Speedy bag off the chair beside me.

Zimako was silent as we departed. He stopped to pay our bill at the till.

"*Oga*, your bill na two five."

Normally Zimako would haggle over the bill—he knew they tended to overprice their services—but today he couldn't wait to leave. He counted the cash and handed it over.

"*Oga*, I see you with that mallam. That man is powerful. The other day when he *tell* one client *make him no travel, the man go travel, come see accident, na* only God save the man."

"I'd rather not discuss this. Listen, could you just give me my change?"

Zimako couldn't wait to get out of the café. I was as confused as ever, wondering at the change in Zimako's mood, the phone call, and the mallam. But I knew I would not accomplish much by cross-examining him in public. Better to wait till we got into the car.

CHAPTER NINE

> *Dear Diary,*
> *So this is it, we are packed. We are now counting the days.*
> *In two weeks we will land in Canada.*
> *It feels surreal. We hope it will be our land of milk and honey.*
> *Anyhow, the die is cast. We cannot turn back the hands of time.*
> *Steadily we march forward.*
> *Onward, to a new world.*
> *In anticipation of a brighter future.*
> *Only change is constant.*

The church service was drawing to a close. This was probably the last time we would be fellowshipping here at our home church. I was filled with nostalgia. Zimako and I had been members of Christ Church since we got married and had wedded here. It was not a very big church by Lagos standards, but it was a congregation of "big leaguers." The congregation topped three thousand, and on an average Sunday, the worshippers spilled over into the overflow extension. Our church was housed in a beautiful cathedral-style building with wonderful acoustics, mimicking classical British architecture. You could feel the presence of God in this place.

The pastor said the closing prayers, and then we shared the grace.

* * * * *

"Wait, wait." It was Bisi, one of the sisters at church, gesticulating to attract our attention. The news of our imminent departure was now common knowledge to most of our friends, and everyone seized the opportunity to engage us in some sort of valedictory conversation. Some wondered why, others wanted to know how; it was quite intrusive but often well meaning.

"When are you guys leaving?" She ran up to us, breathless but unwilling to pause, making every effort to speak at the same time. She was a buxom woman, and usually carried her weight with a sensual elegance, but sprinting with breasts bouncing any which way detracted from her deportment.

"Hi, Sister Bisi, take it easy," I said, trying to get her to slow down. "So, when are you guys leaving? I was planning to come and visit before you go."

"We are still here for another couple of weeks or so, but as it is, we are stretched for time. There are not enough hours in a day to accomplish my to-do list."

"What! I thought you still had at least two months? What's the rush? You have the papers *abi*. E*hh*, you can go anytime now, *haba*."

Zimako looked at me; he knew that if we let this conversation linger, it could drag on for a while. We had an appointment to see the pastor and didn't want to be late.

"Bisi, actually, the general criteria is to land in Canada three months after the document is issued," Zimako interjected firmly. "Listen, why don't you call Anuli later to arrange something? We need to see Pastor Dan."

I realised Zimako was now tugging me along, so I waved sister Bisi goodbye and mouthed a "phone me later" to her.

I turned to Zimako. "Darling, that was rather abrupt."

"Oh, never mind, Bisi. I am hoping we can catch Pastor Dan before the crowd gets there."

I could see his point; Pastor Dan was very popular. He was well-loved in our parish. His schedule was often fully booked. This was the ultimate endorsement that he was a very caring and good shepherd. I mused on how he found the time to call and visit with so many demands on his time. He was one of the first people Zimako had informed of our good news and subsequent departure.

He had greeted the news with astonishment, then congratulations, and had invited Zimako to make an appointment to see him closer to our departure. Zimako had duly scheduled the appointment via the church secretary for today, and did not want to be late. We greeted other friends and well-wishers as we made our way through the crowd of brethren. The "after service" networking and greeting was in full swing. Sunday was a day for relaxing. Most people who attended the service made the most of it and took time to meet and greet and catch up with each other.

* * * * *

Zimako was several steps ahead of me when he turned to see me struggling to match his long strides. My heels did not make it any easier. He smiled indulgently and slowed down, stretching out his hand to me as a supportive crutch. I held onto his hand as we reached the pastoral office.

It was always like an oasis in the dry, hot desert. The air-conditioning system was a sharp contrast to the blast-furnace temperature outside, and the lush, deep beige carpet was a perfect match for the serene decor, which exuded calm. The foyer was a clutter-free zone with comfy chairs, presenting a welcoming ambience to the weary, troubled soul. There was a water fountain in the corner with a cross above it to quench one's physical thirst, as though a reminder that Jesus was the living water and eternal thirst quencher. A glass corner coffee table had some tracts and church information pamphlets arranged around a centrepiece of fragrant, fresh lilies in a beautiful vase. The only adornment on the wall was that cross, bold in its message. The pastor's office was at the end of the hallway; we headed there.

Zimako knocked gently on the door; usually the secretary was seated at the front desk area, but today was Sunday and the desk was unmanned. The door into Pastor Dan's office was slightly ajar. Zimako knocked gently again before peering in.

"Amen!"

Zimako stepped back and I looked at him questioningly.

"There are some people with him; they are praying. Let's take a seat and wait till they are done."

We sat down and waited. I was glad to take a seat. My high-heeled sandals had started to pinch the dreadful corn on the little toe of my right foot. I sank into the chair. "Mmmm," I murmured, smiling.

Zimako turned to look at me. "What?"

"These poor feet are just glad to take a break."

At that moment the pastor strode out, escorting his guests out. I recognised them as the other pastors and prayer warriors. It was their habit to meet for prayers after service before leaving for the day.

"Bro Zimako and Sister Anuli, how are you doing?"

"We can't complain, praise God!" We rose and greeted all the other leaders, exchanging pleasantries as they departed.

"Please come in. I have been looking forward to seeing you again."

We went in and sat in the chairs facing the pastor.

"So tell me how you are really doing."

Zimako proceeded to inform him of what we had done and how much we were looking forward to the new life ahead of us. Pastor Dan smiled and turned to me. "And you, Sister Anuli, how are you?"

I smiled, and then suddenly welled up with emotion. "Let me say okay, I guess. Yeah, I'm fine, Pastor. It has not been very easy, but I've also not had time to dwell on things. It has been a whirlwind of activity."

"Are you happy?"

I was not sure what to say. Zimako looked at me, and we shared a moment of telepathy.

"Let us pray."

Pastor Dan was a prayer warrior. Prior to taking up his post to head our parish, he had been the group leader of the Battle Cry group. Many signs and wonders had been witnessed under his ministry before he was promoted to take on more responsibility. He approached his pastoral role with humility and scrupulousness. He took nothing for granted and constantly sought to know the will of God in any situation.

We held hands and bowed our heads. He began to pray. As if

overcome by something, Pastor Dan paused and sighed heavily before continuing. He kept the prayer session succinct and concluded in Jesus's name. We chorused "Amen" in agreement.

Pastor Dan sat back in his chair and focussed his attention on Zimako. He smiled and cocked his head to the side. "How prepared are you for what the future may hold? I mean, this is a new country. You have not lived there before, nor were you born there."

At that moment, the weight of what we were about to take on seemed to dawn on Zimako. "Pastor, please continue to uphold us in prayer. It will not be easy; I do not know what to expect. I'm trusting God."

Pastor Dan turned to me again, gauging my countenance. "Sister Anuli, you must be strong. You will encounter a lot of unexpected challenges. Write "unexpected" in capital letters, then underline it. But you both have chosen this path; it means you will both be walking as a couple, not alone. Canada is not a place where a lot of Nigerians have any connections. It is a far-off country, cold, and lonely. But though you will seem to be walking alone, you will not be alone. And no matter what you encounter, remember that you must not throw in the towel." He paused to consider Zimako and me, and then continued. "Just now, as we prayed, God showed me a picture."

As soon as he uttered those words, I perked up. You see, I had been praying for a message to know the mind of God on this matter and try as I might, I could not convince myself that I had heard anything definite from the Lord. I felt I had been stumbling in the dark. Maybe this was the illumination I had been hoping for. Secretly, when I knew Zimako had an appointment for us to see Pastor Dan, my hope was for some sort of revelation from God. I did not voice this to Zimako because I knew he was cautious about revelations from "men of God." In fact, he generally disregarded such "revelations." I, on the other hand, listened prayerfully to utterances from men of God and allowed my spirit to decipher God's voice from human opinion.

"It was a narrow, crooked path, sometimes broken and then smoothening out, uneven and then craggy and rugged. Then I saw elevation, and then a dawn. This is what I saw as we prayed."

Zimako bowed his head. "Thank you, Pastor. I thank you for sharing this with us. I know it will not be an easy path, even just getting settled, but Anuli and I are resolute."

"What else did you see, Pastor Dan?" I asked, my inner turmoil getting the better of me.

Pastor Dan laughed softly. "That was it. I don't know what Canada has in store for you, but I can assure you, you'll be in my prayers. You see, you are both in your prime, doing so well here as professionals in your field, and now you are upping sticks." He paused again and looked directly at both of us, then continued quietly. "When you take a fully grown mature tree from where it is thriving and prospering and take it to a different spot, even if it is in the same plot of land, the process of uprooting that tree exposes it and makes it vulnerable. When the tree is replanted, timing, climate, and soil type are key factors to facilitate acclimatisation. Some will wither away. It takes a hardy tree to survive and eventually thrive. But remember, only the resilient eventually thrive, and at that only after it may have dried out and lost some lushness. Then it starts all over again, often different, but usually stronger. Do you understand what I am saying?"

We nodded.

"But no matter how difficult it may seem, if you keep your faith in Christ and love each other, you will emerge victorious."

My eyes welled up with tears; I could feel my heart beating very hard as Pastor Dan spoke. It was not that I expected him to announce that a pot of gold was waiting in Canada, but I suddenly understood from his analogy that it would be okay ultimately. We were not teenagers on an adventure; we were leaving our comfort zone and relocating to a place we were not originally built for. I think my sadness must have shown clearly because I heard him say, "There is a new dawn that awaits you, my sister, my brother. There are many who want to trade places with you, so you must make the best of your opportunity and be good ambassadors for Christ and of Nigeria."

"Thank you, Pastor," we chorused.

"Make sure you keep in touch, by phone and email. You have

all my numbers and my personal email address."

We promised to do just that.

"Let's share the grace."

* * * * *

We headed for Ibadan, making our way to the Lagos-Ibadan Expressway.

Zimako and I had retreated into silence after leaving Pastor Dan. I was a bit disconcerted as I tried to interpret his revelation, but the more I mulled over it, the more a certain peace filled my mind about our journey. I now knew there was a future with hopeful promise. Zimako did not say anything about it yet, but I knew he would have something to say once he digested the information.

"So... " He turned to me and smiled. "You seem happy."

I was neither happy nor unhappy. If I had to describe how I felt, it was more like a calmness, recognising that there would be the usual ups and downs of life and that this was normal, even if we continued our life in Nigeria. I figured that life, being the bed of roses it was, would be filled with petals and thorns.

"Well, I am, in a way."

Zimako laughed. "Well, my take on it is simple. Try not to overanalyse the future. Make the right choices, that will provide the best insurance against any regrets in the future."

"Hmmm, simplistic, but I take your point."

We conjectured and extrapolated, letting ourselves dream fantastic dreams momentarily and discussing plans for how we would hit the ground running once we got to Canada.

We had finally decided we would settle in Edmonton.

We began to consider other day-to-day issues and think about how to decode the system so that we could progress from fledgling immigrants to expert citizens in record time.

"Anuli, *a beg* call Chinazo and see where they are. I had a missed call from her when we were in church, so my guess is they are waiting for us somewhere, maybe at our secret joint near the toll gate. While you are at it, sweetheart, check on Chiamaka as well."

We were on our way to visit my parents. Chinazo and Chuka had promised to come on the trip with us, as had Chiamaka and Ogbo. It helped that Ibadan was just a couple of hours outside Lagos, a comfortable day trip with no time constraints; we could chill out and enjoy ourselves.

As with Zimako's parents, the reaction in Ibadan on hearing our news was shock and sadness bordering on bereavement, but they reacted with love, committing us into God's safe hands. We were asked a lot of questions, but thank goodness there was no drama and no recrimination.

Mummy as usual had laid out the red carpet, and Prof had some fresh palmwine chilled to wash down the dishes. We had a good time. Dad reminisced about his days in England. He'd studied in Liverpool, and then in Newcastle, where he lectured a bit after his PhD. He was sure we would visit home frequently. He said the world now was a global village, and promised he and Mum would visit as soon as we were settled. I sensed sadness beneath his cheerful banter.

The weather was good; the mood was buoyant. Before we left, Dad insisted on his habit of singing hymns and prayers. We joyfully obliged him. The evening drew to a close, we bade them goodbye, and they promised to come along to Lagos to see us off at the airport. We agreed that we would let them have all the details in due course so they could plan the visit.

* * * * *

I was racing against time. I had the responsibility of ensuring that our accommodation and flights were confirmed. It was also down to me to tidy up our affairs with family.

Zimako had done all the legwork with the various professional bodies in Canada to ensure that we had all our Nigerian documents notarised and dispatched to Canada for review and responses forwarded to our temporary new address. He had proactively made contact with prospective employers and sent out our curriculum vitae to executive recruiting agencies. He was in charge of liquidating our prized possessions.

I was too emotional to handle that bit. We had already

inventoried our belongings and decided what we could and could not keep. For now, though, we would keep the house just as a safety net till we were fully settled in Canada.

Our home became a hive of activity. Friends of friends, co-workers, and all manner of people who had heard we were leaving and disposing of our life's belongings were coming over to see if they could score a bargain. The human traffic was constant. Zimako sold the Passat to Buzo. The clothes that were unsuitable for Canada we either sold or given away. Going through my wardrobe was a very sentimental undertaking. Each outfit had a story. It was akin to getting rid of part of my life history. We stowed away a lot of stuff in storage.

We were able to raise a lot of naira, but with the exchange rate, when we converted what we had to Canadian dollars, it did not amount to much.

There was also the business of ensuring that our parents were well taken care of. Zimako wanted to set up a standing order with the bank, but without knowing what our income was going to be for the foreseeable future, we decided to curb our ambitious financial commitments for now. This was a novel experience.

Zimako's bosses had not been able to replace him and had negotiated a leave of absence rather than accepting his resignation outright. Although they agreed to three months, he could take up to six months if necessary, after which Zimako would come back to continue his job, giving the company time to fill his post. He would remain the sole breadwinner till I was settled. I wondered how I would cope when he left.

As if that was not bad enough, at the last minute Zimako decided we should not keep the house empty for fear of squatters and burglars. It made sense to sublet it, rather than to keep two homes since we still had a lease on it.

I felt like my safety net was snatched away from underneath my feet. There was no going back. Luckily, everything was packed. Zimako and Okwe hired a van and transported what was left of our life's possessions home to the village so the tenants could have free rein of the house. The countdown was really on.

CHAPTER TEN

Dear Diary,

Everywhere I go these days, I mentally photograph the moment and ferret it away as a keepsake in my soul.

My days in Lagos are numbered. I'm trying to stay strong, but I must privately admit that going away would never have been my choice.

The flurry of activity and the support have been overwhelming. I will miss Nigeria. Eko for show, Naija forever!

Time is galloping away. We depart in a week, and to my mind's eye, these are the shortest seven days of my life.

I had a thousand and one things to get done. Monica and I had arranged to meet and have a girly night out, which doubled as a leaving-do with some of the other women from work. I was looking forward to it.

Driving from the mainland to the Island at about 6.00 p.m. was easy because the traffic was moving in the opposite direction. I cruised along the highway to the music of Timaya. We were meeting at Double Four on Awolowo Road. Monica was generously picking up the tab.

I was wearing a lemon-green, V-necked, top, which fit perfectly around my waistline, and loosely skimmed my hips, with a pair of cropped khaki chinos. I threw on a pashmina for effect, because I knew most of the other women would be looking sophisticated as usual, coming in from work. I decided on a dress-down, corporate casual look. I finished my ultra-chic look with my oversized Gucci sunshades. Admiring myself in the rear-view mirror, I decided I could pass for an A-list celebrity. I smiled a secret, self-congratulatory smile and thought, *Looking good, girl!*

* * * * *

I slowly brought my Toyota Camry to a halt on the forecourt, BlackBerry in one hand, handbag in the other. Head held up high, I made for the entrance. I was not expecting the whole party to be there yet, but as I stepped in I was greeted by cheers.

"What a wonderful surprise!" I had not been expecting quite so many of the women to be here. Monica came around to welcome me. She hugged me warmly. "Hey, it's Thursday, and what better way to spend the evening than to leave the bosses to do all the work while we skive off? Hmmm? Girls just wanna have fun!" She pirouetted and did a mock catwalk back to the table. I followed closely. We had a nice table by the corner. Emman, who doubled as maître d' and headwaiter, promptly came to take my drink order as I took my seat, air-kissing the other women and catching up on the gossip and news.

Monica held her glass up, clinking it with her fork to draw attention.

"My lovelies," she started, "now that Anuli is here, let's give her a good time so she can feel sorry she is leaving." There was laughter all around. She quickly gave a rundown of how the evening was expected to unfold. Emman came back with the menu and wine list, making recommendations on the specials.

I turned to Monica. "Phew! This is going to set you back big time. You really didn't have to spend all this money. We could have gone Dutch or even Cheapside at your place."

"I agree with you that it could have been cheaper, but how for do, I am not up for the hassle of cooking and tidying up afterwards, and as I always say, why borrow if you can 419?"

"What do you mean, Monica? You've come again!"

"Actually, I was being economical with the truth when I said I was picking up the tab. When I told Segun I was leaving early to send you off, he wrote a cheque of sixty-five K with his compliments; *so na your Oga wey dey fund these small chops, O,* so eat and be merry!"

I was astounded by his generosity and made a mental note to call and thank him. We chuckled at her chutzpah. Monica excused herself to find out what was holding up the drinks. I turned to

Ngozi on my left. She smiled at me. "So what's the real reason you're leaving us?"

Ngozi was one of the women I genuinely liked. She had joined the company at the same time Monica and I did; however, as it always was with starting a race, we ran at different paces. Marriage and maternity leave to have four delightful children had slowed down her career, but we all remained friendly.

I told her about our Canadian odyssey, and how blessed we were, and how it presented an opportunity we couldn't pass up.

"No way! I didn't realise you were leaving the country. Why? To start fresh? Is it a good idea? You are very brave, O!" She was whispering now.

"Ngozi, my dear, we have thought about this carefully and prayerfully; we have not rushed this decision. I thought Monica told you."

"No now, you know Monica. She probably figured you would tell those you wanted to. All she said was that we were sending you off, and only close friends were coming. No, I had no idea at all."

I immediately felt bad. I understood why Monica had not told anyone, but at this stage, I felt there was no point in continuing to keep it a secret. These women here all wished me well. I looked around at the table with nostalgia, calling to mind different memories of shared experiences.

"I am so sorry. You are right; I should have been the one to tell you about it, but the truth is that since the papers came through it's been so hectic, trying to organise ourselves to depart."

"Congratulations! Wow! This is such a big surprise. I mean, your leaving is a big surprise; going to Canada is just awesome. In fact, I don't know what to say. Good luck, my sister. I bet you there is no one around this table who knows the full details of where we are sending you off to except Monica, our hostess; she really kept your secret secret."

"Please don't blame her; I'll tell everybody about it." We noticed Monica approaching with the waiter who had our drinks, and another following behind them with our hors d'oeuvres. Monica's heels clicked on the marble floors as she sashayed towards the table.

"Here we go, girls." The waiters set out our drinks and food. I winked at Monica, and she drew near. "Ngozi is surprised that I'm headed to Canada for good. I take it nobody else around the table is any wiser, hmmm?"

"I did not want to spoil it for you. It's your big news. I just told them what everyone already knew, that you were leaving and we would be sending you forth today. I have no doubt in my mind that there is all manner of speculation, but you know how it is. Once the rumours start making the rounds, it's difficult to turn the tide. I figured if you told your inner caucus today, Chinese whispers would take over and silence the grapevine."

"I hear you. Thank you," I said, casting a look that spoke volumes.

She laughed at my nervousness. "Listen, you are leaving, so what do you care? I'm the one who'll be left behind to pick up the pieces."

We spent the rest of the evening raucously enjoying ourselves. By this time the news had filtered around the table about my leaving for Canada. Once dessert was cleared from the table, Monica took over again and announced to the women that it was time for me to make some remarks. I decided to stand. I looked around at the faces before me, and I felt warmed by their support and friendship. "My dear, dear friends, thank you all for coming today. I am so chuffed that you have all taken the time to make this evening possible. You have all heard the well-kept secret that I am leaving for Canada and some of you are shocked, others surprised, and I'm sure you are all wondering why. Let me just put your minds at ease. There isn't a single answer to the question why. When my hubby first floated the idea, I went along with it, not really expecting anything to come of it. As we started collating the documents, and exchanging correspondence with the Canadian immigration services, the idea became a tangible reality. It has taken all of three years and a more of backing and forthing to finally be approved for an immigrant visa."

This was turning into a speech. I took a sip of my Chapman and continued. "I can tell you that I am happy we have it. Zimako and I were attacked two months or so ago by armed robbers. They almost raped me and nearly killed Zimako; it just brought home to me how lucky we are to have an exit strategy."

I paused as they looked at me, surprised; only Monica had known of the attack. "We escaped that incident unscathed physically, but the psychological scars highlight how unsafe daily life has become in Nigeria. There are many reasons to stay, more reasons to stay than to go, to be honest, but we have an opportunity, we have decided to explore it, and we are grateful to God for it.

"I'll miss so many things about home. I know I will miss all of you, my friends—Monica, Ngozi, Jolomi, Chika, Lara, Naomi, Bimbo, Laraba, Mfon, Ronke, and Ifunanya. I will miss you all, but it is not the end of our friendship. It's a new chapter. Who knows, some of you may decide to come over once you hear how I am doing out there." I began to feel emotional; tears welled up in my eyes, blurring my vision. I couldn't continue to speak as a lump formed in my throat, so I sat down. Monica reached out to hug me.

"So hopefully you will start a family once you get there, *abi*?" that came from Bimbo as she attempted to change the subject, but it was too personal a topic, so when Ngozi started singing "For she's a jolly good fellow… " everyone joined in, and then Jolomi toasted to my good fortune with vodka shots, which instantaneously cheered us up. After that there was no stopping us; we were in high spirits again.

From her end of the table, Lara asked for my Canadian contact details. I hated having to admit that the plans were less than rock solid.

"We do not have permanent telephone numbers yet. We have arranged to stay in a serviced apartment for the first thirty days. Our hope is that we can sort out accommodation once we are on the ground. As soon as we settle, I'll forward the numbers to all of you, but meanwhile, my email address is the same, and I'll be actively updating my Facebook page."

The conversation turned to how to apply to go to Canada, and what the education system was like if one wanted to pursue a master's degree programme. Was it really always freezing? What about shopping? Did they have nice stuff? The mood lightened again; we were all smiling and chatting. The manager must have signalled to Monica, because she abruptly called us to order and said it was time to round up.

"Anuli, we have a gift for you. When the girls heard you were leaving, they had no details, but they all contributed to get you something. Altogether, the contribution came to three hundred thousand naira and a bit over; I thought it would be best to give you the cash to use towards your new life. *Abi*?"

Everyone cheered. I was overwhelmed.

"Thank you, this is fantastic. I don't know what to say. Thank you all so much."

The night was over. I went around hugging all the women as we rose to disperse. Monica handed me the envelope and settled the bill, and we all headed out to the car park. I'm glad I could hide my tears behind my sunshades. My heart felt heavy as I promised to keep in touch, knowing deep down that I might never see some of them again. It signalled the end of an era.

CHAPTER ELEVEN

> *Dear Diary,*
> *It's just Zimako and I now.*
> *We are pursuing his dream. He believes he is taking this leap of faith to give me a better future.*
> *Everyone is rooting for us; we must not let them down. I'm holding on to that Bible verse that says that wherever I step my foot, I will possess the land. I will possess this land. We will triumph. I hope.*

Sunshine filtered through the snowflakes. I snuggled under the duvet with my face buried, clinging to the warmth it provided, not yet ready to venture out of it. Zimako must have been feeling the same because he reached out, wrapped his arms around me, and drew me close.

"Mmmm… " I moaned as I cuddled up to him. He took that as an invitation and explored further. He trailed his fingers down my arms, caressing me tenderly. I spooned in, enjoying the warmth. It was not long before I felt the stiffening of his manhood against my nether regions. "Mmmm, sweetie," I whispered.

He responded by tweaking my nipples till they hardened. "Baby, do you want me? Let me feel you. Touch me, baby, go on, show me the way." He groaned.

I responded by teasing his manhood gently at first. His groans were guttural. "OoOoo, baby, yeah, honey, touch me."

I knew how to light his fire. Increasing the pressure of my grip, I traced my palm down his thighs and slid down to plant feathery kisses all the way down. His sigh told me I was hitting the right buttons. I could feel a throbbing and wetness as my desire mounted and my juices began to flow. His fingers explored my depths, and I writhed and moaned in response as we kissed. I was lost in the moment. The mutual kneading and rubbing increased in tempo and intensity to the music of our murmurs and moans. I groaned softly as Zimako touched and tasted my secret places. I could not control my desire anymore, and I cried out wantonly, "Please, babes, now!" to which he teased, "Are you sure you can handle it?" I was very aroused and couldn't bear to wait any longer. I straddled him and guided him in, and then he took control, plunging deep as he anchored my hips to his. We began to move rhythmically, riding the wave of passion. Zimako filled me completely and I pulsated around him as he cried out, "Baby, are you ready? I'm coming!"

As we lay spent, basking in the warmth of the aftermath, Zimako held me close and whispered in my ear, "You minx, you'll be the death of me." He laughed as I wriggled and then continued, "That was so good, it must be a sin. Trying to ruin a good Christian man. Now I know how Samson felt, naughty girl." He smacked my bum playfully and I laughed as he jested.

This was a side of Zimako others never saw. I wagged my finger at him. "Naughty boy, any more of that and you'll get a spanking." We both laughed, revelling in the moment. "So what's the itinerary for today?" I asked.

* * * * *

We had arrived in Edmonton, Canada, a week ago.

The immigration procedures went without a hitch. Once we showed the border officials our Confirmation of Permanent Residency (COPR), we were welcomed into Canada. Our documentation was confirmed and verified with cursory enquiries about our financial resources to ensure we met the financial threshold for landed immigrants. Zimako had wondered if they would ask us to show further evidence of our finances to prove we had the stipulated amount, but they were satisfied with the numbers we'd filled out on the form: no further questions asked. The application for the Permanent Resident (PR) card was automatic, and forms were handed to us to apply for the SIN card and health care card. We were also given lots of helpful leaflets to help us navigate our way as we made Canada our new home. Zimako and I were excited. The officials at the immigration service were cordial and gave us a warm welcome, a real contrast to Nigerian Customs. Bureaucracy sorted, we were waved through the barrier, and hey presto, we were in Canada. We retrieved our luggage and then walked through the beautiful Edmonton airport, admiring the shops.

Zimako turned to me. "*Obidiya*, how do you like it so far?"

I smiled. "So far, so good. Not bad at all."

Once outside we found it was snowing a little. This was a new world. Unlike the arrivals area at Muritala Mohammed International airport back home, which would have been crowded with sundry persons loitering, everyone here seemed to have a definite purpose. The taxicabs were queued up, picking up passengers on a first-come-first-serve basis. It was all so organised. Zimako and I took the next available cab.

We settled in for the drive, admiring the structure and cleanliness of the city as we drove from the airport to our downtown rental apartment. Our taxi driver, who had immigrated to Canada more than twenty years ago, engaged us in conversation, freely sharing his insights and experiences with us.

"I come from Poland to Canada to find good life too, twenty-one years now," he stated proudly once we told him we were newly landed immigrants. He revealed that he had moved around a bit before settling here. On landing, he had initially lived in Ontario before moving to Regina, then to Alberta. "I am married with three kids! The oldest is now in college. The weather is not bad. I can tell you it is better than a lot of the other provinces; we have the Chinooks!" It was still obvious that English was not his first language, with his broken grammar and disjointed tenses. And on and on he rambled, carrying on a monologue of sorts, flitting from topic to topic, but not providing in-depth information or pausing long enough for questions. He was pretty much like many taxi drivers in Lagos, a font of local knowledge.

Suddenly the focus of his conversation swung towards us. "What brings you come Canada? Is it very bad war?" he asked.

Zimako and I looked at each other, puzzled. Then Zimako

spoke up. "War? What war?"

The driver made eye contact with Zimako in the rear-view mirror and insisted, "You know, the war in Africa." I could tell Zimako's hackles were raised as he responded indignantly, "There is no war in Nigeria. We are here as skilled professionals."

The cabbie paid him scant attention, having jumped to his own conclusions. "Many say they are doctors and engineers back home, but here, they drive the cab just like me," he announced proudly, casually throwing this into the mix before moving on to the next topic.

He left us with more questions than answers. Some of his tales were so fantastic, they must have been exaggerated. He soon announced that our destination was in sight. "We almost there. You gonna love Canada."

He brought the cab to a halt. "Nice place," he said as he looked at us maybe with real interest for the first time. Whilst Zimako lingered to settle the fare, I stepped out of the cab, inhaling the freshness in the air, pulling my jacket closer. We thanked the taxi driver for his kindness and waved him goodbye.

We were unsure what to do next, so for a moment we stood on the forecourt by our luggage, pondering our next move, when a man approached us.

"Mr and Mrs Adiora?" He raised his eyebrows enquiringly.

Zimako responded, "Yes, I'm Zimako, and this is my wife, Anuli." He stretched out his hand.

The man shook hands with Zimako. "I'm Suresh. Welcome to Canada!" He had the smile of a professional greeter and stood almost as tall as Zimako at five-ten. He helped us with our luggage and directed us towards the apartment block. I appreciatively took note of the luxurious foyer as he ushered us into the lift. "How was your flight?" he asked.

Zimako responded, "Smooth and pleasant, but yeah, we are glad to finally be here."

"So what was the weather in Africa like this morning?" he enquired.

"In Lagos I'm guessing hot and clammy, but this morning in London, it was grey and overcast," said Zimako.

Suresh looked confused. "London? I thought you were coming from Africa."

"Yes, we were," we chorused, and then Zimako continued. "We set off from the city of Lagos, the financial hub of the country called Nigeria, the giant of the continent of Africa. We stopped over in London for a few days before continuing out here. We've flown in from London today. It was a nine-hour flight."

The sarcasm was lost on him. We arrived at the fifth floor, where the short-let serviced apartment that was going to be our home for the next month was located. Suresh unlocked the doors, disabled the alarm, and set about settling us in. He showed us around the bijou apartment, giving us "helpful" instructions on how everything, even the most basic household appliances, worked. His manner was patronising, verging on condescending. Zimako and I raised our eyebrows, nudged one another, and smiled. When he was done, he welcomed us again and promised to call round the next day to see how we were doing.

As soon as he departed I exploded with laughter, wiping the tears that sprang to my eyes in my mirth. I couldn't help myself. "Zimako, this is unbelievable. Clearly he thinks we are natives from the jungle-country called Africa." Mimicking his still noticeable Indian accent, I acted out some of his instructions, shaking my head from side to side like he did as he spoke. "Let me show you how to turn on the gas cooker." Zimako laughed uncontrollably at my amateur dramatics.

We looked around, turned on the television, and relaxed. It was a plush and comfy one-bed apartment.

"Welcome to Canada."

I smiled to hear that from Zimako. "Yeah, welcome to Canada too, my darling. I hope Canada is good to us."

The next day, Suresh the agent rang the buzzer at ten a.m., and we let him in. "I hope you rested well?" he enquired with a degree of familiarity.

"Yes, we did. Thank you."

He made himself at home. He was very chatty and made it clear that we could rely on him to offer whatever assistance we required to settle into our new life. He told us a little bit about himself. Also an immigrant, he said he had been in Canada for more than ten years. He was originally from India, where he had trained as an accountant. He was now dealing in real estate and owned four apartments like the one we were renting, which he let out to holidaymakers and new immigrants while they found their feet.

He said the maximum letting period was six months, which offered his clients sufficient time to get to know the city and make alternative arrangements. He suggested that we sign a contract for three months, so that we did not have to worry about accommodation during our stressful settling-in phase, explaining that if we didn't sign such a contract, then he would have to make it available to the next person without giving us an option once our thirty-day tenancy expired. It struck me that as a shrewd businessman, he may have said this to secure a three-month lease from us. It appeared as though our newfound friend was not averse to using underhanded tricks to secure a quick buck. Surprised as we were by his about face from newfound friend to shrewd businessman, we remained noncommittal. As the nominated "accommodation guru," I assured him that we would definitely be leaving to a more permanent accommodation in thirty days, as we had indicated originally. We were paying $1,500/month and knew we had to find cheaper digs as soon as possible; the thought of paying this rate for the next three months was unthinkable. His response was one of indifference as he shrugged nonchalantly.

Suresh was quite curious about our lives back home in Nigeria and what our plans were now that we were here. I said our first priority was to find jobs as soon as possible. Wary as I was of Suresh, I must admit that he projected a helpful, friendly demeanour. He offered to help in whatever way he could. He mentioned that he knew a few people and would gladly help us pass on our résumés to them. "That is what we call networking in Canada."

We realised he was going to be a useful contact. We had wondered about calling home to let our parents know we had arrived safely and asked Suresh how to go about making long-distance phone calls. He smiled in what I was beginning to think of as his "putting his client at ease smile" and recounted how much he did not know when he arrived. He seemed impressed with our questions. "You guys are switched on. You ask a lot of questions and that can only stand you in good stead!" He went on to explain that we could get international calling phone cards, which was the cheapest way to call home. Suresh went on, "I am also thinking you need to get a mobile phone, yes?" He generously spent time with us talking about other essential services, including banking. He shared his local know-how with us. Suresh was a mine of information.

Zimako and I added his suggestions to our to-do list. He seemed very gratified to be of great value and reiterated his availability should we need to contact him with any queries.

When he left, Zimako turned to me. "What a guy. First he thinks nothing of trying to inveigle an extra sixty days' cash from us, hmmm? But then he seems willing to help in whatever way he can."

I shared my husband's amusement, commenting, "Clearly we are low-hanging fruit; we are going to need to stay on top of our game to avoid people taking advantage of us."

It was going to be an uphill task.

Zimako sensed I was getting melancholy and proceeded to provide comic relief in the form of further mimicry of Suresh. "That is what we call networking in Canada!"

I loved it when Zimako monkeyed around like this. I relaxed; everything was going to be okay. Not to let the grass grow under our feet, later that morning we called a taxi to take us to the Resource Centre for Newcomers to submit our Social Insurance Number (SIN) forms. As if for the first time, I took a good look at the address; it looked like it had too many numbers. "How come there are so many numbers, Zimako? This address is quite confusing."

Zimako took a look at the address in question and muttered, "Welcome to Canada." It had become our refrain for all things new and different. We both laughed as we tried to figure out the numbers on the address. It was all fascinating to me as we took baby steps towards our new life. At least with the taxi we would be sure to get ourselves to our destination without getting lost.

The cabbie was obviously an émigré, and in a strange way we were glad to see one of our own. I jumped in, savouring the warmth of the comfortable taxi. We greeted the cab and hoped for an engaging dialogue, but this was not to be; he must not have known we were new in town. He treated us with polite reserve compared with the cab driver from the airport. I was disappointed at his reticence, and almost felt snubbed by it.

The streets were populated with people of different shades of "white" ethnicities, but we struggled to spot anyone we could describe as "black." I noted that in contrast to the streets of London or Lagos, there were no real crowds. It lacked that hustle and bustle I associated with urban cities, so I voiced my observation. "Babes, have you noticed what I'm seeing? This place is not congested at all. Where are all the people?" Zimako suggested they might be sheltering indoors because of the weather.

That got the driver's attention and he chuckled. "Are you new to Canada? Where are you from?" His spoken English was almost without accent, but retained a soft lilt and a certain formality.

"Nigeria," we choroused.

That melted his reserve. "Nigeria is a big country. I am Somalian. So you are new in Edmonton?" he asked.

Zimako answered him, "Yes, we only arrived twenty-four hours ago."

This piqued his interest. "From Nigeria?"

We nodded; it would have been too complicated to explain.

"Ah, welcome to Canada. Are you immigrants or just visiting?"

We confirmed that we were landed immigrants.

"There are not many Africans here; few Somali, but many Indians, many Chinese; yeah, mostly Asians."

Zimako was surprised, and swung into patriotic mode. "What of Nigerians?"

The cabbie, who had by now told us his name was Yasir, said he couldn't be sure, but added, "I think there are some Nigerians.

Maybe you will meet them." He went on to tell us he came to Canada five years ago from Kenya and he liked it here. "But it is different from back home."

We wanted to know about specific differences, but he was vague. "Anyway, I have family here, so it is okay."

We soon arrived at our destination; the taxi had cost us another eye-popping wad of cash. The fare came to nearly $40 Canadian.

That made Zimako grumpy. "Honey, we have to do something about our transportation costs. Yesterday I thought the fare was high, but I kept quiet, reckoning that fares from the airport are usually high. But if we do not hunker down and decode the transportation system real quick, we will be putting our hats out to beg for our supper soon."

I understood his gripe. Thirty-eight dollars for taxi fare when converted to naira was enough to feed a family of five in Makoko for a week. Not that we could not afford it, but without knowing what the future held, we needed to be prudent with our funds.

* * * * *

The Centre for Newcomers was efficient and well organised. We completed the formalities in less than an hour; the official assured us our cards would arrive in the post within three weeks.

As we left, Zimako suggested we make the journey home by bus. I was quite amused. "Hmmm, Canada is a leveller. By the time she finishes with us, we will not recognise ourselves, O!" I continued, "This is only our first week; we have the rest of our lives ahead, but okay, anything you say."

He smiled, and lapsed into proverb-speak to buttress his point. "This is not the time for 'cut your coat according to your size.' Rather, we should be cutting our coat according to our cloth." Then in collo-quial Nigerian speak he added, "If Canada *wan* dey expensive, we go use the same hand follow *am; den we go see who go first tyre.*"

I smiled at him. "Are you saying that life as I know it is about to change?"

He nodded, confirming my interpretation of his wordy speech.

We headed to the bus stop. It was snowing again. It was not like the snow I'd seen in films, which had seemed round and fluffy. The snow was flaky and thin, and turned to liquid almost as soon as it hit the ground. I held my umbrella closer, thinking I might need to get a raincoat. We stood at the bus stop trying to figure out which bus we should be getting on. The bus route signs were not user-friendly to the uninitiated. Our only other experience of public transport was in London, and that was far easier to navigate.

We were determined. This was not rocket science. Soon we had it figured out and waited. Our bus arrived on time. Zimako offered the bus driver a twenty dollar bill in lieu of the fare. The driver looked at us strangely, but said nothing as he fished around for change. We were home in no time. I was happy to be back to the warmth of the apartment, but Zimako was not done. He wanted us to take a tour of our neighbourhood and get a sense of where we lived.

"Darling, I'm freezing. It's so cold outside!" I whinged. He agreed with me, but didn't back down. "Yes, babes, but we need to start getting out and about, if only to get used to the environment. If we keep sitting indoors, we will never integrate. So have a quick drink, ease yourself, and let's do it!"

Zimako had it all planned with a to-do list. He wanted to go downtown and possibly change some of our US dollars to Canadian. I did not hide my reluctance as I struggled not to sulk. I really wanted nothing more than to wrap up warm and savour my cup of hot cocoa.

As soon as we stepped out of the apartment on foot, I realised my shoes were inappropriate. Fine Italian leather loafers, comfortable as they were, were not designed for walking in the snow. I hoped we would not be out for too long. As we headed towards what passed for the bustle of the downtown, shop displays caught my attention. It was a transition period; some shops still had signs for Halloween while others had put up Christmas displays. It was hard to tell which was going up and which was coming down. We did not celebrate Halloween in Nigeria with these displays, and the ghoulish figures and pagan mannequins on display made me cringe.

"Omigod! Zimako, look at this!" I pointed to the vampires and ghosts adorning one of the windows. "How can they put these things on display openly? It's witchcraft."

Zimako did not seem horrified at all. In a blasé manner he glanced at the display and turned away. "Welcome to Canada, baby," he said, laughing. Then he continued. "Anuli, this is a different country. We have to keep reminding ourselves of that. Okay?" He tried to shield me from looking at other Halloween displays, distracting me by pointing out the tall buildings and the clean streets. I let myself be distracted and was soon engaged.

I noted that rather than names, the streets had numbers. "Have you noticed that the streets are numbered, not named?" It was all so different from what we were used to. "And the cabbie was correct; there are quite a number of Asians." And on and on we observed our locale, identifying names of businesses and stores we'd seen or read about.

* * * * *

It did not escape our attention that we were the only black people out walking downtown, and we were attracting curious stares.

Zimako voiced my thoughts. "This is deep inside Oyinbo territory, babes. We are the only black people here. See how they are staring at us."

I had observed the same thing and found it rather amusing that we were truly an object of interest; Zimako spotted one of the big oil conglomerates and pointed it out, stating, "We have to start looking for work soon."

I agreed. "I hope we find work quickly. I'm just wondering if they will hire black people, as we seem like more of a curiosity around here; they are all looking at us so strangely." It was a novelty, being perceived as a creature of interest.

The weather did not feel so bad once we had been out and about for a while.

We walked on, hoping to find a bureau de change. We came across one and went in to enquire about changing some money.

A Chinese woman looked at us from behind a glass screen. "How can I help you?" she asked rather abruptly.

"We'd like to change some money."

She appeared not to understand a word of what we had said and even seemed petrified by us. "What you want?" she demanded, one hand hidden from view.

My limited knowledge suggested she might be about to push a panic button to alert the police of some danger. I looked at Zimako to see if he also observed the same thing, but he was oblivious to her actions. "Money, money, currency, change currency," he said, reaching for his wallet.

I quickly grabbed his hand so he did not reach into his pocket. "Let's go, Zimako. I don't think she wants to do business with us."

As we turned to leave, she called out, "Come back. I change for you."

We were surprised, but settled back to continue the transaction.

We enquired about her best rate for changing $5000 US. She pointed to the display. "Best rate on display. You want change?"

"No thanks." We decided to shop around for the best exchange rate. I asked Zimako if he had noticed the panic button incident, but he had missed it completely. "I hope I'm not being paranoid."

He reassured me. "No, baby, I don't think so; I was busy concentrating on getting across to her because she did not seem to understand a word of what I was saying; maybe it's my accent."

The time was only three o'clock in the afternoon, but it was as if it was seven p.m. in Lagos. It was dark. I suggested to Zimako that we make our way back. My feet were aching. We decided to catch the bus again. We found the nearest bus stop and located our bus. It was a long wait. "Maybe the bus thing is not such a good idea; at this rate we will be late for appointments." No sooner were the words out of my mouth than did our bus arrive. This time we had exact change and paid our fare, jostling into the bus with fellow commuters.

Zimako was ahead of me. He turned to me with excitement in his voice and whispered, "Look, there's a black guy at the back row, and there are vacant seats beside him. Let's go and sit with him." We headed that way. He seemed glad to see us and smiled warmly. Zimako and I smiled back. You would have thought we were old friends.

"Hi," he said, making room. Zimako took the seat beside him, while I sat across from both of them. He introduced himself as Kojo. Zimako did the introductions. Kojo was originally from Ghana, a close neighbour of Nigeria on the west coast of Africa. He had been in Canada for seven years. Zimako told him we'd just arrived yesterday. He was excited to meet us and wanted to know more about our journey. Soon we were chatting like old friends, swapping comparisons between the weather at home and here. He gave us his contact details and Zimako gave him the number at the apartment. As it was only a short ride, we had to get off before long, but Zimako promised to call him on the weekend and arrange to meet up.

"Hmmm, Zimako. Wow! Your first Canadian friend! He seems like a nice guy. You two bonded instantly."

"Well... let's not be hasty, but yes, he seems a decent guy. But when I asked him what he did for a living, I was somewhat disappointed with his response."

"Disappointed? *Eh hen*, why? What does he do for a living?"

"He is an assistant manager at McDonald's."

"Really? Hmmm, that is indeed a bit of a let-down. He seems well-educated, but then, who knows?"

"Exactly. I'll keep an open mind; we'll see."

I changed the topic as we walked towards our apartment block. "So what are our plans for Christmas?"

"Christmas? Anuli, please don't go there. We just arrived, and we should be focussed on how we can get our act together."

I could sense that something was bothering Zimako and decided to leave him with his thoughts.

We spent the rest of the day leafing through the documents we had been given by the immigration people at the airport yesterday. The weather was still nippy, with temperatures of minus fifteen degrees Celsius. We spent the evening indoors, marshalling our game plan.

The next morning, bright-eyed and bushy-tailed, we readied ourselves to venture out again. Like clockwork, about ten o'clock, the buzzer sounded. Sure enough, it was Suresh at our doorstep. "Oh, wow, looks like Team Africa is ready to take on Canada?" he commented with a smile. He was right, we were.

Having been out on our own the previous day, it was no longer so intimidating. We decided the weather was not going to keep us from doing what needed to be done. Suresh chatted with us for a few minutes, making sure we were doing okay, and then he left. Our journey that morning saw us heading back to the downtown area again to sort out banking matters, acquire mobile phones, purchase a laptop, and take care of other miscellaneous to-dos. Afterwards we popped into the Alberta Human Resources Centre downtown. We had been advised to visit the nearest Immigration Settlement Services Centre on arrival. We needed all the assistance we could get to get on the career ladder.

* * * * *

Our visit to the Alberta Services office was a good start towards integrating into indigenous Canadian society. It was very illuminating. We were appointed a counsellor right away. He was friendly and helpful. He came to Canada over nine years ago himself, so he had first-hand experience of what we were going through. Talking to him was very informative. He did his best to put us at ease. We talked about jobs, accommodation, health care, everything. He was interested in us as people, and the icing on the cake was that he knew some Nigerians!

Zimako got excited. "Do you think it'll be okay for us to make contact with them?"

The counsellor pondered Zimako's question for a minute, then responded, "I don't think it'll be a problem, but I need to get their consent; once I confirm with them that it's okay, I will let you have the details."

Zimako and I smiled at each other; this was so different from home, where generally no one minded you passing on their contact details if they could be of help. We accepted it as the way things were done here.

Our counsellor continued, "You both have a very good command of English."

We decided to take this as a backhanded compliment rather than as an insult. We were fluent in the Queen's English, had studied in English back home, and were top-notch professionals.

Either not noticing or choosing to ignore our lukewarm reaction to his comment, he went on. "That would stand you in good stead with prospective employers." He went the extra mile of contacting his colleague in the job search branch about us and asked if he could send us over. We went to her office immediately, keen to get the ball rolling.

"Do you have a copy of your résumé?"

We handed her copies of our curriculum vitae. Each document was four pages long. Mine had a big heading, "Curriculum Vitae." We both had a lot of industry experience and on-the-job training in our fields and wanted to showcase that; we did not want to leave any stone unturned in our quests for our new jobs. She browsed through the résumés quickly, frowning. I couldn't interpret her body language. When she was done perusing the document, she sighed before speaking. "Well, both of you come across as articulate with an impressive command of the English language."

This was the second time today our so-called command of English had been commented on. Rather cynically, I wondered how badly my fellow immigrants communicated in English. Madam "Job Search" was not done. "You are well qualified. Indeed, I will say you are both overqualified."

I listened with shock and trepidation. This did not sound like high praise. If anything it sounded like criticism. I stilled my racing heart as I tried to make sense of what I was hearing.

As she droned on, I could now make out a disparaging undertone. "Prospective employers might have a hard time taking you on even if they want to. You look good on paper, but you lack local Canadian experience."

Zimako and I looked at each other, wondering where this was going.

We did not have to wait long before she dropped the

bombshell. "You have to be willing to accept lower positions to start with. My advice would be that you set your sights lower, get some relevant Canadian experience, and hope for a fast-track trajectory." She said there was nothing in her books suited to our résumés as they stood today, seeing as we were overqualified for the posts she had available.

Deflated and browbeaten to a pulp, we timidly asked some questions, but felt unable to confide our concerns to "Madam Job Search." We did not confide our fears. A picture was beginning to emerge. Zimako and I kept our true feelings bottled in. The consultation came to an end, and we thanked her for her advice and time.

She smiled that cold, reserved smile that signalled good riddance. When we got outside, Zimako looked at me to gauge my emotions and then said out loud, "Welcome to Canada!"

I grimaced at his attempt at humour. "Thanks."

The rest of the day went by in a haze as we discussed the chances of landing a decent job in our professions. It was going to be an uphill task.

The past few days had been full-on, but I felt I hadn't made any headway and wished I could run home to Daddy in Ibadan.

Zimako's voice brought me back to the present. "What are you thinking, babes?" he asked tenderly.

I felt like crying, but I knew I had to be strong. "Oh, nothing, nothing at all." I forced my lips into a smile. We had a lot lined up and a new life to build. We needed to be strong for each other. I had to be strong; tomorrow would be a better day.

* * * * *

Our first week had been an eye-opener. As I lay cuddled up to Zimako, I felt a deep contentment. We had each other, and everything would be just fine. "Mmmm, baby, that's what I call a wake-up call."

Zimako perked up. "What about an encore before we get started for the day?"

I giggled, then teasing, retorted, "Are you sure you can rise to the occasion?"

Not one to resist a dare, Zimako responded, "Hey, don't try me, baby. I am more than equal to the challenge."

As if by magic, I felt him stiffening again and moved my hips so that he fit in perfectly as I guided him into my honeypot. This time it was a masterstroke. Before I knew it, he was inside my creamy warmth and I heard him groan deeply. "OoOoo... "

We sat down to breakfast and watched the news. We went through the papers; Zimako concentrated on the Careers pages, whilst I combed the classifieds looking for rental property. We circled items of interest so we could discuss them later.

I looked up and noticed Zimako writing something on paper. "Find something interesting?" I asked Zimako.

He looked up. "Honey, I'm optimistic. There are a few interesting positions here, and I think finding a job might not be as impossible as that woman led us to believe."

I felt encouraged by his words. "You really think there's a chance we'll get something decent quickly? I am willing to do anything and start anywhere just to get the ball rolling."

I had decided that I would be realistic and take on any post I was offered and do whatever it took to get my foot in the door. That had always been my modus operandi. I confronted challenges head-on, chipping away at them bit by bit till I succeeded. Persistence was my secret weapon, perseverance was my motto. Canada was not going to wear me down. I would overcome.

"You may not have to step down judging by the vacancies I'm seeing. There are quite a few positions here that I believe you'll be perfect for."

"Okay, just circle them and then we'll send out some CVs later today." I had brought several copies of my CV with me from Nigeria and even had my references notarised for authenticity. I was leaving nothing to chance. We made our plans for the day. Top on our agenda would be to complete the banking procedures. We had been holding on to our US dollars and checking rates to see where we could get the best rates before changing our cash. We finally decided it would be better to do it piecemeal and leave what we did not need immediately in US dollars. Our appointment at the Immigration Services Centre was not till next week. We planned to explore some more of the town.

I decided to prepare cover letters to the prospective employers and tweak my CV a little bit to fit the specifications. I crossed my fingers, hoping for the best as I mailed them to the jobs Zimako had underlined for me. I was feeling cautiously optimistic.

CHAPTER TWELVE

Dear Diary,

Not that I'm a snob or anything, but we are having guests today. A guy we met on the bus who is an assistant manager at a fast food franchise. Is it indicative of the social circle we will be moving in? I have heard obodo oyibo is a leveller. I hope it doesn't level us, too. I'll keep an open mind.

We were expecting Kojo, our first friend in Canada, the black guy we met on the bus, and I was curious to know if he had mentioned his marital status during the several conversations he and Zimako had had. "Babes, I wonder if Kojo is married."

Zimako was sitting on the armchair, watching the news. It was a forty-two-inch, flat-screen, wall-mounted TV that nearly dwarfed the room or, if you took a positive view, was a nice centrepiece that made for excellent viewing. I watched him search his mind and try to remember if Kojo had said anything that hinted at whether he had a wife or family. "I am not sure at all that he mentioned it, but, so as not to be wrong-footed, let's prepare for the eventuality of him arriving with a wife and two children."

The menu was simple and hearty. I had made some meat pies and *chin-chin* (finger food) for nibbles as we chatted. Because Kojo was not Nigerian and I didn't really know how to cook Ghanaian, I'd decided to serve *jollof* rice and chicken, which is universal to most parts of the west coast of Africa. In the end I got carried away and also made some *moin-moin*, which is my signature dish. I hoped Kojo had a healthy appetite.

The kitchen was small, but had the essentials, and although

we were not expecting to make a party of it, both Zimako and I were happy to be having a guest. We loved entertaining our family and friends back home and hoped to make friends quickly in Canada. Kojo was the first one of such, and we were eagerly looking forward to building a relationship with him.

"Darling, what are you going to offer him to drink?" Zimako usually catered to the drinks while I looked after the food—that was not going to change.

He turned from the TV to regard me in surprise. "I thought there was some Coke in the fridge," he said, coming into the open-plan kitchen area to investigate. I stopped him. "Zimako, don't be so tight-fisted. You cannot expect our guest to make do with Coke. Even if that is his favourite drink, we ought to be able to offer him a choice of drinks. I was even thinking that some wine will not go amiss."

Zimako looked at me meaningfully. "*Obidiya*, I know you want to make a good impression, but I thought we were going to take it easy with the spending. Moreover, we do not have to impress him, eh. He does not know who we are or where we are from! Let's maintain a low profile, *biko*."

I could see Zimako's point, but still. "The fact that he doesn't know who we are does not change who we are. It is up to us to maintain the standard we are used to without being flamboyant or ostentatious. But I guess you are right. Let's keep it simple, cheap, and cheerful."

Hollow as the victory was, Zimako was happy to win this one, and with a quick kiss planted on my forehead, he headed back to his comfortable position on the armchair.

It had been overcast all day, and I was hoping that would not deter Kojo from visiting. I finished my preparations, tidied up my little kitchenette, and went to join Zimako in the living area. We sat in contemplative silence. I was preoccupied with what the future held.

The buzzer sounded, bringing me out of my reverie. Zimako stood up to get it and gave me a hug. He jokingly suggested I loosen up.

Zimako met Kojo at the door. Kojo had arrived plus-one. As

they both walked in, I did not know how to address his partner. I searched for clues initially to see if they were married, but she wore no ring on her finger, yet they were quite comfortable with each other, and their body language was very relaxed. Kojo introduced his pretty, mixed-race companion as Fifiana without qualifying the relationship or saying any more. I gave up on my amateur detective work and focussed on entertaining my guests. Kojo and Fifi, as she preferred to be called, were good company.

"How do you like Canada so far?" Kojo asked.

Zimako went on to tell about our experience with the Alberta Services. "It seems English is a key issue for many immigrants. I found it condescending every time they said 'Your English is quite good.'"

It was Fifi who responded. "You are right. There are lots of immigrants who have to take classes for English as a second language. It is somewhat unusual to meet an immigrant who speaks decent English. Being black and speaking good English is a double whammy that will elicit a reaction."

I looked at her with new respect. She had just explained something which I hadn't been able to put my finger on. I decided to pick her brain. "What are our prospects of getting a job? They keep suggesting we are overqualified. That bothers me."

Fifi and Kojo exchanged glances, and I thought I saw a certain expression cross her face. Kojo smiled. "Well," he started with his still-perceptible accent, "they will tell you that you are overqualified because of what they know and the openings they are willing to put you forward for. It took me a long time to figure it out. When I first came to Canada, I tried all I could to get a well-paying, middle-management, executive job. I had a first degree in sociology and a master's degree from Ghana, and no one would give me a job. Weeks turned to months, my savings were running low, and there were no jobs to be found. To make matters worse, the bills just kept coming. I was in a difficult situation. Even the low-paying jobs were elusive."

I was watching Kojo closely, and my heart sank into my stomach in fear as I put myself in his shoes. Zimako must have been feeling the same way because he asked, "So what did you do?"

Kojo looked at Zimako, and I saw in his eyes something that stopped me in my tracks. It was barely there, then disappeared. He sat forward in the couch and lowered his eyes. It appeared that even now, years later, the scars of his experience still had the power to cause pain. Fifi slipped her fingers through his. Kojo smiled, and continued. "Canada is tough, believe me. Do not think for one minute that there is a straightforward solution to settling down here, man. A lot of tears, blood, and sweat. It does not mean some people do not have it easy; some do, but I did not."

Kojo tried to laugh off his experience, but Zimako and I looked at each other. I felt overcome by his account and wanted to ask more questions. Zimako sat back and regarded Kojo.

We were silent for a bit. Then Fifi chipped in, "Go on, KJ, you might as well tell it all. It may put things in perspective for these newbies. You are among friends," she said, interpreting the look on our faces.

Kojo seemed unsure about our interest in his story, but with a nod from Zimako, he continued. "Long story short, I ran out of money and was on the verge of homelessness. I moved into the YMCA. At this time I could barely afford one square meal, and you know, looking for a job is not easy. Psychologically and emotionally, I felt pummelled. I felt very ashamed of myself, because I felt I had disappointed everyone who had invested in me. I felt I had let myself down. I contemplated going back home and abandoning the whole Canadian saga. Do you know it got to the stage where I entertained thoughts of suicide? But in my sane moments, I knew it was not an option. I did not stop looking for work, though."

"So how did you manage for food and basic essentials of life?" I asked.

Kojo smiled. "Like I said, it was tough, but I made a few friends at the Y. One of the guys I became good friends with there took me to his church. He helped me out a lot. After a meeting in church one day, one of their members mentioned that his grocery store chain was looking for night stockers."

Zimako wanted to know what a night stocker was.

So Kojo explained, "It is just a night job loading shelves. I did not mind. I had nothing left of my dignity. I was no longer in a position to pick and choose. I told him I was interested. He took my résumé, glanced at it, and told me to remove all my qualifications and keep only my GCE. All I had worked for was suddenly irrelevant. You know what that means?"

Zimako and I were stunned.

"Anyways, I agreed, watered down and restructured my résumé, and gave it to him the following Sunday. Within three weeks, I was hired. That was how I got a foothold in the job market and started digging myself out of the black hole. One thing led to another. I took on a few other roles and began to gain the much-coveted Canadian experience." Kojo laughed and took a swig of his Coca-Cola. "I consider myself lucky. Today, I am an assistant manager, and with some luck and hard work, I will make branch manager," Kojo concluded, nodding to himself. Zimako shook hands with him, pumping hands.

I smiled. "Congratulations, Kojo," I said.

Fifi smiled, too. She positioned herself close to him, holding his hand in solidarity, her thigh rubbing against him, her caramel skin complexion offsetting his ebony-dark skin. These two were in love. "I met KJ when he was just pulling out of the doldrums. It was after church, and I was leaving in a hurry. I did not see him, because I must have been distracted."

I pictured their meeting and smiled. "So you bumped up against him, eh?"

Fifi laughed. It was a beautiful sound, and Kojo wrapped his arm around her shoulder. "No," she said with more laughter, "I tripped up against the rug and the contents of my bag spilled out. He was there; before I knew it he was helping me. I was so embarrassed. We gathered my stuff and then he walked me to my car, and that was it."

Kojo laughed as he took up the story. "When I saw her trip, I was afraid she might have hurt herself, but only her dignity was bruised; she recovered quickly. The least I could do was help her gather her bits and bobs. Anyway, I introduced myself and she told me her name was Fifi. We became friends, and then one day,

I asked her to coffee after church and she said yes. She is without a shadow of a doubt the best thing that has happened to me in Canada." He planted a kiss on her cheek. Fifi blushed.

Zimako was clearly moved. "You are both very lucky."

I felt happy for both of them. "What a feel-good story, Kojo. I am so happy it's worked out for you."

Fifi was definitely a very bubbly person. She radiated sunshine. I stood up to go to the kitchen to get set for our guests, and she volunteered to help me out.

The rest of the evening passed with Zimako and I asking questions and sharing our expectations and anxieties with Kojo and Fifi. It was a good feeling to have company and to be able to share our concerns with people who understood where we were coming from. By the end of the evening, we were sure we had made firm friends.

* * * * *

The Alberta Services hall was located on the main floor of Canada Place in Edmonton. Zimako and I had left the apartment early to make our way to the venue, anxious to get started with our job search. We made sure to take copies of our résumé. We thought we might be the first to arrive, but when we got there about thirty minutes before the appointment, to our surprise, a number of other immigrants had already gathered; they were just as anxious as we were to get started with the opportunity to find a job.

The first thing I observed was the different modes of dress. Zimako and I were dressed business casual, with Zimako wearing one of his pure wool, navy blue blazers; I wore a simple dress that showed off my legs, which were my best asset. I was careful to wear low-heeled pumps for comfort. Others were dressed in a simple shirt and trousers, some wore hooded tee shirts, and I noticed an Indian with a head turban. I was not accustomed to the casualness. Secretly, Zimako had a tie in his pocket just in case it was required. It became clear that we would probably have to adjust our dress code to something much less formal.

I had observed that most signs everywhere were written in

English and French, and there was no exception here. I wondered if lots of Canadians outside Quebec spoke French. My anxiety levels were rising as I contemplated what the meetings would be like. It had been a long time since I was interviewed for a post or hunted for a job; having Zimako with me helped. He was just along to experience what it was like. We had agreed earlier that he would return back home once I was settled in, but he wanted to take the opportunity to get a feel for what to expect. We stood to one side, observing other immigrants who were casting surreptitious glances at one another, occasionally raising a hand in greeting or acknowledgement while passing time, waiting for the doors to open. It was clear that some attendees were old hands, judging from their familiarity with the environment. I thought about how I was already changing and trying to adapt.

At 8.30 a.m., the doors opened and I found to my surprise that not everyone was headed in the same direction as Zimako and I. We found the receptionist and asked directions for the Job Search Workshop. She pointed us in the right direction, and we headed there. It was a large room with a half-moon seating arrangement. Zimako and I chose our seats to the right side of the arrangement. I resolved to overcome my feeling of newness and participate actively in the workshop. Within a short time, the room began to fill up. There were people of different nationalities—Indians, Chinese, brown people, maybe from the Americas. Besides Zimako and me, there did not seem to be other black people. To our surprise, we observed that there were also white people in attendance. It was a full house. There must have been about twenty-three of us in all.

Soon enough, a woman who was clearly our instructor came in. She introduced herself as Chantelle. She had a very pleasant disposition and her smile caused her eyes to crinkle. Her peppered hair was more blonde than grey. I liked that she smiled often.

"Welcome to Canada," she started. I noticed a slight accent and trained my ear to decipher where she was originally from. Dressed in a peach-coloured wrap dress with a dark jacket and a scarf around her neck, I was almost certain she was from Europe. I had yet to see a Canadian woman dress with such simple sophistication. We all responded to her greeting. I began to feel very good about the meeting. I turned to Zimako; he was smiling, too. Chantelle did not waste any time. She introduced herself and gave us a brief intro. Originally from Ukraine, she immigrated to Canada as a young woman in the early '90s. She took English courses, worked admin jobs, and then decided to follow her passion to help new immigrants to Canada find the hopes and dreams that many long for. She went through routine housekeeping, telling us about fire exits, toileting facilities, smoking areas, and mutual respect for other participants.

"Feel free to ask me any questions during the sessions or catch me afterwards. I am available to talk." She wrote her numbers on the board, then continued. "Let's start off by introducing ourselves by name, where you come from, your occupation prior to your arrival in Canada, and for those who have lived in Canada but are between jobs, let us know what your previous occupation was."

It was going to be an exciting session; I could feel it in my bones. I settled down and began to listen while formulating my short intro. Zimako and I were being very attentive, and occasionally I glanced at him. He was like a sponge absorbing every detail. Soon everyone had been introduced. There were top professionals like us—accountants, bankers, administrators, engineers, pilots, sales managers, project managers, university lecturers—hoping the session would offer some help obtaining suitable jobs.

Chantelle continued the job of moderating. "In this room, there's an enormous amount of talent and skill. You were all probably successful professionals in your own right, and I hope that with help from this centre, you can put together your résumé, and begin your path to getting the job you've dreamt about in Canada. The first thing we will start with is networking right here. Before we take a short fifteen-minute break, I will give you all an opportunity to go around, meet and chat with at least two people, introduce yourself, tell them about yourself, and learn about them, too."

She stepped back and gestured, waving her hands. "Go on, I too will go around and meet some of you and introduce myself."

With that said, Chantelle opened up the room. Initially we were all shy; Zimako turned to me, and smiled. "Babes, what are your thoughts so far?"

I liked Chantelle, and the ambience in the room was positive and nonthreatening, but I did not yet understand how that would translate into jobs. "Well, cautious optimism. After all the stories from Kojo, I am really hoping that we do not get stung by the same bee. I am willing to do whatever is necessary."

Zimako regarded me with a smile. "Babes, chill out and go with the flow, and let's trust God for favour."

Behind us, one of the participants touched Zimako on the shoulder. "Hello, my name is Raj. I would like to meet you." As Raj introduced himself, I made eye contact, smiled, and then excused myself to go and make my own contacts.

Anna smiled at me. I walked towards her. She appeared confident, and smart. I stretched forth my hand. "Hi, my name is Anuli."

She took my hand in a soft but firm handshake. "I am Anna, not so new to Canada. I have been here four years."

I was perplexed. I had been under the assumption that most, if not all, of the attendees were newly-landed immigrants like Zimako and I. "Four years?"

"My first foray was as a caregiver nanny. I did that for a while and built up some savings. After spending two years in Canada, I decided to use the money I saved to go back to school to get a diploma in HR. You see, before I came to Canada, I was a human resources counsellor, but it is difficult to come to Canada from the Philippines as a professional, so I opted to come as a caregiver so it would be easy to get my work permit. Once I received my PR status, I could seek employment as a professional, and with my diploma, that is what I intend to do."

I was impressed with her single-minded determination and openness in confiding her story. "That is so brave. Well done, you!" I went on to tell her my own story. "I am very new to Canada. I've been here precisely one week." She was gobsmacked.

"Oh, wow! That is new. How do you like it so far?"

I smiled. "Well, it has been okay. We have heard stories about the horrors of job-hunting, and we want to be sure we get it right."

Anna smiled noncommittally, as though she knew more than she was letting on. She seemed very pleasant. "We are all in the same boat here. I think if we can get the guidance we need, we'll be well on the way to sorting ourselves out by the time we leave this place."

I took that as an indication to move on. "It's been nice meeting you." I moved on to meet some of the other attendees. The next person I talked to was Lu, an Asian man who appeared shy and reluctant to make eye contact. I stretched out my hand towards him. "Hi, my name is Anuli and I am new to Canada." Lu looked at me, and for a moment I thought he would not return the courtesy. Then he smiled and shook hands with me. It was a rather soft and limp handshake.

"My name is Lu. I am new too. I hope this session will help me." He spoke rather hesitantly.

"Me too," I said. "You said you were an accountant. What has your experience been like since you got here? Have you put out any résumés?" I was interested to know the experience of an allied professional.

"I have; not very successful yet, but I keep trying."

I could empathise. "I was a Financial Advisor. Is it very difficult?"

He smiled at me and I saw a genuine emotion from him at last. "I think it depends. Many people from Korea finding it difficult, because of English. So many give up after some time, but I want to try a little bit more."

I warmed to his openness. "Is your family here?" I asked him.

"Yes, I came with my wife and two children. My wife is not working now, but my children are both teenagers in high school. They are also trying to adjust."

I responded by telling him about Zimako. We rounded off, and I sought my next target. So far I was enjoying the conversations and getting a feel for my fellow immigrants.

"Hey." The voice was confident; I turned to see who it was.

"I'm Kayla." A casually dressed woman in a pair of ankle-grazing pants and a colourful jumper was carefully observing me.

"Hi," I responded. She seemed out of place in the manner of her dress. She did not strike me as a new immigrant.

"So tell me," she started, but before she went any further, Zimako was beside me asking that we leave immediately. I was surprised by his sudden appearance, and noticed the look of anger and frustration on the face of the woman who had started to address me. I could not understand his hurry.

"Zimako, I was actually starting a conversation with that white woman. I'm sure you were not trying to be rude. Are you okay?"

Zimako guided me to the coffee table without a word and then offered me some biscuits and coffee. I smiled inwardly. Knowing Zimako, he was trying to deflect from his uncharacteristic highhandedness and rudeness. I was going to take him up on it. I could not erase the look on the woman's face. We spent a few minutes savouring our refreshments, making no actual attempt to depart. We soon re-joined the group. Later Zimako whispered in my ear, "You'd better watch out. I don't like the look that woman is giving you." I did not need to ask which one. I nodded, respecting his observations.

Chantelle began the session on preparing a résumé. I was surprised to see that we would be taught something as basic as how to prepare a résumé. Inwardly I smiled, remembering where I was coming from and wondering what my friends at home would think if I told them that today I was taught how to write my résumé. I felt a little bit patronised and confused by this topic. Why on earth at this stage was it important to teach grown men and women who had built careers how to write résumés? As I mulled this over in my mind, Chantelle began to distribute a two-page document. I dragged myself back to the present to focus on what she had to say.

"Please fill in the gaps as we go along. You may find that a Canadian résumé is quite different from any a lot of you have prepared in the past. Even if you feel you know how to prepare a résumé, it will be wise to pay attention to these classes and interact as much as possible." As she continued to speak, I tried to catch Zimako's eye and cast a sneaky eye around the class at other participants. I wondered how they all felt about being taken back to the very basics. Not even when I graduated from university did I need anyone to teach me how to draft my curriculum vitae. Judging from the deep concentration of the other participants, no one else appeared put out or seemed to share my sentiments. They were all listening with rapt attention, taking notes. I refocussed my attention reluctantly.

The time passed quickly, and as the day wore on, the class became more interactive, with Chantelle engaging us with her stories, sharing anecdotes and successes of other participants who passed through the class.

I also began to identify the faces and match them to names. By the end of the day we had fleshed out draft résumés to be reviewed the next day. I did not find anything spectacular about it, but it was clear that Canadian employers favoured a one- or two-page résumé. I would have to whittle my four-and-a-half-page résumé down. This sentiment was echoed by a few others in the group. At the end of the day, the work was well worth it. Chantelle promised the next day would be even more interesting. "We will polish off your résumé and then work on your two-minute elevator speech. We will also look at what to expect in an interview, and how to negotiate your wages."

As we left for the day, Anna came up to me. "Hi, did you like the classes today?" she asked.

I responded in the affirmative by nodding, but was not sure if I should reveal more. I asked how she found the day; she was very positive and obviously excited. "I liked the content. A friend of mine found a job after this programme and I hope to find a job, too." She said that by the third day we would be encouraged to start calling employers and asking for jobs.

That was news to me. Zimako was beside me and was obviously eavesdropping. "Do you mean that on Wednesday, we will start calling real employers for jobs?"

Anna nodded. "Yes."

I could see why she was so excited. I became very excited, too. Obviously we had come to the right place. We all headed down, chatting about how the day had gone and whom we had met.

Come Wednesday, we had become more comfortable in our wider group. Zimako and I began to dress down a little bit more, although we still kept it business-like. He was wearing a polo neck top and a blazer with a pair of jeans, and I matched his look with a pair of jeans and a cashmere twinset. We did not sit together, as we were encouraged to change our seating positions and interact as much as possible and share our experiences. I was getting to know more of the women in the group. Besides Anna, I had made a real connection with Emily, a Canadian mom who was re-entering the job market after her maternity leave, which she always called "mat leave." Zimako had become friends with Raj and another man called Zack, who was originally from Eastern Europe.

Chantelle came in with a smile and bouncy gait. "Today, I have a surprise for you." Her broad smile indicated it was something pleasant. She continued, "Actually, I've got two surprises. The first is Sara. I will let her introduce herself and share her story."

Sara was all smiles as she walked in. She was a plain woman whose face lit up when she smiled, transforming her into a beauty. We all clapped as she stood before us. She started to share her story.

"My name is Sara. I arrived in Canada from Egypt five years ago." She paused to look around at us and at Chantelle, who nodded for her to go on. "When I arrived, I had a language barrier, because I had little English. It was a very different country for me. The only person I knew was a friend who lived here. It was difficult for me to communicate in the Canadian language.

"I came here as a nurse and was anxious to start working immediately. But with language barrier and no Canadian experience, it was a challenge." As she spoke, her voice quivered with emotion. I put myself in her shoes, and empathised with her predicament. "I discovered that I could not be employed as a nurse in Canada without passing some exams. It was very discouraging. I thought I did not know enough English to sit for an exam in Canada, so when I told my friend, she encouraged me to come here to enroll for the ESL classes to learn English as a second language. I came here and enrolled for the classes. It was a six-month course."

"You know, when you are an adult moving to a new country, there are many challenges. I was in a hurry to settle down, but I realised that I had to go step by step. During the ESL course, I did not want to keep depending on hand-outs, so I got a part-time job as a caregiver for an elderly lady. Though it did not pay much, one of the perks of the job was accommodation; it gave me a roof over my head and hot meals. After I completed my ESL classes, I continued my job as a caregiver, but deep down I still longed to practise as a nurse, because I heard they make a lot of money." This elicited a ripple of laughter from the group.

"So with my new confidence in English language, I began to explore avenues of getting back to nursing. My research revealed it was a tough process. I wanted to be an Intensive Care nurse, but I could not afford the registration fees, even the savings from my job. I was downcast. The exams would have been no problem, but the fees represented an insurmountable barrier. I tried to apply for some loans, but I did not qualify for any student loans. I was so devastated, I considered returning to Egypt. The facilitators here had been supportive during my courses and had become mentors to me. Before giving up, I decided to come by and chat to them about my challenge. They did their best to help signposting me to some agencies they thought would offer help. Sadly, I met brick walls everywhere. I nearly gave up." Sara swallowed and had a sip from her glass of water.

"My friends were my salvation. It is so easy to give up when nothing seems to be working out. I was losing the will to fight and sinking into depression. My friends were an amazing support network. I found I was not the only one struggling. Some friends too were holding temporary positions, hoping for some better job in future. I reminded myself to be thankful I had a job.

"Help came from the most unlikely source. My employer's son, grateful for the diligence with which I cared for his mother, offered to help me get back to nursing."

Sara paused and looked down as her eyes glistened with tears. Hers had clearly been an emotional journey, but she had emerged victorious. She continued. "I was embarrassed to disclose my financial constraints, but he was undeterred and asked me for my résumé and certificates. With his help, I got on a diploma programme, breezed through the exams, and got recertified." Finally Sara's face was brightening up.

"Once I was done, I was back here again, back to square one." She paused at this juncture, and we all laughed, relief flooding our faces. "Seeking assistance with résumé writing and guidance with job-hunting. I got a job before the end of the week. Now, just six months after, it seems like that was the easiest part, but not so. Every stage of the journey is a piece of the jigsaw. I am happy here and I am glad I stuck it out."

Sara was done with her story. It was depressing and scary, yet encouraging. We all applauded her. She wiped away a stray tear and smiled.

Chantelle came forward and gave Sara a warm hug. She was beaming with pride. "Sara and I will take a few questions and then we'll break for coffee, perhaps for fifteen minutes. When we come back, I have another ex-student who will share his story."

★ ★ ★ ★ ★

The day flew by really fast. Daniel's story was more straight-forward. He was an indigenous Canadian. He had quit his last job with one of the tech companies because he wanted to spend more time at home with his family. After three months as a house husband, he got itchy feet and decided to get back to work. Coming to the Services Centre helped him explore his options to achieve work-life balance. He had a passion for teaching. Using his background in the technology industry, he retrained as a teacher and now taught computer studies to high school students at a local school.

Although Daniel's story did not resonate so much with many immigrants, who did not understand how anyone could give up a well-paying job as an IT specialist to take on the less prestigious teaching role, we still applauded him for his courage.

The success stories had encouraged us. We were raring to go. It was clear the mood was upbeat, with members of the group now anxious to begin making those potentially life-changing calls to employers.

When we came back from coffee, Chantelle introduced a colleague. "Logan will work though your telephone role plays with you before you start making calls. You will select names from the phone directory of companies you would like to work in. You need to have a few details about the company, and armed with your elevator speech, which we will get you practice in, you can begin to make calls. I advise you to keep a record of the feedback you are getting, and we can evaluate it afterwards. Please ask questions if you need to. We are here to help."

There was already a palpable air of excitement in the room. Many of us had heard stories of long-term unemployment suffered by new immigrants. This all seemed too good to be true. We all went and grabbed the yellow pages and began researching names of companies.

CHAPTER THIRTEEN

> *Dear Diary,*
> *Canada's people welcome us with open arms, but the job industry is another story. So far no doors have opened to us. All the immigrants I have seen and chatted with have had to step sideways from the professional skills they arrived with. I have not encountered any open racism as such, but I constantly feel everyone is looking at me. Thank God Zimako is here with me, even though these days he is sometimes short-tempered. But this journey is not for one person alone. I hope God gives us favour somehow soon.*

Zimako and I had spotted a church downtown when we were out on Tuesday and decided we would join the congregation on Sunday. In Lagos we were members of a vibrant church and were hoping to become part of a fellowship of believers. Mentioning it to Logan on Friday after a jam-packed session, he enthusiastically found a list of places of worship for us. "Going to church is a great idea, I think," he said. "You know, it is part of the connecting process. You can make friends."

By now Zimako had had enough and was fed up. He responded rather shortly, taking what seemed to me to be a holier-than-thou stance. "We are looking for a place of worship. Appreciate, if you are able, Logan, that everything is not about connecting!" Zimako uttered the last word with dripping sarcasm.

Logan was embarrassed and immediately turned a deep hue of red as he tried to retract his comments. "I meant, with… with… the church community, and like-minded…"

I felt sorry for him. His discomfort was painful to watch, so I stepped in. "We understand, Logan. It's just, I guess we are a bit sensitive."

Logan nodded, mouthed a quick apology, and took off. I felt there was no need for Zimako to take his frustration out on Logan and I took him up on it. "Darling, why did you speak to Logan in that tone? That was not right—you embarrassed him."

Zimako showed no remorse and implied I was taking sides. "No, Anuli, I can understand this talk of connecting when we are job searching, but does it have to permeate and define everything? I know this is the Western world, so they do not see worshiping God as the intimate genuine relationship we do, but at least respect it."

Knowing Zimako, I sensed he was seething, with the combination of frustration and mounting his high horse, defending his God. I decided to drop the matter. My husband is fiercely competitive, and he had believed he or I would get a job offer during the five-day-long seminar. Clearly that had not materialised, and he felt impotent. Two members of our group had good news. Chantelle did warn us as a tip to allocate one month for every $10,000, so if we hoped for a sixty thousand dollar job, it would probably take six months or more to find a job.

Come Sunday, not even the heavy snow was going to keep us away. We were full of hope and excitement as we made our way to our first Sunday service in Canada. I had struggled to find a suitable outfit to wear. On one hand, I wanted to express myself by wearing something ethnic, but I did not want it to define and pigeonhole me.

Zimako eventually helped me decide. "Wear one of your Nigerian print skirt suits, darling. I like that orangey-brown one; you always look very nice in it, it flatters your curves, and you can always wear a jacket over it to keep warm and blend in." I decided to go for it.

Zimako himself was not so adventurous, and played safe. He stuck with his business casual. We headed for the bus stop. It was freezing and I dreaded the wait. In any event, it was not a long wait. In about ten minutes we were on the bus. I had the exact change to hand, and I inwardly congratulated myself on adapting so quickly.

I was getting a lot of surreptitious glances from other passengers, which I found rather unnerving. On the outside I looked different, calm and nonplussed, but inwardly I questioned my sartorial decision.

Service time was advertised as 1000 hours. We were somewhat late arriving at the Victory House on the Rock at 10.25 a.m. and ran as fast as we safely could into the building to avoid the relentless snow. In the reception area we shook off the snow and regained our composure. Zimako and I walked into the populated auditorium, with music blaring from the altar by the band, while enraptured worshippers had their arms raised in adoration. We entered cautiously, trying to find a seat in the crowded auditorium. That was when we saw a woman beckoning to us midway from the front. She had a warm, inviting smile. I couldn't resist and I pulled Zimako along with me. She was middle-aged and, although she could have been older, she appeared to be in her late fifties to early sixties. Her distinguishing features were a sharp, intelligent look and piercing blue eyes.

"Come in. Welcome," she said, making room for us beside her. We took our seats and settled in for the service. The woman stretched out her hand and introduced herself. "I'm Kathy." It was a firm, honest handshake. We responded, "Anuli, Zimako."

We immediately felt welcomed and settled into the service. Kathy was at the aisle, followed by myself, Zimako beside me, and a man with peppered grey hair beside Zimako. The church was cosy and the lights were at a dimly-lit, medium intensity. The music was Pentecostal, but it was not like the happy-clappy worship songs we sang back home. I am sure it was gutsy by Canadian standards, but was definitely subdued by even the most conservative standards in Lagos, Nigeria. The altar had a large projector screen which beamed the lyrics to the songs to the congregation. I had never seen a projector as the altar. There was no cross or anything to depict the altar, just the projector with the words of the songs. I had to overcome my discomfort and focus on the praise worship. Soon, Zimako and I were lifted in spirit, feeling at one with our new brethren. If the order of service was like back home, the next item on the agenda would be announcements, the welcoming of first-time visitors to the church, sermon, offering, and ministrations. Indeed it was. But that was where the similarity ended. The service was so subdued, and so contained, it could only be described as lukewarm. Nonetheless, I felt comfortable enough through the service. By the time the service was over, my stomach was growling for some lunch and I was anxious to leave, but Kathy wanted to "get to know us better."

"Hello, Anuli?" She said my name tentatively, as if trying out a tongue-twister, or perhaps not sure she had heard me correctly.

"Hi, Kathy," I replied, taking her proffered hand and shaking it in yet another firm handshake. She had to raise her face to regard Zimako, and once I released her hand, she passed it to Zimako.

"Zimako?"

He smiled at her and nodded with a broad smile.

"Are you new?" Kathy asked.

I guess my disastrous costume made it a reasonable question. "Yes, we arrived about a fortnight ago."

My answer must have pleased her, and she squealed excitedly. If I closed my eyes, I could imagine her rubbing her hands together in delight. By now the auditorium was emptying and some people were leaving while others were bustling around, as is usual after church gatherings and meetings. This routine clustering seemed as much a part of the Sunday service as the order of the service itself. Kathy drew closer to me and asked, "Where are you from?"

"Lagos, Nigeria," I replied.

"Nigeria? Where is that? Is it close to Congo?" This question revealed her abysmal knowledge of the geography of Africa.

But Zimako was feeling magnanimous and helpful. "No, Nigeria is not close to Congo. Congo is in central Africa, but Nigeria is farther up the continent to the West Coast."

I personally thought Zimako's explanation was lost on her. She was so excited, a minor pedantic detail like that was not going to dampen her enthusiasm. "How do you like it so far?"

Zimako confided that he hated the cold, and this tickled her.

Her laughter rang out deep and sincere. "You'll get used to it. Make sure you wrap up and keep warm indoors and out, because temperatures will continue to drop as the winter progresses."

This was not the reassurance Zimako was hoping for. He expressed his dismay—"Oh no!"—but cheerful Kathy was just getting into her stride and remained very good-natured as she patted my hand and smiled. "You'll be fine."

I then asked her, "Have you been to Africa?"

Her face lit up. "Yes! I have, but that was a very long time ago. In the early '60s, I visited Congo on a missionary trip and spent some time there. It was very beautiful with lush vegetation... " she let her voice trail away and I detected a look of nostalgia in her eyes.

"Did you like it there?"

Again I detected that faraway look in her eyes. "I did. We lived in a small town called Bandundu. I've always wished I could go back." She quickly recovered to focus her attention on us. "So where do you stay?"

We told her where we were staying downtown. She looked surprised. "I stay farther away, but I love to come here to this church because of the young people. It is such a warm and vibrant church."

By some unvoiced token, we all stood up at this juncture, ready to leave.

"How did you come here today?"

When we told her, she offered to drive us home. I was very grateful not to have to wait in the cold for a bus. We gladly tumbled after her to the exit; it was there that we spotted another black face. Zimako and I were excited, but unable to stop as Kathy was ahead, leading the way to her car. We made brief eye contact and waved.

During the drive back, we continued to chat as Kathy nosily milked us for information. She was very inquisitive and had so many questions to ask about us. She wanted to know what brought us here, why we decided to come to Canada, how long we had been married, if we had any kids, how we liked where we were staying, if the food was to our satisfaction, and on and on.

We did our best to answer her questions, although after a while it started feeling like an interrogation. Zimako was in the front seat with her and remained in good form and responded to her patiently, even asking some questions of his own. They were clearly enjoying a good rapport. I sat in the back seat and intermittently tuned their voices out, seizing the opportunity to savour the view on the way home without panicking about missing my stop. By the time we got back to our apartment, Kathy knew our professions, our past work history, our family background, our parents' careers, their middle names, and a bit about the political situation in Nigeria. She was also excited to share stories from her time in Congo and anecdotes of what life had been like back there in those days. Zimako listened with rapt attention respectfully, and let her tell us her story. We also gleaned that she had never married, and had not ever really been in love, but somehow, that suggestion hung in the air and unlike everything else she had openly shared, it appeared she was withholding some vital detail.

When we got to our block, I was not sure if she wanted to be invited up for coffee. I was rather apprehensive, as I had not yet become skilled in cooking Canadian cuisine and did not know if her palate would be ready for spicy Nigerian food. I had planned to make some fried rice with stewed beef and wilted spinach and was not at all sure if she would enjoy that. My worrying was in vain. She halted at the forecourt and kept her engine running, and before I could extend my invitation, she waved us off with a cheery, "I'll call you during the week, to see how you are settling down. Have a blessed week."

I was very relieved.

By Monday, Zimako and I had decided to divvy our time between job and house-hunting. Edmonton was not a crowded city in the manner we knew Lagos to be. In fact, we found the streets to be sparsely populated downtown compared with the streets of London and New York, with which we were more familiar. However, we had never lived outside Nigeria, and had only been tourists in those cities. We did not know what skills and guile, if any, were required to find an apartment. But I was clear about one thing: I would ensure we were careful with our resources to make them stretch. Zimako was going to be with me in Canada for a few months while we both job-hunted in the hopes of securing a job before he returned to Nigeria, so we estimated that we needed to be able to support ourselves for a period of up to six months even if jobs did not materialise—if the urban myth held true that each month of waiting to find suitable employment was worth $10,000, and we wanted jobs that paid at least $50,000.

We went out to continue our settling process. We still needed to convert our US dollars into Canadian. Zimako had been going on about us needing to get our driver's licences. After the ride in Kathy's car on Sunday, he did not want to wait any longer, now convinced that it was more cost-effective for us. So with our long list of to-dos, we braved the Edmonton winter to get the job done.

Our plan after the debacle with the Chinese woman at the bureau de change was to try the bank to get our funds converted and open an account at the same time. There were not many banks in Canada, unlike the situation back home where there were no less than twenty-five major banks. Canada had just five major banks. They were called chartered banks and seemed reputable. I decided we would go for the one that had an immigrant in the front office. The first three failed the test, so we kept looking. Zimako was not sure my method of elimination made any sense at all and had said as much, but I was adamant. I made a promise to him that if we did not find any that had even an Indian at the front office, and then we could go back to the first bank we visited.

He was clearly amused. "So you are no longer interested in going for the bank that offers you the best rate?"

I thought about it before responding. "Best rate is good, but have you seen the difference in rates? It is less than a cent in most cases, literally minuscule."

Zimako was less than impressed with my comeback and seemed keen to have the last word. I could see his brain punching out numbers as he did a quick calculation. "At that miniscule paltry one cent, we lose $50 if we change $5,000 USD, and that is before fees. Look, forget this idea of patronising the bank with an immigrant; after all, how do you benefit if they have an immigrant in their front office? Will they give you a job?"

That amused me and I chuckled girlishly. "Darling, just humour me then, and like I promised, if we do not find one with an *immi*, then any of them will do."

There were two more banks to go in the main downtown street. When we walked into the Canadian Royal Imperial Bank, there were two immigrants. I turned to Zimako with a smile. He was very business-like, keeping a straight face. He approached the counter, made enquiries about our business, and was satisfied to find the rate very competitive. We settled down to open an account, explaining that we were new to Canada. This information got the attention of the front desk agent, who informed us that they had a package for newcomers and wondered if we would be interested in discussing this with the manager responsible for newcomer relationships. I was very excited, and Zimako smiled. The welcome was such that, immigrants aside, I was beginning to like this bank. In short order, our funds were exchanged for Canadian dollars and we were ushered into the relationship manager's office. I was very interested to observe first-hand Canadian banking. So far I was already very impressed and intrigued to know what details our conversations with the newcomer relationship manager would entail. When we entered the office, again I was pleasantly surprised to see it was an immigrant. We settled in and felt immediately at ease. She welcomed us to Canada and showed a genuine interest in learning about our experience so far. She told us she was second-generation immigrant and her parents had come to Canada when she was only ten years old. They spoke very little English, but though it was difficult for them, they stuck it out, and raised her and her younger brother here.

"They must be very proud of you," I said.

She smiled in acknowledgement. We talked a little bit more. It was very comfortable, and once we got down to business, she talked us through what they offered to newcomers and asked us a number of questions to determine what our needs would be, short- and long-term. Many of the questions did not help because we were still too new to appreciate the financial implications or risks, as we were not yet earning a salary or paying into a pension or even paying a mortgage. Thankfully, she was very understanding and did not try to push us too much. We wisely put away a good chunk of our funds into a deposit account, leaving just a little in our new checking account for daily living. As we headed out, I couldn't resist giving Zimako the "I told you so" look.

Our next item was still apartment- and job-hunting. The manager at the bank had advised us to pick up as many free newsmagazines and classifieds as we could find at the bus stops, and suggested some residential areas that were good for a middle income professional family, which we believed we were. We picked as many of those as we could find and headed home. One good thing was that we found it also provided us information about cars, so we could begin to plan our budget for one.

Zimako and I spent the rest of the day at home making calls and pencilling down possible apartments to view. Our plans were so fluid, and by unspoken accord, we prioritised finding an apartment first, then completing our driver's license course, with the ever-present need to find a job lurking in the background.

CHAPTER FOURTEEN

Dear Diary,

I don't want to whine or complain or seem ungrateful—I am still grateful that we are Canadian residents—but some days I wake up with a panic attack and butterflies in my stomach and wonder what I am doing here, in this life with no guarantees. People here automatically "downgrade" us because we are immigrants and assume we know nothing! I know that every piece of information I'm given is valuable and each question helps them provide me with a more tailored solution, but often I find the level of questioning simplistic, stupid, and amateurish. Everything is getting to me now, the uncertainty of money and jobs especially. These were things I took for granted in Nigeria. Zimako and I will spend the rest of the week searching for a place to move to because we cannot afford to extend our lease at Suresh's. Sorting out affordable accommodation is now my priority.

It was snowing again. I was gradually getting to understand the weather. It could be snowing, but sunny and bright, or it could be snowing and cloudy, and even windy and wet or dry. I smiled at all the intricacies of the weather. I was getting accustomed to it, but also tiring of it. It snowed all the time.

I stirred and absently felt around me for Zimako, but he was nowhere to be seen. He had always been a light sleeper, and somehow never slept for more than six hours a night. Since we had arrived in Canada, it seemed he was sleeping even less.

I crawled out of bed to get started with my day. On our small dining table were the papers my dearest hubby and I had been using yesterday to mark out possible apartments and lists with telephone numbers of estate agents and property managers. It was halfway through the week, but we had only managed to find three apartments within budget that somehow fit our specifications. We wanted to arrange viewings without delay, but only one was available to show right away. Zimako decided to wait till we could see at least two on the same day. He did not like the idea of going out in the inclement weather just to see one apartment.

We had better luck with our plans to get a driver's licence, if you could call the outcome of that telephone conversation lucky, but every step was such an accomplishment. We had received our PR cards and SIN cards in the post and were required to bring them along with us, since an Alberta driver's license could only be issued to residents of Alberta. It was not a straightforward process, and the shocker was that we would have to surrender our Nigerian driver's licenses. But that was not all. The process involved undergoing a government-certified driver education course, signing a declaration to say we had more than two years' driving experience, and then taking the driver's license test. We had learnt there were two parts to the test. The first was written and, interestingly, called a knowledge test, which was based on questions taken from the Alberta Driver's Handbook, relating to safe driving practices, driving laws, and road signs. The second was an advanced road test.

Although he had initially tried to argue that he did not require a driver's test since he had been driving for several years, Zimako was keen to get going, once the agent explained that Nigeria did not have a reciprocal agreement with Canada, and therefore we had to undergo a written test and then an actual driving test. We had no choice; rules are rules. The conversation ended with us agreeing to come into an Alberta registry office and collect the texts to study before the test.

Zimako had barely come off the phone before he jumped on his soapbox. "Do you see how far Nigeria has deteriorated? Common driving licence—we do not have a reciprocal agreement with Canada." I found his comment ludicrous and laughed. He did not find it very funny.

"What is so amusing?"

"In Nigeria we were respectable people. Here I haven't quite worked out if it's our Nigerianness or our blackness or our foreignness that makes us objectionable, but certainly we are almost treated as though we were the scum of the earth. I was in no mood for that and querried him gently.

"You are acting surprised that Nigeria does not have a reciprocal agreement with Canada. Do we even have one with our colonial masters in the UK? Or even with next-door country, Ghana? Listen, Zimako, we both know Nigeria has been on the decline as far as governance and international relations, so quit being offended by either Canada or Nigeria and get on with overcoming these challenges, *biko*."

He murmured something and then I heard the door click as Zimako stepped out. I set about getting a breakfast of pancakes and crispy bacon ready.

Not long after, Zimako walked back in. He was wet from the snow and quickly removed his jacket, hanging it to air on the door, and left his shoes at the doorway. "It is freezing out there! Minus eighteen degrees Celsius!"

I smiled, knowing the weather was not going to deter him. He had picked up the day's papers and news magazines. He gave me a hug and planted a kiss on my forehead, then plunked down on the sofa and started flipping through the news channels while I finished making breakfast.

"Babes, did you decide which school we would go to for driving lessons?" I asked. He had been researching the Net for a good and cost-effective one.

"Sort of. I have shortlisted a couple; we could go with either of them. Oh, do you remember Raj from the job classes? He sent me mail and wants us to meet up for coffee. I wonder if he has found a job."

I remembered Raj. "Why not? That sounds good. I have not heard from any of the women I connected with. Have you fixed a date?"

"Not yet. I'll arrange to meet sometime next week. This week we don't need any distractions; we must concentrate on finding a place."

The rest of the morning was spent poring through the papers and making calls to arrange viewings. Sometime around midday, the phone in the apartment rang. Zimako and I looked enquiringly at each other, and I picked up the phone rather hesitantly.

"Hello…"

"Hi, it's Kathy!"

"Hey, Kathy, what a surprise. It's good to hear from you. How are you today?"

"I'm not too bad. And how are my new friends from Nigeria finding the weather today?"

"Freezing but, well, we are acclimatising. Zimako has already been out to fetch the papers this morning."

"Brave man. Sounds like he has taken the bull by the horn. So what are you planning on doing today?"

"We hope to get down to the Licence Centre to pick up the textbook for the written exams, and maybe go and view some apartments, see if we can find something we like."

"Have you made appointments to see some of them?"

"We have a shortlist. We haven't made contact with the agents yet, though, as we thought it best to wait till we had about three for sure. Then we could embark on a viewing spree."

"I would like to help any way I can. I could help you get to the license centre; it is on my way to Joan's, so I can drop you off there. What time were you thinking of leaving?"

"We should be getting ready to leave anytime now, but please, we would hate to take you out of your way or be an inconvenience," I said.

But Kathy was very gracious and magnanimous. "It's not a problem at all. I can be over there in about forty-five minutes. The road conditions are not very good, so if I am running behind, don't fret. I will be there shortly."

I was touched by her kindness and very grateful for her help. "Thanks, Kathy. You don't have to do this, and we really appreciate it."

"You are welcome."

As soon as I got off the phone with her, I quickly brought

Zimako up to speed, but he had deduced the conversation from my responses. "She is a very nice woman. I wonder why she is going out of her way to help us."

"Divine favour. God said he will make a way in the wilderness." We shared a secret smile.

By the time Kathy arrived, Zimako and I were waiting at the lobby. We ran out to meet her in the cold, wet weather. This time I took the front seat while Zimako went to the back. Kathy was smartly dressed in a sky-blue matching skirt suit. I quickly complimented her as I took my seat and fastened my seat belt.

She returned the compliment and then caught Zimako's eye in the rear-view mirror. "I hear you are taking Edmonton by storm."

Zimako gave a full-throated laugh. "What can we do? We have a deadline to move from our current place in about two weeks, so the priority is to find a place to move to. And guess who has to go out in the cold to get the dailies?"

As we headed to the licence centre, it quickly became obvious that Kathy was continuing her interrogation where she had left off on Sunday and had more questions for us.

"You know, both of you sound so well-educated, and have a strong command of the English language. Tell me, where did you learn to speak English so well?"

Zimako responded, "English is really like a first language to us. We speak English in school. In fact, speaking our vernacular is not allowed in most private and public schools in Nigeria, except maybe Islamic schools, where of course they speak Arabic."

"How so? How did it come about that you were schooled in English?"

"Nigeria was a British colony just like Canada. We gained independence from the British in 1960. What happened is that with so many tribes speaking different languages, English became a uniting language that everyone could use to communicate."

"So does every Nigerian speak as well as you both do?"

"Not really. Most people speak some sort of English. It varies from the Queen's English to a derivative patois better known as Pidgin English, which is more colloquial, with indigenous slang."

"I don't need to tell you that some new immigrants have to

take courses in English as a second language. Clearly you don't. In the job market, that is a plus, because most Canadian employers like to know that you can speak and write English fluently."

To curb my growing irritation with this line of conversation, I quipped, "Thanks for the compliment, Kathy."

She smiled. The sarcasm was lost on her, and obviously she was not done with the inquisition. "Your accent is a bit distinct. It's not Nigerian, is it? You do not really have an ethnic accent. Did you school abroad?"

I switched off and left her and Zimako to continue. I should have sat at the back and enjoyed the view. This is what the Nigerian proverb *awoof dey run belle"* meant—akin to the English saying "there is no free lunch." I had to grin and bear being patronised.

"Oh no, not at any stage; we both got all our education back home, but our parents invested in our education, so we did go to good schools."

"Are your parents rich?"

This roused me from my daydream, and Zimako and I laughed. Not at her, but at her assumption that a good education was the preserve of the wealthy. I had a burning desire to set her straight. "Actually, we come from modest, average-income, middle-class backgrounds."

"So what brings you to Canada?"

I was gobsmacked by her directness. It almost seemed confrontational, like we had no business being in Canada; but Zimako was ready with an answer. "We decided to come here because we wanted to be a part of something better. Sadly, things have been deteriorating back home, and deep down, I think it will only get worse before it gets better. So when we saw a chance to emigrate and widen our horizons, we decided it was an opportunity worth exploring."

"Yeah, I hear you, but why Canada?"

I was also interested to hear Zimako's answer, because this was something that I had wondered about too, but never bothered to question.

Zimako paused and took a breath before giving his carefully

considered, well-constructed response. "We looked at the options, Australia, UK, US, New Zealand, and Canada, and decided to settle for Canada because of all of them; it has the most straightforward process. But it is a long process. I guess immigration is always a long process. Australia and New Zealand were not places we strongly considered. The UK is a small island that is already bursting at the seams with immigrants. Canada and the US have active programmes for recruiting immigrants. The US has a lottery system in addition to its normal application channels. The US admits 50,000 people a year through their visa lottery, while Canada has only the application channel. Lottery is a chance thing, so we chose Canada."

"That is so enlightening. How are you finding the weather? Had you experienced snowfall before now?"

"Yes. Anuli and I have travelled extensively outside our country. We've been to parts of Europe and the US and have witnessed snow, although nothing like this much snow."

"You know, you are both very remarkable young people. Canada is very lucky you picked her. I hope you will like it here."

It seemed we had passed the test. I was very touched by her concluding comments. "Thanks, Kathy. There is something I have observed which is totally different from how we operate back home. It's this first name thing; when addressing someone older or in a position of power or seniority, we would be expected to call them Madam, or we say "*Oga*" instead of Sir, or even sir. If it is in a less formal set-up, still to show respect and emphasise hierarchy, as it were, a woman would have her first name prefixed with Aunty, or if she were not too much older you could call her Sister. For guys, it is Uncle or Brother. So if we were back home, I'd call you Aunty Kathy."

She found that rather amusing. "No, that is not necessary here. Everyone goes by their first name, so no Aunty Kathy. Just Kathy will do."

From the back seat Zimako asked, "Are we almost there?" We all laughed.

"Actually, yes, we are. I'll drop you guys off, and I hope you are able to view some of the apartments. In the future, if you need to, you can call me and I will be glad to help you get around."

We were humbled by her generous offer. "Thank you," we chorused. We soon arrived at our destination and bid goodbye to Kathy.

We had barely stepped onto the pavement when Zimako punched the air with alternate hands and bowed to the ground, then grinned as if he had just won a boxing match.

"What is it?" I asked.

"*Meeeen*, that woman can ask questions! *Kai*! If I did not know better I would say she is digging. Imagine asking "What brings you to Canada?" Does she own the place? It almost sounded like, "Go back to your country." I should have said poverty. I guess that would be more in line with what she expected to hear."

I was very much on the same page as he was. "For sure she is a nice woman, but she is a true nosey-parker, and to think she said call her when we need to get around. Ha, ha, she means call her to grill you further with questions; *a beg* if that is friendship, me I don't want." I grabbed a hold of Zimako's arm to steady myself as the walkway was slippery.

Zimako just looked at me, surprised by my uncharacteristic animosity. "I thought she'd offer to wait and take us apartment hunting," was his comment.

I laughed at the absurdity of his suggestion. "Is she our driver? Don't you think that she has done more than enough? She is a total stranger to us, yet for reasons only known to her, she was willing to help us, came and got us from home almost halfway across town, and brought us this far. Be grateful."

He was not done yet. "You mean, she came to get us to grill us for lunch and distract herself from her own issues. Imagine never having been properly in love at this age. Thank God I have you, *Obidiya*."

"I love you too, baby." As I cozied into his warmth, I almost slipped again just as we neared the entrance. "Zimako, I do not think my shoes are appropriate for this weather. I need to get a good pair of boots."

"Just so long as you remember that we do not have the luxury of earning an income, so when you go to shop, bear that in mind."

It grated on me that Zimako would bring that up when all I wanted was a pair of shoes to make sure I did not lose my footing and end up bedridden from breaking a limb or worse. I decided to ignore his comment at this time as we walked into the license centre.

* * * * *

"So how long have you been in Canada?" asked the property manager. Hers was the second viewing, and I kept quiet and let Zimako do all the talking.

"About a month?" he embellished.

She was sceptical. Are you working?"

"Not yet, but we are searching, and I'm optimistic something will work out in the not-distant future."

"May I ask what type of jobs you are looking for?"

"Well, I am a project engineer by trade, and Anuli is a finance guru with an accounting background."

Madam Property Manager was less than impressed, judging from her body language and facial expression, or rather the lack of it. "So where are you staying at the moment, and how are you paying your bills?"

"We are staying at a short let, but have indicated that we would be there for only thirty days, by which time we hope to have secured a more definitive tenancy. We are looking for a place where we can stay for at least six months, and extend it as necessary."

Her questions got more intrusive. "How are you paying your bills? Rent has to be paid in advance at the beginning of the month, and if it is not paid in a timely fashion as per contract, then you will be without a roof over your head."

"We are fully aware of the risks of not honouring any agreements we sign up for. We came here with our own finances. We have money. So don't worry about your bills being met."

She again eyed us rather cynically, playing with her hair. "Do you have any evidence of those funds?"

I had a copy of our bank deposit slip, so I fished it out of my wallet and handed it over to Zimako. Zimako took it, but instead of handing it over to the manager, he kept hold of it and said, "This is a copy of a deposit slip of money we have lodged in the bank. It is confidential, but I will show it to you because you have asked to see it." He placed it on the desk, sliding it towards her. The manager picked the slip up, perused it, and smiled. The content appeared reassuringly satisfactory.

"Fine, let's get down to business. I have three apartments to show you. A one-bed studio, a one-bed apartment, and a two-bed apartment. The rates are $600, $750, and $900 per month. I'll pick up the keys, and if you are ready we can view them straightaway."

She stood, and we followed behind.

All three apartments were in the same high rise-block. First she took us to the two-bed apartment on the fifteenth floor of the building. It was very spacious and bright. She did her best to talk it up and show us the features she thought would engage our interest, highlighting the double glazing, under-floor heating, and ensuite master bedroom. Then as a cautionary note she pointed out the necessary practicalities. "The rates do not include utilities. You will be responsible for your water, electricity, and telephone bills. The gas is included, though."

Our next stop was the studio. It was much smaller than where we were staying, but cosy nonetheless. Finally on the tenth floor we were shown the one-bed apartment. Each one seemed attractive in its own unique way. When we were done, she asked, "So which one will you be interested in?"

I liked all of them, but had not made up my mind. Zimako also seemed to be of two minds and indicated that we would need to confer privately and would be in touch. I was pleased with his response.

The property manager, who by now had invited us to call her Imogen, then handed over her card. "Give me a call within forty-eight hours. These rooms go so fast and I cannot keep them for longer." We expressed our appreciation and parted ways.

Once we were out of earshot, Zimako asked my opinion. "*Obidiya*, so what is your honest feeling?"

"Of her grilling or of the apartments?" Both of us did a little jig and started laughing.

"You know, you are right. What is with these Canadians and trying to know all one's personal business? Is it a cultural thing with them? Back home, people do not ask all these personal questions in this way. If anyone in Lagos dared interrogate me the way I have been grilled these last few days, I would have told them to go jump in *Bar Beach*."

"*Na real wa*, it has to be a cultural thing. First Kathy, and then the first place we went to view, and now here, too. But to your question, I really liked the two-bed. It is not too big; the size feels right. The smaller ones were a bit claustrophobic; certainly the studio apartment is a no-no. I know that at the moment we don't have that much to put in it, but long-term, I think it will be perfect for us."

Zimako did not agree with me. "I was thinking the one-bed was okay. It's just both of us; why do we need an extra room?"

I carefully laid out my case. Firstly, the difference in rental price was not much; secondly, we would not need to move for some time if we had a second room to expand into; and thirdly, what if we had guests from home? Zimako seemed to be coming around to my point of view, but flagged one last hurdle. "Our funds are limited. What if we do not get a job soon? Can we afford a two-bed apartment? Is it not better to start small and upgrade than to downsize because we are struggling?"

My answer to him was simple. "Have faith, my dear. God has not brought us here to disgrace us. I am sure we will get jobs soon enough, especially now that we have done the job search programme."

That clinched the deal. With that, Zimako smiled. I had convinced him. "Okay, let's go for the two-bed, but... pray hard so that a job will come quickly, O."

That settled, a big weight was lifted off our shoulders, and we were in good spirits. Not even the icy wet weather could get us down. It had stopped snowing, but remained overcast. We went to see the third property agent. The attitude of the manager was no different from the last. He was not just sceptical, but openly suspicious and unfriendly. I was almost tempted to remind him that we were in his office at his invitation to view the apartment, but since Zimako was interacting with him and appeared not to notice his rudeness, I kept my peace.

"So do you think we could view any of the apartments we are interested in today?" Zimako asked, after what was a stilted, unfriendly exchange which in my mind had undertones of racism.

"I'm afraid the apartment is currently occupied. I am sorry. I can only show it when the occupant is out." He was very unhelpful and unwilling to suggest convenient times. I nudged Zimako on the knee under the desk to let him know there was no point. He got the message.

"Thank you for your time. We will be leaving now, but do give us a call if you have one vacant to show." With that we stood up and took our leave.

When we got out, I turned to my husband, trying to read his facial expression, but he seemed unperturbed. I wanted to know if he had sensed the vibes I was picking up from the manager.

"You mean his negative attitude?"

"Of course I mean his racist, contrary, reluctant negativity, almost like he did not want us there darkening his doorstep and sullying his apartments."

"Calm down, dear. Oh, Anuli! You don't know what sort of day he has had. And moreover, he has the power. We need a place to rent; it's his prerogative to pick and chose who he welcomes as prospective tenants."

"And we have the money, so we can decide where we go with it," I retorted.

Our business of the day was done and we were finally headed back home. It had been a very productive day. I still wanted to buy a pair of shoes, so I suggested to Zimako that this would be a good time to run into the shops and find something more suited for the weather, since I was sliding and slipping on the frozen ice too much. He was agreeable.

It was quite dark at five p.m. when we got back. The phone was beeping with messages. One was from Suresh; he wanted us to return his call. The other call was from Okwe. He sounded confused, still unaccustomed to the time difference, and was just checking in on us. We unpacked our shopping and I set about getting dinner ready.

Zimako settled in to study the driver's test text, skimming through the book.

"So darling, should we let Suresh know we have found a place?" he called out.

"I don't think so; what is the urgency? After all, we still have nine days here; we can inform him a couple of days before our move."

We discussed the events of the day and how much of our to-do list we had managed to tick off. Zimako was putting a positive spin on things. "Once we move to our place, we can redouble our efforts in finding a job. Hopefully, God helping us, we will not have to go through all the challenges that people complain about." I said a silent amen to that.

Shortly after, the phone rang again. This time it was someone we had not met before; they were friends of my boss, Segun. "He gave us your number and asked us to check on you to see if you needed any help." We were pleasantly surprised to hear from them. They wanted to be sure we had arrived and were settling in nicely, and after some brief chit-chat they promised to call on the weekend so we could speak more.

* * * * *

The next day we started out early. We had discussed getting mobile phones, and Zimako wanted us to have that sorted out. We headed to the BelTel phone company booth. The two salespeople seemed too young to be working. Zimako must have felt the same way because I noticed his hesitation, but he approached nonetheless.

"We'd like to get a couple of cell phones."

The salesperson was quite knowledgeable and enthusiastic. A discussion immediately ensued about the type of phones we were looking for, the latest phone gadgets, and the available promotional plans. Zimako was given three options to choose from. The phones looked cheap but we were quite excited. We reviewed the features, and while Zimako settled for the BlackBerry, I opted for the Android. The phones were quite affordable, and from our research, BelTel had excellent coverage compared with some other providers. Our decision was easy. We confirmed that we could send texts to Nigeria at a price that would not bankrupt us. Once we decided, we made our choice known.

The sales-youth assured us we had come to the right decision, and that we only needed to complete some paperwork; then all would be done. Everything was going well. We gave our personal details, and PR Cards served as our piece of photo ID in lieu of our driver's licences. This was the first concern. The young man took the PR card, looked at it, and concluded that it was not an identification item he was familiar with. He looked at Zimako and me and asked us to wait while he spoke to his manager. Zimako was amused by the look on his face. We waited patiently in the mall and kept ourselves occupied window-shopping. In no time the young man was back, smiling.

"So was the ID well-received?" Zimako asked the slightly embarrassed young man.

He smiled and responded, "Absolutely, sir, this will do just fine." He continued to gather the necessary info, maintaining a friendly countenance. "Credit card, please?"

To which Zimako responded, "Would you accept a British credit card? We do not have Canadian credit cards yet."

The young man looked up from the screen and, blushing deep pink, he excused himself to clear it with his manager. By this time Zimako and I were smiling. It had all been going too smoothly to be true.

Shortly, the young sales-guy returned, struggling to make eye contact, mumbling an apology. "I am sorry; we cannot accept your British credit card. Unfortunately we require the card to set up a contract for you. Seeing as you have no credit history, we will need a full deposit to cover the cost of the phone." As he spoke, his eyes darted from the screen to his shoes and over our heads to an unidentifiable spot on my shoulder. The gist of what he said was that we would need to shell out about $1,500 for phones that just a few minutes ago required a hundred-dollar deposit. This was a rip-off, another way of hitting at poor immigrants.

Zimako was not going to take it lying down. "What! Are you

suggesting that we have to pay for the phones by cash?"

"I am sorry; this is out of my hands. There is little I can do. That is the policy. You are required to provide a credit card with a reasonable balance, and only a Canadian credit card will do."

Zimako knew we had hit a brick wall at this time so he changed tactics. "Is it possible to speak with your manager?"

The young man acquiesced to our request and left to find the manager. A confident, smartly dressed man who seemed more composed approached us. He introduced himself to us, and Zimako introduced us, accepting his offer of a handshake. Without much ado, Zimako brought him up to speed, explaining that we were new to Canada and had yet to build a credit history. We were very willing to provide our British credit cards if that was any help, but we found the request for a deposit for the full price of the phones steep.

Mr Manager tried to show some empathy and explained that the deposit would be returned at the end of the contract period, so it was not a payment for the phone. Still, Zimako was less than satisfied and asked that he reduce it by half, since with the way technology was evolving, the phones would be obsolete in another few months anyway, and that moreover, there were other providers we could take our business to, but we chose to give BelTel a try. The manager seemed to give our proposition due consideration and decided to go with Zimako's suggestion. He directed his staff to accept the deposit of $750 and do the required paperwork for his initials. He thanked us for our business and departed. From then on, everything moved swiftly. We were handed our phones and a welcome package.

As we walked away, Zimako high-fived me.

"Wow! Mr Negotiator, that was awesome!"

Zimako admitted that he did not think the manager would accept the offer, and that he was willing to call his bluff and walk away, even if it meant going to another BelTel booth.

"Welcome to Canada! Well, that was easy. If it was back home, the manager would *bone* for you. These *Oyinbo*, he did not even do proper *shakara*."

We laughed again, feeling happy. Mission accomplished!

CHAPTER FIFTEEN

Dear Diary,

Month four in Canada. Wow! The weather is gradually thawing out. We experienced minus thirty degrees, but what I noticed is that it's a different sort of cold and that when I'm properly dressed with internal thermal wear, lots of layers, and appropriate outerwear, then the cold is not so intimidating.

We have scaled many hurdles and now have driver's licences, having passed our driver's exams and practical driving test, which we took our time with because many of the road signs were new to us and we had never driven in snow conditions before; we are now in our own apartment which, though sparsely furnished, is ours, and definitely cheaper than staying at Suresh's place.

I like it here and finally feel like I'm settling in even though we still have not found jobs. I feel in subtle ways that people are more accepting of us, although there are days when I meet people who act as though I am an alien.

Everything seems to be falling into place. I hope we make it here. Zimako and I have been job-hunting in earnest without any breakthroughs, but we are determined, trying not to be discouraged, and we have each other. I am looking forward to when we both start working. Then we can finally start a family.

Zimako had gone out jogging. I preferred to use the gym downstairs, and even at that, I was not as consistent as he was. I went there perhaps two or three times a week. It was still quite cold and I marvelled at how he had adapted so easily. I dreaded the cold, but he was gutsier and embraced it.

We had turned our dining room into a study of sorts and did

most of our work there. For the time being we'd settled for a radio rather than splurge on a flat-screen TV, which would only distract us. Our laptop, various newspapers, notepads, info for immigrants, *Auto Trader* magazine, and classified ads covered the table. Outwardly we tried to remain upbeat, but for me a certain silent hysteria was setting in. We both agreed that the confirmation of acceptance to Canada would be getting jobs. Our finances were dwindling. We kept our living costs low, budgeting and living like church mice, but certain essentials were unavoidable.

I made myself a cup of cocoa, turned on the radio, tuned into Capital FM 96.3, and savoured my drink. Next I knew, it was almost 8.00 a.m. I made a dash for the bathroom to have a quick shower.

Today we would ramp up our job search.

We had been encouraged during the job search at Alberta Services to form the habit of getting up bright and early every morning, sitting at our desk as though we had a job even if we had yet to find one, with the aim of keeping that professional edge sharp.

Zimako and I took this advice to heart and made sure we did not have a lie-in on weekdays, no matter how much passion and cold made us want to cuddle up and get up to hanky-panky; there hadn't been much of that lately, now that I thought of it.

We took fifteen-minute breaks in between and a longer thirty-minute break at lunch, unlike the way we worked back home, working from morning straight till noon, taking an hour, and then straight till the day ended. I actually liked the shorter regular breaks in between, the Canadian way.

I logged into my email account to see if there was some good news. There was none. It was the same autoresponse mail confirmations that kept coming back, and new email alerts for jobs. I began to scan the messages, reviewing the job alerts. Each one would require an updated cover letter and tweaking my résumé to tailor it for each new job application; we made sure to limit ourselves to jobs we felt confident we could handle, posts that were related to responsibilities we had successfully managed in our previous life.

The good thing was that unlike back home, here most employers required email responses, not physical résumé drop-offs. I smiled to myself as I realised I had become accustomed to referring to it as a résumé, as the Canadians called it, rather than curriculum vitae or CV, as we did in Nigeria. The downside of these electronic applications was that there was no one-on-one contact or even someone to chat to get a feel for the job and company. This sometimes feet disheartening and impersonal.

I was confident that if I had an opportunity to meet face-to-face with an employer, I could sell my personality, enthusiasm, and skills. Yet here we were, more than three months into our job search, and nothing, zilch. We still kept in regular contact with our friends and alumni from our job search agency, Anna, Lu, Raj, Zack, and Chantal. Occasionally we met for coffee to reminisce and share our dreams about finding jobs, but so far, none of us was employed. Lu had taken a job with a relative who owned a Korean restaurant, but was still hoping to find a job better suited to his skills.

I still remember the conversation Zimako and I had, discussing the wisdom of Lu's sideways move in taking on the temporary role.

"I don't think he is doing the right thing, though," was Zimako's opinion following his discussion with Lu.

"Why not? I can see the sense in it and he has a family to feed," I countered.

"He does, and his reasons sounded well thought through, but I think it will only distract him, and once you get distracted from the path, it is a downward spiral from then on."

"Downward spiral or not, it is only the living that can stick to your so-called 'path.' Is it when he and his family die of hunger that you will see that there is a price too high to pay for snazzy industry experience? Is it not wise to make a temporary detour, fend off hunger, and keep applying for jobs? Job-hunting does not have to be a full-time occupation in itself. They could be running out of funds, you know. He has a wife and two kids in high school."

"*Obidiya*, calm down. It's not that I don't understand. My issue is that once you start sliding, the mind-set becomes one of survival, and then before you know it, anything goes."

* * * * *

"Sometimes, something is better than nothing to get your foot in the door, but I take your point." I did not really agree with Zimako, but was in no mood to continue the discussion.

I was still at the computer when Zimako came back from his morning run. He said regular exercise helped reduce some of the pent-up emotions and kept hysteria at bay. I let him kiss me on the cheek. "Hi, babes, already at work? Am I late?" he jested.

"Yes, O!" I responded.

"So, what's new?" he asked as he went through to the kitchen area and refilled his bottle of water. I liked the open plan design, and the kitchen was nicely kitted out with all mod cons sleekly hidden away.

"Nothing, absolutely nothing!"

"Don't fret, sweetheart. We just have to keep at it; something will turn up soon. I can feel it in my bones."

"When did your bones become an accurate predictor of the future? The only thing you can feel in your bones is the cold." We laughed.

I knew he did not want me to feel depressed, because I desperately wanted to get a job; he still had his job to go back to in Nigeria. My emotions yo-yoed from anxiously wanting to start work now to trepidation that I wouldn't be able to deliver; I had deep-seated insecurities about this new country. I had been a banker, and had worked all my life since graduation, picking and choosing the direction of my life. I understood the banking industry back home, knew the industry and trends. I had knowledge, deep understanding, and an innate awareness of the Nigerian banking industry, whilst here I was a novice, or in their words, I lacked industry nous, with no clear understanding of how the banks functioned. I really needed to get in there, get a job, and get it on. Many of the advertised jobs in banking were not in my area of expertise, commercial banking, and this insecurity plagued me.

I had once discussed it with Zimako, but he did not really get what I was trying to convey. He wanted me to get a job, and felt confident in my abilities, believing that I could apply myself and excel. "You have nothing to worry about, babes; commercial banking O, investment banking O, capital market O, you have done all these things back home. The point is getting in first, and starting. *No-how, no-how*, with a little training, you will show them know how."

I let it go, not wanting to be all doom and gloom. Sometimes I really felt all alone on this journey. I masked my feelings and buried my fears.

* * * * *

Our day progressed as usual, with Zimako and me trawling the Internet and searching for jobs. In the evening we would go for Bible study at church. Kathy was coming to get us. I was ready to break for the day when Zimako exclaimed like a miner who had struck gold, "Babes, maybe we need more help with this job-hunting, O."

"More help how? We have done all we were told and gone through the whole Alberta service job search thing. Do you think they will be happy to see us again? And even if they agree, what more can they offer?" I asked.

"Not them. I mean a private job search company. See, look at this," he said, pushing the laptop over to me.

It was an online advertisement by a company which offered new immigrants to Canada private coaching, résumé preparation, and, crucially, a network of contacts to help tap into the hidden job market. My joy at the service this company was offering was akin to sexual arousal.

"Hmmm, how did you find this?" I liked what I was reading, and was getting really and truly excited as I scrolled down.

"Do you like it?" he asked.

I took a moment to look at him before I answered. "Babes, I really need a job, and I'd do whatever it takes to get into the industry. Right now, even though I am searching for jobs, I feel somehow disconnected. The week at the job shop opened our eyes to the expectations of the Canadian market, but I have wondered if that is all there is to it. Reading this stuff, it is clear there is more depth, and maybe with some private coaching, we will be on our way to getting the kind of job we desire. I mean, we have not even received so much as a decent response three months into our job search. We are now beginning our fourth month in Canada, and we are no closer to getting a job than when we arrived."

"Why didn't you say something sooner, babes?"

"Well, I didn't know what to say. You know. I just had this feeling, but I did not know what it was—just that there was a missing link somehow."

"So do we agree that we should look into this? Say we decide to do it, and this is purely hypothetical, we would need more details about costs, outcomes, success rates, time scale, that sort of thing."

I was happy. I felt hopeful. Optimistic even, like a weight had been lifted off my shoulders; I suddenly felt lighter. This would afford me an opportunity for a one-on-one with an employment coach who could really talk to me about Canada. It was at least a month long, and promised that at the end of the intensive period, many new immigrants had landed $100,000 jobs!

I stood up and gave Zimako a kiss on the lips. "Genius, babes. You are simply the best!"

He smiled and responded in our usual way. "Better than not enough, babes. Better than not enough." I hadn't heard that for a long time.

* * * * *

I was in a very good mood as our "working" day drew to a close. Kathy had been a blessing to us in so many ways. She had transformed herself into a guardian, family, friend, and chauffeur all in one, and made it her job to help us with transportation and local advice. She refused payment, but we tricked her by putting gas in her car whenever we could. I remember that the first day I referred to it as fuel, she looked puzzled. "What is fuel?"

I was surprised; surely Kathy knew what fuel was. All cars ran on some sort of fuel, didn't they? It then dawned on me that her confusion could only be because I had used non-Canadian lingo.

I tried a descriptive way to get my idea across. "It's a petrol product that powers the car engine."

She laughed merrily. "Anuli, I learn something new from you and Zimako all the time. Of course I know what fuel is. We just call it gas in Canada." By this time both of us were laughing together. Kathy's inquisitiveness was more endearing than irritating the better I got to know her. I came to realise it was her way of getting to know us, and that the finesse of subtle curiosity did not come naturally to Canadians.

I must be careful about generalising, but another Canadian trait is fairness and respect. To break the monotony of our job searching, one day Kathy had offered to take me to the popular Canadian coffee franchise Tim Hortons. I had been excited to go and had a great time with her. At the end, the waiter asked if it would be separate or joint bills. Kathy said separate. The waiter then presented us with individual bills. I was very shocked! It had been at her invitation that we came out, and the practice back home was for the bill to be paid by whoever made the invitation. I was stunned for a moment, but regrouped quickly, and luckily I had enough cash in hand to pay my way. I decided to be more circumspect about accepting invitations from Canadians. I realise now she did not want me to feel like a charity case.

Now she would be coming over to take us to the Bible study. We now enjoyed attending church at the Victory House on the Rock, and had been connecting with other members through our small Alpha Bible study group. We had become friends with Afaafa, a mixed-race girl who had been adopted by a white couple. Her biological father was Kenyan, and she and I were about the same age. She thought befriending us would help explore her black roots. Our Bible study group was made up of twelve people, including Zimako, Kathy, and I. It was not always a full house. It was a cosy, quiet time to reflect, share our beliefs, and discuss any life issues or private stresses with a support group. They never failed to enquire as to how we were settling down, and offered suggestions and advice where they could.

I liked Afaafa and loved to chat with her after Bible study. She was very interesting and had a great sense of humour. She told me about her job with Alberta Child and Family Services. The stories she told were amazing, sometimes funny and sometimes sad. Even though I had no way of knowing the people involved, she took confidentiality seriously and kept the stories anonymous and light-hearted. I admired the work she did.

When Kathy arrived, Zimako and I were down in the lobby waiting for her. She took care with her appearance and as usual was well turned out and happy to see us. "Hello, Zimako and Anuli, how has your day been?"

"Hi, gorgeous." Zimako greeted her with a kiss to each cheek and made his way to the front seat. I took the back seat and greeted her, telling her we'd had a productive day. The journey to church with Kathy took about twenty minutes. With the bus it was about forty-five minutes, not counting waiting time. We chatted about the weather, a favourite topic, and how much we couldn't wait to see what spring was like. She brought us up to speed with news and current affairs, and soon we arrived and made our way to the basement of the church building where our Bible study group met. I liked that we were a bit early, giving us time to settle in and meditate while waiting. Kathy stood by the doorway, speaking softly with the assistant pastor who officiated the meeting. As I quietly meditated, I felt Zimako leave my side, but continued my meditation, silently praying to God for a decent job and for a successful Canadian odyssey. I took soft, deep breaths and focussed my mind on the Creator, asking for strength, wisdom, and open doors.

Soon the Bible study was underway; it was a simple message on the Good Samaritan. The session was interactive, and for me the message was spot on. We explored its biblical standpoint and its more practical application, highlighting learning points, the take-home message, and ways in which we would change our lives and impact our communities to make a difference. We explored how our actions protect the weak and save the environment. I was still intrigued by the differences in the mode of worship between our new church and the one we had left back at home. Zimako and I exchanged knowing glances, and I could tell he shared my thoughts. This was more like a tutorial than our usual Nigerian-style Bible study. Here, the assistant pastor monitored the interactions, moderating and moving the topic along, allotting time to each section. In Nigeria, though, the pastor led the Bible study and prayer, timing was flexible, allowing the Holy Spirit to lead the way, and one knew to allow for a late finish. Here, Bible study started at 6.00 p.m., and by 7.50 p.m. we said the closing prayers, and just before 8.00 p.m. we shared refreshments of crackers, cheese, and hot or cold drinks.

Zimako was talking with the assistant pastor when Afaafa sprung on me. "Anuli!" I immediately recognised her voice from behind.

"Afaa! I saw you sneak in. How was your day?"

"It was good. I'm glad I was able to get in before the study was over. It was awesome!"

We talked about the study, and then without warning, she dramatically changed the subject. "So where is that handsome-looking man of yours, Zimako? I would not let him out of my sight if I were you." We shared a laugh.

"He is about somewhere."

"Listen, you will not imagine my day today. I met the most gorgeous guy. And guess what?"

"What? Go on, tell me."

"He is black!"

"No waaaay, Afaa! Are you going on a date with him? Did he ask you out?"

"Not yet, but I'm working on it." Afaa liked all things black because she had missed out on so much of that aspect of her life growing up, and sometimes I thought she might be overcompensating. We were still chatting about the new man when Zimako joined us. We joined the rest of the group, and gradually everyone began to depart.

We walked to the car park with Kathy, but we did not take her hospitality for granted, so Zimako thanked her, and seeing as it was late, offered to take a bus home. Kathy accepted, hugged us, and left.

Zimako and I made our way to the bus stop holding hands.

"Did you enjoy the Bible study today?"

"I usually do. We both acknowledge it's different, sometimes lukewarm, a bit didactic rather than spirit-led, but still better than nothing. Having said that, I really liked today's session."

"I liked it too, babes, but what has the environment got to do with the Good Samaritan, *biko?*"

We laughed. Eco-issues and saving the environment were not things at the top of our priorities in Nigeria. It was a new angle for us. I was still in high spirits from our earlier conversation before we came to church, and there was a spring to my steps. Zimako must have been happy, too. He suggested we treat ourselves to some Chinese take-out. I concurred. We stopped to get some fried rice, noodles, black bean shrimp, and sweet and sour spare ribs and spring rolls with chilli oil, and then hopped on the bus home. I was relieved not to have to make dinner.

We arrived home and ran across the road to our apartment block. Thankfully it was not snowing, and the roads were not icy or wet. The lobby was well-lit, and the lifts clean and well maintained. I was carrying our takeaway, and Zimako had his arms across my shoulders. The lift stopped on the third floor, and then as the doors shut, Zimako took the opportunity to sneak a kiss, a proper kiss, full on the lips.

He fumbled for the keys, not wanting to let go of me, and stumbled into the welcoming warmth of our home.

He set the table in the living room area and got the drinks while I dished the meal, happy the day was over. Zimako sat beside me on the sofa and we enjoyed the view of the night sky from our vantage window. The room was dimly lit and very cosy. We were enjoying our meal, intermittently feeding each other tastes from our different dishes.

"Babes, are you happy?" he asked.

"Today? Yes, I am. Are you?" I asked in return.

"Sort of."

I paused, not knowing where this was going and wondering if Zimako was just being the joker I knew he could be sometimes. I did not have long to wait.

"You know, you could make me reeeaallly happy, if you paid

me for what you owe me… "

I smiled. There went my one-track-minded Zimako. "And what do I owe you for, exactly?" I asked, dropping a shrimp in his mouth before he could speak, causing him to pause and swallow.

"Now if I may remind you, before we went off to Bible study… " He was carefully dragging out his sentence, waiting for me to take the bait. I listened intently.

"Mmmm… " I responded, encouraging him to continue, getting in the mood. I took one shrimp and rolled it over my tongue, watching him from the corner of my eye to see if my seductive moves were having the desired effect on him.

"Now, Anuli, when someone does you a favour, wouldn't it be nice to reciprocate and show that someone some appreciation… especially if that someone who did that good thing was your husband?"

I was watched him closely, knowing I had him where I could do anything with him. I pretended it was too warm in the room by fanning my face, and undid some buttons from the top of my blouse, exposing my cleavage.

"You are treading on very dangerous ground, Anuli."

I smiled, noticing the deep guttural tone of his voice.

"Are you hungry, tiger?" I asked, playing games with him. I knew what was to come and I was ready. He did not say any more words. His lips on mine, kissing me deeply and moulding his body to mine was all I needed. I kissed him back, fulfilling a yearning need from deep inside of me. When he stopped, his eyes were deep pools in which I wanted to drown.

"I want you, babes… " He straddled me, framing my face in his hands, kissing me all over, and roughly, manfully tore off my blouse, buttons flying everywhere.

"Zimako!"

"Say my name again!" he demanded.

"Zimako, oh baby."

"Come, babes, yeah… " He stood up, and before I knew it, lifted me up and carried me to the bedroom. He laid me down, stripped naked, all attempts at romantic seduction gone, giving room only to pure animal desire. Zimako was a finely chiselled creature, beautiful in the nude. I was desperate with arousal, writhing in bed as he eyed me lustfully. He lay on top of me and began to caress and nibble and tease, bringing me to the edge. When he sensed I was moist and ready, he plunged deep. Our connection was deep and spiritual. He kept moving at a fevered pace, and just as I was about to climax, he slowed, making me ache and beg for more. His movements were deliberate. He swayed his hips and plunged deep, hitting that mythical erogenous spot, heightening my excitement. His pace increased; we were both losing control, the desire unquenchable, a liquid fire within, and with the next stroke we both screamed out in unison and erupted. He flopped on me, whispering, "Oh, mother of God!"

CHAPTER SIXTEEN

> *Dear Diary,*
> *For all the effort we've put into job-hunting, and now the funds we are pouring into career coaching, I'm just keeping my fingers crossed that it all pays off. I feel my life is on hold or perhaps regressing, from being a success in Nigeria to hanging in limbo here. I'm not getting any younger at thirty-one and my biological clock is ticking. I hope our luck turns soon.*

We walked into the plush offices of Platinum Careers Management Group (PCMG) on the twentieth floor of the TD Tower in downtown Edmonton. The ambience was luxurious, exuding professional success. As we walked in, to the right a marble reception decorated with fresh flowers and plaques of awards lined the walls, and a Barbie doll-like receptionist herself fielded calls with a smile. Zimako and I headed in her direction. Our appointment was for nine o'clock a.m.

"We are here to see Dave Monte. We have an appointment for nine o'clock."

She barely looked up to acknowledge us while rounding off her call. We waited. When she was done, she smiled directly at us, exposing a perfect set of teeth.

"Welcome, please have a seat. I will let him know you are here."

We went to the seats. It was a brief wait. Dave walked out to the foyer to greet us.

"Good morning," he said, extending his hand. "I'm Dave Monte."

Zimako took his hand and introduced himself. I did the same.

"Come with me."

We followed as he led us down a hallway of quietly buzzing phones and humidifiers, lined carpeting, and name tags affixed to each cubicle. We headed to the end of the corridor and there it was—Dave's office. He stood aside to let us enter and then shut the door behind us.

"Please take a seat."

We sat down, and Dave took his seat and invited us to make ourselves comfortable. He started by making casual conversation, asking about our experience in Canada, and how we liked it so far. Then he gradually began to move the conversation to find out more about our professional experiences. He said our education, industry experience, and spoken English was impressive. "I would like to work with you. I have no doubt you will be easy to place, and employers will be lining up in no time to make you offers."

I was excited to hear these words. He began to tell us about the work they did at PCMG. They worked with employers in Canada's top companies—the Pier Thomas Foundation, Toyota, Greyhound Canada, RIM, CTV Media, Telus, and Bombardier, as well as prospective employees in high tech, communications, finance, industry, government, publishing, and consulting. No matter where an individual was in their career cycle, Canadians and new immigrants alike, they were able to help them, but only if they were professionals. He shared their successful history with us, using unique tools, tapping into the hidden market-wide database to connect the two parts of the puzzle.

He was very charismatic and charming and kept it real. "Now you tell me, in your entire career, besides maybe when you took your first job, did you have to respond to job advertisements to get any other job? Or has it been by word of mouth, one friend recommending you or telling you about a position, and referring you?"

He was right, and it resonated with me. I looked to see how Zimako was reacting to this sales pitch. My husband's body language was difficult to interpret, but I could tell he was listening intently and watching Dave closely. Dave was in full flow as he spun his tale of new immigrants who had benefited immensely from their programme. He cautioned us about the limited spaces they had available, as their recruitment coaches were fully booked for much of the year, but he said they might be able to squeeze us in if we were willing to work with them. At this juncture, he produced two packages and handed them over to us. He opened one and began to go over the contents. The glossy, well-ordered package was filled with much of what he had just discussed with us. In addition, it had a price list.

When I saw the prices, my heart sank! Each individual would be required to pay $5,450 for a thirty-day coaching seminar, access to their database, referral, and sundry networking opportunities at a minimum. It went upwards from there. Maybe he saw the expression on my face, because he quickly threw in that if both of us decided to sign on, then we could get a deal, reducing the costs to $3,650 each. He assured us that for the value we would be getting and the jobs he was certain we would land within a few weeks, this was a sound investment. He paused to let his offer sink in. Then he continued. The offer was for a limited time, and the coaches had a limited window, as most employees would soon be closing their employment period, so he advised us to go home with the package and review it, and tomorrow at 11.00 a.m., we could return to discuss the other part of the programme.

With that, Dave thanked us and complimented Zimako and me on being a handsome couple whom he would be pleased to work with.

The meeting was over. He walked us back to the reception area and thanked us for coming, concluding by saying he looked forward to seeing us the next day.

As we got into the elevator, Zimako and I exchanged glances but did not speak, as there were others in the elevator. We were bursting to speak, but it could wait till we got outside. Zimako was in deep contemplation. As soon as we got out, I sought my husband's opinion on our encounter with Mr Monte. He smiled and commented that the man was a sleek salesman. That was not the response I expected, so I probed further, wanting a breakdown and more detail. I wanted to know if he thought the offer was genuine and held any promise. I was anxious to get started; I had bought into the spiel, and if we could meet the costs, I was keen to get started without delay. Zimako was ambivalent; he thought it was expensive and too good to be true.

Zimako took some convincing, but I persisted and suggested we weren't in a position to leave this promising stone unturned. I think he did not want to be blamed if we were still unemployed months down the line, so his resistance wavered.

We arrived at Dave's office as appointed the next day and waited at the lobby.

Within a few minutes Dave was striding towards us, hand outstretched first towards me. "Thank you for returning. I am glad you decided to proceed. Please come with me."

We followed him to his office, along the same long corridor that we'd traversed the day before. It was crunch time. I was having palpitations. Even as we left the apartment I was still unsure as to what Zimako had decided. He had been cagey. I guess in light of my desperate enthusiasm, he was hard put to express any negative vibes. What was there to be negative about— the cost? I considered this an investment.

I had made it clear that I was very interested in the employment coach.

We took our seat in Dave's plush office in the seats facing the windows. In the corner of his office, I spotted golf clubs and asked if he played. He told us he was an avid golfer but found that golf was not just a sport, but a tool for face time with important clients, a chance to meet clients and competitors; in short, for him golf and networking went hand in hand.

We settled down to business. Dave wanted to know if we had had time to review the package, and if there were any questions he could help us with to clarify the offer. I wanted him to explain what he meant by the hidden job market.

"That is a very good question. First, just to define it for you, the hidden job market is a term used to describe jobs that aren't posted online or advertised. Jobseekers can tap the hidden job market by using networking connections to help find unadvertised job openings. It is estimated that only 20 per cent of all jobs are ever advertised, meaning 80 per cent of jobs are filled by companies without ever advertising the position. Instead these positions are filled by referral, the 'who do you know?' method of recruitment. So while keeping an eye on newspaper advertisements and Internet job search sites is important, the percentages are in your favour to get one quicker if you investigate the hidden job market. Remember, as I said before, I am an avid golfer and play golf with many important people. I meet with many CEOs and we are on a first-name basis. I could easily introduce you guys to the right people in the business." He paused, smiled smugly, and then told us about a client who came to them, and after they coached him, within a month, he was in a position much better than his previous role, with benefits he'd previously only dreamed about.

"So what is the catch?" Zimako asked. I was surprised that he'd ask that. The question seemed to catch Dave off guard.

"I—I—I'm not sure. What do you mean?"

Zimako repeated the question. "Here you are, you know, finding jobs for people, and there are so many immigrants out there wanting to find jobs, so how come you are not serving them all?"

That wasn't what I thought he meant when he asked about a catch. Even Dave looked relieved and was smiling again. "Well, we are not here to serve every man and his dog. Those who need our services will find us, and our prices ensure that we remain exclusive enough to put in the legwork necessary for our premium clients. We know the value of what we offer, and we charge appropriately for it." He swung his chair to turn his back to us and face the same window we were overlooking, which showed the Edmonton skyline, high-rise by high-rise, and with a grandiose sweeping gesture he asked, "Do you think that if we were not successful we'd be here?" Then he turned back to us. "Any more questions?"

We had none. So after a loaded pause, he suggested we make a decision one way or the other; he offered us some privacy by leaving the office to give us time to consider.

Zimako and I were alone behind closed doors in Mr Monte's office.

"So, have you come to a decision? What do we do now?" I asked.

"Babes, I know you are very excited about this... " He took my hand in his, then continued. "Are you sure? My concern is the cost implication. $7,300 is a lot of money any way you slice it. Sure, if we get a job, though expensive, we can forget about it, but if we do not get one, is there a money-back guarantee? Will we have lost out completely? You know how much we have, and you know what is left. Babes, tell me, do you still want us to do this?"

Zimako was making a good point; I had not bothered to ask about refunds if the process did not come through with a job. Did they give us an actual job? Now that I thought about it, I could see Zimako really wanted this coaching too, but he feared for us. What would we do if we ended up penniless in Canada? I made up my mind. "Okay, let's tell him we will not do it for now — that we need more time to think."

Zimako could not believe it. "Babes, you know you want this. Are you seriously going to give it up because I am expressing doubts?"

"Partly. I don't want to force you if you are not convinced; secondly, there is no harm in giving it more thought. After all, it is not like he has given us any guarantees."

Zimako looked at me silently. I did not know where I found the strength to even back off, because that was not my style. I would have hounded Zimako till he saw my point of view if I wanted something done, and I really wanted this. I wanted to find a job as quickly as possible, but I needed guidance, and I had felt that this PCMG would clinch it for me.

"Okay, we'll wait. We'll give it more thought, and if they have an opening for us, then fine. If not, I am sure there are other companies offering similar services."

I nodded.

We waited.

Soon Dave knocked tentatively at the door and let himself in. He was smiling very broadly.

"So, have you come to a decision?"

It was now up to Zimako. "Yes, we have. We... Anuli and I

have a couple of questions: one, is there a refund under any circumstances, and secondly, can we pay in installments?"

Dave remained expressionless. "Actually, I will not say our coaching system is fail-safe, but the rate of success is very high, and from what I have seen of both of you, with your determination, transferable skills, and experience, you will not have any problems at all. So that addresses the subject of refunds. To instalment payments, I'm sorry, we do not do that. I have offered you a two-for-the-price-of-one deal, and I would say, take the offer." He clasped his hands, resting his elbows on the rosewood desk.

Zimako volleyed on. "Well, in that case, we will have to decline your offer at this time." He paused for effect. "While we appreciate the value your programme offers us, and understand that there are limited spaces, we really cannot sign on at this price. Our resources are limited, and you do not offer us any guarantees. We really would like to work with you, but we are genuinely constrained. Thanks, Dave." When Zimako finished speaking, he turned to look at me. He had kept his eyes directly on Dave and averted from me while he had been speaking. I smiled at him, and I saw him heave a big sigh of relief.

Dave, on the other hand, seemed surprised. "Oh! Well, I understand your situation. Look I know the price may seem a bit steep, so what if I say, keep thinking about it, and I will discuss your situation with management and see if there is some way we can help you. Will that sway your decision?"

"Perhaps."

With that, it seemed our business with Dave was done. We thanked him, and he politely walked us to the door, and we found our way to the reception area. On the way out I craned my neck to see if I could catch a glimpse of the coaches and any prospective clients who were signed up with them.

Within three days of our visit to Dave, we had a call back from him. Zimako took the call. He was very pleasant and excited when he finished his conversation. I surmised he was happy with the outcome. "Guess what, babes? They are willing to consider us for $5,000 if we make a full payment."

That was music to my ears. I had really wanted to get signed on, but had hidden my disappointment when Zimako had declined. Now he seemed just as excited.

"So how do we know that we are not getting a watered-down package with this discount?"

"No, babes, we are not. He assured me we would be given the full shebang. The way he explained it, he understood that the value of money varied between an immigrant and a Canadian— that he knows that $5,000 probably means $10,000 to us."

I battled to contain my excitement. "So now, what's next?"

Zimako laid out the next steps. We would go to the offices of the career managers and sign the contract the next day, and by Monday start the programme. My heart was filled with joy, I was singing inside. I was convinced I could land a job with their help.

Once the decision to become clients with PCMG was taken, there was a palpable lifting of a weight off our shoulders. Our sessions were billed to start on Monday the next week. For the first time since we came to Canada, there was no search for work or talk of résumés, vacancies, jobs, or classifieds.

Zimako and I agreed that the end would justify the means, with personal coaches, and as Dave said, with our determination and experience, we'd be working in no time. In fact he practically promised that we would be working in ninety days or less. With this in mind, we took our time and put our feet up. I believe this was the first time since we arrived in Canada that we let ourselves relax properly. Zimako offered to take me to dinner and then to see the movies. I accepted.

The next day, we went back to PCMG and settled the business with Dave. He was very pleased to see us and assured us we would not regret our decision. Zimako and I signed our individual contracts and Dave signed his portions. We acted as each other's witnesses, and once it was settled, we thanked Dave and left.

* * * * *

It was exciting to call our families back home and talk to them. We had been speaking regularly with them, and we could tell they were worried for us; four months into our stay, we had yet to report any interviews or jobs or proper positive news. Today was somehow different.

We called my parents. Prof answered. "Hello, Dad, it's Anuli."

Dad was so pleased to hear from me. "Anuli! What a surprise!" He was keen to know how we were doing, and to tell me how much he and Mummy missed us. I asked after their health, and the last time they saw Chiamaka, and it turned out Chiamaka had been in Ibadan the previous week and spent the day with them.

"Are you working yet, Anuli?"

Dad was perhaps the one person who understood how much rebuilding my career in Canada meant to me, and he always asked after my prospects, wondering if there was anything he could do to help. He offered advice and assured me that he and Mum were rooting for us. I quickly brought him up to speed on the career managers with whom we had signed up to help further our job search. Dad thought it was a great idea and felt confident that we would be working soon. Then Mum and I chatted and I updated her; she was very pleased that we would be getting a personal coach, and was equally confident that we would do well. She spoke with Zimako, and she ended their conversation with, "Take care of my baby." He laughed. "Mum, you know I do my best." It was very light-hearted.

After speaking to my parents, we called the in-laws, Zimako's folks, too. They were all concerned about us, especially knowing we had yet to find jobs. Everyone agreed that signing on with career managers was the right way forward at this stage, and were very happy that we remained focussed. Zimako spent time speaking with Ichie, who was sounding rather frail.

"Papa, are you well?" he queried. "You are sounding so tired."

I could tell Zimako was deeply concerned. His brows knit together. Then I heard him reassure his father. "Well, you should see a doctor, Papa, and take your medication. I don't want you falling ill."

They talked a little longer, and then Okpue-umu-agbala came on the line. She was her usual self, milking every ounce of emotion from the call; Zimako seemed immune to her antics; he wanted to know more about his father's health and state of mind. It seemed Okpue-umu-agbala was withholding information to stop her beloved son worrying when he was far away. "You should not worry too much about him; it will only make him feel worse. He worries for you, especially because he knows how tough it can be out there, but you say you are now working with some professionals who will help you get a job, so that is good. How is our wife?"

Zimako passed the phone to me. "Anuli, my wife, I hope you are well and keeping warm?" She called me her wife as a traditional address. I assured her we were well and that I was taking good care of her son, and no, we were still not ready to start a family, and yes, I recognised that time was ticking on.

She kept probing. "O, the job your main focus, eh? When will you give me grandchildren? Will Ichie die without holding his grandson?"

I felt bullied by her remarks. Zimako must have noticed my growing distress. He took the phone and scolded his mother. "Mama, you should not harass Anuli like that!" I liked it when he defended me; he admonished her sternly and then quickly rounded off the conversation by asking to speak to his father again. His voice turned tender as he urged Ichie to look after himself. He promised to call often.

Our next call was to Okwe. "Okwe, my man!" Zimako called out.

"Zimako, you are the man! Bros, I miss you men. How's tricks?"

Okwe brought him up to speed on all the current events he was missing in Naija-country from his unique Okwe funny-man perspective. Zimako was roaring with laughter. "Okwe, can you be serious for once?" he said, still trying to control his laughter when he joked about the president rather irreverently.

"Okay, I'll be serious. I was planning to call you. I have some news. Ireti is pregnant, and we are planning on getting married."

Zimako was blown away. "No way, man! You did it!"

"Yes, O. It was kind of a surprise. We had not planned it that way. Ireti was not sure how I'd take it, but you know how I feel about her."

"Yes, man, I know how you feel about her, but I don't know how Okpue-umu-agbala will feel about her. She'll want to know why you had to pick a girl from another tribe with all the beautiful Igbo women in Lagos," Zimako tried to jest.

Okwe admitted that he was dreading informing the parents, and as if that would change anything, he had started giving Ireti a crash course in Igbo and mentally preparing her for the tribunal that facing Okpue was sure to be. That further amused Zimako, who wanted to know when the "judge and jury," as Okpue was, had been arranged.

Okwe's intentions were surprisingly clear. He was planning on formally seeing Ireti's parents and getting their consent, and then when it was practically a fait accompli, heading to the village to face the "firing squad." He had made up his mind, and unless Ireti's parents refused to give her hand in marriage to him, everything else was mere formality.

"*Na wa, O,* I turn my back and like joke, my kid bro has become a man, O." They both shared a moment of laughter.

It was clear Zimako approved, and Okwe was relieved to have his big brother on his side. He changed the topic. "Well, don't say I don't bring you breaking news, but *e be like say Makua don fall for Tony, O!*"

"Okwe, *you sef! Haba!* How do you know that?" Zimako pretended he was not interested in the juicy details, but he was hoping Okwe would reveal more.

"*Make I leave am like that.* She can tell you whatever you need to know. By the way, how is the job search going? Have you guys found anything yet?"

At that point Zimako shared the gist of the career managers with Okwe, who thought it was an expensive but perhaps necessary step in the right direction. It was getting late, and with the eight-hour time difference the brothers started to bring their chinwag to a close. "Anyway, if you see Makua and Chinazo, you can let them know we'll call them over the weekend." Goodbyes were said, and Zimako hung up.

He quickly brought me up to speed on the conversation with Okwe even though I'd figured out most of what had been said. I was happy for Ireti, but I began to wonder at my own priorities, and how Zimako might feel.

"Zimako, how do you feel about the news? I mean, concerning us."

"Anuli, my baby, I knew you'd feel this way, but I trust you know that Okwe and I operate differently. We agreed we'd wait to have kids, so I don't want you to feel that not being pregnant is an issue. Different strokes for different folks."

I felt reassured that Zimako was not having second thoughts about our plans to defer childbearing. It was always this way when we called home. Okpue-umu-agbala had a way of teasing me unkindly or openly nagging me about having children, and now she was going to get her grandchildren, but not from us— from Okwe and Ireti. I knew that regardless of what Zimako said, now the clock was ticking and I was under pressure to get a move on. I was glad I could rely on him to some degree to deflect her jibes.

The rest of the evening passed in a relaxed mood for Zimako and I. We talked about Okwe's news, Okpue's reaction, our career coach, and what life had been like since we came to Canada.

Zimako mentioned that we needed to make more calls to Nigeria before going out to dinner, him to his office and me to my previous boss. With the Nigerian full-on work ethic, it was almost certain that they would still be at work.

CHAPTER SEVENTEEN

Dear Diary,

Thank God for Shelly. I'm in my third week, and I have her to thank for being out and about networking, meeting new people, gaining confidence, and gathering information on what would be "a good fit" for me. These are things I never considered before. When I left school, I took a job working with my finance company, and that was it. The choices available in Canada are myriad compared with the job market back home. This process with the career managers has changed my outlook. Shelly says that the process of meeting people and getting two names of referrals of "people who can help me" from them will land me the dream job. I believe her. It has helped me stop and think through my decisions, whereas before, the choice always seemed obvious because I did not explore the deeper layers. Seriously, thank God for Shelly!

On Monday morning, we arrived at the offices of PCMG, ready to embark on our coaching. Linda Wallace, the receptionist, looked pleased to see us today. She welcomed us with a warm smile and even called us by name. "Hello, Zimako, Anuli, you are expected. Your coaches are waiting for you. If you will wait a moment, I will call them to come and get you."

I smiled inwardly. Gone was the aloof treatment. She was being warm and friendly. In short order, a gentleman and lady came to meet us. "My name's Shelly and I will be your coach." The lady directed her introduction to me, and the gentleman introduced himself as Bruce.

I had not expected that Zimako and I would have different

coaches, but I guess it made sense. I followed Shelly down the corridor with Bruce and Zimako behind us. Once we got to Shelly's office, the first thing that hit me was the smell of incense, and then I noticed the small Buddha decorated with flowers and other auspicious signs of spiritualism. As a Christian, I was put off by these displays of idolatry, but I decided to concentrate on the reason I was here and hopefully an opportunity would open to introduce Shelly to Jesus.

"Please have a seat, Anuli. That's a nice name. Does it mean something special?"

"Thank you. Yes, it translates literally as joy."

She smiled. "I like that."

We settled in and began to chat. She tried to put me at ease and told me she was a third-generation immigrant. Her parents came to Canada with their parents when they were just in their very early teens. We talked about why Zimako and I immigrated to Canada and the experience so far. She seemed genuinely interested in finding out how we were coping and I quickly laid to rest my misgivings about her idol worship and focussed on the individual and the value she was bringing to my job-hunting. She asked incisive questions about my career before moving to Canada. She was easy to talk to, and soon I let my guard down with her. As she walked me through stories of successful candidates, I became more confident of my abilities to succeed with their help. She laid out the coaching plan and explained that I would have to be willing to do a lot of work to make it happen. She would do her best to provide me with the guidance and tools required to get the job I desired. With that said, Shelly handed me a folder divided into several sections. It was empty but for the first section. She began to explain what we would be doing during the next four days.

She encouraged me to get out and interact as much as I could while job-hunting. "Don't limit your interaction to those who will assist with your job-hunting. Develop other interests, make new friends, go out and reach out. With your being new to Canada, people want to hear your story. Tell them your story. Make it concise and interesting."

As she spoke, she created a picture of a new me, successful, with many friends, just like back home, settled in a happy life in Canada.

"We will begin work now."

She explained the software. It was very comprehensive, with detailed information of contact people in many industries. I would focus on the industry I wished to work in, read up on the industry, and begin to make contact with the industry people, reaching out to them.

We would work on my "new to Canada" story and my résumé, but I was not to give out any résumés at this point. She made it clear that I had to be committed to learning all I could when I approached these industry personnel, not just using the encounters as a means of getting a job. "Ask questions that will help you understand the industry, and seek information that will enable you to determine what you want to do. With that as your primary focus, the pressure to get a job will not overshadow your meetings, and people will genuinely want to assist you."

I asked her questions and she guided me along.

"The next thirty days will be very interesting. You are smart and determined, and I wager you will be working in no time."

Her compliments were good for my battered self-esteem; I felt affirmed, and smiled my thanks. I could see why it cost so much to have personal career managers. The few minutes I'd spent with her added more value than a full day at Alberta Services.

She continued to show me how to work the database, explaining that with each new week, a new password would be required to move to the next level of coaching. "I will be giving you assignments as we proceed. It will help you remain focussed and target different areas of the job hunt."

It was all so new to me. I had never been through a process like this before, and I wondered if this was something we could do in Nigeria as a line of business. No one was doing anything like this back home, and until Zimako stumbled on it, I had never heard of it. I wondered how Zimako was getting on with Bruce.

Shelly and I spent three hours together. It was the most productive three hours of work I had done since coming to

Canada. By the time the day was done, I was spent but exhilarated.

"Thank you so much, Shelly."

We shook hands. "You are a pleasure to work with. Keep the momentum going, and make sure you get all the work done before our next meeting."

I went out to the reception area, and there was Zimako with a man, whom I guessed might be a fellow client. As I came up, Zimako introduced me to him. "Anuli, Nick. Nick, this is my wife, Anuli." I shook hands with Nick and smiled.

"How do you like the course?"

"Well, it's my first day and Shelly is very experienced. I like the way she handled the sessions, and I'm now optimistic that I could find my dream job soon."

Nick smiled. "I have been on the programme for two weeks, so I have another two weeks to go. They do promise contacts and finding a job in a ninety-day window, so we'll see. Okay guys, take care and see you around." With that he left Zimako and me.

"Darling, so, how was it?" I asked Zimako, still buzzing from my experience.

"I liked it, and I like my coach, Bruce. He has a wealth of experience; he's coached lots of immigrants, so I am very comfortable with him."

We continued to share our experience as we left the office, both agreeing that so far it was certainly money well spent and we had no regrets. The conversation with Nick rankled. "What do you think Nick was implying? He did not sound as excited as we feel, or am I imagining things? Did you get that feeling?"

Zimako agreed with me. "We had only been conversing for about three minutes before you joined us. He was grumbling about not being given a list of contacts, and I was just telling him that I was new and not at that stage yet, but he seems pleasant enough, and I guess we will be running into him and other clients in due course."

I took time to digest the info, and then filed it away in the recesses of my mind. I was happy with my experience, and although Dave had hinted at a contact list, I thought Shelly had covered it with the database she had shown me.

* * * * *

I sat at the reception area of the Sterling Financial Management office, waiting to meet with the branch manager, Doug Sedge. He had been gracious enough to invite me to his office in Sherwood Park to answer my questions. I was fifteen minutes early, so I sat patiently, keeping myself occupied. I browsed through one of the magazines on the table to pass time and compose myself. When it was five minutes to the time, the receptionist called me and directed me to his office.

Doug looked fifty-something. He wore a simple blue shirt which looked comfortable, but had definitely seen better days and was in desperate need of ironing. He struck me as an eccentric, jolly good fellow. When I entered his office he stood up and shook hands, inviting me to have a seat. I mentally compared him to Segun, my old boss. Segun was always impeccably turned out and sharp looking. I had found that the dress code in Canada varied depending on the image the company was trying to portray, much unlike back home where the norm was projecting an image of wealth and success. I refocussed my mind, shaking off the comparisons. I was very glad for these interactions, and each one differed from the one before it. Shelly, my coach, referred to my visits as fieldwork, and rated me for the quality of each one, based on what I came away with.

"How are you doing, Anuli? Nice to meet you. I see you are new to Canada and would like to know more about the financial industry."

I agreed with him, and took time to explain my objectives. Though they included understanding the industry, they also extended to gaining his personal insights of the issues, learning from his experience, and understanding the value of social interaction in the workplace. These questions gave me an insight into Canadian experience without having worked in Canada.

"So tell me about yourself."

I was already well-accustomed to the format these interviews took, and was very happy to be on familiar ground. I told him about myself, starting with my personal info, then linking into my professional career. He asked about my family, and the ties I had back home. With nostalgia, I chatted about my family, careful not to get carried away, and we exchanged more peripheral conversation. He knew some people who had migrated to Canada from Pakistan, and told me stories about how they had adjusted. Soon he asked what he could do to help me, which was when I launched into my ten questions. I was always careful in selecting my questions. I wanted to learn as much as I possibly could, and I took notes while he spoke.

When we were done, Doug told me how impressed he was with my understanding of the Canadian market so far, and wished me the best. He mentioned that currently, they did not have any openings for an entry-level person, although they were looking for a management-level finance person, but if a position opened he'd be happy to put me forward for it, and he requested a copy of my résumé. Unfortunately, I had not brought one along! This was the first time someone I had interviewed had requested my résumé. For the most part, I went in and asked my questions with the genuine intention of learning about the industry, and being better informed. I was thankful for their taking time to impart knowledge and that was it. So I was pleasantly surprised and flattered. I admit it also left me somewhat flustered. I promised to email or fax a copy to him. It was at this point that I asked him to refer me to two more people that he thought might be of help to me as I journeyed through understanding and deciding what would be a good fit for me. He looked thoughtful for a minute, and then scribbled down two names. "You can tell them Doug sent you."

I thanked him for his time, stood and shook hands, and left his office. It had become my practice, as Shelly suggested, to send a thank-you note to each one of these gracious hosts, personalising it by highlighting something I had learned from meeting them or a new insight I had gained from the visit.

Flattered as I was by getting the first request to send in my résumé, I was rather saddened that all he considered me fit for was an entry-level position. Back at home, I was not just a management staff, but a well-recognised and indispensable member of my team with an excellent track record. To now be downgraded to an entry-level position, when there was a management position available for which I was not considered suitable, broke my heart. It was a mixed blessing. On one hand, I was elated that he would even entertain offering me a job, but on the other, I was only good enough for entry level. I tried to quell the tears of regret and sadness that engulfed me as I made my way to the bus stop.

We had still not bought a car, and Zimako had decided that could wait. The advantage was that we were getting to know more of Edmonton through the bus routes, and it was cheaper than having a car at this time.

There were additional fees at our condo, a name that Canadians had for high-rise apartment blocks. Rather than apartments, which generally referred to rentals, they called them condos, short for condominiums. Also, there would be the cost of gassing up the vehicle, and then parking fees, which required that you paid at least $2 in the parking metre for every thirty minutes. We calculated these costs for a month, and found that it was much better that we continue with the monthly bus tickets for transportation till at least one of us found a job.

I noticed the weather was turning warmer with the arrival of spring. Zimako was still out on his call to a few offices. Our different coaches followed much the same format, but there had been few differences. Zimako and I shared notes and incorporated the best of what we were learning from our coaches. We were out and about much more in the day, and spent less time at our computers. We added volunteering to our activities, and still found time to attend Bible study on weekdays and Sunday service. Our schedule had suddenly become hectic, but we loved it. There was less time to sit around the apartment moping and reminiscing about home and the life we had before. It was also good to have something interesting to share when we called home. There was always an interesting titbit or something new, and the excitement of our interaction with these people was evident from our tone.

Not all the field visits were upbeat, though. There were visits that left us depressed. Those were the visits that did not yield much information. The host would be somewhat belligerent and unwelcoming, or decide to doubt our qualification and experience and interrogate us on that, then flip to asking why we found it necessary to come to Canada if we were doing so well back home. I remember meeting a man with one of the chartered banks. The experience had left me bewildered. I had been very happy to clinch an appointment with someone who worked for one of the big banks, and was really excited to meet him. That morning, I had dressed carefully, ensuring I looked business-like, and I had all my documents in a soft leather binder. As usual I was on time, and I waited to greet my host, who did not see me till nearly half an hour after the appointed time. I found this unusual, as I made certain to call ahead. Nonetheless, I was very grateful that he was making time for me. When I was finally called in, he was very abrupt and harsh. "Make it quick. I am running late, and I have just a few minutes to spare."

I was not put off; rather, I mentally whittled my ten questions on the industry down to five. I started with a brief intro about myself, and wrapped it up with my professional experience. I could tell that he was doing an assessment of me, and reaching some not-too-pleasant conclusions.

"Are you looking for a job, because if you are… "

I quickly jumped in to deny that this meeting was about job-hunting, and tried to summarize to him the purpose of my visit, which I had earlier stated before being invited to this appointment.

When I was done, as though he hadn't listened to what I said, again he asked, "So are you an African refugee, because we have a programme for people that—" and again, I interrupted him and made it clear that I was not a refugee, but a skilled professional, new to Canada, and my purpose was to gain an understanding of the industry. It was becoming obvious that he had a preconceived opinion, and maybe I was not exactly what he had expected. I considered calling the meeting to a halt and politely thanking him, but decided to persevere.

"Okay, so be quick and let's get to your purpose."

I brought out my notepad, and began my interview. He barely listened and wanted to make it quick. "How heavily would you say the Bank of Canada weighs on banks in terms of regulation?" I asked.

He sat up in his chair, looking directly at me. He responded in a very professional manner, and provided me an insightful response with an assessment of the interest on mortgage rates. I was impressed with his response, which did not betray his earlier impatience, but kept strictly to my questions, deciding to ask only four of my five core questions. When I was done, I folded my notes.

"Is that all?"

"Well, I usually ask ten questions, but I recognise that you are very busy, so I do not wish to take up too much of your time." At this point I stood up. I could sense the regret in his demeanour. Then, as I turned my back, I heard him suggest, "You know, you could do really well if you moved to one of the smaller cities. It might provide you with an easier foot in the door. The bigger cities are very competitive, and although you do seem like a strong and smart individual, without requisite Canadian experience, no one will hire you."

It seemed he was determined to kick me when I was down. I must have misread him. My throat was choked up with tears, making speech difficult, but I steeled myself, turned to face him, and thanked him for his kind advice, which I promised to consider as I continued my search for what might be a good fit for me as I put my roots down in Canada.

What hurt most was his disdain and nonchalance. I expressed this to Shelly when we met the following day; she did her best to reassure me that it was unusual to meet a host so ungracious, as Canadians on the whole prided themselves on being polite.

I was glad that meeting with Doug had proved uneventful. In fact, it had been positive in many ways. During the forty-five-minute ride home, I let my mind wander as we travelled. The weather, which had been thawing out, had left the roads wet and unsightly with black snow and debris. I was looking forward to a quiet evening completing some assignments. When I got home, Zimako was still out and I let myself crash on the bed.

I spent the rest of the day catching up with housework and relaxing. I was meeting up with Afaafa later in the day to catch a film, and was looking forward to that when the phone rang.

"Hi, this is Anuli. Who am I speaking with?"

"Hi, Anuli. It's Anne! How are you?" Anne was from the Alberta Services. We still kept in touch, and met up occasionally. I was pleasantly surprised to hear from her.

"How are you, Anne? Good to hear from you. What's new?"

"Anuli, I have news for you. I got a job!" I could feel her excitement. This was the news we all most wanted to share, the moment we had all been hoping to happen to us. I was happy for her.

"Oh, Anne, that's wonderful! Tell me about it."

Anne had just got a job in a PR company working with the admin department, which also did the HR work. She was elated, and started to tell me how she got the job. It was through a friend of someone she marginally knew who had mentioned she was looking for such a role.

"You mean the six degrees of separation?" I asked, laughing. We shared the joke, which was something I had learned during our job search at the Alberta Services.

"I am so happy, Anuli; I couldn't believe it when they actually called me back to say I got the job. What about you? Have you found something yet?"

I had to inform her that I was still searching, although I was feeling hopeful with the way things were progressing with the job-hunt process as compared to before. Anne, in turn, was encouraging and hopeful for me. "You know, Anuli, we have affiliations with some companies. Do you want me to put in a word for you? I know it's probably not what you are looking for, but it will be a start."

It was very thoughtful of Anne to think of me in that way, and I was quite grateful, but I was on a path to get the job of my dreams, and I did not want to be side-tracked. On second thought, I'd learned that a bird in hand was worth two in the bush, so I responded cautiously to her offer. "Anne, you are such a good friend, thank you. You are right—maybe the jobs they offer won't be what I am looking for, but let me think about it, and I will let you know." We rounded off our conversation, I wished her luck with the new job, and hung up.

I considered my conversation with Anne, and reviewed our progress as compared with the acquaintances we had made. Zack, who was a construction engineer from Poland, one of Zimako's friends from the Alberta Service, was now employed as a shipper receiver with a multinational logistics company. Lu, originally an accountant from Korea, was still working at his relative's restaurant. Raj, a pilot, was still looking, as were Zimako and I. I tried not to let this state of affairs get me down. I was finally on my path to success, and I had to remember that.

Zimako came home much later than I expected. "Baby, what happened? I thought you'd be back earlier."

He looked very tired. He pulled off his jacket and slumped on the sofa. "I got lost!"

I had been lost a few times since I started venturing out on my own, but I couldn't imagine him getting lost. Zimako, unlike most men, had a good sense of direction. I burst out laughing, not able to hold it back.

He gave me the look of death. "You find that funny, eh? It's funny to you?"

I couldn't control the giggles; then he jumped up and grabbed my neck, pretending to choke me. Soon we were both laughing. When we finally pulled ourselves together, I wanted to know details of where and how he got lost. "How could you have gotten lost?"

Rather shamefaced, he explained, "Well, I was trying to be smart, and wanted to take a shorter route, so I changed buses and hopped off at a stop that I thought would help me make a shorter connection. I soon realised it was the wrong stop, and had to wait forever for the next bus, and then when it finally came I had to reconnect to my original route and start all over again. It was just one of those days. The first interview was okay. I dropped off my résumé with them, but the second was just one of those that made one despair."

I liked to hear about his interviews. "I've had a few of those! What happened?"

He said the interview started with him being sent to a junior staff member in the company, who acted as though Zimako was speaking a foreign language. Every sentence was met with, "Huh? Could you repeat that?"

I was laughing again. "I'm serious, Anuli, it was diabolical. He told me I had a strong accent, and was difficult to understand, so could I speak slowly?"

I laughed even more. "Zimako, tell me you are making this up. You don't sound Canadian, of course not; but strong accent? Please. Granted, you sound different, but everyone has an accent, and yet we all manage to communicate effectively."

Zimako continued, "It was downhill from there. I tried to modulate my speech, but even that didn't work. I wanted to be rescued from there."

I held back my laughter, knowing how bad Zimako must have felt. "So what do you do? Are you going to register for Canadian elocution classes?"

Zimako looked at me from the corners of his eyes. "Oh, be serious, Anuli. It was just unbelievable. Anyway, in the nick of time, the chief engineer, the guy I was originally billed to see, came and ended my ordeal. He rescued me and had no problem understanding my accent."

I smiled. He asked about my day, and I told him about my meeting with Doug and how he ended by asking for my résumé for future job openings.

He was happy for me, seeing it as a step in the right direction. I explained my misgivings about the disparity between my self-assessment and Doug's assessment of me. "He only felt I would be suited to an entry-level position, and there were none of those available. The management position was open, but he did not think I could handle that."

Zimako pulled me closer to him. "Come, baby, sit down. We've both had a tough day."

I knew he was trying to make it better; I reluctantly sat down beside him. We were now at eye level; he put his forehead to mine and looked into my eyes, then closed his eyes. I mirrored his actions. After a moment he squeezed my hand. I held back my tears. We sat like that for a moment, then he let go of my hand. "Are you feeling better?"

I was, so I nodded.

"Good, because I am very hungry."

I was now smiling. Everything was back to normal. "Do you remember that I'm meeting up with the girls later? We are going to catch a movie."

Afaafa, Fifi, and I were becoming fast friends. I enjoyed being with them. We had a lot in common.

"Do you mean you are going out for some gossip?"

"Well, we certainly will not be discussing global warming and problems at Parliament if that is what you mean." I got supper ready, and went to get ready for my evening out with the girls.

* * * * *

It was late when I got back, and Zimako was getting ready for bed. I was relaxed but tired, and was also looking forward to a good night's sleep. Once we were settled in bed, Zimako turned out the lights and spooned into me. "Babes, are you awake? Do you want to talk?"

I could tell he was worried about the effect my meeting with Doug would have on my fragile self-esteem. I was reluctant to talk about it, but Zimako knew it was still festering in my mind.

"You know, what you said about your meeting with Doug, babes, is something that we have to accept. The chance of getting a job at the level we were at home is probably less than 50 per cent. I am not saying it is impossible—after all, look at the gains we have made since we started working with the career managers—but I really think if we can get a job in our career path that we are blessed. Look at how many people we know have fallen by the wayside. They came to Canada as professionals, but are now doing menial jobs. Let's keep trusting God."

I realised Zimako was right. That did not stop me from feeling demoted. I had expected it in theory before coming to Canada, and had been willing to do whatever it took to succeed, but the reality still hurt. I was silent as I contemplated the cost of immigration to Canada.

"Babes, are you there?"

"Mmmhm… " He held me closer. "Are you okay?"

"Mmmmhm… "

"You know it could also happen to me?"

"Mmmhm… " I could tell he was now amused.

"Then you'd be married to a labourer… "

"Mmmhm… I like the thought of being with a labourer… "

As soon as I said that, he turned me over to face him and kissed me. "Well, I can be your labourer tonight, baby… "

* * * * *

We were headed to the lifts for our appointment with our career coaches, and had barely caught the lift before the doors closed. A hand was inserted between the closing doors; the door reopened to admit Nick. He nodded to Zimako and me, and we nodded back. He turned to Zimako. "How is it going so far?"

"Good, good," Zimako replied.

"Are you satisfied with the services so far?" Nick asked again.

"So far, so good," Zimako responded.

"I am going in to meet with Dave this morning."

Zimako did not reply to that.

"Do you mind if I have your number?" he asked.

Zimako had no aversion to that and handed him his cell phone number.

We arrived at our destination. "Thanks, buddy. I'll be giving you a call." As soon as the doors opened, he was out in a flash.

I sat in Shelly's office while she went to get some coffee. The music of Yanni was playing softly in the background. I had gotten used to Shelly, her alternative beliefs and her quirkiness, and accepted her that way. I was confident that her methods were effective, and she encouraged me to explore my spirituality, whatever that was. I was more reticent about evangelising her. When she came back, she wanted to review my recent field trips. I discussed my meeting with Doug, and other networking appointments I had attended. As usual, using her grading criteria, she awarded me marks, offering praise and constructive feedback.

"Instead of feeling that Doug was less than fair to you, did you consider mentioning to him that you would be interested in being considered for the management position?"

I squinted at her and shook my head slowly. "That never crossed my mind."

"Can you think of a reason why not?"

I thought for a moment. "I think I assumed he had the right or authority. Okay, I believe that from our interview, he had reached an assessment that I would be best suited for an entry-level position."

Shelly regarded me, and smiled. "Could you have responded that you'd like to try for the management position?"

"I guess so. Yes, maybe."

"Could you?" she asked again, dropping her gaze.

"Yes, yes, I could have, but I don't think I had the courage and self-belief to challenge his assessment, and I was blindsided by the mention of an offer."

She let a pregnant silence fill the room before she spoke again. "You have the power to succeed if you believe in yourself. If you doubt your abilities, you will stymie your chances. Now what is the worst that could have happened if you indicated an interest in the management position?"

"He could have turned me down; he might have gone on to explain why. Hearing the actual words of rejection would have broken my heart."

"Indeed, that is the worst that could have happened, but you'd have left his office knowing you gave it your best shot. But now you may never know. You left his office assuming you were not good enough for the management position when you could have risen to the challenge. You have the education and qualifications. You have the transferable skills. What you need, and why you are here, is to gain help tapping into the market. You have what it takes, but you must also be ready when the opportunity presents itself."

The way Shelly put it, I could see clearly that I had missed an opportunity. I stopped feeling sorry for myself and blaming Doug for thinking I was not good enough for the management position. It probably had little to do with my qualifications and more to do with my attitude.

The rest of the meeting was about becoming adept at communicating my qualifications and skills in compelling terms and selling myself as an ideal candidate.

Shelly gave me the rest of the day off, promising to email my next assignment in the morning. I thanked her for all the work she was doing with me, and took my leave.

When I got to the reception area, Zimako had not come out, so I texted him and then waited patiently.

CHAPTER EIGHTEEN

> *Dear Diary,*
> *Time really does fly! It is almost six months since we came to Canada, and we are now in the early spring. The weather is cool but not cold. What a contrast to the freezing winter we came in to. Sadly, Zimako will be heading back to Nigeria to his old job. We had hoped one of us would be employed by this time, but it has been two weeks since we finished our formal training with the career managers, and no job. Our finances are not what they were, and money is running low, but we are grateful to be here. Fortunately, Zimako did not quit his job back at home, so at least we have his income to fall back on. That is our safety net. Zimako has picked up some of the Canadian slang, and I teased him that when he gets back home, they will find it difficult to understand him. "You betcha!" he responded. I'll miss him.*

We are doing our best to remain upbeat considering our circumstances. When our thirty-day coaching period ended, we were advised that it was not yet over, since we had a ninety-day contract. However, a lot of the work that was left, we had to do on our own. We continued to attend our networking meetings, give out our personal cards, attend Toastmasters meetings, and ask for referrals. The lessons we received with the career managers were helpful. The difficult part was responding to our concerned family back home about why we were still unemployed. We were evasive, reminding them that we were blessed to be in Canada, what a great country it is, and how well the government has cushioned the economy from the collapse that has engulfed the western hemisphere. My dad asked us the other day if we needed money. Zimako was very embarrassed and disturbed by that, feeling he had somehow failed.

It was almost midday. Zimako and I sat at the dining table which doubled up as our home office, scouring the database for contacts, when the sound of the phone ringing jarred us from our preoccupation. "I'll get it." Zimako stood up.

Zimako began to speak to the caller. I tried to discern who the caller was using my usual one-way eavesdropping technique, but I couldn't, so I gave up and realised I would have to wait till he was done. My thoughts drifted to our plans for later in the day when I was meeting Kathy, who had promised to take me to the Royal Albert museum. Kathy was keen that we take advantage of the improved weather to get to know Edmonton better. She generously offered her time and companionship, coming up with places of interest for us to sightsee and explore. I noticed that Zimako had come off the phone and I was chomping at the bit to know what the call was about. "Hmmm, you were on that call for a while. Is everything okay?"

"That was Nick, from our career managers. He was very vexed. Get this, Anuli. He and some of the other clients are getting together, and they want us to come along to discuss the services we got from PCMG. Apparently many of them are not satisfied with the results."

I could not say I was shocked to hear that this was coming from Nick. From the first time we met, I sensed he was not a happy camper. "Does that surprise you?"

"I guess not. I am not sure I totally agree with him. Look at all the value we got from them. They showed us how to navigate our way, and get in front of employers, something we were unable to do before, and hopefully by God's grace, we will break through the glass walls."

"So what was he expecting that he didn't get?" I asked.

Zimako told me it all boiled down to the failed promises, the hidden market, the six-figure jobs, and being put in direct contact with employers.

"They did not hand us a job, true, but apart from that I felt they delivered."

"Well, apparently not in Nick's opinion."

I asked if he would be attending the meeting and where it was taking place. He swiftly and emphatically corrected me. "You mean, will we be attending?" he said, looking meaningfully at me. I had not expected to be roped in, because all along I had assumed he was Nick's target.

"The answer to that is yes. He'd like us both to be at this meeting to discuss the dividends gained for the investment extracted based on the written and oral contract at the time of signing on. We would share our experiences, and see where we go from there. It'll be interesting to know if he has a game plan."

"I am going to the museum with Kathy today, at three p.m., and will probably not be back before five p.m. It's a prior engagement and it'd be rude to cancel at the last minute, so I wonder if I can really be at the meeting."

"Luck is on your side, Anuli my baby. I can tell you are torn between your prior engagement and this meeting. But guess what? The meeting is not till six p.m. and it's at the library downtown, so you don't have to choose, sweetheart. You can do both. Ha-ha." His voice dripped with sarcasm.

I couldn't quite see the sense in the meeting, and Zimako knew I was trying to avoid attending. I refused to let myself get irritated.

"Okay. I don't want to be pushy, but I'd like for you to be there, babes. Think about it, and let me know your decision."

I smiled; Zimako knew I'd sulk for days if he insisted I come along to the meeting against my will, so he was playing it safe. I relaxed into my seat and continued to search for opportunities. I had widened my scope beyond just searching for a job to include activities that interested me where I could meet like-minded people. Shelly said that was a good way to connect with people and possibly get more referrals for job offers.

The rest of the afternoon went by uneventfully, and soon it was time to meet Kathy. Zimako reminded me as I left that the meeting was at 6.00 p.m., and that he'd miss me. I gave him my "don't pressure me" smile and left.

The museum was by the river in the picturesque older area of

Edmonton. "I hope you will find the exhibition of our cultural heritage interesting," Kathy said. "This is one of my most favourite places to come. I never tire of it, and with my Experience Alberta Museum pass, I get free admission to all Government of Alberta Museums for a token fee."

It was clear she was quite excited to share it with me. Kathy had a passion for life. I admired this. Coupled with the wisdom of her years and life's experience, it had made her a role model for me. "I like museums, although I must be honest, the museums back home are a joke. Mouldy and dusty, not designed to be enjoyed, and no one really goes there. I do not recall the last time I was there myself."

As we approached, I was struck by how well kept the grounds were. The old buildings nearby seemed designed to take one back in time. I could sense her pride. The first floor was divided up into two sections, as was the second floor. On the first floor they featured Wild Alberta, showcasing the wildlife of Alberta. The animals were stuffed, but looked so real, protected in glass so clear, you could almost imagine there was no glass, tempting you to reach out and touch them. There were also rusty old tools from pioneer days. Kathy and I joked about how much simpler life must have been back in the day. Something I said must have brought back memories for her. She had that faraway look in her eyes. "You know, Anuli, I still miss Africa."

"But that was such a long time ago, Kathy," I reminded her. I had long come to the conclusion that something had happened to Kathy in Africa that she still yearned for.

All at once she looked sad, lost, and dreamy. I wondered if she wanted to talk about it; but just as that look appeared, in a flash it was gone. She continued as though nothing had happened. I did not want to probe. We continued down the first floor where the many birds of Alberta, their eggs, and their habitats were displayed. Upstairs was a tribute to the Aboriginal culture and people of Alberta. It was amazing to see how they survived with very little in the harsh weather conditions. The Aboriginal Gallery was beautifully and sensitively done, with an exhibit dealing with current aboriginal issues. We continued to the other side of the second floor gallery, gazing at the many moths and brilliant butterflies of Alberta. I was mesmerized by the display of precious stones. Kathy suddenly took my hand, and I let her hold onto it, thinking she was tired, but when I looked at her, she looked very animated; then she whispered to me, "This is one of my favourite places. It reminds me of the primitiveness in Africa. Can you see? Do you understand?" The look in her eyes pleaded with me to understand. All her sixty-five years were written on her face, and I could tell this was important to her.

I nodded.

"I left my heart in Africa, Anuli."

I waited.

"All these years, and it's still so fresh in my mind."

I didn't know how to respond. She was looking at me. I glanced at her, but the sadness in her eyes made me look away. She did not say anything more. We continued and finished our museum visit by visiting the café.

I was pleased to have had the experience of seeing some of the rich history of Canada. We walked to the car after taking in the stunning view of the south side, the university, and the lovely valley.

"Did you enjoy it?" Kathy asked as we drove down the quiet avenue heading downtown. I told her I had a good time, but wished we had more time.

Then I asked her what I really wanted to know. "Kathy, are you ever going to talk about it? Tell me to shut up if you feel I'm prying."

"I will, when I'm ready. Now please drop it and not a word to anyone."

I decided to respect her privacy. She then proceeded to share some of her less poignant childhood memories with me, after which, in true Kathy style, she turned to question me. "So, enough about the museum, the past, and me. How are you guys holding up? I hope something turns up soon work-wise for you. I know you'll do well in Canada; you just have to be patient, keep an open mind, and take in all you can. Don't rush yourselves."

After six months, no one could accuse us of rushing. I told her my concerns about not working, my fears of getting deskilled, the impact on my self-esteem, our dwindling finances, and my dependence on Zimako now that he was the sole breadwinner.

Kathy tried to empathise. "I am sure something will turn up. Just be patient." I was getting tired of hearing the same platitudes, but what else could she say? We continued in companionable silence for a while, and then she asked, "What about those career managers? Did you get any contacts that helped?"

I told her about how Nick and some other clients were dissatisfied even though I thought the experience was worthwhile. "We are supposed to meet later in the evening today to share our experiences, but I'm not keen."

I had decided I'd let Zimako attend the meeting without me. I knew I was emotionally in a very sensitive place, and because of the confidence I had in Shelly, I was not quite prepared to let my mind wander into the possibility that we had been short-changed.

Kathy drove me home and I thanked her for her kindness. Her reply was touching. "You do more for me, young lady. Now, keep your chin up, and remember what I said."

I was dreading confronting Zimako with my decision not to attend the meeting. I opened the door, and saw he was ready but chatting on the phone. I let myself in, hanging up my jacket and leaving my boots by the door. I headed to the bedroom.

"Babes, that was Kojo. Hey, you look tired," he said as he sat on the bed beside me and planted a kiss on my forehead. "Are you okay?"

I knew he'd be disappointed with my decision, but I had to spit it out. "I'm so sorry. I can't come with you to the meeting… " I started, but he cut me short.

"That's fine, babes. I'll go alone and then probably stop by Kojo's. Shall I pick up dinner on the way back? Save you cooking? Just get some rest, okay?"

I felt good enough to smile. "Thanks, sweetheart." With that he gave me a quick cuddle and left for the meeting.

I must have drifted off to sleep, because next thing I knew I heard the front door open. The room was dark. I called, "Zimako?" half concerned it might be an intruder.

Zimako was in the room, turning on the light. "Wow! My sleeping beauty! Have you been asleep the whole time?"

I sat up in bed as he started to tell me how the meeting went. There were six of them in attendance. Each one had come to PCMG with the hope that they would give them access to a contact list of employers. They had expected PCMG to use their network relationships to link them up with the so-called hidden job market.

I was struggling to see what the problem was. "Zimako, I still don't get it. What do they want?"

Zimako continued to explain. "Clearly, they were expecting to be spoon-fed names in the industry, and their claim is that for the amount of money PCMG was charging—each of these people has paid anywhere between $5,000 and $8,500—their expectations were not unrealistic. Worse still, the results have been patchy. Only one guy got a job, which he did through his own contacts. None of the others have converted any interviews to jobs."

"So at least we are not the only frustrated jobseekers."

"I'll tell you what we are. We are the only immigrants in the group. They really wanted to hear my experience, and they believe that our input will be very important if we decide to participate, because it will show how Dave has preyed on innocent and unwary persons to further his greed. Let me tell you, after listening to some of the stories, I feel compelled to be a part of whatever action they decide to take."

I knew that once Zimako got involved in anything, he could be tenacious, and would see it to the end. As I considered his words, he went on to tell me about Mike, Bill, and Larry. These were men who had been laid off and desired to resuscitate their careers. They had gone to PCMG with their life savings, full of hope. He mentioned that there was one other woman who was part of the meeting; her name was Brenda. She was quite emotional about it because she took the money from her retirement savings. "I think she paid $6,800. She's probably in her early fifties."

I considered the information and asked him, "So are you decided? And, if so, what next?"

Zimako maintained that he wanted to think through it. He

said the group really wanted both of us to be a big part of the fight to expose Dave as an unscrupulous scammer rather than the suave businessman he tried to pretend he was.

I could see their point. Certainly we were all seeking jobs, but we were coming from a different place and had different expectations. They were Canadian born and bred, and to them a promise was a promise and had to be honoured. We definitely could benefit from joining forces with them. It became clear that we were the ones who had set our expectations too low.

Zimako mulled over it and two days later suddenly announced, "We should join the uprising, baby. We have to!"

I listened to his reasons and had to agree with him.

"He does not have to give us a full refund. We could work out something where he pays back 50 to 75 per cent of the fee we paid."

He quickly informed Nick of our decision. Nick said the next steps would be arranging a sit-down with Dave and everyone who signed up to the revolt.

The following week, Zimako, I, Nick, Mike, Bill, Larry, and Brenda arrived for our meeting with Dave. We waited in the conference room for him to join us. While we waited, we discussed our expectations for the meeting and hoped for the best outcome. I noticed Nick watching Zimako closely. The wait seemed interminable, and I was getting irritated when suddenly Bruce, who had been Zimako's coach, came into the room. He was very tight-faced and headed straight to the seat reserved for Dave. He looked around the table at everyone, politely acknowledging us.

"Let's quickly get to the purpose of this meeting. I'd like your representatives to tell us what their grievances are. We will try our best to see how we can resolve them."

Brenda took him up. "Before we jump to that, could you tell us why Dave is not here?"

She had spoken what we were all thinking. Bruce seemed embarrassed. I watched him turn beetroot red from his neck up. He stammered through his response. "Dave, Dave... he... has to deal with some issues... immediate issues that have come up, and cannot be here."

There was a silence in the room. Larry, a man who appeared very calm and reasonable, interjected, "Just a minute, Bruce. We need to know that you have the mandate to sit in for Dave, and that the conversations and agreements will not be invalidated."

Bruce nodded, and responded, "Guys, this meeting is exploratory. I do not think there will be any agreements reached today. I am here to hear your concerns and pass them on to Dave, so let's be clear." He paused for effect, and seemed to look directly at me. "There will be no promises or commitments made today."

He went on to speak about the product the company offered, and highlighted the small print which said jobs were not guaranteed at the end of the contract. The meeting spiralled downward once he pointed out the conditions in the small print. He emphasised that everyone was given an opportunity to review the contract before returning the next day or not, there had been a cooling-off period, and there was no pressure to sign on. The mood was subtly hostile. We finally agreed that there was no point continuing the discussion with Bruce. We opted to wait till Dave could spare time from his busy schedule to meet with the group, which Zimako still described as insurgents.

Meeting with Bruce made it clear that PCMG would not cooperate with us, nor was it willing to make any concessions to us as a group. Rather, the company tried to reach out to individuals to divide and conquer.

A few days later, Bruce called to speak with Zimako; obviously they believed he was a weak link in the chain. The conversation did not go as Bruce anticipated, because Zimako was unwilling to compromise once he realised the company's intention was to destabilise the group. Zimako told Bruce we wanted more transparency, a full meeting with the whole group. Bruce could not concede that, and they agreed to disagree.

The next time the group convened at the library, I was with Zimako. The discussion was very lively, and Nick was preaching to the choir. We finally decided to take our case against the company to the small claims court. The disgruntled "Insurgents" v PCMG: Let the battle commence.

CHAPTER NINETEEN

> *Dear Diary,*
>
> *Zimako has departed for Nigeria. It was a tough decision for us to follow through on, but we had little choice in the matter. Being in Canada has been tough without Zimako; I almost lost my enthusiasm to continue our routine. It has been really quiet in the apartment, but thank God for friends. Fifi, Kathy, and Afaafa have been amazing. It was during one of my job searches that I had a eureka moment. Each of the jobs listed qualifications and experience. The phrases that jumped out suddenly to me were "Canadian experience" and "education." Although our foreign qualifications had been evaluated as acceptable by the requisite institutions, employers were still sceptical about giving jobs to untested newcomers.*
>
> *It was obvious that they specified Canadian experience or education for the credibility, familiarity, and uniformity it conferred. It set me thinking, and the more I thought about it, the more excited I became! It was really right there before my eyes, and I had missed it the whole time.*

I kept dialling Nigeria.

The cell phones were not going through. The eight-hour time difference was not helping matters either. Trying to reach Zimako to share with him my latest discovery was proving to be an impossible task. I hung up after several attempts. I did not let that dampen my enthusiasm. I had pencilled some likely courses and schools that were relevant to my background. I continued to work and make calls all day, gathering the information I needed. Another issue of import was the financing for the schooling. I did not qualify for any grants or financial assistance because I did not meet the criteria for the one-year residency status in Alberta. This meant the financing would come from our savings. It gave me palpitations to think of it, knowing we were already so low on funds we were now being even more careful about what we spent our money on.

I decided to send Zimako an email, and hopefully he would call when he could.

I called Anne, whom I had remained in touch with, shortly after-wards and told her about my plans to go back to school. She thought it was a good idea, but was worried that I sounded rather down and wondered if I was getting depressed by a perceived disappointment in the Canada dream. It was a legitimate concern, and I assessed how I was feeling. My mood was often low. "You know what, Anne? Some days are so much better than others, but having friends and people I can talk to who understand helps me get through."

She offered to take my résumé and see if there was a part-time job she could find me from the various companies her company was affiliated with. I thanked her for the thoughtful offer. I immediately emailed her a résumé from which I had deleted my degree and postgraduate qualifications, knowing that would render me overqualified for any jobs she would be putting me forward for. A job of any sort would make a difference. I would need every bit of cash I could lay my hands on to offset the cost of going back to school.

I was feeling overwhelmed and was glad to get out of the flat. Afaafa and I were meeting for drinks that evening; I needed to talk to someone. Afaafa was very fun to be with. With her, what you saw was what you got. She was open and easy to talk to. We had arranged to meet at the Starbucks café, close to the LRT Station. I sat down with my cup of latte, looking out the panoramic windows of the cosy shop, waiting for her.

Within a few minutes, she came running into the shop and looked around for me. She waved enthusiastically, ordered her drink, and joined me.

"Hey," she said.

"Hey, you," I responded. "How was your day?"

She smiled at me. "Well, we'll talk about that later." She sighed heavily. Afaafa's work as a social worker could be emotionally draining, and I knew her compassion for many of the youths and families she worked with sometimes got to her. Almost every time I saw her, she had a heart-breaking story, and even though she tried to put a positive spin on the cases, I could sense her feeling of impotence sometimes.

"I hope you are speaking with Zimako."

I had not been able to connect and speak with Zimako all day, and I missed him so much. "No, we did not speak today. I'm hoping he calls later tonight or at least by the morning. You know how it is. Telecommunications back home can be touch-and-go, so we'll see."

"If I were married to a man like Zimako, I would never let him out of my sight. Girlfriend, you are too trusting."

"No, it's just the principle of it. Zimako would never—I mean, never—do that. He's not the sort."

"Of course. I know, I mean, being a Christian and all, he won't, but sometimes, these men get tempted, and you have to… "

"Afaa, forget the stereotype. Seriously, Zimako is a man of honour. I know he is human, but he would not do anything that will jeopardise our marriage."

"I hope I will have that kind of confidence in the man I end up with."

Her comment reminded me to ask about the new guy she had met. I knew she had been spending time with him, but it did not seem as though things were progressing towards a serious, intimate relationship.

We sat for a while, just to let the heat of the discussion pass, and then I told her my news about going back to school to earn a postgraduate, professional qualification. She was very excited. I was glad to have a friend who was so supportive. She highlighted the benefits for me, and concluded that it would definitely help find me suitable employment, the type I had been hoping for.

In turn I updated her on my research and the feedback I was getting. "It basically boils down to some essential modules, one final major exam, and then I earn the CMA accreditation."

We shared more details about what the professional designation entailed and how much time was required. As I explained the nitty-gritty, I got really enthusiastic, and she shared my joy.

"Ah, Anuli, I am so pleased to see a real light at the end of the tunnel. Are you getting any grants?"

I explained that I was not qualified for a grant, but was going to go ahead and finance it on my own. She looked concerned.

"Why do you look so worried, Afaa?"

"I am speaking from my experience, Anuli. Finances can be a very thorny issue, especially for new immigrants. With no job to replenish diminishing funds, I'd be surprised if it doesn't cause some friction. You do know you are looking at about $2,500 per semester? That is a chunk of change, girl."

I nodded, considering what she was saying, because in my excitement I had steamrolled ahead with my plans without securing the part-time job, or getting Zimako's opinion and go-ahead.

"Anuli, here's what I know," she said, sitting back in her seat and regarding me intently. "Some families that came to Canada with the same dreams you have are divided today because of the financial strains they have encountered. They lost their kids; Child Services had to remove the children from the hostile environment, and the mums and dads separated because of abuse. Its alarming how often this happens and I am always glad to see how you and Zimako have been able to get by without the drama."

I could see her point. I revealed that I was looking for a part-time job to help me fund my living costs, and that although Zimako and I had yet to fully discuss the school matter, I was hopeful that I would get his backing, as he had so far always been supportive.

The statistics about family break-ups in the new immigrant population were scary. I wanted clarification and details.

"Actually, we see a lot of that, and it affects immigrants from across the globe who come here for a new start. The children struggle to adjust to the new environment. When the parents disagree and quarrel about money, the children witness this, and it affects their desire to mingle and socialise in school. Teachers notice their disengagement and detachment and want to know what is going on. They tell their teachers how life at home is too stressful, and that they think they are the problem or contributing to it. Some of them want to run away from home, and that is when Child Services step in."

I listened, horrified. "Afaa, are you saying this is commonplace?"

"For the most part, we see this in the cities. Statistics show that those who are in the suburban areas and smaller cities or towns manage to weather the storm. But like I said earlier, you and Zimako have done so well. I suggest you do a good budget and discuss this fully with him before you embark on it, because I have seen how strained relationships can affect newcomers."

We lapsed into silence as I considered all she had said.

Not one to be quiet for any length of time, before long Afaa was talking again. She was chatting about her day, and as I listened, something she said caught my attention.

"What did you just say?"

"That it's not working out with this guy I was seeing, so I broke it off, and now I am going online!"

Afaa was very cutting-edge and trendy and often came up with ideas I thought were weird and wonderful. "Are you sure? Isn't that dangerous? Moreover, an attractive girl like you, surely you can meet someone without going online."

"Nothing is without risks, but no, Anuli, it's not dangerous at all. Actually, it's a Christian dating Web site, so I'll be in good company. Relax," she said, laughing.

We spent the rest of the evening talking about guys, love, and all that stuff.

* * * * *

I was awakened by the phone very early in the morning.

"Hey, babes."

"Zimako! I am so glad you called. I tried all day yesterday, but couldn't reach you."

He explained that the communication systems were bad on his network the previous day. "Babes, you can always text me if the lines are not going through."

I hadn't thought of that. I asked if he had seen my email. The silence at the end of the phone unnerved me.

"So… " I prompted, "what do you think?"

"Babes, I'm not sure if that is the right thing to do at this time. You promised to keep the momentum going strong, and we already decided we need to keep our focus steady on getting the kind of jobs we had before we moved. I'm surprised by this new angle."

I sensed his resistance and did not want us to argue about it, so I deflected the conversation.

"Okay, maybe you need time to think about it. I have not made any commitments, but I feel that is the right way to go. But let's leave that for now and think about it a little more."

"How much is it going to cost?"

"Around $2,500 per semester," I answered in a very quiet voice. There was more silence at the other end of the phone. When he did not speak, I asked, "Zimako, hello? Are you still there?"

I could tell he was restraining himself as he responded. "I am… Where is the money going to come from?"

I knew the conversation was going to degenerate into an open disagreement if one of us did not back down. "Babes, listen, I have a plan, but let's talk about this later. Tell me, what is the latest back home? How is work, and how is everyone?"

He recognised we were moving in opposite directions and for now conceded to give peace a chance.

"Work is fine. We are already advertising my position, so we'll see how that works out. I will be going with Okwe for the engagement to Ireti's parents on the weekend, and afterwards we will travel to the village to see Ichie and Okpue-umu-agbala. Hopefully, Makua will come along."

I tried to get excited about all the news, but Zimako sensed my heart was not in it. Our conversation ended with the promise to talk again soon.

* * * * *

Zimako gazed out the window of his office. He was very pensive. When he read Anuli's email the previous day, he hoped she was not serious about pursuing further education. That was the last thing he expected her to come up with. He hoped that while he was gone, one of the many contacts would invite her for an interview, and she would be employed by the time he got back. That was how it was supposed to work. "God, why?"

All the best-laid plans about Canada were not working out in the time frame they had expected, and it was disheartening. Thank goodness, he still had this job, but still, he would ultimately have to make his way back to Canada, and then what?

Living in Edmonton was not cheap, and with the exchange rate, the Nigerian currency was at a disadvantage. His first thought was how to pay for Anuli's schooling. With their savings dwindling, this was certainly no time to be forking out huge amounts of cash for school. He did not need this, not now!

Zimako entered the apartment he was sharing with Okwe. He and Anuli had given up their place when they relocated to Canada. He knew, coming back to Nigeria, that it would be quite an adjustment moving in with Okwe, but he was not prepared for the extent of the change. Okwe lived life loudly and to the fullest. That, coupled with the imminent engagement, meant that everything was upbeat, bordering on raucous. His friends called and came by at all hours, and the phone never stopped ringing. There was no moment of respite. Zimako missed his old life with Anuli. Much as he liked being at Okwe's, he began to consider finding alternative accommodation just so he could enjoy some peace and quiet.

The entire gang of Okwe's close friends was there again. Zimako let himself in. They hailed him gregariously as he walked in.

"*Bros, we dey* hail, O. How far?"

"I *dey*," he answered. It had been a hectic day, and all he wanted was to have his supper and rest his head, but none of that would be possible without first spending the obligatory few minutes discussing the preparations for the engagement to avoid seeming antisocial. The guys had obviously been working hard. They had sorted transportation, drinks, *Aso ebi*, favours, cash in crisp mint notes for spraying, and even traditional dancers. They had been busy.

"I see arrangements are going strong?" He sat with them, and soon he forgot how tired he was as the conversation swirled around the plans, marriage in general, and women in particular. Drinks flowed and tongues loosened. Okwe was very excited about his engagement and the prospect of becoming a father. The joy reflected on his face and reminded Zimako of the time he and Anuli were courting, and he smiled to himself. Now from the whirlwind of troubles they seemed embroiled in, a reminder like that was what he needed to see Anuli, the Anuli he fell in love with, as she really was, and not get bogged down by their current short-term differences.

"Hey, guys, I have to leave you. Let me lie down and rest," he said, standing up and slapping Okwe on the back.

* * * * *

I decided to go ahead with my plans for school and find a way to convince Zimako it was the right thing to do. Maybe if I found a part-time job to help defray the tuition from school, he would be more amenable to my plan. It seemed obvious. I knew that a good Canadian professional designation would open doors to the kind of role I could only dream of at that moment. It would require some sacrifice, but it was necessary to get ahead. It was better to make the sacrifice sooner rather than later. I planned on calling Kathy to share my plans, and see what she thought of them, as well as follow up with Anne on the job.

Suddenly everything seemed so complicated. When Zimako and I started out on this Canadian odyssey, we had hoped for the best, but we shared a singular focus and vision. This was the first time I really wanted something which Zimako was resistant to. It was a mammoth challenge, but not insurmountable.

I headed to the University of Alberta. I had completed the requisite forms online and then made an appointment for my registration. It was exhilarating and scary in equal measure.

Zimako had always been by my side, and we made decisions together. This was strange, but if I waited till Zimako came around to seeing my point of view, I'd miss the next semester, and I did not want to waste further time. I was going to the Faculty of Business, where I would be registered for the eight courses that I was required to pass before the final exams that would earn me the designation.

Registration completed, this seemed like the first day of a very bright future. It was a very interesting meeting. I had planned on a one-year programme, but the head of faculty, after reviewing my transcripts, asked me if I'd like to sign on for the seven-month accelerated programme! It was so unexpected, but I did not have to think about it. I took it! It reduced my time in school, and the cost of getting the designation. I went with my gut instinct on this. I would call Zimako again to talk to him. It might take time to win him over, but in my opinion it was for our greater good.

True, further education had not been part of our plans when we arrived. Indeed a lot of money had gone down the drain with PCMG, but this was different.

With little left of our finances, when I paid my fees, we would practically be living on the poverty line. Zimako was right to worry about how we would cope, but perhaps if I could demonstrate my commitment by finding a job that paid something to replenish our now meagre resources, that might assuage his fears.

When I got home, there were messages waiting on the phone.

The first was from Zimako. "Anuli, call me when you get this message."

The next message was from Anne. "Anuli, call me! I have news for you." My heart skipped with Anne's message. I dared to hope.

I quickly returned Anne's call. I wanted to hopefully share some good news about the job when I called Zimako. "Hi Anne, this is Anuli."

"Anuli! Hey. I think I have something for you. Can you come over to our office? We are accepting résumés on behalf of a group that requires temporary workers. It pays a decent wage, and requires some numerical skills. It will be child's play for you. If you are interested, I will let them know you will be coming in to drop off your résumé."

My heart was beating as Anne spoke. I was willing to take any offer that came my way, and if it paid a decent wage, this was a no-brainer. "Yes! I can come down right away. Just maybe give me about forty-five minutes to get there."

"Fine. Be prepared for a little question-and-answer mini-interview when you come down. Good luck, Anuli."

"Thanks, Anne, you are the best."

I put off calling Zimako and set off for Anne's office, armed with a copy of my résumé.

I was shown to the office of the executive assistant to the vice-president. I took a seat and waited.

"Anuli?"

"Yes, good afternoon." I rose to my feet and shook hands with her.

"Thank you for coming at such short notice. It is a temporary position for nine months. The woman has gone on maternity leave, and we need to fill the position. The hours are flexible three days a week, and it requires numerical skills, teamwork, and time management. The successful candidate will work as part of a seven-man team, and have to meet deadlines. Oh, by the way, I'm Julia Samachuk."

I was nodding as she spoke.

"So tell me about yourself and why you believe you are the most qualified person for this position."

"My name is Anuli Adiora. I'm new to Canada, but prior to coming here I worked with a finance firm, dealing with high net worth individual accounts, deposits, and sourcing new relationships. I have excellent customer service skills. I have good computer skills, and I can multitask. I am a quick learner, and think on my feet. If I'm given this opportunity, you will find me flexible and adaptable. My excellent people skills means I would fit seamlessly into the team. I am married; I enjoy swimming, tennis, and gardening."

She asked me more questions, which related to job specifics, and when we were done, she smiled. "Thank you for coming along. We will be in touch with you within the week."

I thanked her and left. My head was spinning. I wanted to sing, laugh, dance, and skip, but I walked out, calmly setting a mental reminder to send her a thank-you note.

CHAPTER TWENTY

Dear Diary,

I got the job! I got the job! I got the job! There is a God somewhere. I can't stop thanking Anne for her help. My act appears to finally be coming together. I am registered to start school in a few weeks, and I have a job to help me pay my way.

I started the job, and though it is not my dream job, I'm on the path to fulfilling my dream. I have not been able to convince Zimako, but when he learned about how much I would be earning, which at least helps with my living expenses, he grudgingly acquiesced. He is still insistent that I should have focussed on getting a job, but I will not let Zimako rain on my parade.

I was elated to be at the bus stop heading to my first day at work. I had attended a second interview which tested numerical skills, and then a third and final one with two managers of the company, which was called a behavioural interview. The questions were about how I had behaved in the past when trying to handle potentially challenging situations. It wasn't something I had experienced before, but Anne had warned me, so I read up on how to answer behavioural questions like "Tell me about the time when you had to deal with a difficult customer," or "Tell me about how you resolved a conflict with a demand that was in opposition to the company policy." I wasn't sure I had impressed them at that interview, but waited in anticipation, and when the call came it was such a wonderful feeling. The only person I thought to call was my sister Chiamaka. She knew my plans and the stress I was experiencing with Zimako's refusal to see things from my point of view. I was glad I had her support. She encouraged me to press on.

The outfit I chose for my first day was business casual. I was in the back office; the job itself involved some responsibility, repetitive tasks, accuracy, and interaction with the front office. I waited to be introduced to the other members of the team. Anita was the lead of our small team of ten. It was on a shift basis, and one shift had ended and the new shift was resuming when Anita brought me in for introductions. She took me to Helen, a wizened lady, and asked her to show me around and introduce me. The first thing that struck me was that I was overdressed. Everyone else was casually dressed, and I was rather embarrassed to be looking so formal. I made a mental note to dress down. I shook hands and smiled, but could not commit all the names to memory at once. Introductions done, I was shown to my work area and handed a binder. It was the bible of our job; it told me the basics of how to get things done. The final formality was going to HR and payroll to complete documentation. Anita then handed me over to Maria, whom I was to shadow. Her remit was to guide me through the necessary induction and train me for the next fortnight, by which time I would be a fully signed on member of the team.

The day went well. During lunch break, the women and four guys who were part of the team treated me well, and asked lots of questions about my family, Africa, and what brought me to Canada. I found them to be friendly, if inquisitive, but I had come to expect that from everyone in Canada. Maria took me under her wing. She was also an immigrant, but had been in Canada for twenty years and had worked in the company for ten, starting out as a temp with flexible hours just like me, and she was optimistic that if I was any good, the company would likely extend my contract.

The job, which had appeared relatively easy, required maintaining records and files, data entry, clerical duties such as filing and faxing, computer work, and some word processing. It required that I paid attention to detail, and I began to understand why Maria said it necessitated utmost focus and following specific instructions. I was just excited to be at work.

Thursday was my day off. It was my second week at work, and I was meeting up with Kathy for a walk in the park. I was so happy I had met Kathy. She was a friend and mother and sister rolled into one. I had come to trust her and count on her support. Now I was more relaxed about my being here. I had a sense of purpose, and I could see a bright future ahead of me.

I saw Kathy pull up and went to meet her. "Anuli! You look gorgeous, my dear. Great minds think alike."

I was wearing yoga pants with a red-hooded fleece top, going for the healthy, sporty look. Kathy was looking very well turned out as usual in a pair of Capri pants and a red top, and I complimented her. We looked well-coordinated. "In Nigeria when people dress so alike, we say they are in *aso-ebi*, which literally translates to uniform for close kin, and Kathy in Canada, you are my kindred spirit." She smiled, and I could tell she was pleased. I had her to thank for so much, not least for keeping me on my toes and helping me discover Edmonton.

We headed to Capilano Park. I was looking forward to the hiking and enjoying the fresh air. I admit that I rarely stepped out unless I was on a mission to accomplish some goal or another, and had not quite spent as much time just smelling the roses. Kathy obviously intended for us to do just that today. She had brought along a small picnic bag of sandwiches and nibbles. I had brought some drinks to cool off.

It was a nice day out. The forecast was for sun and some clouds, but it promised to be dry, and temperatures were average at eighteen degrees Celsius. We started out, and saw others who obviously were out to enjoy the day as well. Some were walking, and others jogged along. After we had been walking for about an hour, Kathy suggested we sit down and enjoy our picnic. This was the life: sun, friendship, and food.

We found a nice spot and spread our mat and sat down to enjoy the meal. We people watched, and Kathy asked me to tell her about my home in Africa. I was always happy to talk about what life was like, and she never tired of listening and asking questions. I knew she loved Africa, but I felt she was not quite prepared to open up about what had happened to her in Congo. I was going to wait till she was willing to confide in me.

"Anuli, I wish I could go back and do it again."

I was surprised she brought it up; I listened attentively with bated breath.

She deliberately unwrapped her sandwich and began to talk. "I have never shared this with anyone. You know already that the time I spent in Africa during a short missionary trip was the best year of my life. I had gone with my family to help build an orphanage in Congo with our church group. We lived in Nkara in the Bandundu province. It was a very beautiful, picturesque town, very green. The people lived off the land and I liked that it was a little bit primitive, very rustic." She paused to look at me, but I smiled. I understood Kathy. She wasn't being rude, just trying to describe what she loved.

"The natives, and I mean the people of the province, were very welcoming, and respectful. I remember they called my mother Teacher and my father Pastor, and they called me Miss Kate. They were lovely, genuine people. There was a certain purity to their way of life that was very endearing. There was none of the modern comforts we enjoy here, and there were bugs, real creepy-crawlies." She laughed, and I with her as she said that because I knew it to be true.

She continued, "Yet, I found that despite all that, I felt at home. I loved the sun, its heat, the enchanting sunsets, the wet rainbows. My friends and I helped with the building by day, and played with the children. In the evenings, we'd sit around under moonlight. We'd gather the orphans and read Bible bedtime stories to them. One day, we were to have a crusade."

I was listening and nodding, knowing that churches held crusades all the time in Africa.

"It was a three-day event. I had never attended one before and I was excited. I was helping with placing the chairs behind the school building under those huge trees that I have only seen in Africa. There were invited speakers from some affiliated churches, and that was where I met Nsala. I... I think it was love at first sight."

She smiled and paused and had a sip of her drink. She wiped

her eye as though swiping off an insect, then went on. "He was about my age at the time, I guess seventeen or eighteen years old. He was dark, tall, well-built, and he had the most engaging smile. He was visiting his father, who was one of the ministers at the crusade. We were tongue-tied with each other to start, but when he looked at me I melted."

Kathy looked at me again, and I could see she was opening her heart in a way that she probably had not done with anyone before. I did not want her to feel embarrassed, but I knew she could not bottle it in any longer. "Go on," I encouraged her, listening intently.

"Well, although we did not say much at that meeting, we became inseparable. We ran errands together, and helped out side by side. Sadly, the three days went by quickly. Before he left, he promised to write to me, and I promised to write back. He did. He wrote to me almost immediately, and I wrote back. I still have his letters. I saw him again only once more before I returned to Canada. He came for two days to help when the orphanage was completed. We managed to steal some private time together. I remember so vividly, we went on a walk by the river, canopied by trees. Then we sat down and talked and talked. We sat side by side. I loved to listen to his voice. He had such a beautiful accent. I told him I wanted to be a teacher; he said he wanted to be a doctor and help cure diseases. We talked about what we'd like our future to look like. We held hands, and… "

She hesitated. I could feel her reticence. I wondered if they had shared some intimacy.

"No, it's not what you think. He held my face and kissed me. I melted, and I gave him my heart. He held me close, and said he did not want to let me go. Before we went back, he said he loved me. For days after he left, I was so lost without him, but we wrote to each other. I lost contact with him after we returned to Canada. I thought those feelings would go away over time, and for a while they lay dormant. But as I have gotten older, they have become stronger. I never did find anyone else who made me feel that way." Kathy stopped and wiped away a tear. I could see she was spent.

I did not know what to say, but I felt privileged to be the recipient of her confidence. When she composed herself, she said, "So now you know. That day, when I saw you and Zimako walk into the church, I was so happy. I felt I had known you from the beginning." I remembered how Kathy had reacted to us, and I smiled.

We sat in silence and ate our sandwiches.

I had known something happened to Kathy in Africa, and now I understood. I did not know what to say, so I said nothing.

Kathy took charge again. "So, enough about me. Tell me, how is work and how is school coming along?"

It was typical of Kathy, deflecting attention from herself. I regaled her with stories about my job and the people I worked with, and my preparations for starting school in two weeks. As usual, she was full of questions, which I had come to expect from her. Soon we were up on our feet. We packed up the debris of our picnic and headed back. Our conversation was light and revolved around my work and colleagues, my preparations for school, and Zimako. I told her I spoke frequently with him, but did not divulge the extent of his resistance to my going back to school.

"He is a very fine young man, and both of you will do well in Canada. You must keep at it. When my mother came here she was a teenager. It takes about two to three generations to get settled here."

Kathy was always very encouraging, and I thanked her for her kind words.

* * * * *

Zimako and I spoke often, but we avoided discussing my decision to go back to school. As much as I loved my part-time job, I also kept those discussions to a minimum because Zimako was not in support of my decision. He seized every opportunity to tell me I was underselling myself, losing focus. "Babes, you will fall into the same trap that we have always said we did not want to fall into. Have you forgotten who you are? You were responsible for a large portfolio of accounts; you headed your own department. Look at you now—in a part-time job where you cannot even tell them you have a degree. You cannot tell your friends here in Nigeria what you are doing. Is that the life you want?"

He had a point, but he refused to see mine. My focus was on the master plan. This was the path to success. I would not be shaken. In my mind's eye, I saw my future and I was going to make the sacrifices necessary to accomplish it. So rather than rehash the same arguments, I encouraged him to tell me about Nigeria—his job, Okwe's engagement, their visit to see Ichie and Okpue in the village, and general current affairs. I updated him on our small court claims against PCMG, and the group meetings. They were safe topics.

Then Zimako sent me a text saying he would be coming back immediately after Okwe's wedding. I knew something was wrong. He had planned to spend six months in Nigeria before returning to Canada. He was barely three months in, and the wedding was in a fortnight. We wanted to stretch his stay so that he could earn a decent sum of money before returning to Canada, so I knew something had happened to change the plan. Our financial situation was not dire, but it was a new lifestyle for us to budget every cent before spending it. We had forgone a lot of luxuries since we came to Canada, and not finding the roles we wanted would keep us living on a budget for the foreseeable future. I replied to Zimako's text, with a promise to call later.

"Hey, babes."

"How far?"

He sounded down, so I skipped the chit-chat and pleasantries and asked him about the text. Clearly something was wrong.

"The company told me that they will let me go at the end of the month since my replacement is already hired and has been doing okay. They plan to give me a package before I leave. Anuli, honestly, I don't know how much more I can take. I have been praying about this whole thing, and it is as if God has turned away. *Haba!* Can you imagine? I mean, what would it have cost to have kept me for an extra three months?"

I wanted to comfort him, but I knew Zimako did not like plat-itudes, so I listened while he vented. He railed against the exchange rate that made our currency weak against the Canadian dollar. He was angry with the Nigerian leadership for the endemic corruption that had reduced the country to a malnourished, leprous nation.

I could tell Zimako was not happy to be returning to Canada earlier than planned. "Look on the bright side, babes. At least we will be together again," I said, trying to remind him that we were stronger together and we could weather this storm.

But Zimako was in no mood for that. "I just hope I get a job as soon as I get back. I am tired of this whole thing."

Canada had been Zimako's idea. I was happy in Nigeria, and now I was trying to claw back some happiness by getting on any which way I could in Canada. But I did not feel a need to state the obvious. I deflected the conversation to what I hoped would be a happier topic, Okwe and the impending nuptials. Zimako told me about the trip to the village. Ireti, in spite of her best efforts, had failed to impress Okpue-umu-agbala, who wanted nothing but an Igbo girl from her tribe for Okwe, but Ichie had done his best to make her feel at home.

I smiled to myself. As far as Okpue was concerned, nobody was good enough for her sons.

Her animosity towards Ireti notwithstanding, Okpue could not suppress her excitement at becoming a grandmother, but she insisted that decorum required the couple to see the priest for absolution; she refused to condone fornication. Zimako said the last bit with some amusement in his voice. Afterwards we discussed his plans for returning to Canada.

On the eve of the wedding, I called to speak to Ireti.

"Welcome to the family." I could tell she was very happy and excited about her future with Okwe. There was a lot of noise, music, and merriment in the background.

"Thanks, Anuli. I appreciate the way you and Zimako have really welcomed me. Everyone has been so nice. Makua helped put my bridal shower together, and Chinazo as usual helped with food. They are all taking *aso-ebi*; I have given your own to Zimako to pass onto to you. Do you want me to get it made for you first?"

We talked a little more, and I congratulated her, and offered her a few pearls of wisdom on marriage.

In Igbo tradition, she would be my junior wife, so she would have to defer to me on issues regarding the family. I liked Ireti, and I was happy Okwe had found someone he loved, and who was a good fit in the family, too.

Wedding over, Zimako started organising himself for his final return to Canada. He was under immense pressure. His job had been our safety net, and I think psychologically knowing he had that backup plan had buffered the frustrations of the failures we were experiencing on the Canadian front. With that rug snatched from under his feet, he was now belatedly confronted with the insecurities I had faced. Worse because he felt that as the man, he had to bring home the bacon. Coming back to Canada now, it was for good. All ties were severed; there was no going back. He had said his goodbyes to the family and had to finally embrace Canada and whatever fate had in store.

* * * * *

Zimako returned to Canada and found a lot of changes.
School was resuming in a week. I was busy with preparations and juggling my part-time job. I was no longer available to him each morning to search for jobs. That was the first rude awakening. In his absence, I had become quite independent and carved out a social life for myself with the girls. While he was gone, I had solidified my friendship with Fifi and Afaa, who both called frequently to arrange girly meetups for movies and coffee. I tried to adjust my schedule so I could also spend more time with Zimako, but the changes caused some friction.

On the weekend, I slept in, and kept my diary free so we could be together in an attempt to recapture the magic.

Zimako was lying in bed with his back to me. I gently rubbed his shoulder and ran my fingers through his hairy chest. "Babes," I called gently, hoping he was awake. He seemed frigid, and I could not discern from his breathing if he was awake and ignoring me or if he was genuinely fast asleep. I decided not to disturb him and crept out of bed to make breakfast. I hoped he was not holding a grudge because I had had a busy week and had not been at his beck and call since his return a week ago. I was making scrambled eggs and pancakes, which I knew Zimako liked, and hoped the smell of food was enough to entice him from his slumber. It worked. I saw him come out of the bedroom.

"Hey, babes, are you finally awake?" I asked. He tried to glare at me, but I was determined to do my best to make the time we spent together happy. "I am making pancakes the way you love them."

He took a seat at the dining table and turned on the radio and rubbed his eyes distractedly.

"Sleep well?"

"Well? Under the circumstances, I guess I did. You were out all night with your friends, so what does it matter to you?"

Fifi, Afaa, and I had gone for coffee, and to see the late movie. I went over, planted a kiss on his forehead, and sat on his lap. "Did you miss your baby? I'm sorry, sweetheart," I said, looking into his eyes.

He was silent for a minute. "Okay."

He was still sulking, so I left him to listen to the news while I finished off breakfast. The way to a man's heart, they say, is through his stomach, so I was hoping breakfast would melt his resentment. I did not want to fight fire with fire. I wanted the time we spent together to be quality time, plus I needed him to be in the right frame of mind for us to have a discussion about our finances and what we hoped to accomplish over the next few months. As things were, most of our original plans had not worked out as we had pencilled them. I knew that if we were to have that discussion, I had to gently guide Zimako out of his dark mood.

Once I set out breakfast, I asked him what his plans were for the day. He said he planned to focus on mapping out his strategy, and rebuild his list of contacts and companies to target for jobs. This time he planned to give it all he had, because if one of us did not get a serious job soon, it would be disaster. I listened to him, and decided to ignore the put-down about my job; but the gloom and doom prophesises were weighing on me, and I wanted us to have a sincere conversation without hyperbole and blame.

"Babes, can we spend time today just going over our finances? I know our plans have not panned out as well as we hoped, but we are not doing so badly. Maybe, if we crunched some numbers and put your wonderful brain to work, we might be able to cut out a few things, and stretch our resources."

He glared at me, but I smiled. I could feel the tension, but I felt I had the moral high ground and was willing to be magnanimous, massage his ego a bit, and stay calm. One of us needed to be rational if we were going to get anywhere.

"You want to talk, eh? Okay, let's talk," he answered. He sounded rather cantankerous, so I focussed on my food even though I couldn't taste it. "Let's talk; you want to talk, *ngwa nu.* Let's talk."

I could tell he was spoiling for a fight. I knew this was pent-up anger about my going back to school, but he was being rather vindictive in my mind's eye. What I did, I did for us, and I wished he would open his eyes and see beyond the immediate financial outlay. I bit my tongue, but by now my hold on my temper was tenuous. "Zimako, there is no need to be like this. If there is anything that is bugging you, spit it out; let us deal with it."

"I will tell you what's bugging me. What is bugging me is that we started out this journey with clear goals, but once I turned my back, you veered off to carry out a plan hatched out of desperation. I expected you to know better, given the state of our finances. I'm bitter and stressed and desperately worried because I've lost my job, and what we have in the bank now is all we've got for the foreseeable future. If I was still working, at least we could augment, but now, we are not even sure where the next dollar will come from, and I feel I don't know you anymore. You've changed."

"What do you mean by that?" I asked, no longer ready to take the high road. "I have a job which at least pays some money that we can try to manage with, and still pay my tuition, and keep some savings."

"I will not touch that money, Anuli! See how easy it is to become complacent? You are working as a data entry clerk, and you think it is something to be proud of? You have already begun to accept the status quo. Well, good luck to you. I will not be dragged down that road." He stormed off into the bedroom, leaving me seething and confused.

Zimako and I rarely fought over anything; we always found a way to compromise. I was upset that he was being so stubborn about this, because I was certain I was doing what was best for our family and me.

I was still mulling over the turn of events when Zimako appeared, fully dressed, clearly on his way out. He ignored me when I asked where he was going or if he wanted company. I heard the door shut. I was now alone in the apartment.

This fight was the last thing I wanted.

I had hoped to win Zimako over to my point of view, but he refused to budge. I would be starting school on Monday, and I had hoped we would walk this path together, but my hopes had been dashed. I fell to my knees and prayed to God to forgive me where I erred, if I had not submitted, and to touch my husband's heart.

Zimako did not return until the evening. I was very miserable without him, and I wondered where he had gone. His phone was switched off, and he did not respond to my messages. When I heard the door handle turn, I tried to compose myself. There would be no point trying to query him on his whereabouts, so I was quiet when he came in. I watched him and tried to read his body language. He went through the kitchen to get a drink from the refrigerator and then came to sit down on the couch.

I did not say anything. I remained silent.

After he took a swig of his drink, he turned to me. "I am really mad at you, Anuli, and it is partly your fault."

I sat there, listening to what he had to say. At least he was trying to have a conversation.

"I know you think what you are doing is right. I do not agree and I'm entitled to my opinion. You have committed our resources again, this time to this school thing, and it is a done deal. It's not just about the money, but time you've committed to it as well. I wish we had discussed it and made a plan together. I would never have taken such a step without consulting you. I still believe we should have kept our focus on getting professional jobs in our fields. We have the right education and qualifications to accomplish that. My greatest fear is becoming like one of those people driving taxi cabs and reminiscing about the good old days back home when they were doctors." As Zimako spoke, his voice quivered.

He had spoken of this fear so often, and wanted to avoid being a statistic. Back home we had jeered at stories of professionals who had left home, chasing the pot of gold at the end of the rainbow, only to become hewers of wood and fetchers of water in foreign lands. I listened, consumed by the maelstrom of my innermost thoughts and emotions.

Zimako continued, "So, I will go ahead with the original plan. I will keep looking for proper work." The conversation was over. He stood up and went in.

I sat in the dim light for some time, confused and worried.

What if I was wrong and it did not turn out the way I had planned? Would I end up like Maria, working as a data entry clerk for ten years? I felt so insecure and alone. Tears travelled from my eyes down my cheeks unchecked.

I joined Zimako in bed. He reached out to me and we made love with a ferocity borne out of shattered dreams. It was wild, and I felt him pour out his frustrations. I was spent, but I hoped we would weather this storm, and that the Canadian dream did not become a nightmare.

CHAPTER TWENTY-ONE

Dear Diary,
My first week juggling school, work, life at home, and making
time for myself has been more than I bargained for. How do other
people do it? I had to change my shifts at work around to
accommodate my school timetable. God bless Anita for being so
understanding. This adult education thing is not a joke; my brain
is not what it used to be. The stress at home is not helping matters.
We have an uneasy truce. We have agreed to disagree.

Dinner today was *ogbono* soup and *fufu; sadly, there is no kponmo in Canada.* I had tried to conserve the little local delicacies I brought from home because they were nowhere to be found in Edmonton. The monotony of Chinese takeaways and Canadian cuisine, which I had yet to develop a fondness for, got boring. At those times, Zimako and I fell back on our "swallow" or a good dish of Naija fried rice, *jollof* rice, or *ewa*.

We had been talking about our day. I was telling Zimako about my professors, and how rusty I was, and that it was going to be a steep learning curve, but I wasn't fazed. My real concern was the subtle racism. "It's like they do not expect much from me just because I am black. Every time I raise my hand to answer a question, they look a bit shocked."

"That is the world of *onye oji.* Do you blame them? All the stories they hear about Africa are stories of war, underdevelopment, poverty, and corruption, so what do you have to contribute to the discourse? If you were Asian, *ehen*, then that is a different ballgame."

"You are justifying their attitude, eh?"

"No, but it might work to your advantage that they have set

the bar very low for you. At least you do not have to work too hard to impress anybody."

"It's not that, darling. The CMA requires a certain competence level to meet the perquisite regardless of where the tutors set the bar for me, and then of course there is the big exam after completing the prerequisites before becoming a CMA."

"Oh well, I wish you all the best."

I could tell he was losing interest so I asked him how his day had turned out.

"Well, I don't want to confess negatively, so I won't say bad, but, it's tough out there. I know there is hope. I spoke to Raj; he is now working at the airport."

"As a pilot?" Raj had been a pilot before he came to Canada, and I had been sceptical of his chances of landing such a role in Canada.

"No, but he wants to gain the experience, so he is doing some work at the airport so that at least he can begin to acquire Canadian experience."

"Is it in a professional role, though, or is he a technician of some sort?" I queried, knowing Zimako was very big on remaining in one's field even if it meant getting in at a lower level. That was an underlying accusation he held against my job as a data entry clerk.

"I'm not sure exactly what the role is. He understands that it may take some time to find an airline that will accept him and his credentials, so he has taken this job. He says it will allow him to interact so that when he qualifies, his hours can be transferred onto his licence seamlessly."

Even though Zimako had over time come to accept my job, and his anger at my going back to school had thawed, it remained an unresolved issue, so I found it interesting that he was putting a positive spin on Raj's job at the airport. "So I guess it is a good move for Raj, this new position, hmmn?"

Zimako went on to justify what Raj had done and how he would do the same if he had an opportunity. I listened to my husband, and inwardly I was shaking my head. Zimako had changed. He used to be fair and objective. I was losing the man I used to know and there seemed to be nothing I could do to reverse the situation. He was being so obstinate, it blinded him to any other viewpoint. He continued to hold rigidly onto a plan we had drawn up before coming to Canada and was not willing to revise, review, or reconsider. A wave of sadness overwhelmed me. I was getting tired of the same old fight, the passive aggression, the sarcasm, the subtle provocation. I was exhausted.

"Enough about Raj; I wish him all the best. But did anything turn up for you today?" I asked, trying to keep us from losing the focus.

"No, nothing really. I went to one small engineering company that Zack mentioned is run by an Italian immigrant."

"How did that go?"

"He was very nice. We talked, and he shared his experiences with me. He was probably in his early sixties. He gave me some real insight on what to expect from the job market. He was brutally honest and said that regarding this, my job-hunting, things would still get worse before they began to get better, that I would get despondent and nearly lose hope, but that if I persevered and kept knocking on doors, I would get lucky eventually." Zimako relayed all this in monotone without any conviction, smiling ruefully.

* * * * *

It was pelting down. The weather in spring was rather unpredictable; one minute it was sunny and warm, the next it could turn very wet. We had just exited the class room after a hard day. I was really proud of my performance in the last quiz. I stood by the doors of the faculty and looked out at the pouring rain. I did not dare venture out there! As I stood and watched, I heard a voice from behind.

"Hey, waiting for the rain to clear up?"

I turned to find the voice belonged to one of the guys in my class. I looked at him absently, and he repeated the question. "You waiting for the rain to clear up?"

"It's pouring down, and I'm trying to work out a strategy for getting out there without getting wet."

He stood beside me for some time in silence. His attention was making me a bit uneasy, but I kept looking out at the rain, ignoring him.

"Would you like a ride?" he asked.

I was surprised at his offer of a lift because I did not expect that from Canadians. I was beginning to understand and predict Canadian behaviour patterns. They kept to themselves and minded their business. I weighed his offer in my mind. If I said no, it might come across as rude, and there was no way of predicting how long I'd be waiting for the rain to abate. I decided to accept his offer. "That's very thoughtful of you, sure. Thanks."

"You can wait here, and I'll go get the car."

He brought his car around and I ran out to join him. I was very grateful, and said so.

"Glad to be of assistance. Where are you going?"

I gave him my address, and added, "But you don't have to take me all the way home. You've been so kind. I do not want to take you out of your way, so please drop me at a bus stop and I will find my way home."

"I offered. Don't even worry about it"

I gauged him to be in his very late twenties or early thirties. He participated intelligently in class, and I had noticed that he seemed close friends with a young woman; they seemed to be together all the time. I wondered about that. I was happy I had decided to take the ride. It was raining cats and dogs, and I would have been drenched before my bus came. "Thanks again. My name is Anuli."

"I'm Ryan."

We continued in silence.

"You know, I actually live on the same block as you do?"

I almost jumped out of my skin when he said that. I had never noticed him in the building, but that was no surprise. It was a twenty-six-floor building with six elevators. What were the chances of running into each other? I tried to make light of it. "Are you stalking me?" We both laughed.

"I noticed you are one of the best students in class."

I smiled at the compliment. "I have to put in a whole lot of hard work. I am studying part-time and working part-time, so every minute is precious."

He glanced at me. "You have a real passion for this?"

I laughed, ha, ha, ha. "You do not know the half of it."

He turned to look at me again, and smiled.

What I saw was a perceptive and considerate person. He probably wanted to ask me so many questions but bit his tongue. He was attractive, with dark brown hair and speckled grey eyes. I figured he was about six feet tall. There was something about the way he was talking to me, as just another human being. It wasn't about my blackness or foreignness.

"So are you in school full-time, or part-time?" I asked.

"I'm currently part-time at the moment, but it depends. I could go full-time, too. I just think it's not worth the stress."

"May I ask what you do for a living, then?"

"I am a contractor. I run my own business. We install heating and cooling systems in commercial properties and some residential."

"Mmmm, and you are in an Accounting class because… ?"

He took time to explain his experience. Building his business, he'd had to depend on accountants and advisors, but somehow he hadn't gotten the impression that his best interests were being served, so he decided to get a diploma in accounting and finance.

His story impressed me—the tough road to building his business and getting the recognition of top-notch construction companies. "It's a small firm. I work with a group of subcontractors whose work is of a standard I trust." It was clear that he had pride and dignity in his labour.

We arrived at the underground parking and I thanked him for the ride. I was quite grateful I had gotten a ride home and avoided getting wet.

"Hey, anytime," he replied. We headed to the lift, I to my fifteenth floor and he to his.

Zimako was not home when I arrived. I prepared dinner and then settled down to my assignments. I was becoming a pro at juggling work and school. Of course, that meant I was spending less time with the girls, but we got together as often as we could. I was glad to have formed a strong friendship with them; they were a good support network. Despite this, I felt it would be disloyal to share with them the ongoing friction in my marriage caused by Zimako's resistance to my decision to go back to school. They trusted that we shared our deepest concerns and would be disappointed to find I was bearing such a heavy burden.

I don't know if it was the Nigerian in me, but in some ways I found that I still had attitudes that were very different from those of my Canadian friends. I was accustomed to keeping things to myself, so while I was supportive of Fifi and Afaa and welcomed their confidences, I was not quite as open to them as they were to me; sometimes I felt they opened up a bit too much. My reticence stemmed from my desire to maintain the facade that Zimako and I were blissfully happy. I was embarrassed to admit that he, my loving Christian husband, was bearing a grudge because I had not been a submissive Christian wife. We had failed each other, but I persisted in presenting the world with an image of perfection. It was necessary for my self-preservation.

I had barely settled down to my studies when the phone rang. I let it ring and get picked up by the answerphone. I wanted to focus and accomplish something before Zimako got back. My time was limited, and I did not want to spend it chit-chatting.

"Hello, my friend, it's Kathy! Call me when you can. We have to talk."

When I heard Kathy's message, I felt bad that I had not made time to call and chat. My curiosity was piqued. I wanted to know what she had to say. I made a mental note to get in touch with her also because I'd been thinking of her.

Zimako came back rather late, by which time I was ready for bed. It was unusual for him to be back so late, but I did not want him to see how worried I was. We hardly seemed to communicate honestly these days. Our relationship was like an onion with so many layers of half-truths and bitterness left unspoken. It never used to be like this. One little incident had turned our relationship upside down. Tonight I did not confront Zimako because I was not in the mood for veiled accusations and uncontrolled outbursts. These days a simple question could trigger a row. I would leave it to him to share whatever he wanted.

"Welcome back, babes. How was your day? Hope it went better today," I ventured as he walked in, pulling off his tie and hanging his jacket on the back of one of the dining room chairs.

"I went for a meeting with some guy who wanted to introduce me to someone who could help me. Honestly, people just want to make a fool out of you. I am not sure if that is because I am an immigrant, or if they think I am desperate."

"Hmmm, what happened?"

"In spite of the rain, I met up with this guy who dragged me to Leduc, a town just outside of Edmonton, to attend some fake pyramid scheme sales promotion for Amway! He never revealed what it was, but kept telling me it was a great opportunity and that he was sure I would get the job. I should have seen that coming."

I asked him what Amway was, and he briefly gave me a nutshell description of the scheme. "It is a gathering of some riff-raff where they tell all types of stories about how they have succeeded by selling some products, and how it will soon explode and become the biggest thing in North America. Amway is short for the American Way; they are supposed to be selling the American dream. It just seems like a scam, or shall I say *419*, to me."

I set out his dinner and contemplated staying to keep him company, but decided against it. With Zimako these days, a frustrating day could manifest as a sour mood, and then I would be the one bearing the brunt of his irritation. "I'm off to bed, darling."

"Before you go, I have to send some money home from the account. My father is ill lately and requires medical attention. I plan to send $1,500 back so they can get him to hospital."

I stopped in my tracks. We were just getting by, everyone knew we were not working and Zimako was planning on sending money home. "Zimako, Makua, and Okwe can bear the cost of that, surely. We are barely managing; we cannot afford to send money home, certainly not such a massive sum!"

"We have to do it, Anuli. Okwe just got married, and Makua,

how much does she earn? You know doctors are poorly remunerated at home; she is processing her papers to leave for South Africa. I cannot let my father die, not after all he has done for me. It is my responsibility. You have to understand that."

I was torn. I did not want to be labelled a selfish, bad wife, but it was our money. If he was deliberately trying to be vexatious, he had achieved his aim. I held back from saying something I would regret and said a quiet goodnight.

I fell into bed face down and sobbed. "Oh God! This is such a mess." I punched the pillows, pummelling them to release my frustration. It had been one thing after the other since we came to Canada. We were in no position to send that kind of money home. Who knew when Zimako would find a job, or what the precarious future he had committed us to held? However, he was right; it was an obligation he had to fulfil. Suddenly I realised how selfish and unsupportive I was being. I was so caught up with balancing our finances, I did not even ask how bad his father was, or what was happening to him at the present time.

I realised I was changing. My circumstances were remoulding me. Canada was changing me.

We went to church as usual on Sunday. I saw Kathy with John, who usually was by her side, and headed towards her. As soon as she spotted me, she beckoned me excitedly. Zimako was mingling with some of the other members, so I knew I had time for a quick chat with Kathy. When I got to her, she hugged me really tight and encouraged John to go and say hello to the pastor.

"Why have you not called me? It's almost three weeks since I called you, and you haven't returned my call."

I had been feeling guilty about not returning her call, but had kept putting it off. "Kathy, I'm sorry," I said hugging her back. "It has been overwhelming, what with school and work. Forgive me, I am so sorry."

"Listen, that is fine," she responded conspiratorially. "Actually, I need to talk to you."

I remembered she had hinted at something in her voice message. "What is it, Kathy? Have you got news for me?"

She took me over to one of the seats. "My friend, I have been thinking…" I waited and watched her anxiously, wondering what she had on her mind. "I told you the other day that Nsala has been on my mind."

I nodded, and she continued. "I have decided to take a bold step. You know, Anuli, I have never done anything risky in my life. I have always been very cautious, and never allowed myself to really live life to the fullest. Since you and Zimako came into my life, I have asked myself about many what-ifs. Now at more than sixty, time is running out. I have made up my mind and I've not taken this decision lightly. Believe me, I have given it a lot of thought."

As Kathy spoke, my heart was beating fast. I did not know what was on her mind, and I could wait no more. "What is it, Kathy? What do you want to do?"

"I want to go back to Africa and find the love of my life." She said it in the softest voice. I almost missed it. Her quiet determination reflected in her steely voice.

"Kathy…" I began tentatively, not knowing what to say to her.

"Kathy… " I started again, and reached out to touch her hands, which had been folded on her lap while she spoke. "You need to carefully consider what you want to do. Firstly, in Africa nothing is the way it was all those years ago. Nsala may be married, or… or… or even dead. It is dangerous for a foreigner to go to Africa unaccompanied or unchaperoned. Kathy would be vulnerable on her own in a strange country where she had no friends. Really, Kathy, can we think this over?"

"My mind is made up, Anuli. I am going."

I thought for a minute, then asked her, "Have you called the embassy?"

"No, not yet, but I… "

"So call the embassy, tell them who you are trying to find, and ask if they can help you. They may be able to put you in touch with Nsala. That seems a reasonable starting point."

Kathy seemed to consider my point, and she smiled. "Okay, I will do just that. Tomorrow, I will contact the embassy and let you know." She paused for a moment, then continued. "I still want to go to Africa. I almost gave up on that dream, but now I know I have to go again before I hang up my boots."

I nodded in full understanding. There was something about Africa that was so real; one good visit leaves you yearning for more. It gets into your heart and winds itself around it; you are never the same after a visit.

Zimako walked up to us. He met Kathy with warmth, and they exchanged greetings and updates. Watching Zimako with Kathy, it was easy to see why she would think of her past love in Africa. Zimako made her feel nurtured and cared for; he treated her with cordial respect. Kathy winked at me and left. As had become part of our Sunday ritual, Zimako and I then chatted with Afaa and some new faces who were visiting the church.

* * * * *

On the bus to work, I reflected on how much things had changed since we came to Canada. I missed my old job, my old life, and our house. It was hard not to think of the good life we had when life in Canada was proving so challenging. I looked at the faces of the passengers on the bus, and wondered if the other immigrants felt the way I was feeling. I was early. As I walked from the bus stop to work, I tried to clear my mind and prepare for the day ahead.

I let myself in using the keypad. It was quiet, but I could tell Maria had arrived. I went into my cubicle and said a quick prayer with my head bowed. Prayer done, I was set for the day. I looked up and noticed Brittany lurking at the doorway, smiling; she had a coffee in hand. I liked her. She had rallied around when I was new, and we had become friends at work. She often helped me navigate the sometimes treacherous politics at work; if she had a fault it was her chattiness. This morning, I did not quite feel like chatting, but I could not turn her away.

"Hey, Anuli!" she said.

I smiled at her, wishing she would continue on her way, but trying not to betray my feelings.

"Have you got a few minutes?"

I tried to be tactful. "A little," I replied.

That was the opening she needed. She came in and leaned on

the wall nursing her cup of coffee, and filled me in on the minutiae of her weekend, and wanted to know what I had been up to. This was typical for Monday morning and I dreaded it. Everyone always had some excitement to report, and I often found myself stretching the truth to make my weekend sound exciting. Suddenly the conversation focussed on immigrants. It was something I found my colleagues had little real knowledge about. They based a lot of their comments on racial profiles and false stereotypes. I had my job cut out, explaining the situation to them. Next she was talking about submitting her tax self-assessment and hopefully getting a tax refund. So far, I had not done any taxes, and was not paying close attention to her till I suddenly heard her say, "... at least the government gives you new immigrants some money to help you settle down. Is that a tax-free allowance?"

I had been distracted, nodding and prompting her intermittently, but now she wanted an answer. Brittany did not have an unkind bone in her body and was naïve enough to believe everything she heard. But idle curiosity or not, I still found her insinuations that as an immigrant I was a freeloader hurtful. I gently put away my work and smiled. Getting upset about the misconception would do little to get my point across. I answered her simply. "Brit, surely you do not believe the good government of Canada will hand taxpayers' money to immigrants? If you know what province in Canada does that, please let me know, and I will consider relocating without further ado, as I did not receive any hand-outs when I landed, nor did Zimako."

Brittany turned a deep hue of red. I don't know if that was from embarrassment over realising her stupidity or from dismay at the bitterness in my response. I did not mean to upset her, so I giggled and moved the discussion on, although she suddenly seemed in a hurry to get to her desk.

The day started in earnest, with the usual suspects going out for cigarette breaks and others lingering too long by the water cooler. It was clear that everyone had heard about my response to Brittany, and there was an undertone of concern in the air. Canadians prided themselves on being politically correct and avoiding confrontation. I was not in the mood to play those games today.

Data entry was conveniently a low-bar, entry-level job, but it required fast typing skills. I had a secretary in Nigeria who did my typing. I never learned how to touch-type despite my excellent IT skills, so in my first few weeks on the job I often had to stay late to complete my work. It had been tough, and some colleagues sniggered behind my back, but Brittany had been so supportive. Eventually my speed improved, and in retrospect, I realised that even in an entry-level job there was a lot to learn. I was learning about the Canadian workplace and developing my social skills. Interacting with my colleagues here was different than back in Nigeria, and I sometimes was glad to have started down the ladder. I could not imagine what it must be like, facing challenges in my career without these basic workplace skills.

During my first week at work, I recognised that everyone was expected to eat lunch in the lunchroom, and go out together for lunches when asked to. It was something I was unprepared for, because I was saving every cent and preferred to bring lunch from home, which consisted of my native rice and vegetable stew. It was always fresh, and I wanted to eat in silence, but that was not to be. There was always such curiosity about what anyone was having for lunch, and I was expected to discuss my lunch in enough detail to satisfy their curiosity, which included explaining the ingredients and offering the recipe with enthusiastic generosity. I caught on, and soon, it became something to look forward to.

The workday went very fast, and the next time I looked up at the clock it was nearly time to go home. On my way out I stopped by Anita's office to chat. From the beginning, she had welcomed me and made the workplace inviting. She monitored my progress, and made herself available when I needed her.

"Leaving?" she asked.

"Yes, I have tons of homework, so I'd better go and face it head-on."

"By the way, are you contributing to the lottery pool?"

I laughed. "Oh, Anita, do you really believe that stuff?"

She went on to explain how much she believed in luck, and that no matter how slim the chances were, one had to be in it to win it. "Who knows, someday we might win."

I promised to make my contribution the next day and left, wishing her a good evening. On the bus heading home from work, I reflected on my marriage. Things had not improved between Zimako and me. Communication was still a struggle; to our friends or on the phone to our family back home we pretended everything was hunky-dory. If Zimako was not telling, I would also not tell. Hope was being sucked out of Zimako. He had attended a few job interviews that appeared promising, but none had crystallised into anything. I saw his confidence leaching away, but he did not come to me for solace and I could not reach out to him.

The more down in the dumps my husband was about his continued unemployment, the more he seemed to withdraw into his shell, away from me. There was the occasional flash of passion and tenderness or honest humour, but it never lasted. Every disappointment hit him hard. It hurt me to see what he was going through and I ached for him in my heart, but since he did not accept my comfort and dismissed what I said as platitudes, I focussed on building my life and not letting the animosity engulf me.

Thankfully, I was excelling at school, and gaining the respect of my classmates. Work was great. It was only part-time, it was beneath my qualifications, but it was a great opportunity.

* * * * *

Again when I arrived home, Zimako was not back. This was becoming a habit. It was hard to tell what Zimako was up to these days. I knew he had an interview scheduled for the day, and hoped this would be his lucky break.

I unpacked my books and started preparing our supper.

* * * * *

Zimako left the interview feeling very disappointed and

browbeaten. The questions had not been what he anticipated. It had been a very technical interview, on systems different from what he had worked with back home. Canadian standards and codes were different and it was clear to him that he had come across as inept. Forlorn, and downcast, he knew they would not be calling him back. Tears welled up in his eyes. He felt like such a failure. He just wanted to do what was best for his family, but nothing he tried seemed to work since moving to Canada. He had attended quite a few interviews, and was beginning to wonder if he had set his sights too high for an immigrant. He had never imagined it would come to this. So much was different now, and he could feel the change in himself.

Zimako was convinced Canada had changed Anuli. She did not listen to him anymore; she neither sought nor took his advice. He knew she was slipping away from him. His life was falling apart. He was in a very dark place, and sadly there was no light at the end of this tunnel. He sat down at the shaded bus stop and cradled his head in his hands, pondering his life and where things were going.

Zimako was not accustomed to failure, and his self-esteem had taken a knock from the repeated rejections. He lost his swagger and self-assurance. Initially, when he got a call for an interview, he got excited, as few as those calls were; now he responded to those calls with trepidation at the prospect of sitting before a panel of judges. He feared for his future.

The fire was no longer burning in his belly, and he was wondering why he had thought Canada was such a bright idea. He had started avoiding calls from his friends back home, knowing those conversations would put him under more pressure.

He was spiralling down into depression, but was powerless to pull himself back. Zimako sat staring aimlessly into space. He did not notice the other commuters around him, and did not care; his dignity had deserted him. He had always found it improbable that he would settle for a blue-collar job, but with limited options, there seemed to be nothing he could do. Before arriving in Canada, he had heard these stories and thought that it was a lack of planning, determination, and persistence that would make a professional succumb to a low-level job, and he had rushed to judge. "That would never be us." He thought he knew better, and was better. Those thoughts came back to taunt him now.

It was getting rather late, but Zimako did not feel ready to face Anuli. Instead he decided to call at Kojo's McDonald's franchise. He knew Kojo would be there; to clear his head he decided to walk.

When he arrived at the McDonald's, it was not very busy. He went to place his order. Kojo must have seen him from the monitor and came out from the back to talk to him.

"My brother, good to see you!" Kojo intoned in his heavily accented English.

"Hey," Zimako replied none too enthusiastically.

Kojo was perplexed by the flatness in Zimako's voice; he had not seen Zimako in this mood before. "Listen, I have another hour before my shift is over. Are you in a hurry?"

"I can wait," Zimako replied, waving him back. He took his tray to the far corner and settled down to his meal.

As he chewed on his chicken, he began to consider what he had given up to be here. He appreciated the quality of life Canada offered. Unlike his home country, Nigeria, Canada had functional infrastructure, with pipe-borne water from a public source, an efficient power supply, a criminal justice system that could not be bought and sold with cash, honest policing, good education, health care, excellent road networks, and a government that cared, and he knew he could go on and on. Zimako shook his head in despair, and the realisation that he could not go back. No one appreciated what he was going through. Life as he knew it had hit a dead end. He was going to have to manage his expectations and reassess his options without his previous bias.

He considered the options he had been offered, including moving to a small rural community. That was laughable. At the moment, living in Edmonton, a so-called multicultural metropolitan city, he still experienced subtle racism and was sometimes treated as a curiosity to be gawked at. He knew life in a rural area would be even more difficult. People tended to be more narrow-minded in the smaller cities, and job opportunities were few and far between. Moreover, Zimako was of the opinion that moving out of the city was a retrograde step. In the backwaters he would rot and decay. He was at the prime of his life; smaller towns moved at a slower pace. What did they have to offer him?

Zimako was confused. What could he do? His heart felt heavy and the darkness that engulfed him was overwhelming. In Nigeria, Ichie's health was faltering, and he had to send funds back home to ensure his father was receiving the best of care. Without a job, how could he even meet all the obligations that he was faced with? He sighed deeply, not knowing what to do. He now began to appreciate Kojo's travails and saw in a new light how he had risen to the challenges that had been thrown at him. He shook his head at the ignorance of his earlier snobbery. Those who settled for blue-collar jobs in Canada were not failures.

He was tired and confused and frustrated and depressed. Zimako bowed his head again.

Kojo came up to Zimako and saw him with his head bowed. He pulled the chair beside him and reached to squeeze his shoulder. "Man, *whatsup?*"

Zimako shook himself up from his brooding reverie.

"What is the matter, my brother?" he asked Zimako, concern written all over his face.

Zimako did not know where to begin. He seemed lost for a moment and looked blankly at Kojo, staring forward without focus. Kojo shook him again by the shoulder. "Talk to me, man. Tell me, what is it?"

Zimako began to speak. He told Kojo of his failed efforts to secure a decent job, and his not-too-stellar performances in interviews. He confided about his ailing father back home. As he spoke, his pain and confusion were evident. He had expected a rosy reception when he dreamt of coming to Canada, but things were going awry. Kojo kept nodding as he spoke. Zimako tried to smile at the end, but it came out as a grimace. "I don't know where to go from here."

Kojo had experienced the same situation and faced those same demons, but he knew Zimako was a proud man who had come to

Canada with high expectations. Kojo decided to broach the subject of lowering his expectations. "Look, man, you do not have to give up hope. What you are going through is the story of many immigrants that have come to Canada. Sometimes it has worked out as expected; other times, it takes longer to achieve the dream. Look at me. I was once destitute in Canada, but now I could be considered a success story. It is not the end of the world. I know it looks bleak, but you can turn it around." He paused to make sure Zimako was listening. "Look at these setbacks as a blessing in disguise. You can start small, get a decent-paying job on a lower level... " He watched Zimako's reaction as he spoke, then continued. "There are many such jobs out there, and it is not permanent, just a way of getting your foot in the door, start earning some money before you run out, while you still pursue your dreams. Hope is not lost. See it as a stepping stone."

Zimako listened intently to Kojo. He was hurt and embarrassed that he had thought Kojo was not successful, and now he saw that he may have judged too harshly. It was difficult for him to climb down from his high horse, and he wondered how much lower he would descend if he started sliding downwards. The dream had become a nightmare.

Kojo continued. "There are many doctors, lawyers, pharmacists, even engineers who had to find a way to just make ends meet initially, but, if you are determined, you will achieve your goal. You have a very beautiful and supportive wife. You have not lost everything."

Zimako was listening as he considered Kojo's advice. It was a bitter pill to swallow. "I will think about all you've said," he said in a low whisper, almost to himself.

Kojo knew it was a difficult situation for Zimako. He had come to know Zimako, and had gotten a glimpse into his life in Nigeria. It was obvious this was a disappointing impasse. Both men sat in silence, each contemplating their lives. Kojo spoke first. "I know someone; his company is hiring." He was hesitant to continue; he did not want to offend Zimako, or appear to be railroading him. He paused midsentence. "Listen, it is getting late. Anuli will be wondering where you are, and Fifi will be expecting me to come home before she leaves for her shift."

They both stood up and walked out into the sunset. As they parted ways, Kojo promised to call and check up on Zimako later in the week.

CHAPTER TWENTY-TWO

> *Dear Diary,*
>
> *I can't believe Kathy is determined to go to Africa. I have tried to give her more reasons not to go, but nothing will deter her. She has even suggested I take a break from Canada and come along. She has received a package from Congo with information on Nsala and has been so excited about it. I do not want her to be disappointed or heartbroken. They say love conquers all, but now I am not so sure.*
>
> *Zimako has been so moody the last few days. He said there is a temporary change in plans. He is now looking for a blue-collar job. I know this is difficult for him. I hope we can weather this storm together.*
>
> *It has not been easy. I miss our old life. I miss how we used to be.*

I had never visited Kathy's home. But when I walked into her apartment, it was everything I imagined it would be. It was bright and airy, and tastefully done up in an eclectic style. I loved the abstract lush rug, in the centre of the living area, which drew in the Victorian buttoned tub-shaped chairs, with floral upholstery on cabriole legs framing a weathered tan leather couch. A bookshelf in the alcove beside the fireplace overflowed with books, and to the corner was her computer and workstation; the aroma of fresh baking wafted from her kitchen.

"Something smells good," I said.

"I baked some blueberry cake. Would you like to try some with a glass of milk?"

I was delighted. I knew this was a special visit. Kathy had

sounded very excited on the phone, and I wanted to hear her big news. Once we were settled with our cakes and milk, the conversation turned to my family in Africa. She always enquired politely about my parents and siblings, and I gave her my updates. She kept current on what was happening in Nigeria and I was impressed with her grasp of the local politics.

"Well, enough about me, Kathy. How are you, and what have you been up to?"

She smiled, and got up to pull a folder from the workstation.

"I received this documentation from Congo. They found Nsala! He is alive. Oh, Anuli, I can hardly believe my luck!"

I could hardly believe it either. It was such a stretch to imagine that Kathy could locate Nsala after such a long time. I cautiously received the news. "The same Nsala?"

"Yes, Anuli, the same Nsala, my Nsala. I have spoken to him. He remembers me! Anuli, I am going to Congo."

This was incredible. Africa was different from Canada and Africans are different from Canadians. I was sceptical about Kathy going to Africa.

"Hmmm, Kathy, give me details. You know I have my misgivings about this adventure you wish to embark on."

Kathy then brought me up to date on how she had hired a private investigator to help find Nsala in Congo with the sketchy details from her youth. She had made contact with the Canadian consulate in Congo as well. The PI worked fast and a few weeks later presented her with a dossier on Nsala. She learned that he had recently retired from the University of Kinshasa. He had lost his wife several years ago and had four grown-up children, the youngest of whom had graduated last year. She had obtained a number where he could be reached and spoke with him. She was very excited.

"Does he know you are planning to visit?"

"Not yet. He was shocked to hear my voice after all these years. We talked for a while, and he has promised to call me back."

I wondered if Nsala was as excited about the reunion as my friend Kathy was. She seemed more alive than I had ever known her to be. She was glowing, and I could not help but share her joy at locating her true love. She stood up and headed down the hallway. I guessed she was going to her room. It was a one-bed apartment, with high ceilings and generous dimensions. I looked around and noticed the beautiful paintings that adorned the walls. One was of particular interest, and I went closer to get a better look. I smiled. I understood why it looked familiar. It was a painting of a city in motion, a small town in Africa. Memories came flooding and tears welled up in my eyes. I missed home.

Kathy returned with a bundle of letters carefully bound in blue ribbon. "Look, I wanted to show you—some old letters from Nsala."

I touched it and smiled. "You kept them all these years."

Kathy nodded. "I did. In the beginning it meant so much to me. Then we lost touch and the memories seemed to fade, but after some time, I would remember and wonder how he fared and what happened to him, and now that is all I can think of."

Kathy and I sat down, and she shared her memories of Africa with me. I let her talk. Her love for Africa was evident, and I found myself hoping that she was not on a wild goose chase.

* * * * *

I sat across the table from Ryan. Our lectures were over for the day, and we had gotten into the habit of stopping for coffee and whatnot before parting ways. Sometimes he dropped me off at home. We had gotten to know each other better, and I felt comfortable with him. He understood the pressures of juggling school and work. He told me about his contracts and details about his work. He was currently working on a new job, which he said was his biggest so far. He discussed the challenges he encountered and his uncertainties with me. "I might have to drop this semester to focus on the business," he said sadly. "I need to make sure I am not screwing my clients over. The demands of school are way too much, and I have been working on getting this contract for the past three years. It is huge, and could be my big break."

I was nursing my cup of coffee as Ryan spoke. I could hear his frustration. When I did not say anything, he reached across and held my hand. It was the first time Ryan had touched me. It sent electric waves through my body. I withdrew my hand as he jolted in surprise, quickly withdrawing his hand. Our eyes met across the table and I knew he'd felt what I felt.

"I am so sorry." He was blushing; I was embarrassed at my own reaction to him. I had not anticipated it and mentally downplayed it.

"It is a tough choice, but you have to decide what your goals are, and that should ultimately guide your decision-making process."

He seemed even more confused by my answer. "I was hoping you'd tell me what to do."

His answer took me unawares. "Me? Why? How?" I was flustered. I think he was enjoying my confusion.

He looked deep into my eyes, unabashed. "Don't you know?"

His voice suddenly sounded husky. I couldn't breathe and my heart was pounding. I felt trapped, yet deliriously happy. I knew what he wanted to say. I waited to hear the three words.

"You're so wise."

I was relieved, but somewhat disappointed at his response.

He continued, "It always seems so black and white to you. You cut through the morass and always get to the point. I thought I could take advantage of your insight."

"Oh, me? Wise?" was all I could manage.

If he felt my disappointment, he did not show it. "I'm at a crossroads now and don't want to make the wrong decision. Will you think it through and tell me what you think? I really respect your opinion."

I promised to give it further thought. I took a final swig of my now lukewarm latte and set the mug down with a force that reflected my mood. "I am just about ready to leave. Are you?"

He nodded, and we headed to the car park.

I had not asked Ryan if he was in a relationship. He knew I was married and had arrived in Canada with my husband. A few women flirted with him in class, but everyone knew we were friends and often rode home together. Sometimes one of the women would walk with us to the car, and I was careful to give him privacy on those occasions. Ryan did not discuss his relationships and I did not pry.

After what had happened in the cafeteria, I wondered if it was wise to continue to ride home with him. I now realised how vulnerable I was. Although Zimako and I had our problems, I had never entertained any thoughts of straying.

The vehicle was an intimate enclosure and I was very conscious of Ryan. I focussed my attention on passing traffic to keep my thoughts from dwelling on this festering attraction.

"Anuli... what happened... eh... " he started; I did not look at him or say a word. I was in turmoil. How could I let myself lust after another man?

"I am so sorry," he finally said.

I did not say a word. We drove home in silence. The silence was not uncomfortable, but it was unusual. He was easy to talk to, and very engaging, but I was so distraught by my reaction to him I wanted to shut him out. I did not want to encourage him. I did not want to betray Zimako. I was a married woman. I was not available. Ryan was good looking, and financially well-off. If I did not guard my heart, I would be in danger.

When we got home, I thanked him politely and walked to the elevator. I wanted to put as much distance between us as possible, but he was not going to let me go so easily. In a few quick strides, he caught up with me, grabbed my arm, and swung me to face him, an action which brought me up against his rock-hard chest. He held me close and looked down at me tenderly; I could smell his natural musk mingled with aftershave. I was overcome by his closeness. He lowered his face and I shut my eyes in a moment of weakness, anticipating what I knew would come next.

I heard his voice in my ear. "I have done nothing wrong." He let go of me gently, and I ran to the stairway, avoiding the elevators. I was breathing hard and my heart was pumping against my chest as I opened the heavy doors of the parking basement and headed up the stairs. He must have sensed my desperation. It was almost humiliating. By the time I got to the fifth floor, I slowed to a walk, having dissipated my emotional adrenalin. I tried to compose myself as I continued to make my way to our fifteenth-floor apartment. What was happening to me?

Ryan.

So now what?

How did I let myself get to this point?

I was utterly confused. Ryan and I had become friends, I knew he liked me, but I had not expected to react to him with such animal passion. I tried to calm down; I took deep breaths and swallowed. I was almost home. I was not sure if Zimako would be there, but I did not want him to ask me questions I wouldn't be able to answer honestly. I leaned against the wall, and checked my appearance in my small compact mirror. I reapplied my lipstick, recapped it, and took the final stairs to our floor.

When I let myself into the apartment, Zimako was in the living room on the phone. He turned when I entered, but waved perfunctorily and went back to his call. I made a quick detour to the bedroom, wanting to rid myself of the clothing that must stink of Ryan. I hurriedly undressed and went in to have a shower. I ran the water till it was scalding hot and stepped in, lathering my soap with my exfoliating gloves all over my body to scrub off Ryan's touch and proximity.

There was a knock on the bathroom door. "Yes?" I wondered why Zimako was knocking.

"I am going out. I need to send some money to Nigeria. I want to take $700 to send by Western Union."

Because the tap was running, I was not sure I heard him, but I knew he had mentioned money. I turned down the tap so I could hear him. "What?!" My heart was palpitating.

He was silent for a while. I was waiting. I couldn't leave the bathroom because I had soap all over my face and body. When I did not speak he repeated, "I am going to send money home by Western Union." I heard his footsteps as he left and the door shut. I was angry. How could Zimako deplete our resources to send money to Nigeria knowing our situation? Why were his brothers and sisters not contributing to help pay the bills for their dad's health care? I finished having my shower, still fuming at Zimako, and waited for him to return.

My emotions were a mess.

I tried to concentrate on getting some assignments done, but I could not get my mind to focus. After a while, I dumped it, and went to get supper ready. I started to feel calmer as I sorted out my thoughts and feelings. Zimako and I needed to talk. I determined to have a real chat with Zimako about our finances. My job covered what I had to pay for tuition, and a bit extra, but our savings were going down fast, and Zimako had yet to find a job.

When Zimako walked through the door, I was ready. I welcomed him home and invited him to have his supper.

He declined. "I already ate something."

I was upset that he had decided to eat out, but decided not to make an issue of it. "Zimako, we need to talk."

"What is it, Anuli? Wait, I know. It is because I sent money home. Well, I have news for you. We both worked for the money in that account, and I have as much right to spend it as you do."

His pre-emptive strike caught me off guard. I had the evening all well planned in my mind, but it was not working out the way it should. I was tempted to respond with similar aggression, but did not want a slanging match. The apartment walls were thin, and if we raised our voices, the neighbours would hear. So I took a seat, and invited Zimako to sit down, too.

He refused. "I will stand. Just say what you need to say."

I swallowed hard to keep my emotions in check. "Zimako, you are right. It is about the money. You know we cannot continue this way. The demands will keep coming, and we will soon find ourselves on the streets if we are not careful."

Zimako laughed in derision. He was laughing at me. "Oh, you are afraid, eh? You think we will become homeless? Well, I just want you to know that I will be starting a job soon. They are processing the criminal and credit checks before I resume."

This information caught me unawares. He had mentioned seeking a non-professional job whilst waiting for his dream job. We had not been communicating, but I was shocked to be in the dark about something so monumental. We had become strangers.

It put a new complexion on the whole situation. I couldn't hide my surprise. "Oh, when?"

"I am sure you think you are the only one who has any sense. Listen, I do not have to report my activity to you. And there is a lot you do not know. So please do not interrogate me. If you are finished with talking, I have to go and sleep." With that, he departed, leaving me feeling redundant and irrelevant.

I sat for a while digesting the bombshell. We needed every dollar, but it was becoming more obvious that we were living separate lives in Canada. He did not know or care what I was doing, and I tried to convince myself without success that the feeling was mutual. He did not provide any details about the type of work. I guessed he was now doling out information on a need-to-know basis. I would just have to wait and see.

I turned to my studies to try and get some work done. My time was so precious, and I was determined to achieve excellent grades. "Please help me, God, so I can finish school and pass my CMA at the first sitting."

I remembered Ryan, and what he had asked me to think about. I wondered about him. Men were funny creatures. Was he playing games with me? Had he sensed I was vulnerable and decided to take advantage of me? Was he looking for something serious or did he just want a fling? What about the hordes of women who kept throwing themselves at him? Or did he just want to sample black meat? If he genuinely liked me, was I in a position to do anything about it?

I dreaded seeing Ryan in school the next day. I was still trying to understand what was going on between us, and was not sure I'd be able to act normal and nonchalant. I planned to avoid him and make a quick getaway at the end of classes. There was no escape. As soon as our lecture was over, he found me. "Anuli, we need to talk."

I did not trust myself alone with him, but did not have a ready excuse.

"Listen, I want to apologise about yesterday. I am not sure what came over me." He looked so contrite, it was almost cute. I smiled as he continued. "Okay, Anuli, I guess you know how I feel. I have wanted to tell you for a while now, but... I... I wasn't sure how you'd respond." I could tell he was watching my reaction. "And I know, I know, there is no future in it, so... if you'll let me, I will just go on being your friend."

When he finished speaking, I still did not know what to say. How did I get to the point where a white man fancied me and I reciprocated his feelings?

"Thank you, Ryan. I... I am so sorry."

"So, can I still keep taking you home? I promise to behave myself. I just want to be with you."

I knew he was doing me a favour taking me home. Although I had a transport card, it was so convenient to just ride with him. I knew I should say no at this point and get out while I could, but I allowed myself to be convinced that it was okay to keep accepting his kind offer to drive me home. I reasoned that as long as we both knew we could only be platonic friends, then I was safe.

We headed to the car park. Everything seemed magically back to normal. We talked about achieving work-life balance as he complained that he had probably bitten off more than he could chew.

"Maybe you really should drop out and focus on the job. Once it is done, you can always carry on from where you stopped."

"Are you trying to get rid of me?" he asked.

"What? And lose my private chauffer? Not a chance!"

We both laughed, and I knew everything was going to be fine.

* * * * *

Zimako suddenly got up and started getting dressed. I guessed he was going out. I was up studying. "Where are you going?" It was almost ten p.m., too late to be going anywhere.

He did not respond, but got his stuff together, and when he got to the door he gruffly said, "I am going to work. I will be back sometime around seven a.m." With that he shut the door behind him.

I knew nothing about what was happening in my husband's life. What kind of job was he doing that would take him out so late in the night? I went to the drawer and started going through his things. I felt bad that our relationship had deteriorated to the extent where I was now snooping to discover everyday information about my husband. Then I saw the envelope labelled "Armed Guards." I hurriedly opened it, and read through. Zimako had been offered a job with them after successfully passing the physical, with a clean security and credit check. His starting pay was $17 per hour for a three month probationary period, and if confirmed, he would then be paid $18.50. I folded it and put it back carefully. As I tucked it away, I espied another letter and reached in to see what it was. It was from PCMG, our career managers! I had often wondered what had become of them. I pulled it out and read through. It was an invitation to a settlement meeting addressed to us and the other members of the group. I put it away. Zimako had never mentioned it to me.

I began to wonder if what we had could honestly be described as a marriage. Zimako was moving on, and I was just a spectator in the side-lines of his life. He had not let me know about his job. I did not even know how his father's health was faring. Should I sit down with him and try to talk things over? All my attempts at rapprochement had been rebuffed. "Zimako, O! Zimako."

I knew my husband was a very proud man and I knew that taking a job as a guard had to be a big blow to his ego. And because he was not naturally a duplicitous person, having to keep it secret from his friends and family back home would be another burden weighing heavy on his heart. Nonetheless, just as I was enjoying my job and giving it my best, I was confident that he would apply himself to the job and become an asset to them. My husband, a security guard, *chei*! "Canada, O Canada! Look what you have done to us."

My heart was palpitating. I clutched my left breast and wondered if there was any remnant in our relationship, in our beings, left to salvage; if after these trials it was possible to emerge unscathed; I somehow had my doubts. I wondered whom I could confide in, feeling so sad, I shut my books. I wanted to call Chiamaka, my sister in Lagos, and tell her the truth of what I was going through. I knew she would feel my pain and side with me, but I was reluctant to wash our dirty linen in public. This was my marriage, till death do us part. What doesn't kill you makes you stronger. I would persevere. We had been good together; our relationship was worth fighting for. I decided to make another attempt, for whatever our future was worth, to talk things over with Zimako.

My first step in the grand plan was to do unto him as I wanted him to do unto me. I had made him place his job schedule on the refrigerator just like I had.

Timing was pivotal. I figured it was best to plan the "Restoration of Harmony" talk for a time when neither of us was likely to be rushing off to work or too tired to engage. I got lucky.

$$* \ * \ * \ * \ *$$

On Saturday, we had just finished a nice lunch of *onugbu* soup and *fufu* and were both relaxed and sated. I had chosen *onugbu* soup because Zimako loved it. It seemed the ideal time to approach the matter. "Sweetheart, *nna'm*, we need to talk about us."

He patted the seat beside him. I thought that was a good sign, because I was seated across from him. I smiled. "Darling, I am serious. We need to talk honestly and openly, please. For the sake of what we had before, we really need to talk."

Something in my pleading tone must have touched his heart. He seemed to settle deeper into the chair, folded his elbows across his chest, and responded, "Okay, I am listening. What is it?"

In a gentle, non-accusatory tone, I told him how I missed my friend and my soul mate, how we had swept so many things under the carpet, how I felt we had let circumstances drive us apart, and that now things were spiralling out of control and we were not taking decisions together as one unit, but as separate individuals. I said it hurt that we were evolving apart and going in different directions. I acknowledged that we both had a role to play in the secrecy, the deception, and lack of trust. As I spoke to him, I noticed his discomfort, but he let me finish. When I was done, he was not smiling.

"For the sake of what we had before? But you, Anuli, are not who you were before. You have changed," he said coldly.

"What do you mean? How have I changed?"

"Were we not doing just fine till you, Madam Know-It-All,

unilaterally registered yourself for school and took a part-time job? Even though as a unit we had agreed we would tough it out and not lower our standards? Who started it? Was it me, or you? I'm not in the mood for your selective memory and accusations."

I told him I was hurt that he seemed to blame it all on me, and not on his inability to see my point of view, his inflexibility, his grudge bearing, and passive-aggressive behaviour.

The gloves were off, we traded blame, and soon we were almost yelling. It became a game of whose voice was louder. I was close to tears. This was not how I planned it. Harmony was supposed to be restored. None of this was making any sense. "Just stop! Stop it!" I yelled. "Why didn't you tell me about the settlement from PCMG?"

"Oh, so I no longer have any privacy in this house, eh? You have been rifling through my stuff?" He rose from his seat and towered over me in an intimidating manner. I was not backing down. I stood up, and it was clear we were both determined to give fire for fire.

"Yes, I have. How else will I find out anything? You have been hiding stuff from me!"

There was so much venom and bitterness between us. The argument raged on with finger-pointing, accusations, and counter-accusations. We argued about money, honesty, and truthfulness. We were going full blast at each other.

* * * * *

Darcy picked up the phone and dialled 911.

"Yes, caller, how may I help you?"

"I think my neighbours are having a big fight. I am concerned."

* * * * *

I was tired of arguing. We were getting nowhere, so I walked out on him and headed for the room. Suddenly, there was a knock on the door.

I heard the latch hold, so I guess Zimako opened the door to the caller. It was difficult to make out the muted voices, but I heard the latch unhook, and I decided to go out and see what was happening.

I saw a Royal Canadian Mounted Police (RCMP) officer and nearly ran back into the room. He called after me, and I heard him ask Zimako, "Is that your wife?"

Zimako was looking really quite frightened. I had never seen him look like that. He was afraid of what I might tell the officer.

"Ma'am, are you okay?"

I nodded my head, just wanting him to be gone. "I am fine." I wanted the ground to open up and swallow me.

He looked at me very closely, then asked gently, "Has this man threatened you?" He looked at Zimako over his shoulder. "Are you afraid for your safety? Do you want to press charges?"

I was taken aback. This was very serious. Zimako was still standing back, and I knew he was waiting for what I had to say. "No, I am not afraid. He has not threatened me, and I will not be pressing charges. Thank you for attending; please leave now."

He looked closely at me, and once he decided to give me the benefit of doubt that I was fine, he nodded and thanked me. "Very well, ma'am. If you need anything, call me." He brought out his card, handed it to me, and then departed.

You could have heard a pin drop.

A few moments later, Zimako got dressed and left the apartment.

It was quiet.

I was shaken; things had indeed spiralled out of control.

Who had called the RCMP?

Were our voices so loud?

I tossed and turned in bed, wondering how we would claw our way out of this prison.

CHAPTER TWENTY-THREE

> *Dear Diary,*
> *Since that police incident two weeks ago, I have hardly seen Zimako. I think he is avoiding me. I don't know how much more of this I can take. Maybe I should see a marriage counsellor or talk to our pastor. I don't want to be unfaithful, but Ryan is such a comfort. He understands me perfectly. I wonder where Zimako goes day and night. Does he have a woman in whose arms he is finding succour? I don't think so; he would never do that. Even now, I somehow know he is an honourable man.*

"Anuli, please talk to me, please," Ryan pleaded. I was not sure I should spill my heart out to him. Zimako and I had had our differences in the past, and had always found a way to resolve them, respecting our differences. Granted, things had been bad, and were not what they used to be, but I had still retained some hope for our future. After what had happened two weeks ago, I was still reeling from the venom that had been spewed by that altercation.

Concerned for me, Ryan had been persistent the past two weeks, wanting me to confide in him. He insisted I talk or else... I was very amused at his playful threat, but he had demonstrated his concern and I was very touched by it.

"Where are we going, Ryan?" I couldn't recognise where we were.

He was looking at me strangely. "Anuli, I want to do something for you that I hope will help you. I want to take you to a spa. Hopefully, some of the tension that you're shouldering can be eased out of your body, and you can relax. Is that something I could interest you in?" He suddenly seemed vulnerable. He wanted me to say yes.

After some consideration, I admitted it was not a bad idea. I was under real pressure, finding it impossible to concentrate on anything. "That's really thoughtful, thank you." I smiled and squeezed his hand.

He seemed relieved. His smile was genuine. "You are a special woman. I just want to try to make things bearable for you in any way I can." He was almost overcome.

We drove in silence, enjoying the weather, and the scenery. It had been ages since anyone had done something nice for me. I did not realise how much the struggles in Canada had taken their toll on me. Ryan made me feel cosseted, appreciated, and surprisingly attractive. We soon arrived at a spa outside of the city; it was like a resort, with a rolling landscape, very picturesque.

We headed to the reception area, where we were welcomed. I realised Ryan had made reservations ahead of time. I was really touched. I began to feel very nostalgic and saddened because it reminded me of the life Zimako and I used to share. I felt tears begin to stream from my eyes. I tried to wipe them away.

The woman handed me some brochures, and another woman came and led me away. I lost sight of Ryan as I was led to the inner chambers. Soft music and mood lighting relaxed me, and I began to feel lighter. She showed me to a room where I was given a fluffy, white bathrobe to change into and directed to the treatment room where I would receive my pampering. I changed and relaxed on the couch, waiting.

My therapist intuitively seemed to know what I needed. The massage was relaxing and rejuvenating. I was rubbed and scrubbed; my face was plumped, massaged, and soothed. I began to feel the tension that had engulfed me dissipate bit by bit until I was languidly lolled into a blissfully hypnotic state of relaxation. I must have fallen asleep at some point because the next I knew, I woke up in the dimly-lit room and realised I was alone. My therapist came back in and suggested I have a warm soak in the bathtub. I finished and got back in my clothes. I felt like a different woman as I made my way back to the reception area. I was hoping to find Ryan waiting for me. The receptionist smiled and pointed to a large bouquet of flowers. "From the man who brought you here. He had to leave, but there is a ride waiting outside to take you home."

It was unlike anything that had ever happened to me. I had been feeling so unloved and depressed, my schoolwork was suffering, and as for work, I had withdrawn into my shell; now I felt so much better. I spied a small card in the midst of the fragrant red and white roses which simply read, *"From Ryan, wanted to make you smile again."* I smiled when I read that. I was sad that I could not take the flowers home. I kept the card. I offered the bouquet to the driver and asked him to give it to someone special.

* * * * *

I was on a high. The longer summer days meant that although it was seven p.m., it was still bright daylight outside. I stepped into our apartment and noticed Zimako was not there. We were virtually living as flatmates. I went to the refrigerator to check his work schedule. He had removed it.

I felt sad.

I settled down for the evening, not sure of what it would bring. Was Zimako coming back later or was he on the night shift? Ironically, I was glad to have the space to myself. I lay on the bed and reflected on what was going on between Ryan and me. Was it platonic? A friend helping out a friend in distress, or was there more to it? I did feel better after my spa treatment, and the tension that left me aching, which I hadn't even acknowledged, had all but disappeared.

I decided to just call it a night and go to bed.

Zimako must have come in very late. I felt his hands moving all over me, caressing me and undressing me. His touch was electric; he was kissing me and holding me so close. It was just how I imagined it would be. He was very gentle. "You know how much I love you," I heard him say. I did not want him to stop. "Please, baby, touch me." He teased and teased till I was unable to hold back. I played his game, too. I teased and tweaked and we had fun. I was laughing and crying at the same time.

* * * * *

Afaa sat on the bench beside me. "I am sure both of you will somehow work it out. You are both great role models for many young people in church."

When I first told her about the problems I was having with Zimako, she was astounded. She planned for us to meet and talk. I had been holding back from sharing, in the hopes that things would improve with Zimako, but nothing had changed. I could not bottle it in anymore. I had tried to be strong for so long, but now I knew I need help. I had run out of ideas. Meanwhile, Ryan was becoming bolder in his advances, and I was hungry for affection. I needed to share all of this with someone who could help me sort through the quagmire.

"Have you sought counselling? You guys have been under tremendous pressure; maybe it is taking its toll on you."

Indeed, we had been grappling with a lot of issues, as individuals and as a couple, and though nothing had gone according to plan, I was still hopeful that we would overcome. I knew Zimako was disappointed that we had aspired for much and seemed to be settling for so much less, but even then, I didn't think he was ready to down tools and hotfoot back to Nigeria.

"Do your sister and parents know what you are going through? Are they aware of the challenges you are facing?" she asked.

"Surely you jest, Afaa. I can tell you how they will react. Dad will offer to send us money, which will upset Zimako. Mum will never forgive him if she thinks he is making me miserable, even if we make up in the future."

"Point taken; so what is the way forward?"

"Afaa, if I had all the answers, I wouldn't be talking this through with you. I need fresh, unbiased eyes. I need help with my marriage urgently because I think I might be falling in love with Ryan."

Before I finished, I realised I had never mentioned Ryan to anyone, and she latched onto the name. "Ryan? Who's Ryan?"

That was a slip of the tongue. How could I be so stupid as to bring Ryan's name up when I was hoping to garner sympathy for my fragile marriage? The genie was out of the bottle. Afaa wanted details. She was waiting for me to answer the question.

Casting my eyes around furtively, I lowered my voice and told her about Ryan, trying to make clear that so far, even though my emotions were confused, we had not been physically intimate. "He is just a friend, a very good friend."

I looked at Afaa. I could tell she was dismayed. "Anuli, you are better than this. What is wrong with you? I know things are not easy between Zimako and you, but you are married to him, and you owe it to yourselves to at least explore all your options before you allow yourself to seek solace elsewhere." She was clearly unhappy about this development, and did not hide her feelings about it, but did not want to judge me. "Anyway," she continued coyly, now smiling, "talking about new lovers, I have found someone."

She had been dating actively online, and she had met a few people from the site with no real success so far. "When did this happen?" I winked at her. "Is it the new flavour of the month or are we talking real potential?"

"I believe it is serious. He and I have been chatting for nearly two months. He is smart and funny, plus we share the same thoughts about life. Actually, I know I am making him sound perfect, but he has told me he is not. He has made his own mistakes in life, and is better off for it. I like him, I really do."

"Afaa, I am happy to hear this. Has Fifi met him? Do we get to meet him at some point?"

"He does not live in Edmonton. He lives in Toronto, and that is something I am struggling with. He's never been to Alberta, and from what he's heard he doesn't think he's missing much. You know, that there are rednecks here, and the people here can be rather prejudiced."

She laughed, and I could see how happy she was about him.

"So we've arranged for me to visit him in Toronto sometime in the next few weeks. I know online communication and chemistry may be quite different than face-to-face, real-life communication and chemistry. Because of that, even though I'm excited and hopeful, I'm trying to rein in my expectations and see the meeting as just a date to get to know someone better."

"Hmmn, seems like you guys are moving quite fast. I hope he is genuine, Afaa. I am rooting for you."

"Did I mention that he is Nigerian? His name is Ola."

I was surprised to hear that. "Afaa! What are you telling me? Wow! What are the chances that you would find a Nigerian online on a dating site, and of all your potential dates, he is the one you fall for?"

"I know!"

I took some time to digest this news. I knew Afaa had always been keen to live out her life with a black male. Now I was not sure if she liked this man for who he was or because he was of African descent. I had to ask her. I did not want her to get entangled for the wrong reasons.

"Afaa, have you properly vetted this guy? What do you know about him? I hope you are not just in it because he is—"

Before I could finish, she jumped in.

"Oh no, no, no! Don't be silly. I did not even see his picture. I did not know he was black when I went online. I was just looking to meet someone, anyone, so I could not have known who I'd meet. Believe me, I did not go out of my way to find him."

I could tell she was being honest about it. "I am happy for you, Afaa. I hope he is all he says he is."

When I got to the office the next Monday, my thoughts were in turmoil and I was finding it difficult to concentrate. Perhaps I should have pulled a sickie, because I was heartsick. Ryan, Zimako, Ryan, Zimako; round and round and round in my head, driving me crazy. I caught myself making errors in my entries and deleting and starting over. By the time it was noon, I was ready to go on break. I was having mood swings, but thank goodness no one had noticed.

Caroline and Deb were crouched in the corner in the lunchroom, sharing lunch. They smiled at me as I entered and waved. I waved back none too enthusiastically. Since I joined the team, I had not been able to connect with either of them. I got the feeling they felt I was beneath them and unworthy of their acquaintance, so kept my distance. I sat at the large oval table in the centre of the room and stretched my feet and reclined, hoping to have a quiet break. My food was in the refrigerator, but I did not have an appetite. I had a few minutes of respite, and then Brittany came in.

"Anuli, hey," she said, coming to sit beside me with her sandwich making its way into her mouth.

"Hey, Brit," I responded, sitting up. I knew she'd want to talk, so I prepared to listen to her natter away. She started talking about the tenants who lived in the apartment below in the house she shared with her boyfriend. They were loud, noisy, and driving her crazy. Caroline and Deb joined the discussion. Soon we were all chatting, and lunch was lively enough to get me out of my gloomy mood.

The conversation took a different turn when Brit revealed the tenants were Mexican. Caroline and Deb did not hide their disdain. "How could you rent your basement to them?" Caroline asked. Brit struggled to explain, but Deb did not mince words. She let her know that she felt Mexicans and various other foreigner groups were unacceptable as tenants. "You should know better."

The tirade against foreigners and immigrants raged on with me as an invisible, silent observer till Maria came in and everyone suddenly became quiet. Maria announced that the next lotto was a jackpot of $20 million. That turned the conversation in another direction. I had joined the pool, and we began discussing what we'd do with the winnings if it ever happened. As soon as I saw my opportunity, I smiled inwardly and stood up. I had had enough. Brit also got up, and we left together. I found she was not very fond of these women either.

* * * * *

Zimako looked at his watch. It was almost six o'clock. He was determined to leave before Anuli got home. PCMG had finally sent a refund of $2,000. He debated what to do with it, and finally decided to attach a note to Anuli, leaving it on the table.

He'd spent over two months on his job, and had learned the ropes.

He felt ashamed because this post was not at all related to

engineering, so in his mind's eye, it was a compromise too far. A position as a security detail with Armed Guards was not what he had imagined for himself in Canada. Even though he felt defeated, he kept telling himself that the job was unworthy of him, and that he was superior to his colleagues.

His team was headed by Sanjay, an Indian in his late fifties, who was very fit and agile. He had extremely sharp eyes and missed nothing. Their team of seven shared shifts and was responsible for the Three Tower downtown. Zimako learned the drills and the security requirements and realised he had a natural aptitude for improving the process. However, he remained a detached, reluctant member of the team. He did not want to get involved or immerse himself in it. He did the minimum and no more. He was not looking to win awards or accolades as the best security guard ever. That was not his destiny. Where was God? Was this really the Canadian Promised Land? To be honest, Zimako blamed God for his misfortune.

He still went to church with Anuli, but he did not know where he stood with his faith anymore.

Over time he relaxed a bit and became friendly with a couple of his colleagues, Osei and Mykola. Osei was of African heritage, while Mykola was East European. They were the only ones in the team who were not Asian. He enjoyed their company and they socialised outside of work. Like Zimako, Mykola was an engineer, but he still struggled with English, and unlike Zimako, Mykola was not bitter, nor did he bear a grudge or feel cheated by the system.

As Zimako settled into his role, he discovered that the Asians were all graduates with MBAs, master's degrees, and various international qualifications. Every guy had a story, and he realised they were just like him—well educated, previously middle-class immigrants who had been unable to get into their original professions in Canada. He was completely humbled, and began to develop a new respect for his colleagues.

This knowledge did not make him feel better. If anything, it increased his fear that what he planned as a brief stint while waiting for the dream job might become permanent.

improve my chances of landing a decent job in Canada that would propel me to the professional status I had enjoyed back home. Things were looking promising.

"I have an offer for you," he said.

We had continued to be friends, but I was very careful to make sure he understood that we could be no more than platonic friends. His comment sounded like a proposition, so with some wariness, I asked him to elaborate.

"You recall that I told you I started this class because I was not impressed with my accountant?" he asked, looking me directly in the eye. I nodded in agreement.

"And I also mentioned that the current project I am working on is the biggest job I have done so far. I pursued this job for the last three years. Now the job has elevated my company's status, and I am going to need to build and establish a more structured organisation."

I listened to him, wondering where he was going with this rigmarole. "What are you proposing, Ryan? Get to the point."

"I need you."

I was about to jump in and put an end once and for all to this innuendo when he lifted his hand and stopped me. "Let me finish… " He continued, "I'd like you to come and work for me when all this is over. I know we will make a good team. Anuli, you could help me get my financial department properly set up. I have seen first-hand how good you are, and I can assure you my company is a company of the future, and you will go a long way."

When Ryan finished, I was not sure how to respond. I was being headhunted—well, kind of—and his confidence in me and the offer rendered me speechless.

To him, my silence was pregnant with meaning, prompting him to ask again. "What do you think? You don't have to give me an answer right now, but please tell me you will consider it. Anuli, I need you."

I did not want to be impulsive. This had come out of the blue. I had to spend some time thinking a bit more about it. So I told him just that. He agreed with me, then suggested we meet later in the evening with some people from his company, in a more relaxed environment, so I could see if they were people I'd like to work with.

I felt Ryan was railroading me. I had to remind myself that with my CMA in hand, the sky was my limit. I had a world of opportunities open to me. I did not want to hurt his feelings and appear dismissive. So I declined the offer of drinks to meet the team and asked for time to consider the offer.

"It's only a drink with a few of my buddies from work, just a harmless evening out; no strings attached."

It was tempting to say yes, but there were many things to consider. True, Ryan had shown me nothing but kindness, but I did not want to give him false hope on any count. He saw my hesitation and revised his offer. "If today is not good, then at least let's meet on Friday; that's fair. You can ask any questions you have, and you will have caught up with some studying and have also had time to consider the offer. Fair?"

I felt pressured, but realised he wasn't going to back down easily. It appeared rude to keep saying no, especially as he was trying so hard, so I gave in. "Okay, Friday then."

* * * * *

Kathy carefully applied her make-up and took one last look at herself in the mirror. She knew she was not the young woman she used to be. Heck, she was not sixteen years old anymore. She wondered what Nsala looked like. Was he still as attractive as she remembered him? Or was she in love with a mirage?

They had been talking on the phone over the past couple of months; sometimes their conversation went on into the wee hours of the night. Kathy was the first to admit she was head over heels in love with him, and wanted a romantic happily ever after with her Prince Charming.

When Nsala said he would be visiting the US on other business, she seized the opportunity to invite him to stop over in Canada. Kathy's heart sang when he said, "I'd give all my treasure to see you again, Kathy."

Today she was driving to the airport to meet him. She had made reservations for him at the Marriot for a week, after which he planned to return to Congo.

If things worked out, Kathy wondered if he would invite her back to make her home with him.

CHAPTER TWENTY-FOUR

Dear Diary,

Mark these words: "What doesn't kill you makes you stronger." That is now my mantra. These days Zimako is always out, and I don't know what shifts he is working. His breath sometimes reeks of alcohol, but I will not ask any questions. I can't remember the last time we were intimate. My final exams are coming up soon, and then, God willing, my dream job will be within my reach. I can't wait for things to finally come together.

Zimako knew he was treading in dangerous waters, but he was either unwilling or incapable of stopping himself. He had become a regular at the bar; he found it relaxing and fun.

When he was at home with Anuli, he felt he was letting her down, and the weight of that guilt drove a further wedge between them. She seemed to have managed to hold her own. In less than a few weeks, she'd be writing her final exams. He noticed Anuli had been spending a lot of time at the library studying. Her diligence shamed him. He had spent so much time blaming her for the deterioration in their relationship, but if he was honest, perhaps he was the one who had failed her.

He wasn't working tonight, and Anuli had gone to the library to meet with her study group. He was meeting with Osei and Mykola at the club and had invited Zack, his friend from the Alberta job search, along. Zimako now frequented a few of the clubs downtown, but he preferred this one on the route from work. The DJ played a good mix of old-school music, the ambience was cosy, and the drinks were reasonably priced.

He dressed carefully to exude casual sophistication. He knew some of the regular women had a vested interest in him and his friends; in fact, Mykola and Osei had enjoyed a few one-night stands. So far, Zimako had drawn the line at that. He nursed his drink and enjoyed the music and flirtations while his more gregarious friends mingled with the women.

But tonight was different. Zimako was excited. Kelly.

In the dimly-lit bar, occupying their usual corner from where they had a vantage view of the dance floor and bar, Zimako sensed he was being observed by a very delectable woman. He had not noticed her in the club before, and was intrigued by her. She was sitting with three of her friends. They looked as if they were enjoying themselves, but that one woman stood out from the crowd; she caught Zimako's attention because, just like him, she seemed out of place.

Before the evening was over, Zimako made her acquaintance, and he was feeling quite sexually aroused. He had initially thought she was modestly dressed, but on closer inspection her sheer top towed the line between racy and conservative, hinting at the feminine assets within. Her tight leather skirt oozed animal magnetism, and she had the elegance of a cheetah in her stilettos. She stirred something in Zimako's loins; she was a fantasy. Zimako could feel himself falling under her spell. When she spoke, her face lit up and her hands moved in a mesmerising, sensual manner that hypnotised Zimako. He devoured her with his eyes, following her every move. He knew he was being sucked in.

As the night drew to a close, Zimako was sure she'd hand him her number like they always did, but she did not. He was not going to grovel. He would play it cool and bide his time.

When he left the bar that night, he knew he would return every night till he saw her again. He hoped he would not have long to wait. When she did not show up the following Friday, Zimako wondered if he had imagined the mutual attraction. He was disappointed and beat himself up for missing a great opportunity, but try as he might to find some other interest, no one else tickled his fancy. He was determined to find her, and if he succeeded, he would be upfront about his intentions.

Then on Saturday she showed up. He was elated. She held

him spellbound with her gyrating hips and pouting lips. Zimako was immune to his surroundings. He was drowning in the pool of her eyes; her voice was music to his ears. He wanted to know more, but his curiosity was not to be satisfied. She was a master at seduction.

The evening ended on a frustrating note. Zimako was bristling with pent-up desire and unsatisfied longing. He could not remember ever feeling such raw and unbridled desire. Kelly appeared oblivious to her effect. She strummed him like a guitar, close enough to touch, but yet barely brushing against him. Zimako wanted more.

As he was gathering the courage to suggest they go somewhere private, Kelly's ride came along. She was with her usual gang. If she was reluctant to leave, she did not show it. Again, Zimako was left with an unfulfilled expectation. That evening he left with his friends, even more determined than ever that the outcome would be different next time.

It was the wee hours of the morning, and most of the guys were still having a good time. Zimako debated staying on or just going home. The night did not hold any lustre for him with Kelly gone, and he did not want to dampen the mood for his friends. He told Osei of his plans to leave; the fun was over for him.

It was almost four a.m. when Zimako got home. He was feeling quite intoxicated. Swaying ever so slightly, he let himself into the apartment. It was dark and quiet. He knew Anuli was fast asleep, so he tiptoed in, careful not to wake her to avoid any confrontation. He went to the bathroom and ran some water over his face and gargled. He wondered if he should have a shower, but he was feeling drowsy.

* * * * *

It had to be a dream. This could not be happening. Anuli lay there frigid; her mind was reeling. It was just like old times; Zimako held her gently and whispered her name. "I need you, babes. I need you urgently!" She was too shocked and exhausted to be aroused. Even though she was unresponsive, he was undeterred. In a swift motion he plunged into her. A searing pain ripped though her tight, dry depths in response to the friction. It was a bittersweet pleasure as she screamed out in climax.

* * * * *

It was Nsala's last day with Kathy. She had kept him to herself throughout his stay. They spent time discovering each other all over again. In their individual lives, they had experienced so much; there was a wealth of memories and anecdotes to share with one another. Kathy wanted to hold him, feel his big hands on her skin, and curl securely into his firm body. She just enjoyed being with him and listening to his voice. Nsala felt blessed to be reunited with her. He treated her like a delicate flower, often just gazing at her in awe. She was beautiful and compassionate, and she had a certain serenity about her. He could not believe he was getting a second chance. It was serendipitous that they were both free and ready to love at this stage of their lives.

They behaved like intoxicated teenagers in love for the first time. Romance injected a new vigour into Kathy, who was excited but maintained a cautious reserve; Nsala was passionate without being sexually aggressive. They laughed a lot; Kathy loved Nsala's dry wit and sense of humour. He admired her intelligence and curiosity. Nsala was very tactile, caressing Kathy's face and hair, and when they walked along, he held her by the waist and made her feel special. Kathy asked him about Africa, all the places she missed, and he obliged her with stories and painted a picture of his life in Congo. They went on walks to the parks; they went camping. Nsala wanted to visit the library, and Kathy took him to her favourite place, the museum. For the first time in a long time, Kathy felt complete. She was glowing. Love became her. She took even more care of her appearance than ever before, and she was gratified when she drove up to see him each morning and he held her in his embrace, buried his face in her hair, and whispered, "My African rose," in response to which Kathy always blushed. They went on lunch dates, they went to the movies, and they even went shopping together. She did not want him out of her sight. She had waited too long for this. She savoured every moment with him.

Kathy was apprehensive about his departure; she did not want to imagine what it would be like when it was time for him to return to Africa. She wanted their time together to last forever.

On his last day, Kathy decided to bite the bullet. Nothing ventured, nothing gained. She would do the unthinkable. She was very nervous because she did not know how Nsala would react. She packed a few items in her overnight case and set off to see him. They had planned to go to the opera later in the evening after spending the day just wandering through the city creating some final memories.

Nsala welcomed Kathy; he noted her small carry-on with some surprise, but tactfully said nothing. He was in a dressing gown and slippers, reading the paper. Privately, Nsala wondered if Kathy would be ready to take things to a more intimate level. He had no intention of rushing her, and was willing to wait till she signalled that she was ready. He invited her as usual to join him for a light breakfast. Kathy politely declined. Her private thoughts tied her stomach up in knots. Nsala came over to her and asked what was on her mind. "Honey, please share your thoughts with me."

Kathy was too embarrassed to tell him. She seemed so helpless, yet utterly delectable. He wanted to woo her. He held her tightly in his arms, and Kathy responded, snaking her arms across his shoulder, wanting more as she pressed her hips closer to his loins.

Nsala's passion, which he had held bridled for too long, could not remain tethered. His lips devoured Kathy's with an animal hunger, and she opened soft lips to accept him. He moulded her body close to his, and a gentle cry escaped her lips. Nsala looked into her eyes to be sure they both wanted this; he had held back for so long. From the time he set eyes on Kathy he wanted her, but dared not presumptuously claim her.

Kathy was crying as she whispered, "Yes, baby, yes! I want to give myself to you."

Nsala reluctantly disengaged and carried Kathy to the bed. He tenderly placed her on the bed and shed his clothing before slowly undressing her. Kathy lay motionless, not sure what to do. Nsala kissed and probed her, eliciting moans and passionate gasps of surprise as he pleasured her. When he could hold back no more, he slipped on some protection, parted her thighs, and straddled her.

Kathy shut her eyes tight. "Please, darling, I… "

Nsala knew to be gentle as he introduced the tip of his manhood into her wet, tight depths. He was losing control. He wanted to be slow, but she was exciting him with an intensity he had never before experienced as she lifted her hips in rhythm to his thrusts. He had reached the tipping point; he could not stop. He mustered the last shred of strength in him, knowing he would obey her. "Do you want this? Are you ready? Do you want me to stop?"

Kathy blushed, unable to speak; she moaned and held his hips in place, pulling him closer, causing him to plunge the entire length of his ample endowment into her. She screamed out in pain and gasped, then moaned. He met the gentle resistance he had known only on his wedding night. Kathy was a virgin. He gently eased himself in and held her close, rocking her till he was fully enmeshed in her. "Don't be afraid, darling. You can take all of me. I will not hurt you."

Kathy trusted him. She relaxed as he gracefully filled her. Then it was his turn to be bewildered. Then Kathy began to move, swaying her hips. Their rhythm was telepathic. He whispered in her ears, nibbled her nipples as he loved her deep. He kissed her, and she caressed him, gently and shyly at first, then more boldly. When they were at fever pitch, Nsala masterfully brought Kathy to a crescendo. Then he began to move to take his own fulfilment from her. "Touch me, my rose," he directed, showing her how to pleasure him till he exploded in her.

They both lay in bed. He discreetly took off his protection and draped his arm under her shoulder, drawing her into himself while one hand caressed her lovingly. "You are awesome. Thank you for giving me such a wonderful gift. What an exquisite surprise," he said.

Kathy was basking in his attention. She had dreamt of this day, but never knew it would come. From the day she picked him up at the airport, her excitement had mounted till she felt ready to explode. It was better than she had imagined. It was breath-taking. Her skin tingled. His proximity made her buzz; she felt like a live wire. Nsala was a gentleman, and Kathy was glad that he had fulfilled her fantasies. Indeed, he was still the same young man she had left many years back in Africa, if older.

They spent the rest of the day indoors. Kathy could not get enough of him, and her newfound womanhood. Nsala's hands and lips were magic; he pleasured her and taught her how to make him happy. By the time they went to the opera that evening, Kathy was a new woman. She had never felt so fulfilled.

At the Edmonton airport the next day, Kathy was in tears as Nsala readied to catch his flight. He held her close, inhaling the scent of her.

Kathy was sobbing. "I'd like to come with you right away. Don't leave me." Nsala comforted her, promising to visit soon, or better yet, get things in order and invite her over if she would like that.

"Final boarding announcement on flight CA427 on DRC Airlines. Please come to gate G15."

With one last lingering hug, Nsala walked away, leaving a very sad, red-eyed Kathy standing and waving.

* * * * *

Zimako quickly responded to the text. "I'm not gonna beat around the bush. I wanna beat around your bush."

He and Kelly had been texting since their last encounter. He was emboldened by sexual frustration, throwing caution to the wind. There was no need to be coy; Kelly was a woman of the world, experienced in teasing and flirtation. Zimako felt like she was manipulating him by remote control through those texts. He was very distracted and seemed to be in a state of constant arousal.

She replied immediately. "Do you wanna sail your boat on my river, sailor?"

Zimako was at his duty post with his co-patrol. It was one of the other guys. "Your wife?" he asked, wondering who Zimako was texting with.

Zimako shook his head with a vehement, "No!"

His colleague laughed knowingly. "Stupid question. It's never the wife. Once you marry them, they no longer sexy."

Zimako looked at him, wishing he were a fly so he could swat him away. He turned from him and kept texting. However, Sanjaya was not easily fobbed off. "So are you sexting?"

Zimako stopped midway through the text he was composing—"Get aboard my sexboat, ma'am. I'm gonna take you on a trip to ecsta"—and glared at Sanjaya. A sharp rejoinder came to his lips, but he quelled it, completed the text, and pressed send, then put his phone away.

They continued their patrol in silence. Zimako was simmering, and he did not like having people butt their nose in his private matters. Sanjaya continued to chatter, oblivious to Zimako's cold shoulder.

Zimako could not wait to get away; he was like a man obsessed. All his thoughts and desires focussed on seeing Kelly again. He was burning up; she alone could quench his fire. His phone vibrated in his pocket. He pulled it out. She had replied, "I can't stop touching myself just thinking about you. How about tonight?"

He replied hurriedly, "I'm sOooo horny for you right now. Can't wait to see you later. Got a not so little surprise for you!"

Not even Sanjaya's innuendoes could dampen his mood. Kelly was willing and he was ready.

Zimako's shift ended at three p.m. He hurried to change out of his uniform in the private area, but he was unaware that Sanjaya was still dogging him. When he was done and turned to exit, Sanjaya was standing by the door. "Good luck, man! I wish it was me."

Zimako ignored him and hurried out.

He did not go home. Rather, Zimako made his way farther downtown to make reservations at a hotel. His excitement was mounting, and the spectre of fulfilling his longing blinded him to reason and the consequences of his action. He wanted to crush Kelly in his arms, demystify her aura, and squeeze her softness. He was beyond rational thought; he was in fantasy land as he gave free reign to his imagination. Tonight would be the night.

The guy at the hotel completed the formalities and handed the key to Zimako. He grasped it and made his way to the escalator filled with anticipation, and texted Kelly to let her know he was all hers for the taking.

Meanwhile, he texted Anuli. "Working a double shift, won't be back till tomorrow morning."

Once he was settled, lying in bed with one leg crossed over the other, Zimako began texting again. He feeling very excited, and filled with anticipation. *Just this once, Lord, just this once.* He did not want to resist temptation. The temptation was too much; his raging libido was beclouding any good judgement he'd ever had. Kelly's responses to his texts intensified his anticipation. She knew she had him on his knees, eating out of her hands.

About an hour later, Kelly texted to say she was sorry, she would not be able to make it after all.

Zimako was livid! He demanded to know why she was standing him up. He had spent precious money, told his wife a lie, and built up his expectations. How could she change her mind?

Then Kelly sent another text. To apologise, she was sending him room service. Could he open the door to whomever knocked in the next few minutes?

Just as he finished reading that text, Zimako heard a knock on the door. He opened the door, and there was Kelly, wearing a full-length, leather chestnut-coloured coat with nothing underneath but her beautifully nude and voluptuous body. Zimako could not believe his eyes as she opened her coat and reached out to hug him.

He scooped her up in his arms and planted a fierce, bruising kiss on her lips. Kelly was no shrinking violet; she gave as good as she got. Both had wanted this for too long. There was no holding back. Zimako's pants were bulging with arousal. He stripped them off, and Kelly gasped in delight. She was excited to fulfil a long-held desire to experience a black lover.

Wild animal mating over, they lay on their backs in a daze. Both were sweating in spite of the cool air-conditioning in the room. Breathing heavily and weakened from their corpulence,

Kelly eventually got up to go the bathroom. This was the first time Zimako had properly seen her in broad daylight without her costume of seduction. He watched her backside and noticed a flaw—she had knock knees. He turned away. He had seen enough.

As he lay there, the enormity of what he had just done came crashing down with reality on him. Now that the pure lust that had held him captive was sated, it was immediately replaced by self-disgust and self-loathing, and then his conscience cloaked him with guilt and accusations of betrayal and stupidity.

When Kelly returned from the bathroom, Zimako was not feeling so friendly. He observed her slightly wobbly stomach and cellulite thighs. She looked at him with come hither eyes and tried to kiss him. He turned away and stood up to go to the bathroom.

He took a good look at the man in the mirror, and he did not like what he saw.

He stepped into the shower and ran burning hot water on himself, scrubbing and scrubbing from his head down to his toes. He wished he did not have to face Kelly ever again.

But Kelly was waiting, and she wanted more.

Zimako now found her repulsive and could not bear for her to touch him. "Enough! Listen, get dressed. You have to leave right now," he said in a very cold voice.

Kelly was chilled to her bones and suddenly started shivering. Where was the man who had just made passionate love to her? Zimako refused to look at her. It was as though she had served her purpose and was now filth he would rather did not exist.

Kelly pulled her clothes out of her bag and slowly got dressed and applied her make-up, wondering what she had done to deserve this. Was it because she had played hard to get? This was very confusing. She had never felt so used in her life. Fully clothed and made up, self-preservation armour in place, Kelly grabbed her bag and was ready to leave.

At the door, she took one last look at Zimako. She threw her head back and left him with one word: "Nigger!" Then she slammed the door shut loudly as she could.

Zimako lay there, wishing he would die.

How did it all come to this? he thought. How did his dreams, his hopes, and his rock-solid love for Anuli all get so twisted that he was here, in a hotel room, knowing that he had just crossed the line. As tears dropped from his eyes, Zimako felt the burden of guilt overwhelm him, and for the first time in his adult life Zimako sobbed.

When Zimako got home the next morning, Anuli was not in. He went into the room which he had shared with Anuli for the past year while they struggled to settle down in Canada. She must have left home in a hurry. He picked his way around the bedroom and opened the closet, running his hands up and down Anuli's clothes. He brought one of her dresses to his face and breathed in her unique smell.

His heart was breaking; how could he have done this to her? His heart was heavy as tears dropped unchecked from his eyes. He could never face Anuli again. He could not stay here anymore. He had wronged her irrevocably. He packed a bag with some of his personal belongings and left a note.

Dear Anuli,

I am so sorry it has come to this. I am only doing what is best.

Do not get in touch. Don't try to find me.

   Zimako

He took one last look at the apartment and shut the door behind him.

* * * * *

Zimako had sent me a text the day before, saying he was working a double shift. I was relieved. It gave me the flexibility of going to bed when I wanted to. With my exams two weeks away, I had asked for some time off work to focus on my studies. This was crunch time. I was in a battle to fulfil my dreams.

This morning I left early for the library to study, I needed to be sure I had ready access to all the relevant texts to ensure that no stone was left unturned. I had to pass. I had to succeed.

When I got back home, it was late in the evening. I was tired. Zimako was not home. Again. I was tired. All I wanted was to unwind, have a quick supper of some chicken and salad, and go to bed.

That was when I saw it on the table. He had dropped a note.

Sometimes we left each other notes, but we mostly stuck them on the fridge with a magnet. There was a deep wrench in my gut when I saw that note. I dumped my bag on the floor and picked the note up. It knocked the wind out of my sails. I collapsed on the chair. I sat there, not knowing what to do. My mind went blank. I sat there staring at the wall. I curled up in a foetal position, rocking myself, and fell asleep.

* * * * *

When I woke up in the morning, sunshine was streaming through the window, but it was fall, and I felt cold. I curled deeper into myself and remembered what had changed.

My husband had left me.

When the phone rang, I listened, but did not answer. It was from Kathy. She was leaving a message telling me to call her; it was important.

Her call jarred me back to reality. I slowly began to sort through my thoughts.

I had failed as a woman, as a wife. What had I done wrong? What had I done to make Zimako walk out on me? What had I said or done? I had not been given the opportunity to defend myself. He was accuser, judge, and jury. His decision was final with immediate effect. I felt my heart breaking in two.

It had never occurred to me through all our challenges that Zimako would ever walk out on me. I thought things would get better for us, and he would come around. I wondered what I could have done differently. I felt in my heart that I still loved Zimako. He was my first real true love. Now he was gone, lost.

Here I was in a strange country, left to pick up the pieces of a broken marriage.

I moved slowly as I began to will myself to start the day. I had a bath, ate some food, and began to talk to myself. I encouraged myself. I saw my books lying on the floor where I had dropped them last night. I picked them up and decided to keep going. I had to meet some of my colleagues in the library, and I was not going to crack now. "I have to get through this somehow, God, please help me; I have to pass this exam. Give me strength, please help me."

CHAPTER TWENTY-FIVE

Dear Diary,

My exams are over. I gave it my best shot. It is my passport to success in Canada. I've still not told anyone that Zimako has abandoned our marriage. Thank God for my job, for the money, and the distraction it offers. Without it, what would I have done? Ryan is becoming more than a friend. Do you think he can be my boss as well as my lover? All this is too much for me to process in my fragile state of mind. I will just take things slow, step by slow step, one day at a time.

It had been three weeks since Zimako left the home he shared with Anuli and moved to the YMCA downtown. He was struggling with so many issues and aimlessly drifting afloat in a sea of indecision, wondering what to do with his life.

Walking out on Anuli was the honourable thing. He had no right to continue to act as if he had been true to his vows and nothing had happened.

Zimako wanted to retreat and rediscover himself and perhaps restore his integrity. Since coming to Canada his moral compass had become disordered, but he hoped it wasn't damaged beyond repair. He reviewed his life and decided he was better than this. Anuli would not understand why he left, but even if they were to get back together sometime in the future, he needed this time away from her to sort out the mess his life had become.

He still spent time with his friends from work, Osei and Mykola, but he no longer went to the bars with them. That era was over. His friends were inquisitive about the changes they had noticed in his demeanour as he become more introverted. Zimako explained that he had some personal issues, without elaborating.

It was Tuesday; he was on a morning shift sitting at the front desk. He did not like working the morning shift because he felt so conspicuous, and the security risks were higher. On the morning shift, they doubled as assistants on reception alongside the single receptionist to help process visitors to the building. He was carefully observing the people moving around while monitoring the security cameras. The Three Towers were at the centre of downtown, and housed one of the major banks and several corporate offices.

Zimako looked up and saw a black guy approaching the desk. In a split second he knew that there was something different about him. It was his quiet self-assurance, which he wore just as comfortably as the perfectly tailored suit that he wore without a tie. He looked every inch an accomplished and successful professional who, even if not wealthy, was comfortable. He represented all Zimako had hoped to become when he left Nigeria for Canada, but failed to accomplish. Zimako was intensely envious of him and wanted to duck to avoid him.

The man walked up to the desk and faced Zimako. "Could you tell me what floor Sudmor Oil is located on?"

Zimako responded with dispatch and turned back to his screen. The man looked at Zimako again, probably recognising his accent, and asked him where he was originally from. "I hope you don't mind me asking; are you Nigerian?"

Zimako was reluctant to admit it, and nerves made him rather verbose in his response. "Why do you ask? No, don't bother answering that; it doesn't matter. For you to ask, I guess you know the answer. Yes, I am." He seemed ashamed to admit this and kept his eyes averted, avoiding eye contact.

"So, again, pardon me for being forward, how… how come you are doing this job? You sound so educated. I know it is none of my business."

Zimako laughed, then said, "Ehm, it's a long story."

The man looked at him and said, "Listen, I am in town for three days. I want us to talk."

Zimako felt his pulse racing. He wanted to ask questions, but figured there'd be ample time for that later. "Thanks! My name is

Zimako." They shook hands, and the man introduced himself as Dede.

* * * * *

Zimako's shift ended at three p.m., but he decided to hang around for some time in the hope that Dede would conclude his business of the day and they could have that chat. He was in luck. He saw Dede emerge from the lifts with some colleagues just after five o'clock. He stepped into view discreetly to make himself noticed.

Dede saw him from the corner of his eye and turned, then excused himself from his team. "Hey, my guy." Dede greeted Zimako with a firm handshake and a hug, clasping his shoulder.

Zimako suddenly realised this might not be a good time, but he had convinced himself that his meeting with Dede was serendipitous and could have the power to get him back on track. It was an opportunity he did not want to miss. "I... I wondered, can we... can we talk?" he asked hesitantly.

Dede looked at his watch, then turned to his colleagues, who were still idling in the reception area, and waved them off. "Guys, I'll catch up with you later." Then he turned to Zimako. "So, what's up?"

Zimako was in awe of this guy who seemed to have achieved his dreams, but his desperation gave him courage. "Let me be frank. I won't beat about the bush. I need your help." Once he had gotten that out, tears welled up behind his eyes.

Dede was taken aback to see his countryman close to tears. "Hey, hey, cool down. Come, let's go and find somewhere to sit down and talk."

They found a coffee shop around the corner, where they sat down. Zimako opened up to Dede and told him of his journey to Canada, and how none of his attempts to find a job came to fruition. Dede listened patiently and at the end was sympathetic but unfazed. "Man, that is not a problem. You say you are an engineer?"

Zimako nodded. He was so choked up with tears, there was a lump in his throat and he could not speak.

"There is so much work for engineers here. Did you ever consider moving to Fort Mc?"

Zimako had heard of Fort McMurray, but nothing he had heard tempted him enough to think of it as a viable option.

"Look, as unbelievable as it seems now, I was once in the same situation that you are in. I suffered and struggled back then. I heard all the stories about Fort Mc and eventually decided to give it a shot, as I had nothing to lose. Within a month, I was working. Look, if you are what you have told me you are, then let me have your résumé tomorrow. I will be heading back to Fort Mc the day after. We have positions in my company. I'll submit your résumé, but I'm not making any promises. We'll see how it goes."

* * * * *

I went back to work straight after my exams, believing it would be therapeutic. Apart from my emotional state, I had been feeling a little queasy, and toyed with the idea of requesting some more time off to help me recover from the stress of the exams and my heartbreak, but in reality, I knew I needed the money. When I got back, I discovered Brit had left. She resigned the week I went on leave. For all her faults, we were friendly, and I was sad to see her go. Maria pulled me aside and asked if I was also planning to leave. I knew that if I passed my exams, I'd be looking for a new job; it would not make sense to continue working this job. It was a difficult question and I felt I owed Maria some honesty, so I let her know that my plans at the present time were quite fluid with many variables, and I couldn't say for sure one way or another. She found my response rather unsatisfactory, and if anything it seemed to exasperate her.

"Anyway, whatever you do, remember you got your break here, so at least stay for a full year before you go."

That was a big ask. I was taken by surprise. Why would I have to stay for a year? Maria still had very traditional values. I would not let it bother me, and I would not be coerced into a commitment that was not favourable to me just to please Maria. I had been through too much for that. I filed our conversation in the back of my mind.

What I dreaded the most was encountering Caroline and Deb. Brit had insulated me from their nastiness. I went back to my duties, knowing in my heart that I would leave the first opportunity I got.

* * * * *

I was on my way into our condo block when the condo manager called out to me and invited me into her office. She started off making small talk, then asked me about Zimako. I was taken aback. She explained that they had not seen him for over a month and wanted to know if he had gone back to Africa. I almost said yes to that, but there were too many uncertainties in my relationship with Zimako. I did not know if he had filed for a divorce or what his plans were. I assumed he would call me sometime and tell me what he intended to do. So far I had not had the courage to call him because I could not handle any more bad news. I decided honesty was the best policy. "My husband is gone. I don't know where he is." That was the first time I had verbalised what had happened to me. I felt tearful. She fell silent, as though waiting for me to say more, but I was finished.

It was at that point I realised she was looking past me to someone at the door. I turned to see Ryan standing by the doorway. I could tell he had overheard the last part of the conversation. The condo manager asked him to please give us some time, as she was busy. She got up and shut the door. "I am sorry to hear this. Do you wish to continue your tenancy? Let me know."

I nodded. She empathised with me and said to keep her abreast of my intentions regarding the tenancy. I nodded and departed.

When I stepped out of the office, Ryan was waiting. I did not want to face him. I tried to get past him, but he detained me. I felt so raw and exposed and even ashamed. I wanted to run and hide. But Ryan was having none of that. He walked with me to the elevator, and rather than stop on my floor, we went directly to his, and he invited me into his apartment. That was my first time in his place. It was an interior decorator's dream. I was pleasantly surprised, having not known what to expect. He must have had professional help. "I like your apartment. It's very tastefully decorated."

He thanked me, then invited me to sit with him on the couch. I sat with him, and he just hugged me close. We sat in silence. I was not sure what I'd say if he asked me, but it was strangely comforting to sit there in his arms. When he stood up, I felt cold, and wrapped my hands around myself. Soon he came back with a bottle of champagne and two glasses.

I wondered what the celebration was. He toasted to friendship and more. He made me feel at home. We talked about school, and the exams. I was in safe territory. Soon the drink was working its magic; I could feel my depression lifting as I relaxed. I was very comfortable. Ryan took my foot and started to give me a foot rub. I was feeling better already. He put on a movie. We laughed and talked. When it was getting late, I told him I had to leave. He was reluctant to see me go, but did not detain me. "I am here if you need me."

I thanked him. As I went to the door, he held my face in his hands and kissed me full on the lips, then let me go. I looked at him in surprise. He just nodded and said, "Go, just go now before I do something I will regret."

* * * * *

Exams over, I could no longer avoid my friends. Afaa and Fifi had been calling and wanted to meet up. I had to tell them. We agreed to meet for coffee and gossip on the weekend. I had enough time to fortify myself. I did not want pity; I did not want to cry. So when we met up, I told them of the break-up of my marriage. Afaa remembered I had told her we were having problems and asked if we had gone for counselling. I explained that it had all happened rather suddenly, that Zimako had walked out on me, and I hadn't heard from him since. They were both shocked. The news put a dampener on the evening; my friends did not know what to say. When they found out he had walked out right before my exams, they thought that was rather cruel. Both had so many questions. I told them I was still too sore emotionally to deal with their questions. They tried to cheer me up the rest of the evening, and soon we were talking about men in general and how relationships evolved. I silently prayed Afaa would not muddy the waters by asking about Ryan at this time.

Afaa told us about her visit to Toronto and meeting Ola, her online love interest. He had lived up to her expectations and they had a wonderful romantic weekend together. "He laid out the red carpet and showed me a very good time."

I had to be happy for her. We asked her to tell us all. She did. When she was done, she said he would visit Edmonton soon and we could meet him then. She brought out her digital camera and showed us pictures of the two of them together, laughing and hugging. He was undeniably handsome and seemed equally enamoured of her.

* * * * *

When Zimako got a call from an unfamiliar number, he considered letting it go to voicemail, but curiosity got the better of him. He answered cautiously with a bland, "Hello?"

The voice at the other end of the phone responded, "Hello, could I speak with Zimako Aidiohrah?"

He knew the caller was having difficulty pronouncing his last name, so he interrupted, "This is he."

The caller introduced herself as the head of human resources and wanted to know if she had called at a good time. Zimako's heart was beating so hard, but he tried to maintain a facade of calm. "Yes, this is a good time to talk."

She discussed his résumé with him and asked when she could set up a phone interview. Zimako said he was ready at any time convenient for her firm. She suggested a first interview in two days' time. He agreed.

After the interview, he was told he would be contacted within a week with feedback. Zimako was ecstatic. He had a good feeling about this.

He telephoned Dede and updated him. Dede told him that if he got another call, it would be to invite him to Fort Mc for a further interview. Zimako expressed his thanks to Dede, and promised to keep him posted. When he hung up the phone, Zimako fell to his knees and thanked God for showing him mercy and grace. He could sense his luck was about to change.

* * * * *

When I opened my email box that afternoon at work, I saw a note from the Institute of CMA. It read Confidential in the subject line. I knew it was my result. I did not know if I was ready. I wanted to know what the result was, but I was scared. The information it contained had the power to change my life. I did not want to open it. After a minute, I clicked on it. It said my result was attached. I clicked on the attachment, and waited. It took a few seconds to download. I shut my eyes and said a prayer. Then, when I opened it, I saw the result. "Congratulations." I jumped, and sprinted out of my office before I realised it. Then I felt an attack of dizziness and suddenly felt wobbly on my feet; everything swam around before my eyes and then I blacked out. Anita witnessed the incident and rushed to my side. "Anuli, are you okay?"

I tried to regain my composure, but felt too weak. She told me I had to go home, and suggested I see my doctor. I was surprised. I'm not one who falls ill. A wave of nausea hit me. I sat down for a bit and buried my head between my legs till it passed. I thanked Anita for her concern, packed my bag, and left for the day.

I had not felt right for a while. Anita was right; I was probably really run down and should see a physician.

I was given a same-day appointment. I described my symptoms to the doctor and explained the various traumas I had experienced in the past year, hoping his diagnosis would be something as non-specific as exhaustion. He listened to me attentively, took a detailed travel, sexual, and family history, and suggested I take some blood and urine tests, including one for HIV and tuberculosis. It was quite comprehensive. They even did a tracing of my heart called an EKG. He said he might need to do further tests, including an X-ray, depending on the outcome of these preliminary tests.

I went home, now more anxious than when I went in. I hoped

all the tests would be negative. I was alone in a strange country. What if he thought this was some sort of cancer? Maybe I should call Makua and see what she thought. But then she would start asking questions about Zimako. I decided to leave it in God's hands and hope for the best.

The results of the tests were out. I got a call from the physician's office and went in, hoping there was no bad news. I was weary already; I prayed they would not find anything, even though I still did not feel right.

"You are very healthy, Mrs Adiora. Your beta HCG was positive. Your symptoms are consistent with a normal pregnancy. Congratulations!"

I was flabbergasted. I sat there agape. This was totally unexpected. "What?"

The physician seemed oblivious to my shock. He continued, telling me what I needed to do now, including commencing folic acid if I wasn't already on it. I sat there numb as his voice droned on and on. All I kept hearing in my head was, "Congratulations, you are pregnant." I can't remember leaving his office; I don't know how I made it home.

Fate was playing tricks on me. I was not sure whether to laugh or cry. Just when I thought my life was getting on track and doors would open for me, now this.

* * * * *

Zimako got a second call, telling him they would like to meet him in person. He held his breath. A date was set for his second interview in the offices of Sudmor Oil in Fort Mc. He clenched his fingers into a fist and punched the air, and with eyes shut he mouthed a "Thank you, Jesus." He put the call through to Dede and got his voicemail. He left a quick update and promised to call back. Much later that day, Dede called back and invited Zimako to stay with him when he arrived.

* * * * *

I lived from moment to moment, not knowing what would

happen next. I was entertaining the possibility of going to work for Ryan, because I did not feel the time was appropriate to start job-hunting. I had not heard from Zimako, and I was seriously contemplating calling him to let him know I was pregnant, but I held back every time I remembered the way he had treated me. I was reticent about reaching out to him. The future did not look bright at all. I could sense my mood getting low again. How would I cope? But what choice did I have? Could things get any worse? I was worn out. It was as if I had been through a wringer. This was not the time for self-pity. I had to keep plodding on. I took on more hours at work now that school was over, becoming a full-time data entry clerk.

Kathy called me. I was happy to hear from her. She sounded so excited. "Anuli, I apologise that I have been under the radar. How have you been?"

I assured her that I was doing fine. I did not want to blurt everything out suddenly.

She continued, "I have so much to tell you, my friend! Nsala might be coming to Canada again. This time he will be here for about two weeks. I can't wait."

I smiled at her news. Everyone else's love life was falling into place.

"Does this mean you will disappear again into the island of love?" The last time Nsala had visited, Kathy had been so engrossed in their reunion that she hoarded him like a precious commodity and had gone out of circulation. I teased her mercilessly and she giggled in response.

"Oh, stop, don't be silly. You know, I'd be happier if I could go to Congo. I'd love to see Africa again, but I am just as happy with what I'll get."

We talked some more and she asked about my family in Nigeria. I had been avoiding calling home because I did not want to be confronted with talk about Zimako, especially as I did not have answers myself. I fudged my responses; luckily, Kathy was currently too self-absorbed to notice, or if she did, then she was respecting my privacy for once. She asked me to make time so we could have coffee or lunch soon, then rang off.

I had just gotten in from work. I sat on the sofa and put my feet up. It would have been nice to have a TV as a form of distraction and background noise. My cell phone beeped. It was Ryan. I picked up the phone; he was calling to see if I was okay. He asked what I was doing and if I'd like him to buy me dinner. I told him I did not feel like going out, but said he was welcome to visit if he liked. He jumped at the invitation. I told him my place was nothing like his. "It is simple, but it's my home. Don't get too excited."

He was undeterred. So we agreed he'd be here in an hour. I quickly put together some salad, crackers, and cheese. I was somewhat nervous to welcome him into my home.

Within the hour, Ryan was at my door. He had a bottle of wine and a bouquet of flowers. I smiled and greeted him with a hug. He looked around and complimented me on what I had done with the apartment. After a few awkward moments, I relaxed, and soon we were chatting freely. He talked about his job, and I asked questions about the project.

"How are you really doing, Anuli?"

I smiled. He looked very concerned. I decided to just come out with it. "I am pregnant, Ryan."

He stiffened. "Are you getting back together?"

I had not even heard from Zimako. "I don't know anything at this time. I'm taking life one day at a time."

He was not satisfied with that answer. He advised me to think through what I wanted. "Look, Anuli, I do not know if you will ever hear from him, but... I... I," he stammered.

I looked at him intently, curious to hear what he was so nervous about saying. He gathered himself and continued. "I am here for you, and I will do anything—anything—to make you happy."

His tone stopped me in my tracks and made me consider the meaning behind the words. "Ryan, what are you saying?" I asked him slowly.

He looked disconcerted for a moment, suddenly shy. He turned to me and looked earnestly into my eyes. "If you would have me, Anuli, I would marry you."

I was taken aback. I tried to say something, but he put his finger on my lips. "Stop. Don't say anything. I want you to know that this is not out of sympathy."

I was looking at Ryan; my head was spinning.

"I would not insult you by feeling sorry for you. You are a strong woman, and I know you are capable. I am saying this because I want to spend the rest of my life with you."

I was blown away. "Ryan, I don't know what to say," I said.

"Then don't say anything, my African Queen. Just eat."

CHAPTER TWENTY-SIX

Dear Diary,

Zimako has now been gone three months. I wish he would get in touch and let me know what he plans to do. Am I a married woman still? Am I going to be a single mother? I keep expecting divorce papers to arrive in the post. Everyone else seems so loved up, and I'm just here in limbo. I'm attaching my twenty-week scan here. At least the baby is healthy. It has started kicking already. I wonder if it is a boy or girl…

I opened the door to the apartment, looking forward to a peaceful evening. Zimako was sitting in the living room. I nearly collapsed. I shut the door slowly behind me.

"What are you doing here?" I asked in a whisper.

He stood up and stared at me in surprise. "You are pregnant."

I ignored his statement and asked him again, "What are you doing here?"

He was flustered. "Is… is it mine?"

I let out an incredulous gasp. "Are you accusing me of adultery?"

Zimako lowered his gaze and apologised. "I am sorry, Anuli. I did not come here to fight with you. Please. Can we talk?"

I was confused. Zimako was here. He was not as I knew him before he left. This was a different Zimako. He was looking dapper—smart, confident, and just different. Like something had happened to ignite his swagger. Definitely, something had happened to him. I was not going to ask any questions. How dare he waltz back into the apartment like he still lived here? He was an intruder as far as I was concerned. Suddenly a wave of anger overwhelmed me. "Get out! Get out!" I said pointing at the door.

He looked at me and walked to the door. When he got to the door, he turned. "I am sorry, Anuli. You deserve to be angry." He opened the door and left.

I slumped on the chair. What cheek!

Seeing Zimako really shook me up. It was so unexpected. Where had he been? What had he been doing while he was gone? Did he come to hand me the divorce papers? I was not expecting to see Zimako. I sat down and tried to think through what had just happened. What did Zimako want from me?

I felt very tired, and decided to go to bed once I satisfied my craving for celery.

* * * * *

I was at work when I was called to the front desk. I went there, wondering who was looking for me. The front desk woman had a huge smile. I smiled back, looking askance at her. She pointed to a huge bouquet of flowers. "This arrived for you."

I took the flowers. My hands were shaking as I opened the envelope. It was from Zimako. It read, "My Anuli, please forgive me."

I did not know what to do. So suddenly he showed up out of nowhere and thought we would pick up from where we left off, just like that? What about his resistance to my getting my professional designation? What about his denigrating my part-time job? What about his meanness and passive aggression? I was so confused. Where was all of this coming from, and why the change of heart? I looked at the flowers. They were beautiful. It was a bouquet of fragrant calla lilies, my favourite flower. He remembered. I placed them at my desk.

When the women saw me carry the flowers to my desk, the office was abuzz. I told Anita they were from my husband. The news soon spread, and everyone was walking by to admire the flowers. "He must love you so much."

I made no comment. No one at work knew we were separated. If he persisted in this vein, their curiosity would be piqued, and I would have to come up with a fitting explanation.

I would cross that bridge when I got to it. I pushed all

thoughts of Zimako to the back of my mind and tried to focus on my job. I could not afford to make any mistakes. When my phone started vibrating, I looked at the caller ID on-screen and noted it was Zimako.

"Please, Anuli, we need to talk. Please don't hang up on me. Please."

I decided to hear him out. "What do you have to say, Zimako?"

He took a deep breath. "I have been a fool. I have. You don't have to talk to me. I let you down. I let myself down. Please, give me a chance. Please give us a chance; let me explain. Can we meet?"

My voice was cold and flat. "We have nothing to say to each other," I said, dripping bitterness and venom.

I heard a gasp escape him. "Anuli, please, I have something important to tell you." There was desperation in his voice. I had never heard him sound desperate. I wondered what he had to say.

"Let me think about it," I said. That seemed enough for him just then.

* * * * *

I needed to talk these recent events through with somebody. Afaa and I met up that evening, and I confided in her and sought her opinion and advice. She was very upset with Zimako. "How dare he breezily come back as though all it takes is a bunch of flowers to repair the hurt and embarrassment and expect you to welcome him with open arms?"

That was exactly how I felt. I'm glad Afaa saw things from my perspective. I was still fuming at Zimako, and I was not sure I was ready to talk.

Afaa continued with righteous indignation. "He put you through so much. He walked out on you when you needed him the most, and just when you are regaining some equilibrium, he comes strolling back. Who does he think he is?"

I agreed with her, but one part of me wanted to hear Zimako out, give him a chance to explain. For my sanity, I felt it was important to know what I did to make him give up on our marriage. What was the final straw that broke the camel's back?

Afaa noticed my silence, then asked, "Are you considering taking him back? Anuli, he would do it again the next time the going gets tough. How can you ever trust him as unshakably as you did before? How will you sleep at night?" Afaa was not shy to air her views.

I was vacillating between hearing what he had to say and perhaps rebuilding our marriage, and shutting him out completely because once trust is gone, what is left? I guessed this was a dilemma I had to work out on my own.

I shifted the conversation back to her. "So… " I said with a smile in my voice, "When is Ola, the super-duper lover-boy, coming to these shores?"

It turned out Ola was planning to visit for the weekend. He would come in on Friday evening and leave on Sunday night.

"He is coming with his brother, so I could meet a member of his family."

Being a Nigerian, I knew the implication of that. It was the sign of serious intentions. "Afaa, this is a big deal. Wow! You guys are getting serious. Are you ready for this? You have to decide what you want before he comes. If you are genuinely playing for keeps, then you'll have to pull out the stops." I gave her a few tips on being a domestic goddess and getting the target hooked. We laughed and chatted, finished our drinks, and planned to chat on the phone soon for updates.

I decided to call Fifi and let her know as well. I knew Afaa might call her later, and it was better that she heard about Zimako's reappearance from me. She adopted a more accommodating, mellow approach. "Do you want to take him back?"

I was still undecided. I was taking it one step at a time. My big decision for the moment was whether or not to meet with him and hear what he had to say. Reconciliation was not in the cards just yet, certainly not on my mind. I was still quite hurt from everything that had happened, although increasingly I was dwelling on the past, our life in Nigeria, our early days in Canada, just remembering the Zimako of old.

"Anuli, take your time. You have been so deeply hurt. You need to step back, reassess objectively if that is possible, and give yourself time. Whatever decision you make will have implications for your entire life. Whichever way you chose to go, know that you have my full support."

I liked what she said, and I took it to heart.

Later that evening, I was already tucked in for the night when my phone rang. It was Zimako.

"Anuli," he said. I did not say a word. "Can you talk? Are you asleep?"

Clearly, I was awake. I remained silent.

"I got a job."

When he said that, I perked up and asked, "So?" I knew he had his security job, but the way he said, "I got a job" suggested something had changed.

"It's with an oil company. I got a job with one of the oil companies in Fort McMurray. It is an opportunity of the type I had been hoping for. I... I have two weeks before I move out there."

The news took me by surprise. I remained silent.

"Are you there?"

"Yes," I whispered.

"They offered me a job as a junior engineer. The pay is very good, and there are added benefits, too. Anuli, I know I have hurt you so much. You may never forgive me, but I hope you do." He paused. "I have no right to ask this of you, but Anuli, can we try again? For me; for our unborn baby? *Obidiya*, please. Please give me a chance."

I was torn between joy for Zimako that he had found his way and umbrage for the wounds that had cut so deep. He had made my life very miserable. "What are you asking for?"

"A chance for us to talk, please."

I knew what I'd say to Zimako. "Okay, I will meet you at a neutral place in public."

We met at a restaurant, and I was quite impressed to see how much he had changed. He was at peace, subdued. We ordered our food; I was interested to hear what he had to say. We made small talk to start with, and then he suddenly moved on to telling me how he got the job.

"Look, Anuli, I was foolish. I want to apologise for being such an idiot when you went back to school. I don't know what possessed me." He did indeed come across as a changed man. He reached his hand across the table and held my hand in his. "How is school?"

I smiled. "I am done with school. It was an accelerated programme." I was not going to give any information away.

"How did you do? Have you taken your exams? Did you pass?"

I looked narrowly at him. "Yes, I passed, thank God. No thanks to you, though."

He had the sense to look shamefaced. "Anuli, I know I am asking too much, but… you are carrying my baby. I want us to get back together. I want you to join me when I go to Fort Mc." He had delivered the message.

"How do you know it's your baby? What right do you have to claim it as yours?"

Zimako fell silent. I could see the question in his eyes, but he did not dare ask. "It is my baby. Our baby, I just know it."

Then he squared his shoulders and continued. "Please, give us another chance. I would really like you to come to Fort Mc with me. I want to look after you."

I did not say anything.

Suddenly all my anger was spent. My emotions were in turmoil, but I could sense the hurt begin to thaw. I wondered if my broken heart would ever heal, if I could rekindle the love that he had trampled upon, if we could ever be happy together again. I did not know any of the answers, and I remembered Afaa had suggested seeking professional help. "Will you go for therapy?"

"Therapy?"

"Yes. Relationship counselling. We have gone through too much. I believe if we are to have a chance in the future, then you have to go for some sort of therapy. I have been burnt in this union, Zimako. I know this Canadian odyssey has at times been very bruising, for both of us, but the disrespect you showed for my ability to think for myself and make sensible decisions was not something I thought would ever happen. I also never thought you would shut down our lines of communication. Your conflict-resolution skills are totally unevolved, and maybe you have some deep-seated issues you need brought to the fore so you can address them."

Zimako's head was bowed. "I am so sorry, Anuli. I will do whatever you ask of me if you will promise me that we can start over. I need that assurance as I leave to go to Fort Mc. Please, Anuli, say yes. Promise me we can start over again, so I can prepare a place for us.

I knew I was not ready to make any such promise. "Zimako, I do not owe you anything, and I cannot make any promises. You are going to therapy, not for me, but for yourself and any future relationships you have, be it with me or someone else. It's for you and you alone." I did not want to be pressured.

"Okay, I understand."

We ate in silence. "I love you, Anuli. I never stopped."

I looked at Zimako and saw tears well up in his eyes.

"I want to watch my baby grow in you. I want to be responsible for my family. Please, Anuli, give me a chance."

I gave him a warning glance, and he went back to his food.

We enjoyed the rest of the evening devoid of the earlier tension. I found myself laughing with him again. As we left the restaurant, Zimako called a cab for me, and when I got in, he kissed my lips lightly and said, "Do it, Anuli. Do it for our baby."

* * * * *

I went to work the next day with a new bounce in my step. As soon as I walked in, I felt something unusual in the air. I went to my office and tried to figure out what was different. That was when my phone buzzed and Anita invited me to her office. I was curious to know what was going on.

When I got there, most of the women were there already, beaming with excitement. Maria was looking thrilled. The atmosphere was buzzing. I was confused. What was happening?

"Anuli, we have won the lottery!" Anita gleefully announced.

I whooped for joy. "No waaaay! Oh my God, oh my God! Details, details."

Anita broke it down. We had won $320,000. That came down to a little less than $70,000 for each of us in the syndicate. I was so excited. It was almost too good to be true.

We started discussing the next steps. Caroline looked at me and asked, "Did you pay into the lottery fund?"

I smiled at her and, overcome with joy, I hugged her. "Of course," I replied, with a wide grin. She was shocked at my reaction. I felt her arms go around me. I jumped and forced her to jump, hugging me.

THE END

GLOSSARY OF WORDS

Chapter One

Obidiya ---------------------- (Term of endearment for a married woman) – Darling

Atilogwu ------------------- Literally means "Wonder." Name of a dynamic dance group

Ogene ----------------------- Gong

Udu ------------------------- Musical instrument made of small neck, wide base pot, and a pad that beats the open end

Imeobodo ------------------- Name of village

Ogbandiogu ---------------- Mediator

Ndi-ogo---------------------- In-laws

Nno O ----------------------- Welcome

Igba Nkwu Nwanyi------- Traditional marriage and payment of bride price

Okada drivers ------------- Commercial motorcycle transport drivers

Mmanwu -------------------- Masquerade

Otimpkus-------------------- Praise singers who herald a person singing praises

Ichie ------------------------- Traditional title for a person who is accomplished

Okpue-umu-agbala ------ Zimako's mother (Pinnacle of attainment for womanhood)

Makua ----------------------- Zimako's sister (Name meaning To embrace)

Chinazo ---------------------Zimako's sister and Makua's twin
(Name meaning God is my saviour)

Chinazo ---------------------Zimako's sister and Makua's twin
(Name meaning God is my saviour)

Okwe -----------------------Zimako's younger brother

Diokpala --------------------First son (Important position in an
Ibo family)

Akpa-ego --------------------Bag of money

Gourd -----------------------Small calabash for drinking the local
alcoholic palm brew

Palmwine -------------------Tapped from the palm tree, a local
alcoholic brew

Schnapps --------------------Popular alcoholic drink for pouring
libation

Ise ----------------------------Agreement (Amen)

Aso ------------------------Material

Aso–ebi ----------------------A similar material worn by a group
of people

Aso–oke ---------------------Gorgeous material for the rich

Sprayed with cash --------The act of plastering denominations
of money on the face, and sprinkling
it over people as they dance

Ofe onugbu -----------------Ibo delicacy, bitter leaf soup

Omenana --------------------Literally, the old ways or custom

Kolanuts --------------------Used as a traditional welcome
gesture

Dugbe Junction ------------A popular intersection in Ibadan,
Nigeria

Omalicha nwam -----------My beautiful child

Nwam ----------------------My child

Nwanyi oma -------------- Beautiful woman

Palmi ---------------------- Traditional alcoholic brew from
palm tree

Umu-ada ------------------- Women of a certain locality

Iku-aka --------------------- Traditional Ibo engagement

Big-man ------------------- Person of influence

Acada ---------------------- Short for academic

Egunjerize ----------------- To pay homage or bribe

Face-me-I-face-you ------- Shanty or slum

Nwam, nnoo -------------- My child, welcome

Osu ------------------------- Old caste system in Igboland where
some with slave ancestry are labeled
as outcasts

Chapter Two

Thisday ---------------------- Newspaper

Jos ------------------------- City in Northern Nigeria

Boko Haram -------------- Fanatical Islamic cult that despises
Western culture and education

Na wa, O ------------------- Used to express surprise or
scepticism

Kai -------------------------- Exclamation (What?!)

Oyinbo --------------------- White people (Foreigners)

Wash it --------------------- Celebration

Awon----------------------- Those people (Group)

Haba na wetin?! ---------- What is it?! (Exasperation)

O! -------------------------- Expression for emphasis

Bad belle --------------------- Envy

Full ground ----------------- Very present

Suya ------------------------ Delicacy of kebab

Jollof–rice ------------------- Sauteed rice with tomatoes

Moin-moin ------------------ Mashed bean cooked in spices

Chapter Three

Moolah --------------------- Money

Dosh ------------------------ Stash of cash

Igbo ------------------------- Marijuana

Wetin ----------------------- What

Something dey hungry me   I am hungry
                        (In this context, rape)

Wetin dat one go reach do? ------ Expression of dissatisfaction

Chop ------------------------ To eat

Naa-------------------------- Now

Gbagbuo -------------------- To kill

Oga-------------------------- Sir

Wahala --------------------- Trouble

Chapter Four

Ewoo ewoo ----------------- Expression of sympathy

That is not your portion   To forbid something from happening

Hair no dey my armpit -- Expression of being transparent

Aluta continua ------------- The struggle continues.

Chapter Five

Ndi----------------------------- People

Nid-Lagos ------------------- Lagos people

Am ------------------------- It

E ---------------------------- It is

Dey ------------------------- Available

Nne ------------------------ Dear one (Lady/mother)

Biko ------------------------ Ibo language (Please)

A beg ----------------------- Pidgin English (Please)

Nwanyi ji ego ole? -------- Female yam seller, how much for your yams?

Fifteen thousand naira --- = 15,000 naira for one US dollar

Ochoo passenger ---------- Gofer (Helps fill empty seats in a commercial bus and gets paid a commission for the job)

Pata–pata ------------------- At the very least

Oye agu --------------------- Marketplace

Oye ------------------------- Market day

Ugba ----------------------- Ibo delicacy

Chapter Six

Anata go! ------------------- They are back!

E lu te go -------------------- They have arrived.

Broda ----------------------- Pidgin English (Brother)

Ha anatago ---------------- They are back.

Umum Nno-nu ------------ My children, welcome.

Mma Nnu-kwu ------------ Respected mother

Ichie Kwa'n ----------------- Where is Ichie?

Ofe ora ---------------------- Ibo delicacy made of vegetables

Ogiri-ishi -------------------- Ibo spice

Obi -------------------------- The obi was a modern outbuilding with a thatched roof out at the back of the compound.

Ndi okenye e ke ne'm unu   Greetings to our elders

Papa a nata o yo yo! ------ Papa is back! (Happiness all the way)

O yo-yo --------------------- Happiness all the way

Kposkia: -------------------- Superb

Wrapper -------------------- A cloth tied at the waist to cover from the waist to below the knee

Ngwa ---------------------- Right away

Chei, e gbuo mu, O! ------ I am at a loss.

Gbuo AWOL -------------- Missing in action

Dogo turenchi ------------- Long talk

Gba nu oso ----------------- Run

Chapter Seven

Gbagharia ------------------ Being too busy

Capice? --------------------- Understand

Jo ----------------------------- (Yoruba) Please

Yeye yeye ------------------- Rubbish

How far? ------------------- Whatsup? What is the progress so far? Sometimes used as a form of greeting

You dey, no be small ----- Complete, with nothing to add

Chapter Eight

Baba Adura ---------------- A white garment church pastor

Jagba-jagba ----------------- Nonsense

Nyama nyama ------------- Bullshit

Im wan --------------------- He wants to. (Pidgin English)

Pally ----------------------- Friendly

Kpalava --------------------- Trouble

Nothing spoil -------------- It's A-Okay. No need to worry.

Siddon ---------------------- Sit down.

Je je ------------------------ Quietly

How for do now? --------- What more can I do?

Abokis ---------------------- Security man

how for do now?.---------- it cannot be helped

Mallam --------------------- Islamic cleric with psychic powers

Chapter Ten

Eko for show. Naija forever!   Lagos (Eko) is all about
                                   image. Long live Nigeria.

Abi ------------------------- Do you agree?

Obodo Oyibo ------------- Abroad

419 ------------------------- Advanced fee fraud (Scam)

How for do? --------------- It is what it is.

So, na your Oga wey dey fund these small chops, O..............So,
                                   it's your boss who is paying for the
                                   meal.

Chapman ------------------ Cocktail drink made from Swedish
                                   bitters

Three hundred thousand naira -----------$2,000USD

Chapter Eleven

Somalian emigrie --------- Immigrant from Somalia, a country in the horn of Africa

Who go first tyre? --------- Who gives up (blinks) first?

Oyinbo ----------------------- White person

Eh hen ----------------------- What if?

Chapter Twelve

Obodo oyibo -------------- Abroad

Chin-chin ------------------- Deep fried sweet flour

Chapter Thirteen

Immi ------------------------- Immigrant (Short form)

Chapter Fourteen

Awoof dey run belle ----- No free lunch

Meeeeen, that woman can ask questions
Wow, that woman is inquisitive.

Bar beach -------------------- The Atlantic ocean that borders Lagos (southern Nigeria)

Na real wa ------------------ This is huge.

Bone ------------------------- Silent treatment

Shakara ---------------------- Call one's bluff

Chapter Fifteen

No-how no-how ----------- It is do-able.

Chapter Sixteen

Na wa, O -------------------- It surprises me.

E ---------------------------- be like say Makua don fall for Tony,

O! -------------------------- Seems like Makua is in love with Tony.

You sef ----------------------

Et tu? ----------------------- Make I leave am like that
Let's leave it at that.

Chapter Seventeen

Chapter Eighteen

Chapter Nineteen

Bros, we dey hail, O ------ Greetings

How far? ------------------- Whatsup?

I dey ----------------------- I am fine.

Aso ebi --------------------- Group attire

Spraying bank notes ----- A cultural practice to show wealth.
Cash is sprinkled over a person.

Chapter Twenty

Haba ----------------------- Exclamation (What!)

Ngwa nu ------------------- Okay

Chapter Twenty-One

Ogbono soup and fufu ---Melon seed and vegetable soup and yam powder

Kponmo --------------------Boiled beef hide (skin)

Onye Oji --------------------A black person

Ehen -------------------------Come to think of it.

419 ---------------------------Advanced Fee fraud (scam)

Chapter Twenty-Two

Onugbu soup and fufu --Bitter leaf soup and yam powder

Nna'm -----------------------Father (Also used for husband)

AUTHOR CHINENYE OBIAJULU

Chinenye Obiajulu was born in Lagos, Nigeria and at an early age developed a passion for reading. She attended the University of Nigeria, with a major in Accounting; and qualified as a Chartered Accountant in Nigeria. Afterwards, she obtained her MBA from the University of Navarra (IESE) in Barcelona, Spain. Chinenye has several years of experience working with some of the best banking institutions in Nigeria and Canada. She is married to her hero and they live in Canada.

Lightning Source UK Ltd.
Milton Keynes UK
UKOW03f2146090414

229721UK00001B/84/P